THE OPAL KING

ALSO BY AERIN APELTUN

THE OPAL KING

THE CURSED WEAPONS: BOOK 3

AERIN APELTUN

Elsewhen Press

For Tarragon

CONTENTS

THE BLOOD RULE DECREE OF AERBA

1. There will be three Blood Classes – High Bloods, Middle Bloods, and Low Bloods
2. The High Bloods will consist of the Royal family and extended relations
3. The Middle Bloods will include other Nobles, high status citizens and Priests
4. The Low Bloods will include all other citizens
5. Sexual Relationships outside of Marriage are strictly forbidden
6. All Sexual and Romantic Relationships, including Marriage, between Blood Classes is strictly forbidden in order to keep the Blood Classes pure
7. Entering into Marriage or Relationships with citizens of other Lands of the same Blood Class will be permitted but are greatly discouraged and Royal Approval will be required
8. Entering into Marriage or Relationships with citizens of other Lands of a different Blood Class is strictly forbidden
9. Entering into Marriage or Relationships with members of the same sex whether in the same or different Blood Class are strictly forbidden whether Aerban or from another Land
10. All Citizens names will be taken from the Father's Family Line/Land
11. All Citizens Blood Classes will be taken from the Mother's Blood Class
12. Citizens born out of Wedlock will automatically be Low Bloods and their parents Demoted
13. The King has the power to Demote a Citizen from their birth Blood Class as he sees fit
14. The King has the power to enforce the Execution or Imprisonment or Demotion of any Citizen found to be disregarding any element of the Blood Rule Decree at his discretion

As laid out by King Cinquefoil in the year 3929. Rules 7, 12 and 13 amended by King Finule the First in the year 5643

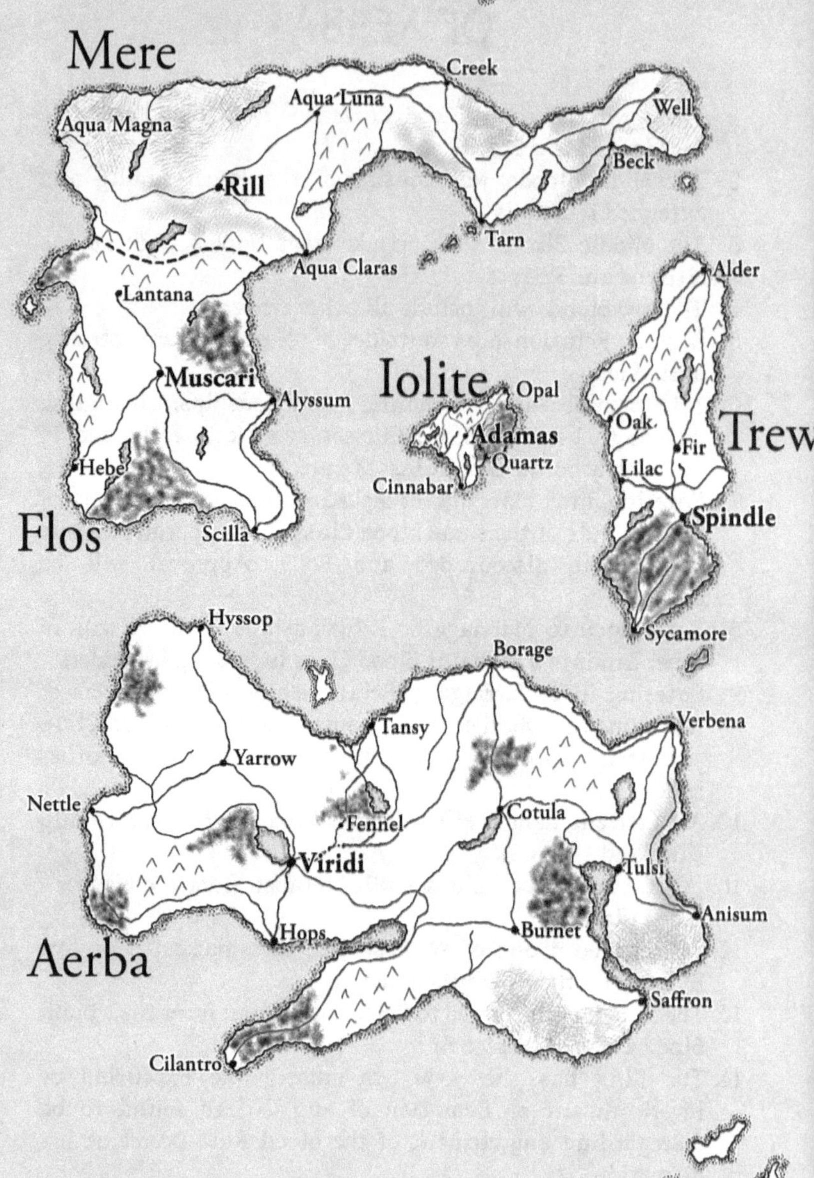

Mere
Aqua Magna
Aqua Luna
Creek
Well
Beck
Rill
Tarn
Aqua Claras
Lantana
Muscari
Alyssum
Hebe
Flos
Scilla
Iolite
Opal
Adamas
Quartz
Cinnabar
Trew
Alder
Oak.
Fir
Lilac
Spindle
Sycamore
Hyssop
Borage
Verbena
Tansy
Yarrow
Cotula
Nettle
Fennel
Viridi
Tulsi
Hops
Anisum
Burnet
Aerba
Saffron
Cilantro

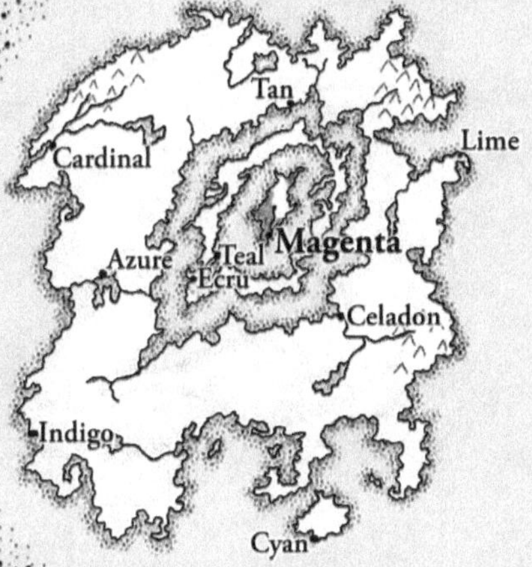

THE SIX LANDS

CHAPTER ONE

The Spirit of the Seas cut through the water like a blade, desperate to force its way through to freedom. I stared out at the white horses breaking around the ship, and at the distant coastline of the Land of Trew.

We'd been at sea for almost two weeks since we'd rescued my elder brother, Malachite, from the Malign Prison on the Third Isle and freed him from our stepmother, Juniper's, grasp. I took a deep breath of salty air, the wind catching my copper hair.

The one thing that I clung on to was that *she* hadn't won, and she wouldn't.

Warm arms slipped around my waist, and hot lips kissed my neck as the smell of sandalwood engulfed me in a loving embrace.

'Captain Pol says we'll be at Lilac by late afternoon,' Rian said in his rich voice. 'We'll take rooms at an inn and she'll start off for Spindle.' The former Prince Valerian of Aerba turned me towards him, his amber eyes glowing in the sunlight, his handsome rose-beige face framed by his long maroon hair.

'I still think it's the best decision,' I said, looking up at him. He was a few inches taller than me and, having recently turned twenty, once more two years older. 'Tarragon and Willow will appreciate being on land, and it'll be the quickest way to get to Spindle and the Trewan Royal Family. Captain Pol will arrive after we've had a chance to finish our business.'

Rian nodded. 'Then we can head for Chroma.'

'Assuming it really is still there.'

'Let's hope so.' The ship lurched, and I grabbed for the rail.

'How's Mal today?'

I sighed. 'I suppose he's getting there, but it's very slow. Juniper's brainwashing is going to be hard for him to overcome, but at least he knows who I am now, and his memory is coming back. It's Onyx I feel sorry for. Mal remembers nothing about their relationship, and it's killing Onyx.'

'I think Anise is right, though. We shouldn't fill in too many details for Mal. He needs to do it himself where he can.'

'I just wish Anise could use his Earth Magic and make him better now.'

'It doesn't work like that, and you know it.'

I huffed. A gull cried plaintively overhead, mirroring my mood.

Rian turned me to look at him, his eyes searching my soul.

'And how are you doing? Really? I know this has come as a shock.'

'Being a Quintessence Angle Spinner? Just slightly,' I said, still coming to terms with the revelation from almost a fortnight ago. 'I'll get used to it eventually, just as you have with your Fire Magic. How long had you and Anise known? About my Quintessence?'

Rian shrugged. 'We hadn't *known*. I think we'd both had our suspicions for some time, but you were so adamant you didn't have a Magic Angle that we didn't take too much notice. Freeing Mal changed all that, though. It was obvious what was going on by then.'

'I didn't even know,' I said. I glanced towards my freckles, hidden under the Iolite Coterie of Assassins' tattoo—or, what I'd always thought were freckles on my pale skin—now covered by Rian's sandalwood-smelling wrist strap. 'I'd read things in Father's book, but I'd never even entertained the possibility that my freckles might actually be the Quintessence birthmark.'

'Why should you? You'd spent your whole life thinking you were a Middle Blood—only High Bloods ever had Magic.'

'I suppose so, but I do feel a bit daft that I didn't work it out earlier. That white light; I should've realised it always coincided with something I was willing to happen. That's why I felt so tired afterwards, because I was using Magic.'

Rian smiled his lopsided smile at me, the one that made me go weak at the knees, as he looked into my amethyst eyes. 'But now we know for sure. I believe it's why you survived the Cursed Weapons for so long—your Quintessence was somehow helping you stay strong. Otherwise, you'd have succumbed a lot sooner, and never broken the Curse.'

I nodded, glancing down at the purple diamond sword, Deorwine, and shield, Glædwine, as Rian had named them now they were no longer cursed. They sat near me, resting against a barrel, otherwise their lingering Magic would have them on my back in no time. The ship lurched again as it hit a large wave, and Rian grabbed me, stopping me from sprawling headlong on the deck.

'I suppose it helped me save you from your poisoning, too, and broke Mal's enchantment and brought him back to us,' I said.

'Maybe that's why Juniper inducted you into the Coterie when she did. She has the same mark. If you're right, and she's a Quintessence Angle Spinner, too, she'd have recognised your freckles. By getting you into the Assassin Coterie, she had the perfect opportunity to cover them up with the tattoo so no one else would spot them, realise what you were. And if you died as an assassin, it didn't matter.'

That hadn't occurred to me. 'Maybe.'

'Carnelian said you were a threat to her now. This is what he meant. He knew. He said "freckles". Working for Juniper, and as an assassin himself, he knows exactly what's been going on. He knows that Juniper is a Quintessence Spinner, too, just like you. And she knows you could stand against her—*would* stand against her, try to stop her from taking the Five Lands, from destroying the Crystal Vortex.'

I nodded slowly. 'That would explain so much. Once I'd evaded Lord Flint, though, and he'd failed to kill me, maybe that's when she decided to use Mal against me with the enchantment. She'd have known I'd try and rescue him once I knew the truth.'

'And turning Mal against you would be the worst torture, for both of you.'

I sighed. 'She really must hate me.'

Rian pulled me closer. 'I don't know if she actually hates you, or just sees you as an obstacle that could get in the way of what she wants, but either way, she's damn dangerous. So tell me, how are your nightmares now?'

'Don't you know? You hold me every night in bed.'

'You haven't elbowed me recently.'

'I beg your pardon?'

He grinned at me. 'Just joking. You only did it once.'

I huffed. 'I didn't mean to.'

'I know you didn't,' he said, squeezing me. 'Seriously, though, I'd say they've improved because you haven't been restless for sometime now.'

I nodded. 'And neither have you.'

'Mine are pretty much better, too. I just hope they stay that way.'

'So do I, for both of us.'

He leant towards me, brushing his hot lips against mine, his Amethyst Talisman slipping out from his tunic. It had once been mine, but I'd given it to him the day we pledged ourselves to each other, the day he'd given me his gold and diamond thyme-engraved ring. Our vows in the dungeon of Viridi Palace back in Aerba may not be technically legal, but they were as binding to the two of us as any formal marriage contract.

'Are you trying to take my mind off things, husband?'

'Now why would I want to do that, wife?' he asked, smiling as he gently kissed me. I wrapped my arms around his neck, kissing him back, then moved one hand and raked my fingers through his hair as we continued to kiss. He turned my blood to wildfire. This young man had set up home in my heart, become my best friend, my soulmate—and my husband. Eventually, we parted.

Rian looked over my shoulder. 'Sage looks pleased with himself.'

I turned and looked, Rian holding me around the waist. At the stern of the ship, Sage stood with Anise, concentrating on the billowing sails, his forehead furrowed but an expression of satisfaction on his face. He looked immaculate as always. His brown eyes, long brown hair and rose-beige skin were typically Aerban. His Air Magic Angle was not. He'd only recently discovered it, and I wasn't sure who was more excited about it, him or Anise.

'He's glad he's worked out his Angle, that's all,' I said, and giggled. 'Anise is so proud of him, look.'

Anise, his violet-blue eyes sparkling in his beautiful, unblemished rose-beige face, stood next to Sage, wearing a broad grin. He smoothed his long black hair over his shoulder as he proudly watched Sage filling the sails with a stiff breeze.

'And I'm proud of you,' Rian said, turning me around and kissing my forehead.

Blood rushed to my face. 'I'm glad Anise and Onyx encouraged him to try and find out which one it was. Perhaps we should have already guessed, though. The first time we faced the sea morgens, Sage got angry and the wind got up. Not that you'd remember – I'm afraid you were unconscious,' I said, wincing, my hand clenching involuntarily at the memory of hitting him and the pain afterwards.

'Oh, yes, thanks for reminding me,' Rian said, a slightly embarrassed expression on his face.

I smiled at him. 'It wasn't your fault,' I said, tapping him gently on the nose with my finger.

'Maybe not,' he said, grabbing my hand and kissing my fingers. 'But it's still embarrassing.' He paused. 'You know, when the wind got up and saved us from the morgens before we got to Mal, for a moment I wondered if I'd got it wrong, and you were an Air Spinner, not a Quintessence Spinner, after all.'

'I didn't think I was either at that point, but I definitely knew I hadn't done anything to start that breeze. I didn't think I was special at all.'

'Magic Angle or not you'll always be very, very special to me,' he said, tilting my head up towards him. His lips met mine, and for a few moments, I lost myself in our kiss.

'I'd be grateful if you'd put my sister down.'

Mal stood behind Rian, smiling at us. His face was still paler than normal, but his silky, deep green-blue, sea-like eyes were more alert than they had been since we'd rescued him. His strawberry-blond hair swished in the wind as it caught on his low Iolitian ponytail, and he flicked a few loose strands back over his shoulder.

'I can assure you I'm taking the utmost care of your sister.' Rian grinned.

'I'm aware of that,' Mal said. 'And I wouldn't let her be with anyone who didn't treat her well.'

I stepped away from Rian, putting my hands on my hips. 'Excuse me? Don't I get a say in this?'

'Not really. I'm just looking out for my little sister.'

'So you know, I think she can look after herself,' Rian said, glancing sideways at me.

'I know that, too,' Mal said, looking as if he was having difficulty suppressing a grin.

'I'll go and check the others have made all the preparations for when we disembark,' Rian said, kissing my lips again and walking back to the cabin, humming to himself as Onyx came out.

The ex-assassin nodded in response to Rian's wave. I was so glad that, after a rocky start, the two of them were now friends. Onyx's black hair, tied in a low Iolitian ponytail, shone in the sunlight as he walked to the opposite rail of the ship and took hold of it. He glanced towards us. His Rose Quartz Ring, a Water Artefact that enhanced his Water Magic, sparkled on his finger. I sighed inwardly at Onyx's sagging shoulders as his hazel-brown eyes looked longingly at Mal and then back out to sea, his sienna skin catching the light.

'How's your memory?' I asked Mal.

'I'm piecing things together,' he said, his oval, porcelain face yet to regain its generally cheerful look. There were moments when I caught his wicked sense of humour flickering across his face, like just now, but it was yet to reassert itself properly. 'It doesn't all make sense and there are things that won't come back to me yet, like how Juniper caught me in the first place, where I've been these last few months.'

'I think you may never remember all of that,' I said, putting my arm around his shoulders. Three years older than me, and a little taller, I found it hard to wrap my arms around him. He was strong, despite Juniper's best efforts, and had quickly put weight back on after his ordeal in the Malign Prison. My brother was the rightful

Master of Iolite, a position that Juniper had, in effect, stolen from him. He was supposed to take over on his recent twenty-first birthday, but instead, Juniper had taken him prisoner and continued her regency. The bitch—as Onyx would say.

'Maybe not. Maybe it's a good thing if I don't. I do remember you giving me this ring, though.' He raised his right hand and admired the vibrant malachite ring I'd given him for his birthday two years previously. 'And that I gave you that malachite War Fan of yours,' he added, gesturing to the Fan clipped to my belt.

I glanced down at the weapon, its polished silver cover, embossed with the sun, moon and stars, glistening in the sunlight. The faceted stones of dusky rose, sky blue and spring green set in the silver, glittered, sending little rainbow sparks across the deck.

'So what's the last thing you remember?' I asked.

He rubbed his head. 'I'd just arrived back at the Crimson Castle. They told me you'd been sent to Aerba to kill Princess Angelica—I wanted to come straight after you. I knew how dangerous it would be. I was hoping you'd be home soon so I could...'

'Could what?' I asked.

He frowned. 'There was something I wanted to tell you. Something *really* important.'

'Oh?'

He chuckled. 'I remember. Onyx.'

'Onyx?' Had he remembered? I hoped for Onyx's sake he had.

'Yes, that new kitchen maid, what was her name?' He scratched his head, screwing his nose up as he thought. 'That's it. Ruby. She was cosying up to Onyx, and he was absolutely terrified of her. Couldn't get away quick enough whenever he saw her coming. She was all over him, but he...'

'He what?' I asked.

Mal frowned and shook his head. 'No, that wasn't the important thing I had to tell you. It was something else entirely. Blast. Whatever was it? I'm sure it was about Onyx, though... I...'

I wanted to blurt it out. That he and Onyx were in love. That's what was so important, but Anise had said that it was probably best if Mal remembered some things for himself, rather than being told everything—and I fancied that this was one of those things. Better he remembered himself than I told him. After all, those new feelings should be his to rediscover, not for me to tell him about. Anyway, would he believe me if I just came out and told him point blank? A little nudge wouldn't hurt, though.

'You had something important to tell me about Onyx?' I pressed.

Mal frowned, his face contorting almost as if in pain as he reached into his mind, desperately searching for the missing pieces of the puzzle.

'That's it!' he said suddenly, clapping his hands together in excitement at having remembered. 'I hadn't had the chance to tell you yet. We weren't ready to before I left Iolite on my last mission. We decided to wait until I got back so we could tell you properly, together.' His face flushed. 'You see, Ama, Onyx and I...' His eyes widened. 'I'd forgotten. By the Stars, how could I forget something like that?' He looked at me. 'Onyx and I love each other.'

CHAPTER TWO

I nodded and smiled. 'I know,' I said. 'He told me.'

Mal froze, looking horrified. 'What must he think of me, that I forgot something so important? How could I forget I love him? No wonder he's been looking so peaky.'

'He understands,' I said, patting his arm reassuringly. 'He knows what you've been through—well, some of it, anyway.'

'Where is he? I have to find him,' Mal said, frantically looking around the deck.

'Over there,' I said, pointing. 'I'm pleased for you both, you know.'

He turned and looked at me. 'Really? I know Onyx sort of liked you for a while.'

'Not really, at least not in the way you mean,' I said. 'If you remember all those times we spent together, you were there, too. He was with me to be near you. I think he's had a thing for you for ages.'

Mal grinned, his eyes lighting up. 'You might be right. I admit I've always fancied him.'

That was the first proper smile I'd seen on his face since we'd rescued him, and the way his eyes sparkled with it made tears well in my own.

'I'll be back later,' he said, running over towards Onyx. He dashed over the deck and caught the assassin in a huge hug. Onyx's expression fell somewhere between shock and delight.

'What's going on?' Rian asked. He'd just come out of the cabin.

'Mal just remembered about Onyx and him,' I said, smiling.

'Good,' Rian said. 'Onyx's been like a bear with a sore head, pining after your brother.'

I watched for a moment as my brother and Onyx rested their foreheads together and started talking softly to each other, holding hands. I took hold of Rian's hand.

'Have you been to Trew before?' Rian asked.

I nodded. 'A few times. The weather's usually cold, quite often wet, too. It's not the most enchanting of countries.'

'I've only ever been once, a long time ago when I was quite small. Can't say I remember a lot about it. There was a Trewan State Visit to Aerba about three or four years ago.'

'The fact the Trewans don't educate the girls, unless they're High Bloods, has always rankled me.'

'I don't know why they don't. It's always been a bit of a mystery to me, not to mention an injustice. Girls are just as smart as boys, sometimes even smarter.'

'At least they taught us in Iolite.' I glanced at him. 'Come on,' I said, taking him towards the cabins.

'What is it?' he asked.

'I just want to be alone with you for a while,' I said, glancing up to the ship's wheel where Rian's cousin, Tarragon, was deep in conversation with Captain Pol.

The young Aerban man, about two years older than Rian, listened intently to whatever Pol was saying, his golden-brown eyes glistening in the sunlight. His brown, sun-bleached hair in its messy ponytail was currently in the high, Aerban style, catching the breeze; he'd have to change that to Iolitian when we reached Trew. His rose-beige skin glistened with sweat in the warm sun, and at just over six feet tall, similar in height to Rian, his lithe, strong frame exuded confidence. He shifted his arm and his Rose Quartz Wristband, an oval stone set in black leather, shone in the light—a Water Artefact given to him by the Dryads of Flos to enhance his Water Magic. I was very fond of Tarragon. His caring, fun nature had endeared him to me very quickly, and I could see why he and Rian had grown up as best friends and confidants. In some ways I was beginning to see him as another big brother.

I scanned the deck, but couldn't see Tarragon's girlfriend, Willow, anywhere. She must have been in the cabin somewhere with one of Anise's seasickness remedies. She didn't do well on sea voyages.

'Tarragon's busy right now, so he won't be able to interrupt us like he usually does,' I said.

Rian rubbed the back of his neck. 'You were alone with me all night, and Tarragon didn't interrupt.'

'So? We can never have enough alone time. Don't you want to kiss me?'

'I didn't say that.' He grinned at me, and we went into our cabin.

The bustling port of Lilac was filled with merchants and townsfolk all going about their business. The smell of salt and fish hung in the air, along with a hint of freshly cut trees as men loaded lumber onto ships for the other four Lands. The people of Trew were very practical. Their leather and woollen clothes afforded them warmth in the cool, wet climate, and many carried wooden bows. We passed Middle Bloods in their brown leather coats, Low Bloods in grey, but no High Bloods, who wore black in Trew.

The Trewans were tall, mainly over six feet, with skin golden, yellow or green eyes, and brown or blond hair. They generally wore their hair quite short, in contrast to Iolite and Aerba. We looked nothing like them. I could see Juniper and Elm in their rectangular faces, maybe even a little of Father in the hair. Mal and I had inherited none of that. Although, my twin sister, Beryl, had the white-blonde hair and similar-shaped face.

We kept to our Iolitian clothes and hairstyles to enable us to move around freely, and purchased extra blankets and sheepskin jackets to keep out the cold, wet weather. I even bought a pair of fingerless gloves, just in case I needed the extra warmth. Onyx rolled his eyes to the sky when he saw them.

'What?' I asked.

'It won't be that cold, Ama,' he said.

'I don't like cold hands.'

'Suit yourself.'

'I will.'

Rian and Tarragon arranged horses and tents, and we then took rooms at an inn on the outskirts of the town.

'We need to get to Spindle as soon as possible,' I said as we all sat at a table in the inn. 'Warn the Royal Family about the assassins in their midst. Do you know any of them well?' I asked Rian as he put down two mugs of Pine Tea. He'd taken one look at the others drinking mead, screwed his nose up at the mere whiff of alcohol, and made straight for the kitchens to ask for the tea.

He shook his head as he sat beside me. 'Only a little, really,' he said, passing me a mug then taking a sip of his own drink. 'King Ash and Queen Photinia were quite good friends with Father.'

'Didn't they try and marry you off to Princess Hazel?' Willow asked, grinning, her deep brown eyes sparkling. Her black hair was tied back, keeping the frizzy locks from getting in her eyes. Her light sienna skin shone. A year older than me, and a good fighter like the other Aerbans that had once been King's Warriors, she'd become a great friend over the last months, her infectious smile never failing to lift my spirits. She'd also grown close to Onyx, having discovered he was a distant cousin.

Rian gave Willow a long look. 'For all of about two minutes. Chervil took an interest in her, but she turned him down.'

'Wise woman.'

'Princess Hazel, eh?' I gave Rian an enquiring look.

He sighed. 'Father spoke about her marrying into the family, but I told him I wasn't interested, and that was before I'd met her. I don't think I've spent more than five minutes in the same room as her. I was only sixteen at the time. Not the slightest bit interested in girls, and certainly not marriage.' His hand slipped under the table and squeezed my thigh. 'Unlike now,' he murmured in my ear. 'And that interest is solely reserved for you, wife.'

I stifled a giggle.

'Prince Birch was interested in anything in a skirt, from what I remember,' Tarragon said in his deep, husky voice as he scratched his chin.

'Chased me down a corridor once,' Willow sniffed.

'You never said.'

She shrugged. 'I trapped him in a guest bedroom. Used my picks to lock him in the south wing. Bobbins. He might still be there, for all I know,' she added, sniggering.

'Better not take you to the palace then,' I said.

'We need to warn them, whatever happens,' Sage said. He looked at his younger cousin, making the single silver earring shaped like a sprig of Thyme that dangled from his right ear jingle.

Rian nodded. 'I know.'

There was a year between them, but Sage always deferred to Rian because of rank. Sage sat straight, a hint of lemon and violet perfume—his favourite—surrounding him.

'Where are Mal and Onyx?' Anise asked, his voice like butter.

'They're eating in their room,' I said. 'Mal was quite tired, and Onyx thought it best if they stay in the quiet.' Although, I guessed Onyx might have had an ulterior motive, now Mal had regained most of his memory.

We ate a good meal of lamb and vegetables, covered in a thick, herby gravy, followed by a delicious treacle tart. Tarragon went back for another helping.

'Pig.' Willow giggled as he returned.

'We're on an important mission and I need to keep my strength up,' he said, glancing sideways at her as he sat down.

'You're always hungry, even when you've eaten,' Sage muttered.

'I happen to have a good appetite,' Tarragon said, totally unperturbed by his cousin. He bent his head towards Willow. 'Y'know, as Rian and Phire are sharing, and Anise is with Sage, I took the liberty of booking us a double room.'

Willow raised an eyebrow. 'You weren't thinking of booking us *separate* rooms, were you?'

Tarragon looked a little taken aback. 'O—of course not. Although, I wasn't quite sure what you'd want to do?'

'No one knows us here, and we've left Aerba so we can do what we want,' Willow said, coughing a little as her asthma got the better of her. 'Besides, I wouldn't want to be alone.' She fluttered her eyelids at Tarragon who coughed and turned pink.

Sage looked to the ceiling and shook his head in exasperation, but I caught the smile flickering on his lips. The Aerban Blood Rules meant nothing to us now.

'I'll make you some of my liquorice and sophora tea, Willow, to help your cough,' Anise said as his Jade Amulet, an Earth Artefact, caught the light.

'Thank you,' Willow said with a smile.

'I'd like to stretch my legs before bed,' Rian said, standing up.

'I'll come with you,' I said, following him out the inn.

He took my hand and we wandered down the street. 'I hope you don't mind, but the smell of alcohol was giving me a headache. I needed some fresh air.'

'It's fine,' I said as we walked along. 'There's nothing wrong with an evening stroll, especially if it's with you.'

He glanced at me, a broad grin on his face that lit his eyes as he squeezed my hand, sending tingles throughout my body. 'You like evening strolls, do you? I didn't know that.'

I laughed. 'Neither did I. Maybe we should make this a new habit. An evening walk together?'

'Not sure it can be a regular thing at the moment, but perhaps once things have settled down, maybe we could.'

'Settled down? You think they ever will?'

He glanced at me. 'I hope so. Then we can live in that little cottage I talked about before. Swim every day, and take a walk every evening. Maybe even in the moonlight.'

'Are you turning into a hopeless romantic?' I asked, grinning at him.

'I think that perhaps I've always been one and never realised it,' he said, pausing to give me a little kiss. 'Not until you, anyway.'

We ventured on down to the docks, and as the sun set we made our way through the dim backstreets to the inn. As we walked along, tendrils of mist began to swirl across the ground around us, winding around our legs, quickly becoming thicker and thicker until we were in a fog. The hairs on the back of my neck rose as I scanned what little I could now see of the alleyway.

'Something's not right about this fog,' I said, my hand reaching for my sword hilt.

Rian looked around. 'You're right. This isn't… natural.'

Rounding a corner in the alleyway, a shadow loomed out of the fog.

'Rian!' I yelled.

'What the—'

Rian never got to finish. The shadow lunged at him, fist flying, and knocked Rian into a wall. A hand reached out of the thick fog behind me and grabbed my shoulder, pulling me backwards. I lost my balance, tried to spin around, but a fist connected with my cheek.

Pain streaked through my face as I hit the ground, stunned. Warm, salty-metallic blood trickled from a cut on my lip into my mouth as I shook my head, trying to clear it, but before I could, great hands took hold of my tunic, pulling me to my feet. I caught a flash of straggly blond hair, the hint of sweat, as someone roughly yanked me around and pressed a knife to my throat. A muscly arm wrapped around my waist as Rian scrambled to his feet, swords in hand and eyes wide. In front of him, stepping out of the rapidly dissipating fog, stood a huge man with spiky white hair and deep green eyes. His full lips curled into a vicious sneer as he looked at us both.

Hell's teeth.

I knew these two men. These two assassins. Sunstone and Hematite. Both great brutes of men; thick necks, muscles of iron, incredibly strong. They were also sword masters, usually lurking somewhere at the Crimson Castle acting as Juniper's bodyguards when they were in Iolite. So why were they here?

I tried to move, but Hematite had such a hold on me I could do nothing, the Cursed Weapons pinned to my back between me and him. I couldn't even get my hands to my War Fan that hung at my hip.

Hematite chuckled. 'Did you like my fog, Lady Merciless?'

His fog? Hematite was an Air Spinner? I tried struggling again, but he just pressed the knife harder into my throat and squeezed me around my waist.

'We're taking you back to Iolite, Lady Amethyst,' he said, his foul breath on my neck making me shudder. 'You have an appointment to keep with Serpentine.'

I froze.

The thought of being taken to Serpentine, Juniper's personal torturer, made me feel physically sick. The stories of his barbarism and savage techniques were infamous throughout the Castle, as were the results of his many elaborate torments which he'd taken to a whole new level and called "artistry"— torments he also delighted in. Most victims didn't survive. Thankfully. They weren't meant to. Dying quickly was a mercy. Those that did survive lived in agony, sometimes unable to live with the pain and disfigurement he'd wrought on them, and ultimately finishing Serpentine's work for him themselves.

I wouldn't be allowed to survive.

My death would be a long one. Lingering in the extreme. Painful, but not quite enough to let me pass out into the welcome arms of oblivion. It would probably be a result of one of his tried-and-tested perverted procedures—or, even more terrifying, a newly devised one that he could use me for as a source of practice and refinement—and would last for days.

And Rian knew it.

I'd told him all about Serpentine's perversions in the past.

The look of desperation in Rian's eyes almost broke me. He knew exactly what we were up against, and the others weren't here to help. We were alone. Rian's eyes tore from mine as Sunstone moved.

I watched in horror as the great assassin swept towards Rian with his huge sword.

Hematite may have been a brute, but Sunstone? *Savage* was the only word I could think of. Rian stood no chance against him. He parried the assassin's blow, bracing himself for the impact, but it was greater than he'd anticipated, jarring his muscles, making him groan with the effort of deflecting the great man's sword away from his body. Each time my husband parried a blow, he staggered backwards under the force of the strikes raining down on him.

Sunstone swiped at Rian, who deflected the strike with both of his swords, but the assassin quickly lashed out with his free hand, catching Rian across the face before he could step away. Rian stumbled backwards, gingerly touching his jaw. Sunstone laughed. I struggled against Hematite, but he only held me tighter; so tight I could barely breathe.

Grinning, Sunstone lunged at Rian again. As he moved, Rian twisted sideways, but the assassin's sword caught Rian across one hand and sliced the side of his ribs. Rian sucked in a breath, stifling a yell of pain, and dropped a sword as blood ran from the back of his injured hand.

Hell's teeth.

Sunstone moved back, a satisfied look on his face. 'And now you will die, Prince Valerian, and we'll take Amethyst to Serpentine.'

Rian staggered, fell to one knee, blood seeping into his tunic from the wound. He leant on his remaining sword, its sharp tip sinking into the ground, and he clutched his bleeding side with his injured hand. He took a great, shuddering breath and looked up through his dishevelled maroon hair, his eyes like agates, face grim. Blood ran down his wounded hand in a rivulet of red, a drop of blood at one corner of his lips. His voice had a steely edge.

'You're *not* taking her.'

'Yes, we are.' Sunstone laughed. 'We're taking her to her overdue death,' he said, voice grating. He glanced at me. 'And it will be a long one, Lady Merciless. Your suffering will become legend inside the Coterie and across the Five Lands.'

Rian's eyes hardened further as his hair shifted in front of them in a whisper of a breeze that wove its way through the alley. Flames moved in their amber depths, and he was now verging on positively feral. Never before had he in any way frightened me, but at that moment I finally saw the Fire Spinner he could truly be. The two assassins had pushed him too far, and when he spoke his voice was white-hot metal, each word coming out slowly, with precision and determination.

'You're…not…taking…my…wife…anywhere.'

He remained on one knee, raising his bloody, free hand. His face took on a look of intense concentration, and a fireball suddenly burst to life in his palm.

Sunstone's eyes widened. 'What th—'

Rian launched his fireball at the assassin. Sunstone screamed in agony as the fire slammed into him, his clothes immediately catching light as if he'd been struck by lightning. I sensed Hematite go rigid with shock behind me. Then he relaxed his grip on me for a split-second as he looked on in horror. I took my chance. I slipped free of him, ducking down below the knife before swiftly rising and planting my elbow firmly in his face. I twisted around, moved behind Rian, and prepared to draw Deorwine and Glædwine, but the prince was already on his feet, lunging forwards.

Rian's sword burst into flames as he sliced between Sunstone's ribs, then spiralled around and struck at Hematite before he could use his Air Magic, ramming his fiery blade into the shocked assassin's stomach, taking him down, too. Hematite slid backwards off Rian's sword, hitting the ground in a pool of blood. Not far from him, lying in the dirt, Sunstone took a final shaking breath and ceased all movement, still smouldering. The smell of burning flesh made me gag.

Rian, breathing heavily, turned towards me. His eyes were wild, full of raging flames. Blood beaded at the side of his mouth, a purple bruise appearing on his lower jaw, his dishevelled hair catching the wind and sweeping into his eyes as the fire around his sword dulled, and the weapon returned to plain steel.

'Damn, that was close,' Rian said, panting. 'Are you okay?'

I didn't reply, just ran into his arms.

'Ow!' he gasped.

'I—I'm sorry. Are you all right?' I asked, looking at his blood-soaked tunic and injured hand.

'I'll live,' he said, a wry smile playing on his lips. 'Which is more than can be said for those two.'

I glanced down at the dead assassins. 'How did you do that? With your sword and the flames?'

He shook his head. 'I don't really know,' he said softly as he winced in pain. 'I just knew I'd die before I let them take you.'

I swallowed. 'I know. And I love you for it, but I really don't want you dying for me.'

'If not for you, then who?' He looked at me earnestly. His eyes still had fire in their depths.

'I'd rather you didn't die at all,' I said.

He nodded, his smile quickly replaced by a wince as he grabbed at his side. 'I'll try not to.' He looked at his dull blade. 'The sword just took on a life of its own. I don't know if I could do it again. It just sort of happened.'

'Come on, let's get you to the inn,' I said.

We retrieved his other sword and I ducked under his arm, helping him walk slowly back to the inn through the alleys.

'Were they the ones you saw in Flos?' he asked, leaning heavily on me.

'Yes – Hematite and Sunstone, Juniper's bodyguards,' I said. 'No one's ever bested them. You were amazing.'

He started to grin, then flinched, his face twisting with the pain from his jaw. 'I try,' he said.

'But why didn't you use your Fire earlier?' I asked.

'I guess I'm still getting used to using it in a fight, and I didn't want to wear myself out too soon, either,' he said. 'Besides, I don't necessarily want to incinerate *everyone* who attacks me.'

I grunted. 'You have a point.'

'Good thing no one saw us,' he said, glancing around at the empty alleyways. 'We'd have had trouble trying to explain all this to the authorities.'

The inn wasn't far, and we entered as the others were heading towards the stairs. Tarragon glanced at us then ran over.

'Bugger me, what happened to you?' he asked, taking Rian's other arm.

'We had a disagreement with a couple of assassins,' Rian said.

'They're still after you? Or is it all of us, now?'

'Neither. They wanted to take Phire back to Iolite and she didn't want to go.'

Tarragon raised an eyebrow.

'Let's get you upstairs and I'll look at your wounds,' Anise said, wincing as he saw the blood seeping into Rian's clothes on his side.

We made it up the stairs and went into our room. Rian sat slowly on the edge of the bed, and I helped him remove his tunic and shirt.

'You're lucky it was only a glancing blow,' I said as Anise arrived with his Herb Chest and looked at Rian's wound.

'It doesn't feel like a glancing blow,' Rian muttered.

'Phire's right,' Anise said. 'It's just a flesh wound. The blood is out of proportion to the injury, really.' He opened his Herb Chest and started rummaging through it, tongue out like usual as he worked.

Willow came in with a bowl of water and a clean cloth. 'Here, I thought you might need this,' she said.

'Thanks,' I said as she left with Tarragon, who'd been hovering at the door until he could be sure his cousin was all right.

I cleaned the wounds on Rian's face and hand, then gently started on his lean, muscular chest.

'Ow! That stings,' he protested.

When we'd left Iolite and I'd touched his naked chest by accident, I'd been embarrassed, but now no shyness or awkwardness existed between us. That was well in the past. We were completely comfortable with each other now, and each other's bodies.

'I've got to clean it,' I said. 'You don't want an infected wound.'

He groaned.

'I've got some salve you can put on once it's clean that will help with the pain. Then it needs to be bandaged up for a day or two with these,' Anise said, placing some white bandages on the bed with a little glass jar of yellow cream. 'You can put the salve on your face and hand, too. They should heal quite quickly.'

'Thanks, Anise,' Rian said. 'I think we can manage now. You get to bed.'

Anise frowned. 'Are you sure? I'm happy to stay.'

'It's fine – we'll be all right,' Rian said, nodding. 'I have an exceptional nurse.'

I raised an eyebrow. 'Have you indeed?'

'Yes, I have.'

Anise smiled. 'Very well. You know where I am if you need me,' he said, leaving the room and shutting the door.

'You really trust me to do this?' I asked with a grin.

'Like Anise said, it's not that bad.' Rian smiled, then winced as I continued cleaning.

'Maybe I can help even more,' I said, finishing cleaning – the bleeding had stopped and I got the salve out, preparing to apply it, but first, knelt beside the bed. I gently ran my fingers across his skin before kissing near his wound, three little kisses parallel to its trail.

He moaned. Was that the pain? Or something else?

'Did I hurt you?' I asked anxiously.

He shook his head. 'No,' he said, reaching out and tilting my head up. He looked into my eyes. 'Not at all. You could never hurt me.' He leant forwards and tenderly kissed me, his lips gentle and soft. My blood turned molten at his touch, and I gave myself over to the kiss, melting into it. Suddenly, he pulled back. Unshed tears stood in his eyes. 'I'm so sorry.'

CHAPTER THREE

'Sorry about what?' I asked, frowning.

'I'm sorry about the fact that m—my body doesn't show I still desire you,' he said, staring at the far wall as he sat back up. 'And I do, truly and completely.' He shook his head. 'I want to make love to you so badly that it hurts.'

I frowned, tears welling in my eyes. He hadn't mentioned the side effect from his Mandragora Berry poisoning for sometime, and I'd thought he'd now finally come to terms with it. I was wrong. I reached up and moved his hair from the side of his face, leaving my hand resting on his warm, uninjured cheek.

'I know,' I said, smiling in an attempt to comfort him. I took his good hand. 'I feel the same, but you don't need to worry about not showing how you feel, because you do show it.'

'I do?' The look of surprise and hope on his face tore at my heart.

'Every time you kiss me, when you hold my hand, when you touch me and your fingers linger a little longer than necessary.'

'Oh,' he said, rubbing the back of his neck. 'I didn't realise—you can still tell, even though…?'

I turned his red face towards me. 'Yes, absolutely. And don't go stopping what you're doing now.'

He gazed into my eyes, then looked at our joined hands. 'Don't worry, I won't,' he said, leaning towards me again and kissing my lips before gently parting them with his tongue. As the kiss deepened, I pulled him towards me. His tongue tasted of treacle as I ran my fingers through his hair. He held me close, my blood turning to liquid gold, his breaths growing heavier. We parted, our foreheads touching as we still held each other close.

'If that wasn't desire, I don't know what it was,' I said, my voice hoarse.

He gave me a wan little smile. 'I thought I'd sort of got used to it, but sometimes… sometimes it's like a knife in my chest, knowing I can't show you how much I love you, how much I need you like *that*, like I so desperately want to. I ache for it.'

He had such a forlorn expression that I took his face in my hands, his eyes still glistening, full of longing.

'And I ache for it and want it, too, but we need to be patient while the side effects wear off,' I said. 'I love you, Valerian. I love you to distraction. The side effects make no difference to my feelings because I love being with you, holding you, kissing you.

You're mine, and all the more precious for what you've lost.'

'*We've* lost.' He pouted.

'All right, *we've* lost – but it's not permanent. You know that. We just have to be patient, and wait for the poison to work its way out of your system.'

'You still think it will?' he asked, his breath hitching as a glint of hope appeared in his eyes.

'Of course, it will. Anise said so. You know it will. We just need to give it more time.'

'Then I'll hold on to that – and to you,' he said, a little smile slowly creeping across his face. 'I could never have imagined finding someone as special as you, my Samphire Amethyst, someone so understanding and compassionate. You're my assassin, for you took my heart when we met and no one else will ever be able to claim it,' he said, taking my hand and placing it over his heart, his skin like fire under my hand, his heart pounding under my fingertips as he spoke.

There wasn't much I could say to that. 'You're my assassin, too. You killed any chance there would ever be anyone else in my life, or in my heart, but you. It's all you now, and you fill my head every minute of every day.'

He grinned back at me, a rather self-satisfied look in his eyes.

I sighed.

'You promise you'll always be mine?' he asked.

'I do, as long as you stay mine,' I said, grinning.

'I'll always be yours, don't worry about that.'

I kissed him on the head. 'Good. Now, let me get this salve on and bandage you up.'

He nodded. 'And as much as I love kissing you, and I really do, perhaps we should stop because it's really quite painful.'

I looked at his injured face. 'It hurts to kiss me but you were doing it anyway?'

He nodded, a wry grin on his lips. 'Couldn't help it. I needed to.'

'Well, that's desire right there,' I said. Even now, I was amazed at his love for me. I grinned back and gently applied the salve to his chest wound. He flinched, but made no other protest as I finished applying it, bandaged him up and then tended to his hand and face.

I awoke, tangled in bedsheets and Rian. I could see no way I'd be able to extricate myself without waking him, so I lay there, content, his slow breathing making my neck warm. The steady rhythm of his heartbeat echoed through me as he rested against me, his hot Fire Spinner body keeping me warm. I rather wished we could stay like this, but eventually he woke up. He smiled at me, kissed my neck, making me giggle, and then kissed my lips like it was the first time, hesitantly, gently, tenderly, sending a little thrill cascading through me.

'And a good morning to you, too,' I said, kissing his nose. 'I take it your face is feeling better?' His bruise had faded and his cut had healed, thanks to Anise's salve.

He nodded. 'It feels fine. You know I'd like to wake up like this every day,' he murmured, trying to kiss my neck again, but I twisted out of the way. 'In fact, I'd like to stay entwined like this with you forever in a warm, loving embrace.'

'Me too,' I said, still tangled up with him and the sheets. 'Would you stop that, though, it tickles.'

'I'm sorry.' But he wasn't. He took hold of me, carrying on with his barrage of kisses until I was laughing.

'Oh, you think it's funny, do you?' he asked, feigning a pout.

'Not in the slightest,' I said, trying to compose myself. 'It's just the effect you have on me. You make me happy.'

He smiled smugly at me. 'That's all right, then, because you make me very happy, too.' He straddled me and kissed me again, this time with purpose.

A sharp knock sounded at the door.

'You two ready to go?' Tarragon said through the wood.

Rian looked at me, rolled his eyes, and sat back on his ankles. 'Be down in a minute,' he called back.

'All right.' Footsteps moved down the corridor.

'I swear, with Tarragon around it's probably a good thing that things are the way they are. He has this nasty habit of interrupting us when we're about to… you know.'

I laughed. 'Tarragon's knack for interrupting at inappropriate moments means that Silphion will never be required.'

Rian gave me his lopsided smile. 'Hmm. Unfortunately.'

I pulled him down to me for one last kiss.

He groaned.

'Your wound?' I asked, looking towards his bandages.

'No, I'm just really stiff from the fight.'

'Sunstone did give you a clobbering.'

'Is that what you call it in Iolite? When someone keeps coming at you like a wagon-load of bricks?'

I smiled. 'What do you call it in Aerba?'

'"Beating to a pulp" usually suffices.'

'It wasn't a beating – you stood up to him. I've never seen anything like it.'

Rian grinned. 'I was quite good, wasn't I?'

'You were better than good,' I said. 'You were magnificent.'

Rian beamed from ear to ear, his eyes sparkling with pride. My magnificent husband, who had quite literally saved me from a fate worse than death. He leant down, kissing me again, his soft velvet lips caressing mine as I wrapped my arms around his neck.

'Mmm, this would definitely be a lovely way to start each morning,' he murmured, his eyes dark, voice husky.

'I'll remember that,' I said. 'Now come on, you – we'd better check your bandage then get dressed, or Tarragon will be knocking on the door again.'

He groaned, but duly got off me. I really wished we could linger, but it wasn't an option. One day we would, but that morning was far off in the future somewhere.

On inspection, Rian's wound had almost healed, so we applied a little more of Anise's salve and then used the spare bandage, before meeting everyone downstairs, having a quick breakfast and starting out.

Grey clouds hung low in the sky and I pulled my new warm sheepskin jacket a little tighter. We rode at a steady rate, making good time across the undulating grassland. Sheep dotted the shallow hillsides, forests reaching away into the distance in dark green walls. The road was more dirt track than anything, rutted by the great lumber wagons pulled by teams of horses. We passed one stuck in the unrelenting mud, the wagon master whipping at his horses as he tried to get the cart free.

'He'll kill them if he keeps on like that,' Onyx muttered. He rode beside me while ahead, Mal chatted to Rian. 'But maybe he doesn't care about that. What's a dead horse to him?'

'I couldn't do it,' I said. 'Too cruel.'

Onyx glanced at me. 'Could you have carried out your orders if Carnelian hadn't done your killing for you?'

'I've asked myself that over and over, but I don't think so. In a fight, in self-defence, maybe, but not in cold blood, however well I'd been trained.'

'What would you have done then?'

'I truly don't know. I never figured that out. I was so lucky I never had to, and in a way, I'm grateful to Carnelian for that.'

Onyx sniffed. 'But not for other things,' he said, his gaze straying towards Rian.

'For other things, I'd like to throttle him,' I said.

'So I noticed, although, "slit his throat" might be a better phrase.' He grinned at me.

'I almost did it,' I said, remembering how I'd held my War Fan at Carnelian's throat back in Mere. Had even drawn blood. 'But I'm glad Rian stopped me.'

'So am I. You don't want that millstone around your neck.' Onyx fiddled with his reins.

'Is that how it feels? A heavy weight?' I asked curiously.

He shrugged. 'Sometimes. Sometimes not. Depends who it was, really. There are some people I killed who were innocent of anything - the millstones - but there are others who the world is better off without.'

'But someone else shouldn't make that choice.'

'I was the executioner, not the judge and jury, and besides, I did it all to keep my mother safe,' he said, his eyes glistening as he remembered his dead mother. 'I didn't have a choice any more than you would've done. You'd have done it to keep Mal and Beryl safe. You'd do it now to protect Rian.'

'I wonder...' I glanced at my elder brother. Would I have killed to keep him safe? I turned back to Rian. Would I kill to protect him? In my wedding vows I'd promised to be his shield. I shivered. 'Let's hope we never have to find out. I wouldn't want to discover I wasn't up to the task.'

'When it matters, when the lives of your loved ones are on the line, you do what's necessary – at least, that's what I've learnt. What's more important? A loved one's life or your scruples? You'd find the courage.'

Would I?

We rode on, camping in a little valley in the hills. The air here had a real chill to it. Rian lit our campfire with his Magic, and it did its best to keep us warm as Sage produced a hot stew for our evening meal.

'Do we need to set a watch?' Tarragon asked.

'Normally, I'd say no. There's nothing out this way to bother us,' Mal said.

'You remember?' Onyx asked, raising an eyebrow.

'I remember coming out this way with you once and almost freezing to death because you forgot to bring the tent, but there was never any suggestion of it not being safe.'

'True.'

'But… That was before we had the Coterie breathing down our necks, so maybe we should?' Mal glanced at Rian.

'I'd certainly be happier with a watch,' Tarragon said, throwing a twig into the fire.

Rian nodded. 'Then we'll take turns,' he said.

The others murmured their approval.

We rose early the next morning as dawn painted the sky in silvers and golds. My breath lingered in the air when I exhaled. It reminded me of winter in Iolite – a time of year I didn't enjoy. I was also glad of my gloves, whatever Onyx had thought, and smiled to myself when I noticed him rubbing his hands together to warm them before he mounted his horse.

As we rode along, mist still lingered in little hollows in distant valleys made pink by the rising sun. Mal rode at the front of our party with Onyx, Willow and Anise not far behind as Sage and Tarragon chatted with Rian.

Riding at the back of our group, I gazed around at the green landscape. We'd reached a section of roadway where the track ran along the top of a cliff, a fast flowing river running below, a winding snake of foaming white water. Around us, scrubby thickets of Trewan Broom grew scattered around the countryside like dice.

Mal said we'd reach Spindle tomorrow evening, or the next morning at the latest, and as we rode, I ruminated, as Onyx liked to call it. The discovery of my Magic Angle weighed on me. I wasn't really sure how to use it, how to control it – even what I could do with it, other than I'd helped save Rian's life from the poisoned berries Carnelian had left for us. I'd somehow broken the Curse that had been placed on me when I'd taken up the Cursed Weapons that sat on my back, and had even broken Mal's enchantment, but I was still none the wiser as to how. All I knew for sure was that I'd *thought* something. Willed it to happen, and by some miracle it had. But it had never been deliberate. If I did do something deliberately, what would happen then? Quintessence was allegedly the strongest, purest form of Magic. It remained to be seen what I could really do with it.

Rian's horse suddenly shied.

My horse jumped sideways. Snorted. Reared, his nostrils flaring.

Hell's teeth. Whatever was wrong with the creature?

The path under us began shifting as if a mynogre pounded at it from below. We weren't that close to the cliff's edge, but close enough. The horse reared again, snorting loudly. Rian turned in his saddle, his eyes widening in horror.

I slipped from my saddle, landing hard with a yell, the wind knocked out of me. One hand caught in the leather reins of the spooked horse, and the beast started to drag me towards the shuddering cliff edge in its frenzied state.

I desperately tried to free my hand. I grabbed at the tangled reins, shaking and twisting them to no avail. The flailing horse pulled me closer to the yawning space. I grabbed my War Fan, flicked the green malachite leaves open, and pressed the amethyst button at its base. The thirteen knife points shot out and I immediately sliced through the leather. I was free. I lay on my back, forcing air into my lungs as I clipped the Fan back onto my belt.

My horse shrieked.

The disintegrating edge crumbled away and the beast staggered, then tumbled into the abyss opening beneath it. The cliff edge continued to expand towards me. I tried to scramble away, but with every move I made the ground beneath me shook and became less solid.

I glanced up.

Rian had jumped from his horse and was sprinting back to me, his eyes wild as he ran, Tarragon not far behind him. Shock registered on Mal's face as he realised what was happening.

The ground gave way.

I fell.

I came to rest clutching a root of some sort, my feet dangling over a one hundred foot drop and the wide mountain river below it, raging within its banks. White water streamed around jagged rocks poking up out of the deep, swirling torrent. If I survived the fall, surely I wouldn't survive a trip down the river?

A hot, strong hand grasped my wrist.

'I've got you,' Rian said, lying on the ground, reaching over the cliff edge. I took hold of his wrist as he made a grab for my other hand. Our fingers brushed against each other's, but he couldn't quite reach far enough to get a hold. 'Reach. Give me your other hand,' he said, stretching further, voice as strained as I'd ever heard it.

I glanced at the cliff.

'Phire, your hand – reach for me,' he pleaded.

But I couldn't.

The cliff edge beneath him was crumbling. I so wanted him to pull me to safety, back into his arms. Neither Quintessence nor Fire could help us now.

'Leave me,' I said.

'What?' A look of confusion crossed his face as cold dread filled his eyes.

'The edge is crumbling. You try to pull me up and you'll just come over, too.'

'I'm not leaving you,' he said, his voice steel.

'You must.'

'I c—can't, dammit,' he said, fear overtaking him, the look in his eyes breaking my heart.

'Rian, if this is to be the last thing I ever do, I want it to be saving you,' I said, fighting back the tears. 'You said if you were going to die for anyone it would be for me. I feel the same – I'd die for you, to keep you safe. You have to let me go.'

'I...' The broken sound of his voice, the look in his eyes, were knives twisting in my gut. 'I love you.'

'I love you, too, and I don't want you to die,' I said, painfully aware of the ground crumbling under him as little pieces of rock and earth broke away, falling towards the unforgiving river. He didn't have much time. 'Tell Mal I love him. Now get back while you still can.'

I let go of his wrist.

'No, Phire, *please*, don't do this.' He tried to grab my free hand with his other one.

Missed.

'Tarragon!' I yelled, knowing he wouldn't be far away. 'The cliff's giving way. Pull Rian back. Now!'

'No!' Rian's eyes clouded, full of pain, tears and despair.

'I love you,' I said again.

My hand started to slip from his. There was a jerk – Tarragon pulling Rian back as I'd asked?

The cliff edge crumbled.

Rian lost hold of me.

My last glimpse of him was his horror-filled face, drained of all colour, his eyes wide with disbelief and the deepest despair. It tore my soul.

'No! Samphire!' Rian's anguished screams echoed around the cliffs as air rushed past my ears.

CHAPTER FOUR

My hair streamed around me. Above, the cliff edge broke away in a shower of earth and root.

No Rian.

Thank the Stars he'd not fallen, too.

Chaos… Swearing… Tears. What was happening up there? Were they pinning him down to stop him from jumping after me?

I hit the water.

The river was like a solid wall of ice, knocking any air I had in me straight out of my lungs. The angry water roared around me, filling my ears with whispers of death. Its cold hands clutched at my arms and legs in a desperate attempt to keep me under its surface, under its control. I struggled to reach sweet air as it twisted and pulled me around, banging me uncomfortably into rocks that littered the riverbed, one hitting my face, others pummelling my body, arms, legs – none of me evaded the beating. I'd be black and blue if I ever escaped this hell.

My head broke the surface. I was vaguely aware of a huge rock in the centre of the savage torrent looming ahead, ready to finish me, just as the current pulled me down again. The river grasped at me, holding me under.

Air… I need air.

My head broke the surface and I gasped in a lungful of delicious oxygen, but I was almost upon the boulder.

Miss it, miss it—

The river violently yanked me to one side, away from the white, churning water around the rock and into a deeper channel where the river appeared less intent on drowning me.

I had no chance to analyse what had happened, whether my Quintessence had played any part in my near miss. The cold chilled my bones, and an ache seeped through me. I glanced up, but the cliff was far away now.

I would see Rian again. I swore it.

Although the icy water was quickly sapping my strength, I started to fight against it again as it swept me along. My fingers were already numb, my toes quickly following. Gradually, I managed to swim over to a slack area of water at the side of the river. I dragged myself up onto a rock and scrambled onto the river bank, shaking.

I lay looking up at the grey clouds scudding across the sky. My cold, wet clothes clung to me as I shivered. I wanted Rian. Needed his warmth, his touch. The Cursed Weapons still sat determinedly on my back, digging in uncomfortably. Groaning, I rolled onto my side.

Where was Rian? What was he thinking? Was Mal with him? A hundred questions were replaced by a thousand more jumbling around in my mind. I was just glad Rian hadn't fallen, too. I'd have lost him in the watery madness if he'd joined me in the maelstrom. I really had to teach him to swim.

My fingers wouldn't move, they were so cold, and I couldn't feel my toes at all now. I tried to get up. I had to keep moving – if I were a Fire Spinner this would be so different – but although my mind screamed at me, my body had other ideas. I needed to rest, just for a moment. I sank down onto the soft, grassy bank. I had to be covered in bruises from my journey downstream, and between that, the cold sapping my strength, not to mention the shock, I wasn't in a good way.

Rest for a moment. Then I'd carry on and get back to Rian. Amber eyes swirled in front of me. Maroon hair shifted in an invisible breeze. I had to get back to him. What would he be thinking? Did he know I'd survived, or did he think me dead? Knowing he wasn't by my side, when he had been every day for so long, suddenly filled me with fear. I needed him. More than I realised.

Darkness beckoned.

Survive. I must survive. For him...

I awoke, shivering. My whole body shrieked. I pulled myself to my knees, then used a rock to get to my feet. I leant on it, the world tilting and dancing before my eyes. Something wet irritated my eye. I rubbed it. Winced. My hand was red with blood from the bang to my face.

How had this even happened? One minute I was riding along happily, the next I'd been cruelly ripped from Rian.

I managed to stagger away from the river, but in what direction I should head, I didn't know. I was cold, damp, exactly as I had been when Rian had found me in the Samphire Creek in Aerba. So long ago, now – but I remembered the shivering and the feeling of the cold knife blade at my throat. In that moment, I'd thought the Prince of Aerba was going to kill me for the assassination of his sister. But he didn't. Something had stopped him, and instead of seeking revenge, instead of me persisting in my dislike of High Bloods – against all the odds – we'd fallen in love. We'd conquered those odds stacked against us and had come out stronger for it.

We'd both changed so much. Learnt so much. Become better people as a result of our adventures and our love for each other. He was a wiser, stronger man than he had been when we'd met – he had an inner confidence now that he'd lacked before. I'd learnt to trust again, to break free of the assassin Coterie. Together we'd become strong, become one. Without him now, I had an ache in my chest and a feeling of loss and incompleteness.

I'd fallen in love with Rian without even realising it. By the time I had, he was so lodged in my heart that there was no way I was ever going to prise him out again. But by then, I didn't want to. I'd never been happier than when he confessed his true feelings to me, if you put aside the Curse. Things had been bleak, but we'd stuck together, determined to grab whatever time we had with each other. Eventually, we'd found the answer to the Curse and with Rian guiding my hand, we'd broken it together.

I missed him.

I longed for his touch, to touch him, to hold him.

Staggering on, I grasped at bushes to support my onward plunge across the scrubby grass and into a forest of pine trees. The smell hung heavy in the air, twigs and pine needles crunching underfoot as I fought my way along to... to where? I shivered in the cold air. I had no idea what direction to go in. No idea where Rian and the others would go now. I assumed they'd think me dead and go on with the mission – or would they? They had no Quintessence Spinner now; they couldn't restart the Vortex without me. But they could still try to stop Juniper. I hoped they would. And I hoped I could catch up with them, but my battered limbs had other ideas.

I tripped on a branch and fell to my knees. I attempted to get up again, but didn't have the strength. Sinking to the ground, I collapsed into an inky blackness.

Birds chattered overhead. The sun had started on its downward descent from noon. I grabbed hold of a tree, pulled myself upright. How long had I been unconscious? It didn't matter. All I had to do was carry on. Get to Rian.

I moved along, lurching from tree to tree for support, my head aching, my body shaking from the cold, my still damp clothes doing nothing to help me. I staggered along for what felt like hours, but was more likely minutes, as the uneven ground tried to trip me up. I grasped a tree, trying to stay on my feet. Failing. Sliding to the mossy ground.

A figure stood before me, back turned, maroon hair loose.

Rian?

No. It couldn't be. This person had wavy hair. The figure turned around. I stared at a woman with the same amber eyes as my husband. Who was this?

She smiled at me, a gentle smile, and held out a clasped hand. Slowly her fingers unfurled and resting on her palm, sparkling in the ethereal light, lay Rian's ring, my wedding ring. It slowly evaporated into glistening sparks. I glanced at my hand, and watched as it slowly materialised around my finger.

I looked over to her. The woman continued to smile, then gestured with her hand. Did she want me to come to her? Suddenly, a spinning wheel of multi-coloured light appeared behind her. Was that what she'd been doing with her hand? She vanished.

I moved. Groaned. Opened my eyes, but the bright sunlight made me squeeze them shut, my head aching as if a summer storm rumbled away inside it.

'Still with us, then, Amethyst-sweetie? I thought for a moment you were already dead.'

My heart skipped a beat. I slowly opened my eyes and turned to look towards the voice. On a log not far from where I lay, a broad grin on his pale face that lit his watery grey eyes, sat Carnelian. He was busy whittling a large twig with his knife, his right eye twitching slightly as he blew his dark, lank hair from his eyes.

'Go away,' I rasped, my throat feeling swollen, as if lined with gravel.

He laughed. 'Don't you want someone with you when you die?'

'Not you, no.'

He smirked. 'As you wish.' He put the wood down and got up, his knife still in his hand, and stepped towards me.

I shrank back. I could do nothing in the state I was in and he knew it. I didn't have the strength to reach for my War Fan, let alone the Cursed Weapons.

He grinned, reached down towards me, and moved my hair from the side of my face. 'Nasty. I don't think I need to do anything here. You'll die of exposure soon enough; no point in me curtailing your agony.'

'You d—don't want to take me back to Serpentine?'

'Why would I want to do that? My orders are to kill you and your prince on sight. No. I'll let you die here. It might take a few hours, but I think you deserve it, really.' He sat down again. 'I've been practising with a slingshot, you know. The stone is of course completely silent when you let it go, and no one knows what's happened until it's too late. Did you know you could send a stone over a thousand feet away?'

I grunted as he blurred for a moment.

'Hiding in a broom thicket was so easy, all I had to do was wait for you to pass,' he continued conversationally. 'I didn't actually mean to hit your horse with the slingshot – I was aiming at Valerian's – but the beast shied at a fly or something, and my stone hit your horse instead. Still, it doesn't really matter as I was after you both. You're accounted for now, and as for your princeling, well…'

My heart froze. 'W—what have you done to him?'

'Nothing. I didn't have to. When I last saw him he was close to dead, too.'

'What? What do you mean?' My voice came out high-pitched, but thin and weak.

'He seems to be taking your death rather hard – in fact, it looked to me as though your loss was killing him. He'll probably be dead of a broken heart before too long – just give it a day or two. He really does love you, doesn't he? I wish Topaz loved me like that, but I think it's more lust on her part.' Carnelian stood up and stretched. 'Well, nothing left for me to do here. It's all turned out rather well, really. The two of you have saved me the bother, and there's something rather poetic about the both of you bringing about your own desperately tragic demises.' He chuckled, resheathing his knife. 'Quite exquisite, really.' He glanced around. 'Can't stand chatting all day. Must go – I need to report back to Juniper the two of you are dealt with, now. Permanently. She will be pleased. I might even get a promotion. Farewell, Amethyst-sweetie.'

He turned and disappeared off into the undergrowth, the sound of his feet breaking dead twigs gradually fading into the distance.

I rolled onto my back, my bruised and battered body screaming at me again as the Cursed Weapons dug into me. I reached towards my War Fan. Felt my belt. Grasped air. I groaned. I must have lost it in the river. A little tear fell from the corner of my eye. Mal's present to me. Losing it after all this time hurt more than the bruises.

I took a deep breath. I had to get back to Rian. Had to show him I was still alive before…

I tried to move, tried to get up.

Cold and darkness swamped me…

A red shadow loomed in front of me. Menacing. Aching for death. I couldn't move. Tired. No energy. Everything hurt.

I was falling. Falling with no end.

I lay on the ground.

A sudden pain twisted in my gut like cold flames, and pure agony followed in its wake as a shadow stood in front of me.

'Compliments of Juniper,' the shadow said.

A purple mist swam around me and I was back in the dungeon under Viridi Palace, gazing at Rian's ring with its tiny diamonds that circumnavigated the golden band.

The stones caught the torchlight, sending little rainbows across the cell. Rainbows of fire.

The diamonds started to glow white.

I stood in the Viridi Throne Room, mist twisting around my feet and the skirts of a purple silk dress. A small child ran across the room, laughing, as Rian, dressed in his burgundy and gold Aerban coat, his hair in its high Aerban ponytail, playfully chased after her…

The crack and snap of a fire sounded across from where I lay. The smell of freshly cut wood, and herbs, lingered in the air. Warmth surrounded me. I opened my eyes. My heart raced. Just ordinary dreams. I squinted. I lay on a low bed in a cabin under several blankets, my clothes now dry, still wearing my new fingerless gloves. Grey twilight was visible outside the window high up in one of the wooden walls. I groaned. Almost night?

'You're awake, then,' came a deep, gruff voice to my right.

CHAPTER FIVE

I pulled myself up on one shoulder. An oldish man, face crinkled like parchment, hair and beard of salt and pepper, sat opposite me. His eyes belied his age, their piercing blue containing an element of youth. His clothes were thick wool and leather in dark, shabby colours.

'I—I...' My throat scratched; I hadn't realised how dry it was.

'Here,' he said, passing me a mug.

My muscles protested as I sat up and reached out, the bruises I'd acquired on my journey downstream making themselves known. I looked suspiciously at the mug's contents. On the far side of the room Deorwine and Glædwine sat winking at me in flickering golden candlelight and firelight.

'Only mead,' he said.

Good thing Rian wasn't here. *Rian.* The thought of him brought me up short. Not having him here with me filled me with such unease that for a moment I found it hard to concentrate. I glanced up at the man.

'Who are you?' I asked, going back to eyeing the liquid in the mug, reluctant to take a drink from a stranger.

'I'm Ostianzis,' the man said. 'And you're a Quintessence Spinner.'

I choked. 'H—how do you know that?'

'I can feel the Elemental Magic coursing through your veins.' He grinned, the parchment around his eyes crackling. 'Stew?' He moved over to the fireplace where a blackened pot sat above the flames. Only now did I realise he had to be a good seven feet tall.

My forehead furrowed. 'Are you one of the Senex?' I asked, remembering the stories Onyx's grandfather had told us in Mere about the old, grizzled men with exceptionally long life spans who had a feel for Elemental Magic.

I took a sip of the mead. The sweet, cloying liquid eased the discomfort in my throat.

He smiled as he handed me a bowl of vegetable stew and a spoon. 'You've heard of my kind?'

I nodded, putting my mug down and taking the bowl, my body aching.

'I am one of the last,' he said, a faraway look in his eyes for a moment. 'I can feel your power within you. It's very strong.'

I wish I could.

'I've met your kind before,' he said. 'Many times.'

'But there haven't been any Elemental Angle Spinners for years,' I said, enjoying the hot herby stew full of succulent vegetables that warmed my core.

'Five hundred or so,' he said, nodding. 'I think that's when I last met a Water Spinner, and he didn't know what he was.'

I coughed again, wild carrot catching in my throat. 'How old are you?'

He grinned. 'Just shy of a thousand years.'

'Oh.' Someone could really live that long? I continued eating, the aches slowly beginning to ease.

'I found you in the forest, battered and bruised,' he said, looking intently at me. 'What happened?'

'I was with my friends riding along the road and the cliff edge gave way. My horse went over, then I fell, too. I managed to drag myself out the river and into the forest, but passed out.'

'And your friends are Magic Spinners, too?'

It seemed more statement than question. I nodded, hoping I could trust this strange man.

'Well, then, just as I thought,' he said, rubbing his chin. 'Maybe you are the ones.'

A chill ran down my back even as I ate the warm soup. 'I've heard that before.'

'Indeed. Then you should listen.'

'No one's said exactly what it is we're supposed to do, though. I mean, I assume it's to do with the Vortex and nature?'

He nodded. 'The Crystal Vortex is failing – I can feel it and see it in the nature around me. Only the right Magic Spinners can restart it with the Fire Opal, but I can see you already know that.'

I nodded, putting my bowl down. 'But why us?'

'Because you're here, now. You already know you have to, and you're the only ones who *can* do it. You are the most powerful Spinners there have ever been.'

'Rubbish. We're nothing special.'

'Of course you all are.'

'You mean the things we've done… They're greater than an ordinary Spinner could have accomplished?'

Ostianzis nodded. 'You didn't know because you had no one to compare them to.'

'But we didn't even know about our Magic until recently.'

'And yet it's always been there, hasn't it?'

What he said was true. Looking back everyone else now realised their Magic had helped them sometimes in the past, they just hadn't realised it. Apart from me.

'You say that, but I don't even know how to use my Magic,' I said, taking a sip of mead. 'My Angle hasn't been there until recently.'

'That is because you are a Quintessence Spinner, and they are always the last to show their Magic. But I can sense you, too, have already done great things with it.' He glanced at the wall where the Cursed Weapons sat benignly, their purple crystal sending rainbows into the corner of the room.

'By accident,' I said. 'I found out my Talisman was a Magical Fire Artefact, and Artefact could be used against Artefact.'

'That wouldn't have been enough on its own to negate the Curse of Aldorbana and Cwicsusl. That Magic was too strong. It wasn't an ordinary Curse – if there is such a thing. It was a special enchantment. There must have been something else.'

'No. I slammed the Talisman into the shield – with Rian's help, of course. I wasn't very well at the time.'

'Rian?' Ostianzis leant forwards. 'Who is Rian?'

Thinking of Rian felt like a knife twisting in my gut. Being without him after so long together physically hurt. 'Prince Valerian of Aerba – well, he was prince until his brother, Chervil, became King and removed him from the line of succession.'

'He has a Magic Angle?'

I nodded. 'He's a Fire Spinner.' I finished my mead and set the mug aside, shifting position in the bed.

'Then there you are. That's it. A Quintessence Angle Spinner using a Fire Artefact with the help of a Fire Spinner against the Cursed Weapons? That's extremely powerful Magic. The two of you could have split Elvedon in two with Magic like that.'

My eyes widened. The whole world of Elvedon? The Six Lands *and* everything beyond?

He chuckled. 'Well, not quite, but it's some of the most powerful Magic alive, and Fire Spinners are almost as powerful as Quintessence. Together you're quite a force to be reckoned with.'

Is that how Rian had been saved from Mandragora Berry Poisoning? Using Fire *and* Quintessence Magic? Somehow, together, we'd been strong enough to burn the poison away and save his life; but at a cost.

'That's as powerful as any Magic,' he continued. 'Your Quintessence would've kept you alive while you were Cursed, too, kept you going far longer than a normal person.'

I looked up at him. 'My brother was enchanted. He fought me with an Artefact, the Malachite Dagger.'

Ostianzis' head tilted to one side. 'The Magentan Dagger?'

'I—I don't know what that is.'

'A block of malachite was once created by the Vortex. The Artefact was taken to the Chromian capital of Magenta and forged into the blade. Some called it the Eternal Dagger.'

'Yes, that's the one. I haven't heard it called Magentan before, though.'

'I thought the Artefact lost long ago, rather like the Time Ring and the Nightfall Crystal.' Ostianzis scratched his head.

'The Dagger has been in Iolite – but I don't know for how long. I've never heard of the other two. What are they?' I asked, frowning.

'Both were deemed powerful Artefacts, rather like the Dagger, although the Time Ring's power was never Released.'

What did that mean? He continued so quickly I had no time to ask.

'For centuries the Ring was owned by the Aerban Royal Family. When Chroma began gathering up Artefacts after the Great Pestilence, nigh on five hundred years ago, Queen Cicely of Aerba left it with her dear friend, Electra, the Queen of Calperion, for safekeeping.'

'Calperion?'

'One of the Far Eastern Lands. She felt it would be safer there, what with the Chromians gathering up as many Artefacts as they could find. Whether it was ever Released or came back to Aerba, I don't know.'

'And the Nightfall Crystal?'

'Ah, that was a strange Artefact. A true anomaly. Created by the Vortex eight centuries ago, it always had a malevolent aura. Once Released it called to evil and evil responded. The Chromians could find no way to destroy it, and deemed it so dangerous that they sent it across the ocean in the hopes of concealing it forever. After that, no one knows,' he said waving his hands. He paused. 'Do you still have the Dagger?' He looked intently at me.

I shook my head. 'It was destroyed when I fought my brother with the Cursed Weapons, not that they're Cursed now.' Memories of that fight with Mal still sent shivers down my spine.

'Your Quintessence could have done that, I suppose. Did you break his enchantment, too?' he asked.

I nodded.

'That's powerful Magic as well – do you know who enchanted him?'

'My stepmother, Juniper, Mistress of Iolite.'

He sucked in a breath of air through his teeth. 'I always wondered about her.'

'You know her?' I asked.

'When she lived on Trew as a young child I knew her. Grew up all wrong, though – too much anger in her.' He paused for a moment. 'So what are your intentions?'

'We need to get to Spindle and warn the Royal Family there may be a Coterie assassin in their midst, preparing to strike if they don't do as Juniper wants. Then we're going to Chroma to restart the Vortex.'

'You have the Fire Opal?'

I shook my head. 'We're hoping someone in Chroma may know where it is.'

'You'll need a Magic Spinner for each Element, and a Waker, to save the Crystal Vortex.'

I frowned. 'We have the Spinners, but what's a Waker? Another crystal?'

'No, no, no,' Ostianzis said, laughing. 'A Waker is a Middle Blood. Artefacts cannot be used until their power is awakened – Released.'

So that's what he'd meant by "Released".

'So a Waker had already awoken my Amethyst Talisman for Rian to be able to use it?' I asked, wondering who had done it and when.

Ostianzis nodded. 'At some time in the past that would have had to have happened. The Fire Opal, though, has never been used by Magic Spinners, its true identity always kept secret. Because of that you'll need a Waker to first Release and awaken the Magic at its heart.'

I frowned. 'But it looks as if there's a flame at its heart now.'

Ostianzis chuckled. 'That is its natural state. Nothing compared to what it will look like when it's Released. Its inner power will be unquestionable once freed. Once this has been done, you must hold the Fire Opal as your Elemental Spinners channel their Magic Angles into you, or it, whichever you prefer. You alone are the one who can contain all the power. You must focus your Quintessence on the Fire Opal, then channel everything into the Crystal Vortex to restart it.'

Hell's teeth. I swallowed. 'But I still don't really know how to use my power.'

'You'll learn.'

That wasn't helpful. 'I don't have much time.'

'You'll have enough, my girl.'

'So why are we all Elemental Angle Spinners?' I asked.

'You say your prince is of Aerba?'

I nodded. 'Yes, and two of his cousins are with us, along with my brother and three friends.'

'In these lands, Magic was always strongest in the blood of the Aerban Royal Family. That'll be why.'

'Rian, Tarragon, and Sage all share an ancestor with my brother and me. So we have it because of our bloodline, but what about Anise and Onyx? We have no blood relation to them, as far as I know.'

Ostianzis smiled. 'Magic Blood calls to Magic Blood. Unconsciously draws you together. You would have attracted the others without even knowing it.'

In the case of Sage and Anise, and of Mal and Onyx, attraction was the right word – and for Tarragon and Willow, for that matter. *And look at me and Rian...*

'Thank you for everything you've done, everything you've told me, but I need to go now,' I said. The wind whistled outside the cabin window.

Ostianzis peered out into the night. 'No, not now, it's dark,' he said. 'You can stay here. I'll take you to the nearest settlement at dawn.'

'But I need to get back to Rian.' My heart twisted as I considered the torment he must be going through without me, not knowing what had happened to me. What misery was he in? 'I just don't know where to start looking for them.'

Ostianzis scratched his chin. 'If they followed the main road towards Spindle, they'd probably be arriving at the Dentro Settlement around now.'

I stood up. 'Then I have to go. Which way is it?'

'I'll take you there at dawn. There are wolves out here in the forest at night.'

'There are?' I shuddered.

He nodded. 'You must be patient.'

I didn't want to be patient. I needed to get back to Rian, but without Ostianzis' help I wouldn't have a clue which way to go, and I definitely didn't want to run into any wolves. I'd have to do as he said, even though my heart ached for my husband. I so wanted him to know that I was fine.

I managed to get some sleep, exhausted from my ordeal. The warm cabin and blankets weren't quite the same as having my husband beside me, but at least I wasn't cold now. Even so, the night passed slowly. My mind kept going over all the things that Ostianzis had said, all spinning around in my head like a maelstrom. How I'd survived the Curse, how Rian had survived his poisoning, how to start the Crystal Vortex, and the fact we needed a Waker. And when I did get those thoughts into some semblance of order, my mind turned to Rian. Was he coping? Was he awake, in despair and grieving my loss, or sound asleep in a place where he could forget what had happened, at least for a little while?

True to his word, Ostianzis woke me just before dawn, made me eat a breakfast I wasn't sure I really wanted, and then led me from his cabin heading out into the pine trees surrounding his home. He strode along, a large wooden bow on his back like so many of the Trewans had. My muscles strained with every step, my newly acquired bruises making themselves known as we walked. Everything still hurt. I also felt the loss of my War Fan. Keenly. I was so used to it banging on my thigh as I walked that the fact it was no longer there left me feeling quite bereft, almost naked, even if the Cursed Weapons did dig into my shoulders from time to time to remind me that at least they were still there.

The air had a cool, fresh tinge to it today, the heady smell of pine lingering amongst the trees as we walked. The silver light of dawn gradually turned into pinks and golds as we followed a little trail through the pines until we reached the river, then walked along the bank for a good hour. Ostianzis was a mine of information about Elemental Magic, and he told me more as we walked – if only we'd found him before. He told me of the Senex, of their long life increased by their exceptional sensitivity to Elemental Magic. I'd had no idea anyone could live as long as he had. He also mentioned something about Quintessence Angle Spinners and having prophetic dreams when they were ill, which started me wondering about my hallucinations back in Cilantro when I'd taken the Moonflower Elixir. At least, I'd thought they were hallucinations.

Finally, the Dentro Settlement he had spoken of loomed in the distance. A large group of wooden buildings stretched along both sides of the river. Smoke drifted lazily from chimneys as the folk cooked their breakfasts and warmed their houses. We crossed over a wooden bridge and made our way into the larger part of the settlement. The question was, if Rian and the others were here, where would they be? Too few people were out and about yet to ask.

'There's an inn just down here,' Ostianzis said, pointing to a good-looking, two-floored building along what classed as the main street.

I nodded. A good place to start making enquiries. As we approached, I noticed a young man with his back to us, standing just outside the inn door. Another young man came out holding two steaming mugs and joined him, handing him a mug.

'By the Herbs, you should never have let him near that Pine Wine. I told you not to,' the first said, taking the proffered mug.

The other closed the inn door behind him and shook his head. 'I didn't. He got hold of it all on his own. I think his only intention was to get hold of some sort of alcohol, then get himself blind drunk. I've never seen him so determined, or so upset. He was verging on feral. Even when his mother died, he didn't react like that. Mind you, given how that happened, that's probably made this all the worse. He's completely broken.'

'He was unconscious until dawn – still tipsy even now, if you ask me,' said the first. 'I don't think he ever wants to be properly sober again. Not that I blame him. I'd probably feel the same in his shoes.'

'I'm quite glad he did turn to drink. For a while there, I wasn't sure if he was going to set light to us or self-combust.'

I stopped. Tarragon and Sage stood just up ahead, backs to me as they talked… And they were talking about *Rian*?

Tarragon turned. His face blanched. 'Bugger me! Samphire?' Tarragon dropped the mug of hot tea he'd been holding.

'What? Really?' Sage turned and looked at me, mouth gaping open.

'Phire!' Anise yelled, barrelling out of the inn and grabbing me in his arms. I flinched, my bruises protesting. 'You're alive? Thank the Herbs. We thought you were dead!'

'Just,' I said, 'but I won't be for much longer if you continue to squeeze me like that.'

'Sorry,' he said, stepping back and grinning, a tear escaping his eyes.

Tarragon swept towards me and picked me up, spinning me around. 'I can safely say I've never been so happy to see anyone,' he said, his voice thick with emotion as he kissed my cheek.

Sage pulled me from Tarragon's grasp for a hug and I couldn't help but flinch with the pain. To my amazement, he copied Tarragon, kissing my cheek. Never the most demonstrative of men, Sage's actions actually shocked me. He looked at me, his brown eyes glassy.

'How did you survive?' Sage asked.

'With help from Ostianzis,' I said, introducing the Senex.

'And her Quintessence,' Ostianzis rumbled.

'That, too.'

They looked at the towering Senex in awe.

'Thank you,' Tarragon said, reaching out and shaking his hand.

'Assuming anyone feels like eating anything, breakfast will be ready soo—' Onyx stopped dead as he came out of the inn. He swallowed, his face blanching. Sniffed. 'Mal, you might want to come out here.'

'Blast it, Onyx, why?' Mal's voice was tired and drained. 'I really don't want to. I've got a headache and just want to be left alone. What is it?' He peered wearily out the door. His red-rimmed eyes almost popped out of his head. He dashed out of the building and grabbed me, tears running down his cheeks. 'Ama? We thought you were dead,' he said, hugging me fiercely. I gasped as he squeezed my bruised body. 'How did you survive? Are you hurt? Is it really you? How?'

'Slow down, I'm fine, just a bit bruised,' I said, hugging him. 'I'm all right.'

He stepped back and rubbed his tear-filled eyes as Onyx hugged me.

'We thought we'd lost you for good this time, for sure,' Sage said, shaking his head and making his earring jingle.

'You can't get rid of me that easily.'

'I'll go tell Willow,' Tarragon said, grinning.

He'll probably be dead of a broken heart before too long, just give it a day or two. Carnelian's words suddenly forced their way into my head.

I looked around. 'Where's Rian? Is he all right?'

The grin faded from Tarragon's face and he glanced at Sage, then pointed along the street. 'Down by the river. Sage and I were just going to get him.' He hesitated. 'By the Herbs, Phire, he was utterly broken after losing you. Inconsolable. Last night he, well, he...' Tarragon either couldn't finish or didn't want to.

Sage sighed. 'He got drunk.'

Tarragon flinched. 'Totally wasted, you mean.'

'Rian? Drunk? Don't be daft, he never drinks.' I looked from Sage to Tarragon to Anise. 'Does he?' I shivered as an icy hand grasped at my heart.

'He did last night,' Sage said, screwing his nose up.

'Admittedly he never has before, which was part of the problem,' Tarragon said. 'He's not used to it.'

'Drank himself senseless, into an oblivion the likes of which I've never seen before, Ama,' Onyx said, a slightly wild look around his eyes, 'and I've seen plenty of drunks in Iolite.'

'So have I,' Mal said, nodding. 'It was an awful sight.'

'And it's something I hope I never see again,' Tarragon said, his brow furrowed.

'It wasn't pretty, Phire,' Anise said. 'And to see Rian, of all people, like that, was…' He shuddered.

'Let's just say that last night the world seemed rather upside down without you here,' Tarragon said.

'Really unnerving, that's what it was,' Sage said sourly, looking away.

My heart stuttered. 'But he's all right?'

'He'll be fine when he sees you and knows you're all right,' Anise said, frowning slightly. 'We kept an eye on him all night last night, just in case.'

'In case of what?'

Tarragon glanced at Anise, then looked at me. 'Losing hold of you destroyed him. He was so devastated we were really worried about him, especially with his Fire Magic. We didn't know what might happen if he somehow lost control of it.'

I swallowed. Carnelian had been right. 'I'll go to him.'

'Be gentle with him – he's got the mother of all hangovers,' Anise said.

'He was utterly crushed, losing you like that,' Tarragon said.

'We all were.' Mal looked at me, his eyes still watery.

I squeezed my brother's hand and nodded, then turned and headed in the direction Tarragon had indicated. As I walked along, the walk became a jog, then the jog became a sprint.

Rian had got drunk? Because he thought I was dead? He never drank alcohol, hated the stuff. What pain had he been in – was still in – to make him crave the drunken oblivion Tarragon and Onyx had spoken of? Maybe Carnelian had been right after all, maybe

Rian really would've died of a broken heart – but he wouldn't now I'd been able to get back to him. But where was he?

I reached the edge of the water, looked down the river, then up.

Rian sat on a rock near the water, head in hands, long maroon hair loose and dishevelled. His body shaking.

Utterly broken.

I stopped, gasping in horror.

Hell's teeth.

My heart shattered.

Tears welled in my eyes.

'Rian!' I yelled, running along the bank, my breaths coming in gasps, my chest tightening. He ignored me. 'Rian!' I loosened the weapons from my back, letting them fall to the ground.

This time he looked up through red, glassy eyes that struggled to focus properly, misery resting in his soul. How much had he drunk? He stared. Wiped his eyes, eyes that widened so far I thought they'd pop out of his head.

'Phire? Phire!'

He ran towards me, stumbling over the rocks. I reached him. He caught me in a hug of such joy and delight I didn't think he'd ever let me go. I flinched as his strong grip crushed my bruises and still-aching limbs, one warm hand pulling me against him around my waist, the other across my back and up to my neck, holding the side of my head, holding me to him. I didn't care about the pain; being held by him was far more important – just as kissing me had been more important to him than the pain after having fought Sunstone. A strangled sob escaped his lips as his body trembled, still holding me tightly.

'Are—are you really here?' He choked the words out, resting his head between my neck and shoulder, breathing me in to reassure himself. 'Is grief making me go mad? Am I imagining you?' He stepped back, holding my face in his hands as he searched my eyes for the answer he feared. His eyes, bloodshot from drinking, shone as hot tears slid down his cheeks.

'No,' I said, my voice catching. 'I'm here—*really* here.'

'I thought you were dead; I never thought I'd see you again,' he said, his face stripped bare, his voice cracking with emotion. A look of wonder filled his puffy, red-rimmed eyes – but a deep pain lingered in their depths, too. Deep enough to have killed him? The great anguish etched into his drawn face made him look at least fifteen years older.

I took his face gently in my shaking hands. 'I'm all right, really. A bit bruised, but I'm fine.'

He hugged me tightly once more, then picked me up and spun me around, making me wince. He gazed at me again, as if to make sure I was still there, then pulled me in, urgently kissing me as if he'd never kissed me before and had been saving everything up for this one time. This one moment. This one searing kiss. I felt his pain, despair, misery, desperation – and his joy. Tasted his salty tears, the lingering alcohol on his tongue, felt his warm velvet lips – more intoxicating than ever. His body still shook as he wrapped his arms around me, holding me close, and I felt his heartbeat through my chest as it sped along. He rested his forehead on mine, one hand going to the side of my face.

'I love you,' he murmured, a longing in his voice that twisted in my chest. 'I thought you'd gone forever.'

'No, not forever,' I said, wiping tears from my eyes.

He looked at me, his amber eyes pools of love, the pain that had been behind them now slowly easing and drifting away, replaced by ecstasy and elation as he realised he wasn't dreaming.

He flinched, rubbing his head.

'What is it?' I asked, resting my hand over his.

'Headache.'

'You were drinking.'

He winced at the statement. 'You know?'

I nodded. 'The others told me.'

'It was the only thing I could think of to do that would block out the pain... at least for a while,' he said, bowing his head.

'You had to be in a great deal of pain to turn to drink when you hate it so much,' I said, shifting his tangled hair from his eyes.

He looked at me. 'I didn't want to believe you were dead. Couldn't. I prayed to the Herbs you were alive. My heart desperately wanted to believe you were, but my head told me you couldn't possibly have survived that fall. So, all I wanted was to drink myself into darkness, forget you were gone. Forget how I'd lost hold of you. Forget everything.'

'And I think you did for a while, if what Tarragon and Onyx said is right. But you didn't lose hold of me – I let go of you.'

'But—'

'This wasn't your fault, and don't you dare start thinking it was.'

He nodded slowly.

'Did it help? Getting drunk?' I asked, resting my hand gently on his cheek.

Shame filled his eyes. He shook his head ruefully. 'Not really, not in the end. To begin with it did. Last night. After I'd passed out. I suppose unconsciousness has its benefits – but this morning I'm so nauseous, and my head feels like it's going to split open. I'm never drinking alcohol again, not a drop, whatever happens to you,' he said, flinching once more at the raging headache.

'Can't Anise give you something for the pain?'

He nodded. 'He did offer before I came down here, but if not for the headache, I feared that I wouldn't feel anything at all. I'd just be numb. The pain helped me focus, feel I was still alive, even if inside my heart was dead.'

I slipped my hand into his. 'I think now's the time to take that remedy of Anise's, don't you? You look awful.'

'Thanks,' he said drily.

I turned his head towards me. 'But still the most handsome man I know,' I said, kissing him on the cheek.

He wrapped his arms around me again, his touch scorching. My bruises protested. His mouth met mine, and as we kissed his hot tongue no longer tasted of alcohol. Had he burnt it away with his Fire Magic? He was certainly stone cold sober now, whatever Sage had thought earlier. All I knew was that I didn't want to let go of Rian ever again. However much it hurt. And as for him, the way he was holding me to him, it felt as if he was actually attempting to make me a part of him as he grasped my body tightly.

'That's enough, you two. Stop buggering about,' Tarragon yelled from along the road. 'Breakfast's ready and you probably need something in your stomach to go with all that alcohol, Rian.'

Rian groaned as he reluctantly pulled away from me, muttering darkly about Tarragon always interrupting us at important moments.

I smiled. 'He's probably right about the food, and anyway, you need to see Anise.'

He nodded, taking my hand. 'I won't lose hold of you again,' he said, kissing my fingers.

'I didn't want you falling with me,' I said, holding back more tears. 'I didn't want you to die, too.'

'I know,' he said, 'and I love you for it. But next time, I'd rather go with you. If it hadn't been for Tarragon, Sage and Anise holding me down, I would've followed you over the edge.'

I blinked. 'All three of them?'

'Yes,' he said, screwing his face up. 'It took them all to stop me from jumping after you.'

I gazed at him. Carnelian had been right. Rian's love for me was so strong it took three grown men, and all Magic Spinners at that, to stop him from jumping off the cliff after me.

'You'd really have jumped, even though you can't swim?'

'I'd walk into hell for you,' he said, looking into my eyes. Flames burnt deep within his amber irises, the depths of his soul on display for me, and only me.

I swallowed. 'Tarragon said he was scared you might burn someone, or yourself.'

Rian bowed his head. 'So was I. Keeping my power in check was... so incredibly hard. Took almost everything I had not to burn up. Literally.'

It hadn't quite been twenty four hours, but in that time Rian had nearly shattered into pieces. Despite his strength, when it came to me he was fragile — as fragile as I was about him. Any hurt to him, hurt me; any pain he felt, I felt. I loved him so much I ached. In many ways our love made us incredibly strong, able to stand against so many things in the Lands, but we had a chink in our armour — each other. If one of us fell, the other would, too. Our love was strong, we were unassailable together, and yet it also made us weak in a way I could never have imagined. To me it made him even more beloved, adored and cherished. Our love was something precious to be protected and defended at all costs. I would guard him with my life, be his shield as I had vowed — and yesterday morning I'd done just that. But now I understood.

From now on we would stand together and we would fall together.

I owed him that.

'Another time — if there is another time, and I hope there isn't — I won't let go of you,' I promised.

He sniffed. 'If you do, I'll come straight after you, whether Tarragon, Sage and Anise are there or not. I couldn't stand to go through this misery again.' He took hold of my hand, his grip warm and firm.

I nodded, once more moving his matted hair from his face. 'I know. And I'd come after you.'

'Like you did in Iolite. Twice.'

I gave him a little half smile and nodded. 'Exactly.'

'I had no idea I could ever feel like this. I guess with great love you risk everything, you risk the huge pain and grief of losing that person. But it's worth it. You're so precious to me, Phire. I've learnt you're like air — I can't live without you.'

'You're being poetic again,' I said with a smile, leaning towards him and kissing his nose. 'I like it.'

He smiled, his eyes full of love. 'The truth is, I need you, and I'll need you for the rest of my life.'

'And I'll always need you, too,' I said. 'Did I ever mention that I loved you?'

He grinned. 'Once or twice.' He looked at me, took a deep breath, and sighed a long, happy sigh.

I smiled, squeezing his hand. 'Come on, let's get back before Tarragon comes down here and drags us to breakfast.'

'And you must tell me what happened, how you survived. You're sure you're all right?'

'A few bangs and bruises, that's all.'

'You'll have to show me later. Maybe I can kiss them better.'

'You're impossible,' I said, smiling up at him.

'I keep trying,' he said, grinning..

'We have a lot to talk about – and there's someone I'd like you to meet.'

'Oh?'

'The Senex, Ostianzis,' I said as we headed back to the inn. I glanced at the grey sky as low clouds moved in from the east on a stiff breeze.

'The Senex are real?' he asked, the Weapons attaching themselves to my back.

I nodded. 'He found me and took care of me.'

'Then I want to meet him and thank him.'

People now bustled about on their morning business as the Settlement came to life. Rian led the way into the inn where the others sat around a table eating. Willow jumped up, knocking over her chair, and ran over to me to give me a huge hug. It only lasted a couple of seconds before Rian prised her off me and took hold of my hand again. I wasn't sure how long it would take for him to get fed up with holding on to me. It might be a while, though, not that I was about to protest anytime soon – I rather wanted to hold on to him, too.

I looked around the table. 'Where's Ostianzis?'

'He's gone,' Tarragon said.

'What?'

'I think he was rather uncomfortable with the number of people moving about now,' Onyx said.

'He said for us to say goodbye to you,' Mal said, sitting me beside him.

Rian glanced at Tarragon who screwed his face up and moved along a seat so Rian could sit beside me, taking his plate with him.

'Thanks,' Rian said.

Tarragon grunted. 'As long as I get to eat I don't really care where I sit.'

'You and your stomach.' Willow giggled from opposite him.

Mal moved my hair from the side of my face and grimaced. 'That looks like it hurts,' he said, studying the cut and bruise.

My hand went to it, and I winced. 'A little.'

'Let me see,' Rian said. 'I hadn't noticed. I'm sorry.'

'It's fine, really.'

'I have something you can put on your bruises, preferably after you've had a warm bath,' Anise said. 'It works better that way. And something for your cut, too.'

'Then maybe we should rest here today,' Mal said. 'Captain Pol won't get to Spindle for a few days yet. If we delay here for one it won't make much difference.'

'I think after yesterday some of us could do with a rest,' Tarragon said, only he wasn't looking at me.

Rian shifted uncomfortably in his seat. There was more they weren't telling me. I'd get it out of Rian later.

'It would give Phire a chance to recover,' Rian said.

'I'm fine,' I said.

'Can you pass me the salt, Ama?' Onyx asked, sniffing.

I smiled and reached out for the salt cellar. Winced. A little involuntary gasp slipped out my mouth as my bruised body protested. Onyx smirked. He'd done that on purpose just to make a point. I glowered at him. I could ride – if I had to.

'We rest today,' Rian said firmly, his hand resting on my thigh.

'So, tell us what happened, Phire,' Anise said as more food arrived.

CHAPTER SEVEN

The story of my survival, Ostianzis, and the information I'd picked up on breaking the Curse, Magic Spinners and Wakers ended up being told over breakfast and beyond. I told them how Carnelian had precipitated the whole incident.

'I swear I'll kill him,' Onyx said.

'You are aware there's a queue?' Anise asked. The dryad massacre still weighed heavily on him.

'A queue?' Mal asked, raising an eyebrow. 'You'd better put me at the front.'

'I think Rian already has that pleasure, even more so now,' Onyx said.

'No. If he's anyone's, he's mine,' I said, clenching a fist under the table.

Rian slipped his hand over mine. 'I thought we'd talked about this before.'

'But things are different now.'

'Why?'

'Because he's tried again.'

Rian shook his head. 'No, it's no different.'

My shoulders sagged. 'I still think you should let me,' I pouted.

My husband gave me a long look.

'Rian's right, Ama,' Onyx said. 'You don't want that millstone.'

I grunted. 'Not sure it would be a millstone.' Although deep down I knew they were both probably right.

'Looks like you need to fight it out with Onyx and Anise then, Mal,' Tarragon said with a chuckle.

'We don't need to fight, just leave it to the three of us.' Onyx grinned. 'Perhaps we can take it in turns to carve bits out of him?'

'Interesting suggestion, but don't tempt me,' Anise said.

'I wasn't – I was being deadly serious.'

Willow and Sage looked at each other and shook their heads.

Once we'd eaten, mugs of tea arrived with biscuits and we continued talking. Mid-morning I glanced out the window. The grey clouds cried as rain came down in buckets. It was a good thing we hadn't set off after breakfast – we'd be miserable and soaked to the skin by now, depending on how well our sheepskin coats performed.

Anise prepared his salves and sent me off to the bath house behind the inn with Rian. I lingered in the hot water, Rian joining me. The heat, increased by Rian, soothed my aches and pains until they drifted away.

'Time to get out or you'll turn into a prune,' Rian said eventually, climbing out and drying off before pulling me out and handing me a towel.

As I got out he gave a little gasp. He hadn't seen me get in – too busy sorting out the towels and Anise's salves. Now he saw the extent of my bruising.

'You didn't say it was that bad – you're black and blue all over,' he said, grimacing.

'It's nothing,' I said, trying to dry myself off without wincing. I failed.

'Don't rub – here, let me.' He gently dabbed the towel over me to dry the worst of the water off. 'I hadn't realised you were this bad. How did you manage to let me hug you earlier?'

'It hurt, but not hugging you hurt more.'

He stopped what he was doing, one hand going to the uninjured side of my face. 'I know exactly what that's like. I love you.' He kissed me tenderly, brushing his lips against mine, not touching me anywhere else in case he hurt me. 'Now let's get these salves of Anise's on you.'

He was true to his earlier words. He kissed every bruise before he applied the salve.

'So what happened? After I fell?' I asked.

'You're supposed to be resting, remember? Anise's orders,' Rian said, lying beside me on the bed in our room, hands behind his head. The rain had continued to hammer down all morning and into the afternoon, the street now a quagmire of mud and puddles.

'I can rest and listen.'

He groaned. He obviously didn't want to tell me.

'Carnelian said something about how upset you were, but I'd like to know the truth rather than his warped version,' I said.

Rian glanced at me, then looked up at the ceiling, one hand over his forehead as he grimaced, but he remained silent on the subject.

'Then I'll ask Tarragon,' I said.

He groaned again. 'No, I'll tell you. He'll only embellish it.' Rian turned towards me. 'I lost hold of you as Tarragon pulled me away from the cliff edge.'

'I wondered if that's what happened.'

'I wasn't exactly happy about it. I swore at him – quite a lot.'

'He only did as I asked. Have you forgiven him?' I moved onto my side with a wince.

'Just about. Anyway, I tried to get up, tried to get back to the cliff edge, but Sage pretty much jumped on me, Tarragon had my legs, and Anise grabbed my arms. They held me down for a full ten minutes while I yelled some rather unpleasant things at them.' Rian's eyes had an agonised, ashamed look in them.

'I'm sure they understood.'

'They did, and I did apologise later. But at the time I was so angry, so broken, I couldn't help myself.'

'And Mal?'

'They may both be smaller than him, but Onyx and Willow had a good hold on your brother. He took it all a lot better than me and didn't try to throw himself off into the river.' He reached out and took my hand. 'After I'd finally calmed down they got me on my horse, Sage on one side, Tarragon the other, and held my reins to make sure I didn't try to get away. The rest of the journey was a blur. I don't remember much other than my Fire burning inside me, an excruciating ache in my chest, and...' He glanced at me, then away to the wall rubbing the back of his neck. 'Tears.'

I moved a little closer to him, flinching as I did so, and wrapped my arms around him, snuggling into his warm chest. He slid his arms around me, pulling me to him even more so I could feel his heartbeat.

'I was exhausted by the time we arrived here. It'd taken everything I had not to burst into flame and to stay on that horse, not ride off and find the nearest cliff edge. I didn't know how I was going to go on without you, how I could bear to even contemplate such a thing,' he said, stroking my hair as he spoke.

'You would've done.'

'Would you? If I'd died after the berries?'

I frowned, glad he couldn't see my face. 'I'd pretty much decided to go back to Iolite.'

'Why?' he asked, his voice incredulous as he moved back slightly to look into my eyes. 'Why, by the Herbs, would you go back there?'

I couldn't meet his gaze. 'I—I was going to go back and kill Juniper, Beryl, Carnelian, and anyone else who got in my way, then jump from the highest tower.'

'You were?' His eyes widened. 'I'm sorry you were hurting so much, too.'

I shrugged. 'It's like you said, when you have a great love...'

'You're open to huge grief,' he said, giving me a sympathetic little smile.

I lay on my back. 'Anyway, that's what I told myself I'd do – it gave me something to focus on while you were writhing in pain on the floor, dying.'

He slipped his arm around me, pulling me back to him. 'The most I could focus on were the advantages of getting drunk out of my mind and the oblivion it would bring me. That's all I wanted. Darkness to hide in. To forget. After that, I hadn't decided.' He glanced at me. 'And now I don't have to – and neither do you.'

I smiled, a tear leaking from my eye. He brushed it away.

'Are you really all right now? After yesterday?' I asked.

He laughed. 'I should be asking you that.'

'You were hurt just as much as me.'

'I suppose so, but in a different way. I think I'll heal quicker than you, though. You know it was strange, without you with me. I'm so used to us being together now I almost felt – no, not almost – I *did* feel scared. I've never felt like that before. Ever. You not being near me was torture. And terror, too.'

My nose tingled as tears welled in my eyes. 'I thought that was just me.'

He looked at me, looked into my soul, shook his head. 'No, it's not just you,' he said, his voice thick with emotion.

'Carnelian said he thought you'd die of a broken heart.'

Rian frowned. 'What?'

'When he found me in the forest after I'd dragged myself out of the river, he said he'd seen everything – including your reaction. He said he thought you'd be dead of a broken heart in a day or two.'

My husband sighed. 'Perhaps he was right. It's true I was hurting more than any injury I'd ever had, more than any pain I experienced during my poisoning. Maybe he could see it, too. I don't know what would've happened to me, and I don't want to.'

'When he said that I—I...' Words failed me and tears stung my eyes.

'Hey, it's all right. I just love you a lot, that's all.'

'And I love you.'

'Why didn't he kill you? You never said before – I mean, he had the perfect opportunity.'

'He said I'd be dead of exposure soon enough and didn't want to "curtail" my agony, then ran off back to Juniper to tell her the good news.'

'Bastard.'

'If he hadn't left me, I wouldn't be here now.'

Rian glanced at me. 'Maybe I should thank him one day, then.'

I smiled. 'Maybe you should.'

He leant towards me, kissing me with his hot lips. 'Now, try and sleep for a while. You'll need the rest if we're going to continue tomorrow.'

I nodded and snuggled back into his warmth and love.

In the early hours of the morning a hand smacked me in the face.

'What the—'

Rian shifted restlessly beside me. From the look on his face he was in the grip of a fearsome dream. His hand swept towards me again, just visible in the dim light from the little candle flickering at the side of the room. This time I was prepared and grabbed his hand before it hit me.

'Rian, wake up,' I said, holding his hand to stop him from striking me again, but he continued to thrash about. 'Rian!'

He murmured something unintelligible. His other hand flew through the air.

I grabbed both of them and straddled him, trying to keep him from injuring himself, or me, further. His body was hot and sweaty from his nightmare, which had him firmly in its grasp.

'Rian, please, wake up.'

'Phire! Phire?' He opened his eyes; eyes full of anguish and tears. He looked at me, took a deep, shuddering breath that bordered on a sob, and yanked me to him. I collapsed onto his chest as he took great heaving breaths, holding me so close I could feel his heart slamming into his ribcage as it thundered away. 'I'm sorry...'

'Shh, it's all right, everything's fine,' I whispered into his ear as I stroked his head. 'It's just a nightmare.' And a formidable one at that.

We lay like that until his breathing calmed and his heart rate steadied. I sat up a little, looking into his puffy eyes, and brushed his hair from his face.

'Any better?' I asked.

He nodded.

'Want to talk about it?'

He swallowed. 'It... I...'

'You don't have to.'

He took a breath. 'You were hanging onto the cliff edge and I couldn't reach you and… and…'

He didn't need to say any more.

I gently kissed his lips. 'I'm here, everything's fine.'

He looked into my eyes, flames stirring in the amber depths of his.

Suddenly he pulled me to him again and kissed me, urgently, in a long, fervent kiss, rolling me onto my back as he held me close, tongue exploring as he rested on me. His grip was firm, his kiss ardent and intense. He'd never kissed me like this before. Not with such need, such urgency and longing. Tears filled my eyes, my heart aching for him and his inner turmoil as he let out a low little moan.

He pulled back, face flushed, eyes full of so many emotions. 'I'm sorry, I just had to do that. I needed it, needed you. I didn't mean to—'

I pressed a finger against his lips and smiled at him. He had nothing to apologise for because after everything we'd endured, I wanted him in exactly the same way. And just to prove it to him, I pulled him back to me, my mouth claiming his as we kissed again, long and deep.

'I know. I needed it like that, too. You don't need to apologise,' I said.

He moved off me and lay beside me, looking at the ceiling. 'That nightmare was worse than when you almost died from the Elixir, worse than the dryads.'

'Those dreams passed, and these will, too,' I said, pulling myself up onto one shoulder to look at him. 'It'll just take a while for us both to settle.' No need to mention to him that I'd already been having a restless night because of my own bad dreams – dreams of falling, dreams of searching unending forests for him.

'I know,' he murmured. He turned to look at me. 'Hold me?'

'Always,' I said, snuggling against his hot body and wrapping my arms around him as his arms slid around me and held me close.

The next morning dawned clear as we prepared to leave. I walked outside into the muddy street, Rian holding my hand, looking sideways at me periodically as though he still didn't entirely believe I was really there. He even squeezed my hand every now and then as if to check he wasn't dreaming me up. We'd both managed to sleep a little, but I think it had been more like dozing for both of us, and we hadn't let go of each other all night.

The horses were waiting patiently for us, but we were one down.

'You're riding with me,' Rian said.

I smiled. 'As if I'd ride with anyone else.'

Rian nodded to someone over my shoulder, and two strong hands suddenly had hold of me. Tarragon had me up on Rian's horse in one smooth movement, just as he had when we'd first met. Rian climbed up behind me, slipping an arm around my waist.

'I don't want you running off,' he whispered in my ear, his breath warm on my neck.

'You think I will?' I asked.

'I think you thought about it when we first met and you were sitting in front of me on my horse.'

'I did, but I quickly realised I wasn't going anywhere, particularly once you had your arm around me.'

'That was the general idea. I'm glad you didn't run. We'd never have got to know each other. And this time, I don't want you falling off behind me. You have form there, too.'

I rested a hand on his arm and we set off.

'I'm sorry about last night,' he whispered in my ear.

'Don't be daft, you've nothing to be sorry for,' I murmured back.

'Other than that extra bruise I gave you.'

'That's all right – I hadn't got one there,' I said, trying to lighten his mood a little.

He gave a little snort. 'Anise's salve will work quickly on it.'

'I know.'

'So am I one of these Waker thingies?' Willow asked with a little cough as we reached the edge of the Settlement.

'I was hoping to ask Ostianzis a bit more about it before he left,' I said. 'I don't know if all Middle Bloods are Wakers, but let's hope so.'

Willow beamed. 'See,' she said, glancing at Tarragon. 'You need me *too*. I'm important.'

'Who said you weren't important?' he asked.

'With you all being fancy Magic Spinners I was feeling a little left out. Bobbins. Seems you need me after all.'

'*I* always need you,' Tarragon said smoothly.

She fluttered her eyelashes at him. 'That's all right then.'

'He knows how to keep in her good books,' Rian whispered in my ear. I tried to stifle a giggle, but he was quite right.

We rode steadily, the track turning to stone, making our going good. I still felt tired from the previous couple of days, but it had obviously affected Rian immensely, too – more emotionally than physically, perhaps, but his fatigue was obvious. Late in the afternoon I felt his hold on me relax; his tense muscles released and his head dropped forward, resting on my shoulder. He started, muscles tightening, and sat up straight.

'Don't nod off, you might fall,' I said, holding onto his arm.

'Sorry. I'm so tired, that's all. I think the drink's after effects are still leaving my system, not to mention the emotional strain of losing you, and last night. I feel like I could sleep for a week.'

'We can rest soon.'

'Together,' he whispered in my ear.

'Together,' I whispered back.

By nightfall, lights glimmered in the distance as the sun's final rays bounced off the faraway sea.

'Spindle,' Onyx said, a satisfied note to his voice.

'Do we go straight to the palace?' Sage asked, looking out over the wooden buildings and the smoke drifting into the hazy sky towards a large, grey limestone building at the city's centre. It had an imposing look to it, with great ramparts and towers along its walls. It reminded me a little of the Crimson Castle back in Iolite, and a little shudder rolled down my spine.

'Not tonight,' Rian said, shaking his head. 'Let's go first thing tomorrow. Best to face it fresh.'

'Then I know a good inn we can stay at,' Onyx said with a sniff.

'*The Ship*?' I asked.

Onyx nodded. 'That's the one.'

'We stayed there a couple of years ago, remember, Mal?'

Mal frowned. 'Was that the place with the candles in the blue glass bowls?'

'Yes,' I said, smiling and casting a quick glance at Onyx. Things were coming back to my brother now, much to my relief. Onyx grinned and nodded.

'It was quite nice, from what I remember,' Mal said. 'Fantastic fish suppers.'

Sage groaned. 'Tell me they serve something other than fish?'

'Yes, they do,' I said. 'They have really nice meat pies with herbs, vegetables and gravy.'

'You had me at pies.'

'And tea?' Rian asked.

I nodded. 'Yes, they serve tea, too.'

'Sounds the perfect place to spend the night, then,' Tarragon said, rubbing his stomach.

We rode into Spindle, through a large wooden gate and walls, and into the main city. It sprawled across three hillsides and on down to the sea. On a small rise at its centre sat the Trewan Palace, and beside it the Temple of Trees. The large buildings' grey limestone didn't help to improve the drab appearance of the city with its dark wooden buildings. We rode down the main thoroughfares and towards *The Ship Inn*, which stood not far from the docks. We stabled the horses and took rooms at the inn.

They still set their candles in blue glass bowls to protect them from going out each time a door opened and closed. Sage grinned when his meat pie appeared, and went into raptures about it as we ate. Tarragon ate his fish supper with gusto. As we finished our meal, a flash of brilliant white light filled the room, followed by a deep rumble of thunder.

Tarragon looked up. Swallowed.

'We're quite safe in here,' Willow said softly, patting his cheek, then coughing gently.

Tarragon grunted.

After our meal we retired to our rooms for an early night. I rested Deorwine and Glædwine against the wall and sat looking out of the window at the flashes of lightning, thoughts cascading through my mind as I listened to the rain that had started to fall relentlessly onto the rooftops and into the streets. I was nervous about how we were going to be received at the palace. I just hoped the Royal Family wouldn't try and arrest us on the spot and turn us over to Chervil. Fighting our way out wouldn't be pretty. Lightning lit the scene. It was as if a white, gossamer sheet had been thrown over everything for a moment, and the Cursed Weapons flared with purple in the reflected light as thunder rumbled. My thoughts turned to what Ostianzis had said about Quintessence Spinners and prophetic dreams, and I shuddered.

'What is it?' Rian asked as he undressed, his tunic and shirt already lying crumpled on the bed.

'Hmm?' I turned towards him.

'You're leagues away.'

'I was thinking about something Ostianzis said.'

'About what?' He stopped what he was doing, britches still on, chest bare. For a moment his half-naked body distracted me.

I swallowed. 'Prophetic dreams and Quintessence Spinners,' I said.

He came and sat on the end of the bed, sandalwood swirling about him. 'Tell me.'

'You remember after I took the Moonflower Elixir?'

Rian screwed his nose up. 'That's not something I'm going to forget in a hurry.'

A rumble of thunder rattled the window.

'I had those dreams.'

'Hallucinations.'

'I was thinking that some of what I dreamt has kind of come true.'

'Go on,' he said, leaning forward intently.

'Well, there was the bright blue glow around Beryl.'

'The Blue Death Worms?'

I nodded. 'Then there was Mal chained up, his eyes blank.'

'The Malign Prison and the enchantment,' Rian said, eyes widening. 'What else?'

'I saw a pine tree, fire.'

'The dryads.'

'Beryl saying she was going to kill you, and you lying on the ground dying…'

Rian sucked in a breath as a flash lit the room. 'Damn. The Mandragora Berries.' A crack of thunder echoed around the city.

'I even felt like I was falling and water was rushing past my ears.' I glanced at him. 'Am I stretching this too far, or were those dreams really about the future?'

He chewed on his lip. 'In all honesty I don't know, but it's just a little too close to the mark for my liking.' He hesitated. Rubbed the back of his neck. 'Was there anything else? Anything that hasn't happened yet?'

I wasn't sure I wanted to carry on with this, but now I'd started I'd have to. 'We were in a crystal cave full of glowing light.'

'The Cave of Crystals where the Crystal Vortex is?'

'I don't know,' I said, reluctant to continue. I hesitated. 'Then this red shadow came out of the walls. It had a blade – a knife, I think – in its hand.'

Rian shook his head. 'That could mean anything.' He looked at me. 'There's something else, isn't there?' he asked, taking my hand.

'It's probably nothing.'

'I'll decide that – what is it?' His eyes searched mine for answers.

I hesitated. 'I—I had this cold burning pain in my stomach, a really sharp, agonising pain. It may have been the Elixir, though, rather than anything prophetic.'

He nodded slowly. 'I suggest we take extra care, just in case. If it was part of your prophecy we don't want it coming true. *I* don't want it coming true.' He stood up and pulled me to my feet. 'You're sure that's it? Nothing else?'

'No, there isn't anything else I can think of that would make any sense.'

'Then let's get some rest. We've a lot to do tomorrow – and don't worry about your dreams. I'm not going to leave your side until all this is over, and even then, I may not ever let you out of my sight.'

I smiled at him. We climbed into bed and he held me close as the storm blew itself out, but a feeling of foreboding now lodged uncomfortably in my chest, which didn't help induce a good night's sleep or sweet dreams. Rian suffered, too, but not as badly as the night before. Hopefully this time our nightmares would calm quicker than before.

CHAPTER EIGHT

The following morning we met at breakfast to discuss our next move.

'We'll have to assume the Trewans know about what's happened in Aerba,' Rian said as we ate. 'That we're fugitives.'

'They could just decide to throw us in the dungeons,' Sage said, a sour expression on his face.

'Hopefully their knowledge of the Fire Opal and the Crystal Vortex, along with the letter from Onyx's grandfather, will make them think twice,' Tarragon said.

'Let's hope so,' Onyx sniffed.

'I think it's a risk we need to take,' I said.

'Maybe some of us should stay outside, though?' Sage said, playing with his earring. 'In case you need a rescue party.'

Willow nodded, coughing.

'I'll go with you to hand over Grandfather's letter, and anyway, I've done business with King Ash before,' Onyx said.

Mal frowned. 'When?'

'Last summer.'

'That's where you went?'

'Yes.'

'I'll come, too – I can't trust the two of you to stay out of trouble for more than five minutes at a time,' Tarragon said, looking at me and Rian.

We decided that Sage, Anise, Willow and Mal should stay behind, while me, Rian, Tarragon and Onyx went to the palace. Willow's asthma had got worse, and she and Anise had gone off to make some of his special tea. We changed into our Aerban clothes and adjusted our hair, Onyx remaining as he was, then set off for the palace. In a strange way I was glad to be back in my purple coat with its white border. I found it strange seeing Rian and Tarragon back in their burgundy Aerban coats with their gold and black borders, hair swishing in their high ponytails. In the Prince of Aerba I once again saw the young man I'd first fallen in love with.

'What?' Rian asked, looking at me.

'Nothing,' I said, smiling to myself.

He took hold of my hand. 'What is it?'

'I was just admiring the view,' I said quietly. 'I always like to admire the view when it's you.'

'Like when I was getting changed last night? I did notice you watching me, you know.' He lowered his voice as he spoke. 'You seem to like looking at me when I'm naked.'

'You're a fine one to talk,' I said, feeling the blood rushing to my face. 'You do it to me all the time.'

'That's because you're beautiful and it's still all very new to me – this love and marriage business – and I find you extremely addictive, particularly when you're taking your clothes off. You've enchanted me, and I can't get enough of you.'

Blood rose to my cheeks. 'Oh. Really?' I couldn't argue with him. 'I feel the same about you, actually. That's why I have to look at you.' I caught Onyx and Tarragon glancing back at us. 'And you'll still want to watch me when I'm old and grey and wrinkly?'

'I'll still want to watch you when you're old and grey and wrinkly,' he said, nodding as he gazed at me. He bent toward me and whispered into my ear, 'I'll want to carry on watching you forever. You see, I adore you.'

'I adore you, too, but you really should stop talking like this,' I murmured back, giving him a playful slap on the arm. 'This isn't the time.'

'Are you asking me to save it for later?'

'Yes. When we're alone and not surrounded by a whole city – and Tarragon and Onyx, who keep looking at us and grinning from ear to ear,' I said, giving Rian's cousin and my old friend a friendly glower as they glanced at us again and smirked. I raised my voice. 'Yes, I have noticed the two of you.' I lowered my voice again. 'I think they've heard every word.'

'They can't have done. They're too far ahead.' Rian frowned.

'We're downwind and voices travel on the breeze,' Onyx said, not turning around this time. 'And red-heads don't go grey, they go white.'

Rian looked at me, eyes wide and face slightly mortified, a rosy blush appearing high on his cheek bones.

'Told you,' I said, slightly smugly.

'I'll keep the rest of what I was going to say for later,' Rian said softly.

'Not on our account,' Tarragon said, turning and beaming at us. 'I was enjoying it almost as much as Phire.'

'Tarragon – shut up,' Rian said, but his tone didn't match his words and he had a little smile playing at the corner of his lips.

'Wait until I tell Willow.'

'If you do that she might just want you to behave in a similar manner to my husband,' I pointed out. 'Just bear that in mind.'

'What, displays of affection in public?' Tarragon asked. 'She doesn't really like that sort of thing.'

'Oh, I don't know – I think she's getting more comfortable with it these days,' I said.

Tarragon didn't look quite so sure of himself now, and Onyx started chuckling.

'She has a point, Tarragon,' Onyx said. 'Willow is mellowing.'

Tarragon raised an eyebrow as Rian started laughing.

'Don't know what you're all talking about – I didn't hear Rian and Phire say anything,' Tarragon said, turning away and striding on ahead. 'And neither did you,' he added to Onyx, pulling the still-chuckling ex-assassin along with him.

Rian glanced at me as he continued laughing.

Citizens of all three Bloods Classes filled the streets, moving around on their errands. The smell of cinnamon drifted on the air along with freshly baked bread. Salt and fish wafted up from the docks and mingled with the rose and lavender that came from a Flosian Perfume Shop. Little bottles of coloured liquid filled its window.

'Don't tell Sage about that place, or we'll never get him out of there,' Tarragon muttered as we passed it.

'Sage likes perfume?' Onyx asked, eyebrows raised. 'Well, how about that?'

At the palace gate we caused a certain amount of chaos, once we'd announced who we were, but they soon granted us admission and an audience with King Ash and Queen Photinia.

I took in the opulent surroundings as we were shown to the Throne Room – a far cry from the shabby wooden homes of their people. The walls were festooned with coloured paint, the floors polished cream limestone, and the drapes at the windows thick-piled red velvet.

The Throne Room stood with a huge ornamental fireplace on one side, windows to a garden on the other, and servants scattered along the sides. At the far end sat a raised dais with two silver thrones – on one, King Ash, a man in his late fifties with grey hair and a beard, wearing an exquisite black velvet jacket embroidered with silver thread. Beside him sat Queen Photinia. She wore a dress of similar material and with elaborate silver detailing as she perched on her throne. Behind them on the left stood a young man who I assumed to be Prince Birch. His blond hair was swept back, and his golden skin almost seemed to shimmer in the light. His expression was one of self-approval, as if he believed himself to be extremely handsome and the Trees' gift to women. Something about his yellow eyes made me shiver; something that looked a little too much like my step-brother, Elm, for my liking.

We walked across the room, Rian still holding my hand, and approached the thrones, bowing as we stopped.

King Ash nodded. 'Prince Valerian. We are surprised to see you here, and with the assassin, Lady Merciless.'

I winced.

'Your Majesty, she is known as Lady Samphire now, and is no assassin,' Rian replied.

'Shouldn't that be princess?' Onyx whispered in my ear.

I elbowed him in the ribs.

'Indeed?' Ash squinted.

'Aren't you supposed to be dead, Valerian?' Prince Birch asked from where he stood.

'Chervil did try to arrange my execution on false charges, but I was able to escape,' Rian said.

'I didn't believe a word of it when I heard,' King Ash said. 'I know you and Chervil, and if anyone was going to commit treason it wasn't going to be you.'

Queen Photinia nodded. 'I'm so glad you were able to escape your brother.'

'I had help,' Rian said. 'Quite a bit of help.' He squeezed my hand.

'I'm amazed you're still alive, Lady Samphire,' Birch said, stepping forwards and giving me an appraising look. 'We heard the Cursed Weapons had killed you.'

'They very nearly did, Your Highness, but not quite,' I said, smiling sweetly. 'As you can see, I'm quite well.'

Birch fiddled with his sword hilt. Definitely too much like Elm.

'Tarragon, it's good to see you,' King Ash said.

Tarragon nodded.

'Onyx, you're in very strange company,' Queen Photinia said.

'Your Majesty, we are here on urgent business,' Onyx said. 'My Grandfather, Prince Beck, has asked me to give you this letter,' he said, pulling it from his tunic.

Onyx's grandfather was a prince? First time he'd mentioned that. Rian cast me a little frown. All I could do was shrug.

A servant quickly took it from Onyx and passed it to the king. Ash opened it and raised an eyebrow.

'Come with me,' he said, passing the letter to Photinia. He led us out of the Throne Room and into a smaller antechamber where only he, the queen and the prince followed. The room had a central table and a number of chairs, and we all took a seat. Birch shut the door behind us and sat down.

'What your grandfather says here is grave news, but something we've wondered about for a while,' King Ash said as the prince read the letter. 'The theft of the Fire Opal caused us great concern. We know its true power, and in the wrong hands it can indeed destroy the Crystal Vortex permanently, like your grandfather says.'

'We've had men looking for it ever since we received the news,' Queen Photinia said. 'It was never going to be in Flos like Chervil insisted.'

'He was only doing that to make trouble with them, and to give himself the excuse to go to war,' Rian said.

King Ash nodded. 'I thought as much.'

'We've been able to track it down,' Queen Photinia said.

'You have?' Rian asked, an eagerness in his voice. 'Where to?'

'Magenta, the capital city of Chroma.'

'They stole it? But why?'

'They knew they'd need it to restart the Vortex and restore balance to nature, so they had it stolen and taken to them. They decided your father wouldn't give it up willingly and so took it.'

'They were probably right,' Rian muttered.

'So the Emperor of Chroma has it?' I asked.

'That we don't know,' King Ash said. 'But we've tracked it to Magenta.'

'Do they have all the Angle Spinners on Chroma that they need to restart it?' I asked.

Ash shook his head. 'Not that we know of. At least, not yet.'

'The rumour is that they're searching for some,' Birch said. 'But there's a problem.' He glanced at his father.

'You must tell them,' Photinia said.

Ash rubbed his beard. 'There is someone who is intent on destroying the Crystal Vortex, on bringing chaos to all six of the Lands. Her mother was a Trewan High Blood, but demoted because of a transgression with a Middle Blood. The daughter now seeks revenge, not just on Trew, but on the other Lands, too, for their Blood Rule Decrees and, as she sees it, harsh laws.'

I couldn't pretend I didn't have a certain amount of sympathy with this daughter of a demoted High Blood. I was in a similar position, and the Blood Rule Decrees were, as Rian liked to say, positively asinine.

'But how does destroying the Vortex and bringing chaos help her achieve revenge?' Onyx asked.

'She intends to step in and rule,' Birch said.

I shuddered. It rather reminded me of... *Hell's teeth*.

'No,' I said. 'You can't mean...'

Ash nodded. 'Your stepmother, Juniper.'

My heart froze. We knew she wanted to take over, but not really *why*, other than power and domination. Now it all made sense.

'She'll need Magic Spinners, though,' Tarragon said.

'She is one, as is her son, Elm,' Photinia said. 'We already know that much – her Trewan High Blood has seen to it.'

'Unfortunately Magic Blood calls to Magic Blood – she won't need to look far for other Spinners,' Birch said. 'They'll gravitate to her.'

'But who else?' Onyx asked.

'Beryl,' I said. 'If Mal and I have Magic, she's likely to as well.'

'That still leaves another two,' Tarragon said.

Rian blanched. 'We know Chervil is working with her.'

'You think he's one, too?'

'I am. Why shouldn't he be?'

The room began to close in on me.

'Wait. Hematite was an Air Spinner,' I said. 'Now he's dead, Juniper's going to be at least one short.'

'What's this?' Onyx asked as Tarragon quirked an eyebrow in surprise. Rian and I had neglected to tell them this detail about our encounter with the two Iolitian assassins, and so we quickly filled them in.

Just as elation rushed through me at the thought of Juniper being on the back foot, another terrifying thought followed in its wake.

'What is it?' Rian asked, taking my hand.

The words came out in a whisper. 'Ostianzis said Magic was always strong in the Aerban Royal Family.' I looked at Rian and Tarragon.

'No. It can't be.' Tarragon shook his head.

'It's probably how he survived the poisoned moat,' Rian said with a groan.

'Who?' Ash asked.

'My cousin, Sorrel.'

'Sage will be pleased,' Tarragon muttered.

'She'd still need a Waker for the Fire Opal,' Onyx said, sniffing. 'But that could be pretty much any Middle Blood in Iolite.'

'And it's assuming they're all different Angle Spinners,' I said.

'The difficulty will be for her to find a Quintessence Angle Spinner,' Photinia said. 'Only two are ever in existence at any one time.'

'She's one,' I said. 'I'm the other.'

Ash's face lost its colour, and he exchanged worried glances with his wife and son. 'Then it's imperative that you get to the Vortex first and restart it before she can destroy it for good.'

'And kill her, too, while you're at it,' Birch said, an evil glint in his eye. Of course, he was related to Elm – that's why there was something about him that unnerved me so much. 'She can't be trusted. She's mad with vengeance and will do anything to rule the Six Lands.'

Ash nodded. 'My son is right. You must stop her, whatever the cost.'

Rian nodded. 'We'll do what we can.'

'Do you have Magic Angles?' Onyx asked suddenly.

Queen Photinia shook her head. 'Magic never came as a certainty with being a High Blood, although it was very common, at least at one time. Now it is much, much rarer. We believe there are still clusters in some High Blood families but even then a daughter may have it and a son may not. Your Aerban family, Prince Valerian, still has it strongly, though.'

Tarragon looked at Rian. 'So we're going to have to stop Chervil, too.'

Rian grimaced and nodded. 'Do you know where Chervil or Juniper are?'

Ash shook his head. 'We know she was gathering her group in Iolite. Chervil left Aerba for Adamas two weeks ago, but whether she's left there yet, or is still there, we don't know. We're concerned our operatives may have been compromised in Iolite. We're working to find out what's happened.'

'We have to assume she's either left or is preparing to leave,' Photinia said. 'We didn't know she had Quintessence. We'd assumed she still had to find a Quintessence Spinner, but with what you've told us she's an even greater threat than we thought. She could leave Iolite at any time. You don't have a moment to lose if you're to save the Six Lands.'

CHAPTER NINE

I'd heard no mention of Princess Hazel since we'd arrived, and when Onyx asked after her, the Queen told us she'd been ill and confined to her rooms. Photinia said it was all part of the Vortex collapsing, that not just the land would be affected, but the people would be struck down with illness, too.

'Maybe we can help,' Rian said.

'How?' Photinia asked.

'We have an Earth Spinner with us. He may be able to help with her ailment.'

Onyx and Tarragon returned to the inn to get Anise, and when he arrived, the King and Queen took me, Rian, and Anise to Princess Hazel's rooms. They were some of the most luxurious chambers I'd ever seen, rivalling the Viridi Palace, with deep-pile green carpet, green velvet curtains, and various couches and chairs. Hazel lay on a bed of satin sheets and pillows, her golden skin pale, face sweaty as her dark blonde hair fell across the pillows. Her breaths were coming in little gasps, and a maid sat beside her, mopping her brow. The princess' bear arms displayed a rash of bright red, angry-looking wheals. The room had an aura of despair and uncertainty, and as I watched the ailing girl, I feared for her life.

'How long has she been like this, Your Majesty?' Anise asked, feeling her pulse.

'A week,' King Ash said.

'She suddenly took ill one afternoon, collapsed,' Photinia said, stroking her daughter's hair. 'She's been unconscious ever since with a fever and that rash you can see on her arms.'

Anise nodded. 'Interesting. I'll see if I can do something to help her,' he said, opening his Herb Chest and, with tongue out, started to sort through his remedies. He pulled out his pestle and mortar and started adding dried herbs and leaves.

'Wait.' King Ash stepped forward. 'What's that?'

Anise looked up. He had just placed into the mortar a small red leaf with a shimmering surface.

'It's a special kind of Moly,' Anise said, gazing at it. 'A herb once common in southern Aerba, but I found this variety only recently. I believe it may help with the princess' ailment.'

'But I've only ever seen drawings of it in books,' Ash said, peering at it.

'My husband is something of a scholar when it comes to botany,' Photinia said, still stroking Hazel's hair.

'I thought this species was lost.'

'It's still growing strong in Cilantro Forest, in the Chamber of Earth,' Anise said.

'The Chamber of Earth? It still exists?'

'We stumbled across it by accident,' Rian said.

'And you got in?'

'We never really did understand how,' I said.

King Ash looked at us, his eyes widening. 'My studies indicated it could only be opened by two bonded Elemental Angle Spinners – only they could open the door to the Chamber of Earth.'

'Bonded?' Rian asked.

'Married, pledged to each other.'

'But we weren't married then. We hadn't even told each other how we really felt,' I said, looking at Rian.

'You're married?' Queen Photinia asked, looking at us. 'I hadn't realised.'

'It happened a little while ago,' Rian said, taking my hand. 'I would have introduced my wife as Princess Samphire, except for my new circumstances.'

If only Onyx was still here…

The queen smiled. 'I'm pleased for you. Congratulations.'

'The fact you weren't married wasn't relevant,' Ash said, shaking his head. 'The Chamber knew what was in your hearts and what was meant to be. That's why it opened for the two of you. It was destiny.'

I glanced at Rian, my face warming as a rosy blush appeared on his cheeks. He winked at me, making it worse.

'You have a book on the Chamber of Earth, Your Majesty?' Anise asked, eyebrows raised.

Ash nodded. 'When you're finished here I will take you to it.'

Anise smiled and got back to work. After a few moments he frowned, then cursed. 'I forgot, I need some White Elderflowers.'

'We have some,' Ash said, heading for the door. He spoke a few words to the servant outside who scurried away. A few minutes later they returned with a small bowl and handed it to the king with a little bow. 'Here, Anise, White Elderflowers.'

Anise took the bowl and frowned. 'I should've said, Your Majesty, they need to be fresh.'

King Ash shook his head. 'There won't be any fresh ones around here until next year now.'

Anise's shoulders sagged.

'Do you need them to be fresh?' Photinia asked, concern in her eyes.

Anise nodded. 'For this to have the best chance of working, I do.'

'Can't you use those ones?' I asked. 'Do to them what you did to that blue flower on board the ship?'

The Earth Spinner's eyes brightened. 'Of course. I'm sorry, Phire, I keep forgetting about my Magic Angle.'

'It takes some getting used to,' Rian murmured, glancing at me.

Anise took four of the flowers into the palm of one hand and took hold of his Jade Amulet Artefact with the other. He gazed at the Elderflowers with the same loving look he'd had with the blue flower, and slowly but surely, the little petals unfurled and plumped up into fresh, brilliant white flowers.

'Amazing,' Ash gasped as he closely watched Anise at work. 'I've never seen anything like it – only heard of such things. You have a rare and special gift, Anise.'

Anise smiled, his cheeks growing rosy. 'Thank you.' He quickly got back to work and he'd soon prepared the tincture. With Photinia holding Hazel up, he gave a few drops to the princess, and they then laid her back down. 'Take the rest of this,' he said, pouring the straw-coloured liquid into a little glass phial. 'From now on, three drops in water, six times a day until it runs out. I hope it'll bring her some relief, but it may take a day or two for you to start seeing results.'

'Thank you, Anise,' Photinia said and gave him a hug. 'How can we ever repay you?'

'I don't need payment.'

'Nonsense – I'll start with taking you to see that book,' Ash said, opening the bedroom door.

'I hope it works,' I said as we left, glancing back towards Hazel's rooms.

'So do I,' Rian said, nodding.

A short time later Anise returned to the inn, grinning from ear to ear about what he'd learnt in Ash's book. Ash and Photinia had agreed to furnish us with all the supplies we'd need, and as soon as Captain Pol's ship arrived in the harbour two days later, they were loaded aboard. She'd made good time, despite a squall at sea.

Rian and I went back to the palace to say our goodbyes before heading to the docks for the evening tide. Rian had some business to discuss with King Ash, so I left them to it and waited for Rian in a small Courtyard garden. I'd had the distinct impression that even before the initial reports of Chervil's plans to execute Rian, the king and queen had taken against the new King of Aerba, but with the new information we'd provided they were definitely no friends of Chervil's now, and Anise's assistance had rather sealed his fate.

I walked around looking at the flowers. Some of the sweetest smelling Trewan roses I'd ever come across were nestled in little groups of red, white and pink, and small trees filled the spaces between them as I moved along the path. I went over to the far wall to inspect a vine that trailed up the limestone.

A cough over by the entrance made me turn.

Prince Birch walked over, a big smile on his face, a wooden bow on his back. 'Lady Samphire, I'm so sorry I haven't seen more of you – I had to go out hunting with Lord Sycamore. It's such a shame you have to go already, but I do hope you will return to us again one day.'

'I hope so, too, Your Highness,' I said, wondering what was taking Rian so long.

Birch reached out, took my hand and kissed it in a gentlemanly fashion. 'You're quite the beauty with your flaming red hair.'

I raised an eyebrow and swallowed when it became apparent that he wasn't letting go. I didn't want to start a diplomatic incident, particularly when the king and queen had been so helpful. 'You're most kind.'

He paused, waiting for something.

'No, Lady Samphire,' he said with a laugh. 'You're now supposed to tell me I'm the most handsome man you've ever met.'

The nerve.

Admittedly he was quite good looking with his swept-back blond hair, but he couldn't hold a candle to Rian, at least as far as I was concerned. He turned my hand over and went to kiss my palm. I instinctively snatched my hand back. His eyes narrowed.

'That's no way to treat a new friend,' he said, moving closer. 'We've helped you, now you can return the favour.'

Not in the way he wanted.

'You must excuse me. I'm sure Prince Valerian must be ready now, and I know your parents are eager for us to leave as soon as possible,' I said, trying to pass him, but he planted himself firmly in my way. I took a deep breath. Take him down to his knees? Elbow to his stomach? I stepped back into the vine-covered wall and cursed inwardly. Which would be more diplomatically acceptable?

He braced his hands against the wall, one either side of my head. 'Now be nice. I'm not asking for much, Lady Samphire. All I want is one kiss.'

'You do ask for too much.'

His eyebrows knitted together.

'Prince Birch, have you seen my wife?' Rian came striding purposefully into the gardens, a fist clenched.

Thank the Stars.

Birch looked at Rian. 'I'm busy, Prince Valerian, can't you see that?' he asked, annoyance filling his voice as he turned back to me. His eyes narrowed as he looked at me. He hesitated, turned back to Rian. 'Wife?'

'Ah, husband, I wondered where you were,' I said, taking the chance to duck under Birch's arm and hurry over towards Rian, hoping the hint of flames flickering in Rian's eyes wouldn't amount to anything. Burning the place to the ground wouldn't help diplomacy, either.

Birch frowned. 'Husband?'

'Yes, we're married, didn't you know?' Rian asked, his jaw set. 'I'm sorry, I thought you knew – your parents do. We have been for a while now, actually. I thoroughly recommend married life, Prince Birch. You must find yourself a wife. Come, Samphire.'

I took Rian's proffered arm, and he led me from the gardens leaving Birch fuming behind us.

'Thank you,' I murmured.

'I realised what was happening from the throne room, and although I know you can take care of yourself, bloodshed inside the palace grounds really isn't a good idea,' Rian said quietly, although there was a little edge to his voice, reserved for Birch. 'Particularly when they've been so cordial.'

'I didn't start it,' I said indignantly. I was happy to end it, though. Emphatically.

'I know that as well,' he said, pulling me to a halt in the passageway. 'I saw from the Throne Room how he cornered you. Quite professionally, I thought. He's done that numerous times before.'

'I'd never look at another man,' I said, pouting. 'You know that, too.'

His lopsided smile appeared, and the little flames in his eyes flickered and died. 'And I'll never look at another woman. Just take care – he knows you're an assassin. I think he was just living dangerously.' He started to move on.

I pulled him back.

'You were more worried about him than me?' I asked.

Rian raised an eyebrow. 'No... and, yes. He doesn't have your singular skills or experience. He was in far more danger than you ever were.' He glanced over my shoulder at the Cursed Weapons.

I crossed my arms over my chest, unsure whether to take this as a slight or a compliment. 'And I thought you were being chivalrous, protecting my honour.'

He smirked. 'Do you want me to be chivalrous?'

'Might be nice, once in a while.'

'I thought you liked being independent.'

'There's a time and place for everything,' I said primly. 'And as much as I can take care of myself, it's nice to know you're watching my back.'

'I was. That's why I came to rescue you.'

'You mean him.'

'I came to rescue both of you from each other. Now, let's go,' he said, taking a step forward.

I didn't move. 'Do you really recommend married life?' I asked softly.

He stopped and rubbed the back of his neck before turning back to me. He smiled, the look reaching into his eyes like starlight. 'Wholeheartedly.' He leant towards me and kissed me. 'Without hesitation. The best decision I ever made. Now, you get back to the inn and get everyone and our luggage down to the ship. Pol should be getting ready to leave on the next tide and we don't want to be late. I've a few more things to settle with King Ash, then I'll be straight along to the docks.'

'You don't want me to wait?' For a moment I considered protesting, telling him we should stay together, but he was obviously comfortable letting me out of his sight for a while, so I stayed quiet.

'I'm not quite sure how long I'll be, and I don't want Prince Birch to get any more ideas and corner you again – for both his *and* your sakes. It's daylight, so go back the way we came through the busy streets – no shortcuts. I'll meet you down at the docks.'

'Fine, I'll go, then. But the same goes for you – busy streets, or I'll be back to find you. And don't be long, we don't want to miss the tide, and we're not leaving without you.'

'I'll be as quick as I can,' he said, kissing me on the head. 'See you soon.'

I nodded and left the palace, weaving my way through the busy streets on my way back to the inn. As I reached the building I noticed a group of rowdy young men outside, a little worse for drink, to say the least.

I hesitated.

They were blocking the doorway. The Coterie rule if outnumbered? Run. If extremely outnumbered, run fast. But running wasn't an option, and the tide wouldn't wait for them to get bored and move on, so I strode confidently onward towards the door.

'Now, what do we have here?' one of them asked, stepping forward and running his pale green eyes up and down me in a less-than-pleasant manner, his greasy, short blond hair sticking up at odd angles.

'She looks just your type, Cedar,' said another with straggly brown hair, his golden skin glistening with sweat.

Cedar ran his tongue over his lips. 'She does, doesn't she, Hemlock? Delicious.'

He certainly wasn't *my* type.

'Let me pass, please,' I said, standing my ground.

'No.'

With no War Fan, my hand went to the hilt of Deorwine, pulling it a little way out of its scabbard so they could see the purple crystal blade. I looked menacingly at them. I would fight if I had to, render them unconscious if need be, but I really didn't want to mortally wound any of them. 'Let me pass.'

Cedar narrowed his eyes. 'Give me that sword and maybe we'll let you pass then.'

I sighed. Why did they have to be so stupid?

'No,' I said. 'It's mine.'

CHAPTER TEN

'Then maybe we'll take it,' Hemlock said, leering at me.

'I'd genuinely like to see you try, but overall, I wouldn't recommend it.'

Behind the group, in the doorway of the inn, stood Sage.

'You really don't want to be doing this,' he said, stepping out.

Tarragon followed him into the late afternoon sunlight. 'Best to move along, friends.'

'We don't want any trouble,' Anise said, joining them.

'Bobbins,' Willow said, standing beside him, her two swords drawn and shining in the light. 'We'd love to give them trouble. Wouldn't we, boys?'

Willow had definitely been hanging around with the young men for too long.

Tarragon grinned and stretched his neck. 'Gladly. I haven't had any exercise today. What do you say, Sage?'

'It could be fun,' Sage said, his eyes taking in each of the young men in turn. 'Do you want to take them all at once or shall we do one at a time? Or we could just take pieces off each one until they decide to give up.'

Cedar looked at Hemlock. 'I think we're needed elsewhere,' he said, backing away.

'Do you know, I think we are.' Hemlock nodded, and the group quickly moved away down the street and off into an alleyway, picking up speed as they went.

I glanced towards the Aerbans. They all had silly big grins plastered on their faces, even Sage. What a long way we'd come. Especially Sage. I had true friends now. I didn't just need to rely on myself – or on the old fall-back position of Mal or Onyx – or even on Rian, now, for that matter. My new friends trusted me, and I trusted them with my life.

'Thank you,' I said, releasing my hold on my sword hilt.

'I'm sure you could've handled it,' Sage said, 'but we need to get to the docks in good time and any little side adventures could take time we don't have.'

'I'm always glad of the help,' I said, smiling at him.

He winked at me.

'Did we miss something?' Onyx asked, coming out with Mal, packs on their shoulders.

'Not really,' Anise said. 'We were just encouraging some local lads to leave Phire alone.'

'Encouraging?' Mal raised an eyebrow as he watched Willow sheath her swords.

'Y'know how it is,' Tarragon said, buffing his fingernails on his coat. 'They were a little excitable, that's all. But they've calmed down now and gone on their way.'

'Thank you – for watching out for my sister.'

I could watch out for myself, but I saw little point in arguing.

'She's one of us now,' Sage said, fiddling with his earring. 'Like you and Onyx. And we look after our own.'

I chewed on my lip to stop tears welling in my eyes. Their friendship, their love, after everything that had happened in the Coterie, was almost overwhelming. From the look Mal gave me, he felt it, too, and Onyx's smile said the same thing. The three of us had found a new family – in fact, all eight of us now had a new family. Each other.

'Rian's finishing up at the palace with King Ash,' I said. 'He said to get everything down to the ship and he'd meet us there shortly.'

Tarragon nodded.

'He better not be too long,' Onyx said, looking through the buildings towards the setting sun. 'The tide will be turning soon.'

'Then let's get a move on so we're not the ones holding things up,' Willow said, heading back into the inn.

We gathered our things and made our way down to the docks, boarding *The Spirit of the Seas* just as the sun caressed the horizon and slid behind the western hills of Trew. Rian arrived shortly after and joined us in the cabin. He had a strange look in his eyes, almost as if he was incredibly relieved to see me there.

'Your wife's been entertaining the locals,' Tarragon said with a grin as Rian sat down.

'What?' Rian's forehead furrowed in confusion.

'To be fair, they wanted to entertain her,' Willow said. 'Not the other way around.'

'True.' Tarragon nodded. 'Although I'm sure she would've humoured them, if pushed.'

'Would you stop?' I gave Tarragon a friendly slap on the arm.

Rian looked at me. I rolled my eyes up towards the ceiling, then explained what had happened, with Tarragon still attempting to add embellishments wherever he could.

'She was fine, Rian,' Mal said, picking up an apple from the table and taking a big bite.

'It really wasn't anything to worry about,' Anise said.

'We had her back,' Sage said.

'Truth was, we were bored waiting, saw what was happening, and rather than let Phire have all the fun, we decided to amuse ourselves,' Tarragon admitted.

Rian looked at me. 'You're okay?'

'I'm fine,' I said, squeezing his hand.

'They're the ones that might not have been.' Onyx laughed. 'I'm sure she'd have whipped that Fan of her's out if she'd needed to.'

My War Fan.

I flinched and turned to my brother. 'I lost it,' I said, tears springing to my eyes.

'What?' he asked.

'When I fell into the mountain river. I lost it then. I don't know what happened to it.'

'The way you were bashed about in the water, I'm not surprised,' Rian said.

'I miss it, though,' I said. 'It was very special to me.' I glanced at Mal through the unshed tears. 'I'm sorry.'

'Don't be daft,' he said, smiling at me. 'I can get you another one.'

'Really?'

My brother nodded. 'You'll just have to wait until all this is over.'

'Thank you.'

He grinned back. 'Anything for you, Little Sister.'

We changed back into our Iolitian shirts and tunics, not knowing what or who lay ahead, as they would allow us to move more freely. As we set sail, Anise regaled us with information he'd picked up from King Ash's book.

'There are so many herbs in the Chamber of Earth that I could cultivate and use,' he said, his eyes bright.

'Well, I'm not going back,' Sage said sourly. 'Whatever happens in Chroma.'

Anise flinched. 'But it could be so helpful to have the use of these new, or old, remedies, Sage. We could heal all sorts of things we can't at the moment.'

'No.'

'I'll come,' Onyx said. 'By the Stars, I wouldn't mind seeing those mynogres of yours.'

'You really don't want to,' I said, chewing a nail. Onyx slapped my hand from my mouth. 'Anyway, the two of you wouldn't get in – only bonded Elemental Angle Spinners can open the door.'

'So you'll have to come,' Anise said, grinning at Sage.

'No,' Sage said, turning away.

'Maybe Mal could come, then,' Onyx said, glancing out through the open cabin door to where Mal was on deck chatting to the First Mate, Holm.

'He's getting better, isn't he?' I asked quietly.

Onyx nodded. 'Slowly, as Anise said, but he's making good progress.'

Mal certainly seemed closer to his normal self now. In the first few days after we'd rescued him from the Malign Prison I'd feared the worst, feared Juniper might have done my brother permanent damage, but now I could see she'd failed. He was returning to the Mal I knew, and between us, Onyx and I were pulling him back – although Onyx's love had a lot to do with it. At least, that's what I thought.

Even though we were now back on *The Spirit of the Seas,* Rian seldom left my side for more than a couple of minutes at a time, and when he was beside me he either held my hand or had his arm around my shoulder. I caught a glance he gave me the next morning that seemed full of relief and amazement. He looked away quickly, rubbing the back of his neck. He was still trying to reassure himself that I was really here.

'You still think I'm a figment of your imagination?' I asked, amused. We stood out on deck watching the ship cut through the waves.

He sighed. 'Not exactly, but there's a bit of me that keeps thinking I'm still unconscious in a drunken stupor, dreaming about you, and I'll wake up in a moment and you won't be here.'

'I was surprised you let me go back to the inn from the palace on my own.'

'I regretted it the moment you'd left,' he said. 'I was so busy trying to keep Birch away from you that it was only after you'd gone I realised what I'd done.'

'So you *were* worried about me?' I grinned.

He looked to the deck. 'Yes.'

'I was fine.'

'I know, but... I didn't want you thinking I was being overprotective, stifling you. But you didn't say anything at the time?'

'I knew you were busy, and anyway, I thought perhaps you were comfortable leaving me again.'

'Not exactly. I just wasn't thinking. I was so relieved to find you okay back at the ship. I won't make that mistake again in a hurry. I really hate this sensation that I'm going to wake up and you won't be here.'

'I had something similar for a few days after your poisoning,' I said, slipping my arms around his waist and hugging him. At least both our nightmares had eased.

'You did?' he asked, his eyes softening as he gazed at me. 'You never said.'

'You were still recovering. I didn't want to bother you.'

'I always want you to bother me with things that worry you. It's what I'm here for – I'm your husband. It's my job to worry if you're worried,' he said, running his hand over my hair.

'Well, I'm not worried at the moment – other than about the Vortex, Juniper and the Fire Opal – so, just the usual.' I grinned. 'And I'm not going anywhere, so you can stop worrying about that.'

He smiled, but behind his eyes a little flicker of concern remained. I should never have told him about my prophetic dream, or at least the bit about the cold flame in my gut. He was probably worrying that that was going to happen, too, but there was nothing to say it hadn't been a random sensation from the Moonflower Elixir. After all, they'd told me I'd been very ill, and I did remember some of the stomach cramps. It was probably just those seeping into my dreams. Wasn't it? I kept telling myself that, but I didn't entirely believe me. I had this niggling feeling that the Elixir had nothing to do with the pain I'd sensed.

'We'll put in at Pax tomorrow,' Captain Pol said. She was a typical middle-aged Merean: dark hair and eyes, burnt sienna skin, beautiful round face, and a strength that belied her sex. We all sat at the table in the main cabin, eating our evening meal. 'We need to stock up on supplies, water, that sort of thing.'

'Have you been this way before?' Mal asked.

'Many times,' Holm, said. He was sitting beside Pol, his arm around his partner's shoulders. He, too, was Merean through and through. In his fifties, he was dressed in the lilac and pink of a Merean Middle Blood, his skin a burnt sienna. 'We're one of the few ships that brings them supplies and keeps them secret.'

'But not beyond, Aunt?' Onyx asked, slurping some soup.

'Never,' Pol said. 'As far as we know, no one travels further.

Beyond the Pax Archipelago are The Great Doldrums. No ship's captain in their right mind goes that far. If you do, you're becalmed quite quickly. Die of thirst.'

'But we have an Air Spinner with us.'

'The only reason we're even going to attempt it.'

'Even so, we're going to stock up on extra water, just in case,' Holm said. 'Food, too.'

We planned to stop for a day, partly to give the ship's crew a rest, and partly for the reloading. Pol assured us that the leader on the island, a man named Zabell, would be happy to entertain us. He was an old friend, and had known her and Holm for many years.

She was right.

The middle-aged man greeted us off the ship with open arms. I wiped perspiration from my brow as we followed him up through a little coastal village to his sprawling villa complex that nestled over the side of a hill. Beautifully positioned to take in the views of the surrounding landscape, it had white limestone walls that shimmered in the sunlight, and verdant gardens around it with ponds and fruit trees. The smell of jasmine lingered in the air, much to Sage's delight

Zabell allocated guest quarters to us near the main house and we settled into the beautifully furnished rooms with their pristine white bedsheets and views of the gardens. He even arranged for small bowls of fruit to be placed on the little tables on either side of the double beds, full of sweet grapes, aromatic apples and ruby red strawberries.

For the first time in months I actually felt safe on dry land, well away from my dear stepmother.

Our evening meal took place in his personal dining room where we were treated to breads, pastries, fruit, salad and cold meats. Tarragon was in paradise.

'So the Blood Rule Decree isn't followed here?' Onyx asked.

Zabell nodded. 'That's right, young man.'

'And do you allow new people to move here?' Mal asked, an eager note in his voice.

Zabell smiled. 'I take it the two of you are together?'

They both nodded.

'Indeed we would welcome you both, if you wanted to make a new home and life here,' Zabell said.

'Perhaps, when this is all over, we could come here, too,' Anise said, looking at Sage.

'I think we'd all like to settle here, if we could,' Rian said, taking a pastry with white icing and sultanas.

'You would all be welcome,' Zabell said.

'And can we marry?' Willow asked.

'Of course.'

Tarragon blanched, then beamed at her, trying to cover his tracks.

'But for now, we need to concentrate on getting to Chroma,' Pol said.

Zabell nodded. 'We, too, have noticed the unbalancing of nature. The days have become much hotter – the nights, too – and freshwater is becoming more of a concern.'

I had noticed the dry patches on the lawns at the front of the villa, but had thought nothing of it.

'It will take you a week or so to reach the outer island of Chroma and sail up river to Azure City,' Zabell continued.

'Outer island?' Sage asked, raising an eyebrow.

'Chroma is made up of three islands, two outer ones which are concentric rings around the main island. You sail east from Azure City into the Second Water, across to Ecru Town on the coast of the middle isle, then ride to Teal. You'll then have to cross the First Water and sail across that to Magenta City. The Cave of Crystals is there, at the centre of the island.'

'Why wasn't the knowledge about Chroma lost here?' I asked, shifting Deorwine slightly from its position where it rested against the table next to Glædwine.

Zabell smiled. 'We've never followed the ways of the other Lands. Our histories weren't erased or destroyed, so we still know about Chroma, that it still exists. Just like the Far Eastern Lands of Ithia, Nyssia, Calperion and Axandor.'

'I thought they were lost, too,' Tarragon said. 'I've studied history, and there's no mention of them after Chroma disappeared.'

'They're still there, about a three week sea journey from Chroma. It is possible to get around the Great Doldrums and get to Chroma, but that's a four month trip, all told, usually in extremely bad weather. Most people aren't aware it's even possible, so Chroma, and the Far Eastern Lands remain "lost". Those lands all have strong trade links with each other, though, for instance in the markets of spices and perfumes.'

Sage sat up straight. 'Perfumes?' His eyes sparkled. 'What sort of perfumes?'

'Calperion Perfumes, from the land of Calperion,' Zabell said. 'They're quite potent, or so I hear.'

'Do you have a map of Chroma?' Rian asked.

'I do. Come, let me show you.'

'That would be so useful,' Tarragon said, nodding.

'And would help with navigation,' Holm said.

They got up and followed Zabell into a side room, Pol going with them. It was the first time in ages that Rian had left my side. I took a deep breath. It felt quite strange. The hot, humid air made my shirt stick to my back, so I took off my tunic and decided to go for a walk outside in the gardens to hopefully cool down a little while they were busy. Mal was in deep conversation with Onyx, Willow, Sage and Anise, so I left them to it and slipped out the open glazed door and into the cool gardens.

I took a deep breath. A refreshing, salty breeze blew in from the sea, rustling the leaves of the fruit trees as I passed them. The Cursed Weapons that had been in the dining room joined me as I wandered along the pathways away from the villa, drawn by the distant sea that sparkled in the moonlight. It reminded me of the light in Rian's eyes when he smiled.

He'd been smiling more, recently. After his brush with the Mandragora Berries he'd been quieter, but lately his smile had come back. After our talk at the inn in Lilac I knew the side effects still bothered him, but at least we were able to talk about it, and he was slowly coming to terms with things.

Mal was so much better, too. He appeared more his normal self as all his memories gradually returned. Onyx was really helping him, and he didn't particularly need me. Seeing my brother with someone who so obviously loved him deeply and would do anything for him warmed my soul. They were rather like me and Rian.

I sighed.

So much had happened – good and bad – but at least some of it appeared to be falling into place. We just had to get the Fire Opal, start the Vortex and stop Juniper. The problem was, none of those things would be small or easy to achieve. From what Zabell had said, crossing Chroma to get to the Cave of Crystals would be a monumental effort in itself.

I looked around. *Hell's teeth.* I'd wandered too far, much further than I'd meant. I'd walked beyond the gardens, past a grassy area and into a little copse of trees. The lure of the sea breeze had been too great. I started to head back through the trees and up a bank. The snap of a branch made me turn.

Suddenly, a cold, agonising fire raged in my stomach.

CHAPTER ELEVEN

I gasped as the pain coursed through my whole body, centred at my core. A cold flame burning at my insides. I fell backwards in agony. Glanced down in confusion, sweat springing up on my forehead.

The handle of a small knife protruded from my stomach.

My white shirt quickly turned dark red and sticky in the moonlight.

I groaned.

Tried to scream.

But the pain only increased and I lay back, the Cursed Weapons digging uncomfortably into my back, cold sweat plastering my hair to my face as I tried, unsuccessfully, to keep my breathing under control.

The figure of a young woman emerged from the trees. She smiled, her long brown hair glistening in the starlight.

'With the compliments of Juniper,' she said. In the silver light the scar on her face – the result of a disagreement we'd once had – and her watery blue eyes made her look even more evil than normal. I could see why Carnelian loved her. 'Although, it was my pleasure, really.'

'What took you so long, Topaz?' I managed to get out. I hadn't seen her since the day I last stepped into the Crimson Castle to rescue Rian from Juniper and Beryl. 'You're getting sloppy.'

She sneered. 'I don't think killing you is sloppy. I've succeeded where Carnelian and the traitor, Onyx, failed. There'll be no confusion over whether you're dead this time,' she said, grinning at me. 'Carnelian's hubris got in the way when went to kill you. He thought you'd die out in the forest, alone and full of despair. I won't make that same mistake. I'm just going to sit here on this log and wait for you to die, which shouldn't take too long, by the looks of you. Then I can tell Juniper you're dead, with certainty.' She sat down, watching me.

'I'll come back and haunt you,' I said, gasping for air. I'd started to wonder if I could move enough to get hold of Deorwine's hilt without the knife ripping me open further. But as a surge of cold fire swept through me, I knew it wasn't an option; the pain was nigh on unbearable.

She laughed. 'I doubt that very much. Oh, by the way, she's ahead of you.'

'What?'

'Juniper. She passed here this morning on her way to destroy the Crystal Vortex on Chroma.'

A cold shiver spread through me – how could she be ahead of us?

She inspected her fingernails in the moonlight. 'Carnelian's waiting off-shore for me. He wasn't overly popular with Juniper for a while, having messed up your kill. Still, all sorted now. I have to say, you were the mark I'd been looking forward to the most.'

Hell's teeth.

I stared at the gold hilt of the knife, encrusted with blue and gold topaz. It wasn't the longest knife, but it was long enough. I looked around, my vision blurry. Why had I walked so far? I'd been a fool. I'd thought myself safe here, out of the Coterie's reach, but it seemed that Juniper's arm was longer than even I had realised.

I tried to get up. Pain tore through me. I sucked in a breath and fell back.

I was dying.

The cold flame burnt in my stomach. The dream I'd had back in Cilantro flashed in front of my eyes. It wasn't the cramps from the Moonflower Elixir seeping into my dreams after all. This was another prophecy come true. An icy dread filled me.

All I wanted now was to see Rian one last time. See his face. Feel his touch on my skin. His lips on mine. As the moon sailed higher into the sky I feared I'd never see him again.

'By the Stars, this is taking too long.' Topaz got up and marched over to me. She bent over. 'Sorry about this, Amethyst.' She twisted the knife.

I screamed.

How I managed to stay conscious was beyond me. The pain was ferocious. I'd truly never experienced anything like it in my life.

'That'll speed things along nicely,' she said with a vicious grin.

I gasped for air. I hadn't realised it would take me so long to die. The knife was probably doing its bit to stem the flow of blood, but even so, my wound was bleeding and I was getting weaker, and quickly. The metallic smell of blood made me queasy. My breathing had become erratic, my pulse thready at best. I swallowed, but my throat was as dry as a Merean desert. They'd never find me in time, now, assuming they'd even realised I'd gone. *Idiot.* Why had I left without saying anything to anyone? Not that that would've stopped Topaz.

So, Juniper was getting her way, after all. Beryl would be pleased. No one left in Iolite would mourn me.

My hands felt like blocks of ice. My feet numb. I shivered. Only my stomach was on fire. But it was a strange, cold fire that burnt my insides, raging in my veins. Throbbing. Meanwhile, the Cursed Weapons dug into my back, adding to the pain.

My thoughts began to jumble. I could see very little in the starlight that filtered through the canopy of leaves above me. The stars themselves seemed to move in some sort of joyous dance in the dark velvet sky. I asked them to protect Rian. To look after Mal. I wouldn't be able to anymore.

Voices drifted on the air.

Hallucinations?

But the voices got louder.

The flickering, orange light from a torch started to illuminate the trees. Shadows twirled around me. The world tilted.

Topaz looked up. 'Damn.' She took the knife hilt, and twisted again.

The pain in my gut increased a hundredfold. I screamed, the agony spiralling through me, my mind blank with the torment.

'Phire!' Tarragon's voice sliced through the night air.

'T-Tarragon!' I yelled.

He appeared through the trees, a flaming torch in his hand, quickly taking in the scene.

Topaz swore as she stood up.

A torrent of water rushed down the bank, picking up twigs and branches, roaring as it swept all before it. It gushed from where Tarragon crouched, one hand on the grass, the other on his Artefact, his torch rammed into the ground beside him, his expression one of pure concentration. The water parted as it reached me, flowing either side of my body as it thundered past, before meeting again just below my feet and grabbing hold of Topaz. She screamed as she lost her footing, and disappeared into the raging torrent, taken away in the flash flood, caught in the unrelenting, churning water. It swept her through trees and out of sight, into the darkness. I had a niggling feeling she couldn't swim.

'Rian! Get over here! Now!' Tarragon yelled, scrambling down the wet bank towards me. He crouched beside me, raising his flaming torch. He gasped as he saw the stones in the knife hilt twinkling in the torchlight. 'Bugger.'

Then Rian was there, falling to his knees beside me, dropping his torch onto the damp grass. Swearing.

'No! By the Herbs! No, dammit!' He glanced at the knife, then reached out to move a lock of hair from my damp face. 'Phire? Can you hear me?'

'R—Rian?' I tried looking at him in the flickering light, but his face kept dancing in front of me like the stars high above. Why wouldn't he stay still? He was making me feel sick. He took my hand. His skin was hot against mine – more so than usual. 'Tell Mal. Tell him *Topaz*,' I managed to croak.

Rian frowned. 'Topaz?'

'Yes. Tell Mal – Topaz.'

'We need to get you to Anise first.'

'No, it—it's important.' I bent double, trying to reduce the pain as much as I could, but it really wasn't working. 'Juniper is ahead of us.'

'Bugger,' Tarragon muttered again.

Rian cast him an anxious look.

'We can't worry about any of that now,' Tarragon said, shaking his head and sighing.

'I wasn't going to – Phire's all that's important right now.' Rian glanced back at the knife that quivered with my failing heartbeat, and from the look in his torch-lit eyes, he knew it. The knife was still stemming the blood flow, but Topaz's efforts had made the wound bleed considerably.

'Do we take it out?' Tarragon asked, looking at it with a frown.

'I don't know,' Rian said, anguish plain on his face even to my blurry eyes. Not to mention the fear in his voice.

'If we don't and we move her, we could do more damage, but if we remove it she may lose so much blood that getting her to Anise will be useless.'

'Then we take her as she is, but we'll have to be very careful.' Rian looked over at Tarragon. 'I can't lose her again. I won't. Not after everything.'

Tarragon reached out, placing his hand on his cousin's shoulder. 'We won't.'

'Damn. I should've realised she'd gone sooner. And with her prophetic dreams – we knew this might happen.'

Tarragon's forehead furrowed. 'What prophetic dreams?'

'I'll explain later. This is my fault for not keeping a closer eye on her.'

'I—it's not your fault, it's mine. I shouldn't have wandered off,' I said, my voice thin, my breathing shallow. 'I'm sorry.'

Rian looked at me. 'Maybe it's no one's fault.' He took a deep breath and kissed my forehead. 'Tarragon, can you take her weapons?'

Tarragon nodded. Rian carefully propped me up as his cousin unbuckled my sword and shield.

'Right, let's go,' Rian said, scooping me up easily and gently in his arms. 'I've got you. Just stay with me, Phire,' he murmured in my ear, his words and warm breath comforting.

'I—I'll try,' I mumbled back. The cold fire raged. I shivered, and gasped again.

Rian held me tighter as we headed up the bank and through the trees, but his hot body did little to warm my core. Tarragon carried both torches in one hand, my weapons in the other, leading the way back towards the villa. I heard voices to my left somewhere. Mal's voice – Onyx's, too.

'You found her? Where was… By the Stars…' Mal's voice became strained and full of fear as he saw me and the glittering knife.

'Back in the copse,' Rian said as he kept walking. 'She said to tell you *Topaz.*'

Onyx choked, torch in hand, holding it high as he looked around. 'She was here?' he asked, his eyes wild. 'By the Stars, how did she find us?'

'Doesn't matter, and she'll be long gone now,' Mal said, taking Rian's torch from Tarragon. 'Forget her.'

'Juniper is ahead of us, too,' Tarragon said.

Mal shook his head. 'Blast.'

'What do we do?' Onyx asked, looking at me.

'Go find Anise,' Rian said, his voice taut, but he did not break his stride. 'Get him to our room. Tarragon, go, too. Find him!'

Tarragon passed my weapons to Mal, and he and Onyx ran off in different directions.

'I'll take you back,' Mal said, one hand holding the torch, the other carrying the Cursed Weapons. He kept glancing around, looking for any sign of trouble – or Topaz – as we headed across the grassy field in the direction of Zabell's villa.

'How long ago?' Mal asked, glancing at me then at Rian.

'Not sure, but from the look of the wound, a while,' Rian said, grimly.

'Deep?'

'Deep enough. She's bleeding badly.'

Another pain tore through me. I tensed. Rian held me tight, making sure I didn't slip from his grasp.

'Stay with me, Phire,' he said, looking at me. 'Anise will be with us in a minute.'

'You think he can do something?' Mal asked, his voice quavering.

'He better.'

We reached our villa building, Rian carrying me back to our room. Mal propped Deorwine and Glædwine up in a corner as Rian gently laid me down on the bed, then climbed onto the other side, sitting beside me.

Mal turned back, took one look at me, and swore. 'I hadn't realised she'd lost that much blood.'

Rian grunted. He pressed on my wound, trying to stop the steady flow of blood.

Another jab wrenched through my stomach and I cried out, unable to contain the pain. Cold sweat covered me, sticking my clothes to my skin, making me shiver again.

'Damn, where's Anise?' Rian said, his voice tight as he pressed harder with his hot hands. They seemed hotter than normal, but then I felt so cold. 'She's bleeding too much. I—I can't stop it.' He pressed harder.

I gasped, eyes wide. Then moaned in pain. 'Please, no, don't do that, it hurts too much.'

'Don't be a baby, Ama,' Mal said, though his voice didn't match the flippancy of his words. 'By the Stars, you've been through worse.'

That stung. 'When?'

'When Topaz stabbed you in the leg.'

'Oh, th—that.'

'What's this?' Rian asked, still pressing hard. I couldn't be sure if he was asking to keep me distracted or because of genuine curiosity.

'Ama and Topaz had an argument,' Mal said. 'They were supposed to be training, but Topaz said something about Father which Ama took offence to, and they started fighting for real.'

'Practice in the Coterie was always for real,' I muttered, wincing, my breath catching.

Rian glanced up at me.

Mal made a face. 'True. But this time they really tried to kill each other. Ama caught Topaz across the face and Topaz stabbed my sister in the leg. She was hobbling around for weeks.'

'T—Topaz still has the scar,' I said, a little smug smile creeping across my face – until the cold fire reminded me of its presence and made me bend double again. 'I don't.'

'Where is she?' Anise came running into the room with his Herb Chest, Tarragon and Onyx close behind with Sage. 'Let me see,' he said, kneeling beside the bed as Mal moved out of the way. He got his knife out and cut my shirt away from the wound.

'How bad is it?' Rian asked.

'I don't know, Rian – it depends how deep it is. She's lost so much blood. I'm not sure if I can…'

A hand came to rest on his shoulder. 'You can do it, Anise. Really, I know you can,' Sage said, his face pale as he looked at me.

Anise nodded. 'I'll make something up. We're going to need to take the knife out.'

'I'll do it,' Rian said, tenderly moving my hair from my cold, sweaty face.

Anise nodded. 'We'll also need bandages – but I don't have any. I used them all up back on Trew for you, Rian, I haven't been able to get any new ones since.'

'Take this,' Tarragon said, pulling his shirt off.

'And mine,' Rian said, tugging it over his head.

'Tarragon, tear yours up; we'll use Rian's as a pad,' Anise said, rummaging through his Herb Chest, his tongue out as he worked. 'I've got something I collected from the Chamber of Earth in Cilantro Citadel that I think may help stop the blood loss.'

At some point Willow had arrived, and she started to help Tarragon with his shirt. Whatever Anise was concocting, he was holding his Amulet as he did it. Whether that was out of habit or because he was using Magic, my addled brain couldn't tell.

'Hey, you still with me?' Rian asked, running his hand over my hair.

'At the moment,' I said, my voice raspy. 'C—can I have some water?'

'In a minute,' Anise said, moving over to us. 'Get those bandages ready. We'll need to stop the bleeding as soon as the knife's out and I've put this on her wound.' He had a little pestle and mortar in his hands. 'We haven't got much time.'

'No Moonflower?' I asked.

'And no Saliivia?' Rian checked.

Anise smiled. 'No. No Moonflower or Saliivia.'

Rian nodded and folded his shirt, handing it to Sage.

'Tarragon, get ready to hold her shoulders so she doesn't move when Rian pulls the knife out,' Anise said. 'Mal. Hold her legs. Any sudden movement when the knife is removed could tear her open. Maybe fatally.'

'Th—this isn't fatal already?' I asked, frowning.

Anise swallowed. 'Let's just concentrate on getting this knife out first, shall we? Everyone ready?'

'Ready,' Mal said as he moved down to the end of the bed.

Kneeling beside me, Tarragon said, 'Sorry about this, Phire, but it's for your own good.' He took a gentle hold of my shoulders, and Mal did the same with my legs.

'W—what are you doing?' I asked.

'We're going to take the knife out,' Anise said. 'This is going to hurt, Phire.'

'Please d—don't,' I mumbled. Everything hurt enough already. 'I'll be fine.' What was I saying? I shivered.

'I'm sorry, my love, but we have to.' Rian leant towards me, his mouth meeting mine, his lips hot as he kissed me gently. 'I love you.' He looked over at the others. 'Ready?'

As they nodded, a stab of pain shot through my stomach and I cried out.

Rian grimaced. 'Anise, can you give her something to knock her out before we do this? Or at least something for the pain?'

Anise shook his head. 'I'm sorry, Rian, but there's no time.'

Rian sighed, and squeezed my hand reassuringly. 'All right then, let's get this over with.' He glanced at me, love and fear swirling in his eyes. He grasped the knife hilt and took a deep breath. 'One, two, thr—'

I looked wildly around me. 'No, please don—'

He pulled.

I screamed.

CHAPTER TWELVE

Tarragon and Mal pinned me down as I instinctively tried to move. I longed to pass out with the pain, but I didn't, despite the fact it twisted and spiralled through me like some ravenously insane beast clawing frantically for freedom. I gasped for air, desperate for anything to quell the storm in my gut as the pain tore at my insides.

I just wanted this pain to stop.

Anise spread something over the wound, holding his Amulet as he did so. Whatever he put on it, it stung like hell, making me cry out even more. Sage passed Rian his shirt, and Rian pressed it to my wound as Tarragon and Mal moved me enough to allow Anise to wrap the makeshift bandages around my middle and tie them in place. My heart raced. I couldn't breathe properly. I gasped for air.

Was there a green glow? Everything tilted and finally, I just couldn't take the pain anymore. Dark oblivion welcomed me into his arms.

The crystals in the cave walls glowed in blues, greens and purples. The colours melded together, giving an ethereal glow that reached into every nook and cranny of the underground chamber. Rian stood beside me, watching something. I turned to look.

A great rotating golden light spun in front of us, fracturing, sending prisms of light across the cavern. It stuttered. Stopped. Started again. The mesmerising light appeared like a living thing, shrieking as it clung to life.

Something to my right caught my eye.

A deep red shadow loomed out of the crystal wall. It moved towards us, the glint of steel in its hand.

It lunged towards Rian.

I screamed a warning, but no sound came from my mouth.

I tried to move, but I was frozen in place.

I tried to shut my eyes, but they remained stubbornly open as the red shadow plunged the blade into my unsuspecting husband's chest.

I gasped. Opened my eyes. My heart raced. Was that another prophetic dream? My mouth was as dry as the desert.

My head rested on Rian's chest. He was still shirtless, his bare skin hot. His Fire Magic burnt within him all the time, and his warmth nourished me as I tried to calm the rising panic I felt inside. Early morning sun spilled into the bedroom, landing on the Cursed Weapons that winked at me from where they leant against the wall.

I must have slept all night. I shifted slightly, immediately wishing I hadn't, expecting the pain to burn cold inside me again – but it didn't. There was no pain. Nothing.

I moved the blanket that covered us both. The bandage still sat in place, wrapped tightly around my stomach. Blood had soaked through, but it was dark and old.

'You're awake,' Rian murmured. 'How are you feeling?'

'Tired,' I said, slipping my arm around him. 'Like a newborn lamb.'

'And how do you know what that feels like?'

'Just a guess.'

'Phire, how are you?' Anise asked, getting up from a chair on the other side of the room.

'A bit woozy. What happened?'

'You passed out. After that, Rian bathed you down and then kept an eye on you all night. You were quite restless.'

'Anise and Sage stayed and looked after you, too,' Rian said. Only then did I realise that in another chair sat Sage, slumped in sleep, snoring gently.

'Let's take a look at this wound,' Anise said. 'Rian, can you hold her?'

Rian shifted position and sat behind me, propped up against pillows. My upper body rested on him as Anise moved the blankets and then carefully unwrapped the bandages. He peeled the blood-soaked shirt away from my stomach.

Anise raised an eyebrow. 'Interesting...'

'How...?' Rian asked in wonder.

There was no open wound. No new blood. Just a shiny white scar where the knife wound had been.

I stared at my stomach then at Anise.

'I don't understand it,' Anise said, rubbing his head. 'I mean, how could that happen?'

'You really need us to spell it out for you?' Sage asked, getting up and coming over. 'I think it's fairly obvious.'

'Earth Magic? But that strong?'

'We always knew you were good with herbs,' Rian murmured. 'There was that green glow...'

I hadn't imagined it. 'Earth Magic,' I said.

Sage shrugged. 'Don't know, but probably. I thought I caught a greenish tinge, too.'

'Thank you, Anise,' I said, my eyes still wide. No wonder I hadn't felt any pain when I woke up. The wound had healed completely, thanks to Anise's Magic.

'The wound may have healed, but you'll probably feel quite tired for a few days,' Anise said. 'You still lost a lot of blood, and it'll take a while to recover from that.'

I nodded, preparing for the worst.

'We can rest here, can't we?' Sage asked. 'Zabell won't mind.'

'No, we have to go today,' I said, shifting position. 'Juniper is already ahead of us. We can't let her destroy the Vortex.'

'I don't care about the Vortex at the moment,' Rian said. 'I care about you, and you need to get your strength back before we go traipsing after her. We can worry about her later.'

'But—'

'He's right. We're going to need you when we get to Chroma, and if you're not strong enough, we won't be able to stop her and restart the Vortex,' Sage said.

'I can rest on the ship.'

'You'll rest here,' Rian said firmly.

Anise nodded. 'Maybe we could still leave tomorrow as planned, if you promise to rest properly today.'

Hell's teeth. I didn't want to delay any longer than we had to, but there was logic to what they said. 'All right. Tomorrow, then.'

'Now, get some rest,' Anise said.

A light knock at the door sounded, and Mal peered in. 'You're all right?' he asked, coming in with Onyx.

'Yes. I can't really believe it, but yes,' I said.

'You need to tell us what happened with Topaz.'

'There's not much to tell. I went for a walk—'

'Without telling us,' Rian cut in, his voice disapproving.

'I'm sorry. I was only walking in the gardens, I didn't mean to go so far.'

He pulled me closer. 'I'm not letting you out of my sight again.'

'And Topaz?' Onyx asked as Tarragon and Willow entered the room.

'She just appeared out of nowhere,' I said. 'I didn't realise she was even there until she'd thrown that damned knife in me.'

'You should have been keeping a better watch on your surroundings,' Mal chided.

'We're on an island. I went for a walk even *I* didn't know I was going to take. I thought I was safe.' I grimaced.

'You were just unlucky, that's all,' Rian said, kissing my head.

'I can't say I'd have been that on guard, going for a walk at night here,' Onyx said, sniffing. 'Until now.'

'Hmm. You're probably right,' Mal conceded.

'Topaz always was a good knife thrower – better than Citrine, really.'

Mal grinned. 'Except when she fought with Ama.'

'True.'

'Topaz said Juniper sent her, that she was ahead of us on her way to destroy the Crystal Vortex. Then Topaz left, sure she'd succeeded where Carnelian had failed,' I said with a shudder. 'I think he was waiting for her on a ship somewhere.'

Onyx screwed his nose up. 'She could have been lying about Juniper being ahead of us. She has a tendency to do that.'

'Not sure I've ever known her to tell the truth about anything,' Mal said.

'Even if she was lying about Juniper being quite so far ahead of us, if we assume she was on whatever ship Carnelian was waiting on, she's still several hours ahead, even now,' I said, glancing at Rian, but he shook his head. We wouldn't be leaving today and I just had to accept it.

'She must have thought she'd finished you off properly this time,' Mal said, looking at me. 'Or she never would've left like that.'

'To be honest, I thought I *was* dead,' I said. I raised my hand to Rian's cheek. 'I just wanted to see you again.'

He took hold of my hand and kissed my fingers.

'You're a strong old thing. I've learnt that,' Rian said.

'We'll go and get you some breakfast,' Sage said.

'If you're sure you're all right, we'll go and eat. Then I'll arrange for a couple of new shirts for you boys,' Willow said, looking appreciatively at Tarragon's bare chest. 'Not that I dislike the views on offer.' She smiled, turning to Rian as she stifled a little cough.

'Thank you,' Rian said with a grin, his cheeks turning pinkish.

'Hey, you look this way only,' Tarragon said, turning her chin towards him. 'No wandering eyes. And anyway, Rian isn't available.'

'Tarragon's right, Willow. I'm sorry but I'm taken,' Rian said, kissing my hand again. 'And I won't be available ever again.'

I smiled at him.

'Wherever you go, Willow, I'm coming, too,' Tarragon said, looking at her. 'Just in case that Topaz is still about.'

'I think we should all stay in at least twos from now on,' Mal said. 'And preferably with either me, Onyx or Ama, seeing as we know who we're looking for.'

'Although it's likely she's left the island by now,' Onyx said with a sniff. 'She probably was telling the truth about that.'

'Let's hope she's gone. If not, she'll rue the day she was born when I find her,' Mal said, his fist clenched.

'We're going to leave tomorrow, as planned, if that's all right with Captain Pol and Zabell,' Rian said.

'We'll go and speak to them,' Onyx said.

They all headed for the door.

'Tarragon. Last night... Thank you,' I said.

He turned back and grinned at me. 'My pleasure, Phire,' he said, with a little nod. He left the room, shutting it behind them all, leaving me alone with Rian. I lay beside him, wondering if I should mention my dream. I really didn't want to worry him. He may have said he wanted to know that sort of thing, but I feared for his life more now than ever, and I didn't want to increase the burdens he already shouldered. My dreams were coming true and I had to do everything I could to stop this one from turning out the same way.

'What are you thinking about?' Rian asked, looking at me intently.

'How stupid I was going off without you,' I lied – although it was also the truth.

'You didn't know she was here; none of us did.'

'I know, but still...'

'No going off alone again, understood? You're not just my dearest love, you're my best friend and soulmate. I want you safe, wife, and I'll do whatever it takes to keep you that way, but you need to do your part, too.'

I nodded. 'And I want you safe, which means I need to keep an eye on you now more than ever, as well.'

He laughed. 'Oh? And why's that?'

'B—because Juniper and Beryl may have sent others to get you.' I was having to think quickly and my brain wasn't sure it really wanted to quite yet. I had this light-headed sensation that periodically swept over me, making thinking straight – and lying – difficult. 'And because I love you to distraction, and I need to keep my soulmate and best friend alive, too.'

Anise and Sage returned with two trays of food for us.

'This soup is for you, Phire,' Anise said, passing me the bowl of steaming hot soup. 'It's quite salty to help you replace your lost blood.'

I took a sip and screwed my nose up. 'You really do mean it's salty.'

'You need to have a few of these today, then we'll let you leave tomorrow, as long as you rest today, too, and Rian agrees.'

Rian nodded. 'Just do as Anise says.'

I grunted and sipped at the soup.

Early afternoon, Rian relinquished his charge of me – he'd been like a mother hen all morning, clucking around me – and had a rest himself. Anise said he'd been up most of the night with me until they were sure I was going to be all right.

I'd been allowed out of bed to sit with Mal in the garden not far from the bedroom. When I'd first stood up, I'd almost keeled over immediately as my heart raced and I broke out in a sweat. Anise assured me it was to be expected, and Mal guided me to a bench in a shady spot.

We sat watching turquoise dragonflies dancing on a large pond, the gentle breeze moving the flowers, making them dance.

'What is it?' Mal asked, squinting in the sunshine as he looked at me.

'Nothing,' I said. 'Just tired.'

'Liar.'

'Hey!'

'I know you, Little Sister. Something's on your mind. Tell me. I will drag it out of you one way or another, you know that.'

I sighed. 'I had a dream last night.'

He raised an eyebrow. 'So?'

I explained to him all about the hallucinations I'd had after the Moonflower Elixir. 'Ostianzis said Quintessence Spinners could have prophetic dreams when they were ill.'

'And they've all come true?'

'Most of them – including the one about you chained up and enchanted.' I hesitated. 'If I'd known it was real…'

'Hey, you rescued me. You broke the enchantment. Your power saved me, not to mention your fighting skills.'

'I managed to stop you from killing me, if that's what you mean.' I grinned.

He looked a little sheepish. 'Sorry about that.'

'You weren't yourself.'

'What I meant was you were able to free me, not kill me in the process.'

'That, too.'

'Anyway, what more could you have done?'

'I could've done it quicker.'

'Don't be daft. You saved me, and that's all that matters.' He rubbed his forehead. 'So, you had another one last night?'

I nodded. 'There was this red shadow in a glowing cave. I—*it*—killed Rian.'

Mal sat silently for a moment. 'You told Rian about this?'

I shook my head. 'I know he's said he wants to know this sort of thing, but I'm worried about telling him something like that. How do you broach it? *Oh, by the way, last night I dreamt you were going to be stabbed to death, and as you know, my dreams have a habit of coming true.*' I bit back tears. I worried that simply telling him might even make it come true, somehow.

'Just because you dreamt it doesn't mean it's going to happen, you know,' he said, taking my hand.

'You hope.'

'Look, I'll help you keep an eye on him – Onyx will, too.'

'Don't tell Onyx about it. Rian will be livid if he finds out later that Onyx knew and he didn't.'

'Then I'll just say something about keeping a closer eye on him after Topaz's attempt on your life, and Carnelian trying to get him.'

I nodded. 'I suppose that'll be all right.'

'Now, stop worrying and rest, or Rian will never let us leave tomorrow if he thinks you're not up to it.' Mal hesitated a moment. 'You know, I would have done your killing for you, if I'd been able, but Juniper kept sending me in the opposite direction. I had no idea it was Carnelian doing it. You should've said what was happening.'

'I didn't want to worry you.'

Mal laughed. 'There you go again. It seems to me you spend your life trying to protect people and stop them from worrying.'

I squinted ruefully at him. 'Like protecting Beryl.'

'Hmm,' Mal grunted, a bleak look in his eyes. 'If only we'd known.' He slipped his arm around my shoulder and pulled me closer.

'We could've left years ago.'

'But then you'd never have met Rian. You love him a lot, don't you?'

I nodded. 'Very, very much.'

'Was it love at first sight?'

I laughed. 'Not exactly – he had a knife at my throat.'

'He what?' Mal's eyes widened. 'By the Stars, Onyx didn't tell me this when he was getting me up to date with all the news, and you and I haven't really had a proper chance to talk with everything else that's been going on.'

'And you've been recovering, too – I didn't want to overload you with too much information too soon.'

'I'm fine now, really. I think everything's pretty much come back.'

'Anyway, I never told Onyx how Rian and I met in a Samphire creek. I thought he might kill him, at least at the beginning.' I went on to explain to Mal what had happened in Aerba, our visit to Iolite, mynogres, Moonflower Elixirs and Curses.

'Blast it, I had no idea you'd been through so much,' he said, squeezing me to him. 'I mean, I knew about the Curse, but the execution and how you defeated the Curse – I'm so glad you found a group of friends to help you. And you found your prince, too.'

I gave him a little playful jab in the ribs. 'It didn't start off like that. After all, he's a High Blood, and you know what my feelings were about them a few months ago.'

Mal grinned at me. 'Yes, I do. It's a good thing you were able to get past that.'

'It is, isn't it? But it took me a little while.'

'What'll we do?'

'What?'

'When this is all over, what'll we do?'

I shrugged. 'Come back here? Preferably without Beryl.'

'I'd like a long talk with our sister,' Mal said, his jaw set. 'She betrayed us, time after time. I can't believe she'd do something like that. I really thought we were keeping her alive.'

'So did I. Just shows how wrong you can be.'

He paused for a moment to flick his strawberry-blond hair over his shoulder. 'Do you really want to come back here to live?'

I gazed out at the dazzling ponds, the jewel-like dragonflies, the verdant gardens and the azure sea far in the distance. 'It is a kind of paradise here, isn't it? Somewhere we can all be with who we want, live the way we want. But I don't know.' I glanced at Mal. 'You're the rightful Master of Iolite.'

'And if we defeat Juniper and Chervil, Rian's the rightful King of Aerba.'

I swallowed. 'I don't think he wants that. Anyway, Chervil erased him from the line of succession.'

Mal took a deep breath. 'The problem is, if he's anything like me, and I think he is a bit, he'll feel duty-bound to go back and look after his people.'

I twisted around to look at my brother. 'You'd really go back to Iolite and do that?'

'I'd do more than that – I'd dismantle the whole blasted Coterie,' he said, his eyes hard.

I nodded slowly. 'You are like Rian – he wants to tear up the Blood Rule Decree.'

'I wouldn't mind doing that, too.' Mal glanced at me. 'And where would you go?'

'That one's easy – wherever Rian is. You've got Onyx, now. You don't need me.'

'Of course I need you, you plum. I'll always need you, you're my sister. But you're right, your place is beside Rian, now, and mine is with Onyx.'

'We're getting ahead of ourselves. We haven't saved the Vortex yet – and there's still my dream.' I shivered.

'We'll keep Rian safe, don't worry. If we do end up here, though, I won't be sorry.'

I smiled. 'Neither will I,' I said, resting my head on his shoulder.

CHAPTER THIRTEEN

That evening, I lingered in the bath until the water began to cool, then wrapped a towel around myself and went back into the bedchamber. Rian lay languidly on the bed, one hand under his head, eyes shut, his lower half covered by the sheet, and one knee raised, his bare chest rising and falling as he breathed slowly. My Amethyst Talisman twinkled in the light, his hair still damp from his own bath.

Was there a hint of rose in the air? Had he been at the perfume he'd bought me back in Flos? For a moment I stood there, enjoying the view. I walked across the chamber and climbed onto the bed, pushed his knee down, and straddled him.

He opened his eyes, an eyebrow rising. 'Did you want something?' he asked.

'Just you,' I said, smiling at him. 'And I'm wondering about where my perfume is?'

'It's in your pack, where you left it.'

'You mean you put it back.'

He grinned. 'Of course.'

'And you've had it out because…?'

'I like it. It smells of you. Now, what did you want with me? I'm tired.' But his amber eyes said otherwise, and so did the pilfering of my perfume. 'And you're supposed to be resting.'

'I'm feeling fine,' I said. 'And you don't have to do anything, you can stay exactly where you are.'

'Oh?'

His eyes widened as I moved the Talisman out of the way and to one side of his bare chest. As I did so, I sensed it almost quivering in my hand. I'd never noticed the Artefact feel like that before – maybe my Quintessence was picking up on it? Or was it that I was now more in tune with Magic in general? Either could have been the case. Rian and I may have even been able to see the little glow in it now simply because our Magic Angles were known to us and we were sensitive to the Elemental Magic that surrounded us.

I gazed at his toned body, then started peppering it with little kisses.

'Oh,' he murmured contentedly.

He let me continue for a few minutes, then grabbed my arms and rolled me over onto my back until *he* was straddling *me*. That perfume was quite something. The effect it had on Rian…

'How's your wound?' he asked.

'Better, really,' I said.

'I think I should check it, just to make sure it's healed okay,' he said, taking my towel off as if it were the wrapping on a present. He sucked in a little breath. 'By the Herbs, you're beautiful.'

'You're impossible,' I said, trying to stifle a giggle.

'I try.'

'Not hard enough.'

He ignored me. 'Hmm. Are you sure your wound's all right?' he asked, intently studying the scar on my stomach, gently running a finger over it.

'Well, maybe it twinges a bit,' I lied.

He smiled, and when he spoke his voice trembled slightly, a warm breeze brushing gently against summer flowers, making a silken thread knot in my stomach. 'I thought that might be the case. Then I should kiss it better.'

And he started to kiss it, reverently, devotedly, before moving lower and lower and lower...

The early morning sun streamed through the window as I opened my eyes to find Rian's face inches away from mine. He grinned at me, then pressed his warm lips against mine, leaving the taste of strawberries behind.

'Good morning,' Rian said, grinning at me as he lay beside me, raised up on one shoulder.

'Good morning to you, too,' I said. 'Have you been at the strawberries already?'

He glanced over at the fruit bowl on his side of the bed. 'I might have been, why?'

'I can taste them on your lips.'

'A strawberry kiss?'

'Hmm, a rather lovely one.'

He smiled as he lay back down. 'They smelt so good when I woke up that I just had to have a couple. How did you sleep?'

'Well, thank you. You?'

'Not bad. Not bad at all.'

I'd worried that he might start having nightmares again after my close encounter with Topaz, but maybe he was going to be all right this time. Or maybe his stunningly passionate display last night had just worn him out, rather like it had me. I sighed happily. Glancing out of the window, the anticipation of setting off on the midday tide started butterflies fluttering in my stomach. I sat up and stretched.

'You know, I've been thinking – certain Artefact gemstones enhance a Spinner's power, yes?' Rian asked, still lying in bed.

I nodded.

'An Amethyst Artefact enhances a Fire Spinner's power,' he said.

'Yes, so?'

He sat up, reached out to me and pulled me towards him. 'You're Amethyst and you enhance my power,' he said, kissing me, making my heart thunder.

How long had he been thinking that one up?

'You certainly know what to say to a girl,' I said breathlessly as he finally let me go.

He gave me that lopsided smile of his that never failed to weaken my knees as he raked his fingers through his hair, just making me want to melt into a puddle even more.

'I try – but I've only ever had you to practise with, so if it's working, I'm doing quite well, aren't I?' he said, a smug little expression creeping across his face.

I'd wipe that smug grin off right now. I pushed him back onto the bed and climbed on top of him. Suddenly he looked a little less sure of himself.

'And I think I do rather well, too, Valerian,' I said, starting the little kisses across his chest that had had such an effect on him last night.

His breathing hitched. 'I suppose you do,' he said, a little hoarsely, then suddenly took hold of me and pulled me into a kiss filled with urgency and passion. The desire that was there in his touch, the longing in his kiss, tore at my heart as his mouth claimed mine. I collapsed on top of him, his bare skin hot as usual. I held him as he stroked my hair and sandalwood swelled around us.

'I thought I was losing you – again,' he murmured. 'You're making a bad habit of this, wife, and I don't like it.'

'I'm not doing it on purpose,' I said, knowing I should've stayed with him and not wandered off alone. I'd broken the promise I'd made to myself after the river, to never leave him. I wouldn't break it again.

'I know. And although I don't want to smother you, until this is over I'm not leaving your side for a single moment.'

'You've said that before.'

'This time I mean it.'

'You know you're in just as much danger as me?' The deep red shadow loomed large in my mind, shining blade in hand.

He nodded. 'I do. So we stick together. Look after each other. Watch each other's backs. Agreed?'

'Agreed, we stay together,' I said, forcing the shadow to the edges of my mind. 'I'll be your shield until my last breath,' I murmured, my vision blurring as I remembered my vow to him in the prison back on Aerba.

'And I'll protect you until my last breath leaves my body.' He turned my head to look at him. His eyes were glassy, too. 'No more wandering off without me, and especially not without telling me where you're going,' he said, running a finger down the side of my face. 'Promise?'

'Promise.'

'You up yet?' Tarragon's voice drifted through the door as he knocked.

Rian sighed and gave me a long-suffering look. 'We'll be with you in a few minutes.'

'Don't be long or breakfast will be cold.'

I screwed my nose up. 'Don't care about breakfast.'

'Neither do I. You know, one of these days I might lock Tarragon up so we can have a few hours to ourselves, uninterrupted.'

'Then you'd better take Willow's lock picks away and lock her up with him. He'll have a distraction then and won't be able to get out.'

Rian laughed. 'I'd almost say you've been planning that, too.'

'Maybe I have.'

'I hear Captain Pol wishes to leave on the midday tide,' Zabell said, coming out into the sitting area where we were all relaxing before our journey, enjoying cold fruit juices. I'd slipped Topaz's knife into my boot – a reminder to stay with Rian, and to be more wary. And the hilt was quite nice.

'That's right,' Rian said. He and Tarragon were wearing the new shirts Willow had arranged for them. 'We can only thank you for your hospitality.'

'Don't mention it,' Zabell said, raising his hand. He looked around at us. 'Do you all know how your Magic works?'

'Sort of,' Tarragon said. 'It's to do with concentrating on what you want to happen.'

Zabell nodded.

'Is this a good time to mention I'm an Air Spinner?' Mal asked.

I grinned at him. 'And how did you find that out?'

'We did what you did, Ama,' Onyx said. 'Process of elimination.'

Sage's eyes widened at the news. 'That's so good – another Air Spinner. We'll have to compare our powers, see if I can help you, not that I've done a lot yet.'

'I'm still getting my head around what I can do,' Mal said. 'Your help would be great.'

Zabell smiled. 'If what you want to do is within the realm of the power of your Elemental Magic then, with enough effort, it will come to pass. But it will sap your energy.'

'Y'know, I've noticed that,' Tarragon said ruefully.

'And Artefacts can make us more powerful?' Rian asked, holding my Amethyst Talisman in the sun, the purple crystal shining in the light.

Zabell nodded. 'Depending on the crystal. But their power doesn't last forever. It will eventually drain.'

Anise looked at his Jade Amulet and tucked it inside his shirt as Tarragon admired his Rose Quartz Wristband and Onyx glanced at his Rose Quartz Ring.

'Not that I'm quite sure what Quintessence does, though,' I said, chewing on a nail. Rian took hold of my hand and pulled it away from my mouth. He then kept hold of it to stop me from carrying on nibbling.

'Quintessence allows you to bind the other four Elements together and use their power as one – which is what you'll need to do to restart the Vortex.'

'But surely to control the power of the other four Elements takes a lot of energy, not to mention it must be highly dangerous,' Rian said, glancing anxiously at me.

Zabell nodded. 'That is true. Wielding it is not without risk, but sometimes the positive points outweigh the negative – it gave Samphire the strength to withstand the Cursed Weapons, and to aid in healing.'

'But I thought it was Anise's Earth Magic that healed Phire,' Sage said.

'I was referring to the prince's poisoning.'

Rian flinched at the word "prince".

I frowned. 'So Rian was healed from his poisoning by a combination of Anise's Earth Magic and my Quintessence...'

'And Rian's Fire Magic burnt the poison from his blood?' Anise pondered.

'That would work,' Zabell said. 'The cure would have been almost instantaneous with that level of Magic in play.'

'It was,' I murmured, looking at Rian. 'Once it was *all* in play.'

'I was tired for a while, though,' Rian said.

Zabell nodded. 'You were healed, but your body still took time to recover.'

'So, in a way, Quintessence can provide an added burst of energy to the other Elements?' I asked.

'Exactly.'

'And on its own?'

'It is pure energy, the most powerful Element – you could light up the night if you wanted to.'

That would've stopped Topaz in her tracks.

'But with such great power you have to realise you will tire quickly,' Zabell said.

'What sort of crystal Artefact would enhance Quintessence?' Willow asked.

Zabell scratched his head. 'Any sort of Diamond Artefact would do that.'

I glanced at the Cursed Weapons sitting beside me. Maybe they could still be of greater use than just a pretty crystal sword and shield.

'How do you know all this, Zabell?' Sage asked.

He smiled. 'My mother's line goes back to the Chroma High Bloods. The stories were handed down over the generations. A lot of what you're all doing at the moment is instinct, but you need to learn greater control over your Magic, and that will come with practice.'

We left Zabell and the Pax Archipelago on the noon tide with Captain's Pol's ship restocked and ready for our trip to Chroma. Zabell had given her maps to help us with our voyage to Middle Isle.

This was all new to Pol and Holm, and I could sense a certain trepidation along with their excitement. Onyx hadn't had to do too much persuading to get her to agree, especially once she'd known we had a couple of Air Spinners to help us across The Great Doldrums. As *The Spirit of the Seas* cut through the ocean, Sage and Mal practised their Magic in preparation for the calm seas ahead. They'd decided to take it in turns to move us through the slack water so neither one became too tired. At least, that was their hope.

I spent some time with Rian watching Mal and Sage's attempts at perfecting their Magic as Tarragon and Onyx got into a friendly competition trying to fill and empty a bucket with water as quickly as possible. Willow and Anise looked on, chatting quietly, as the sailors moved around the deck. In some ways I'd have liked to try out my Quintessence a bit more, but on board the ship didn't seem the cleverest of ideas. Rian had also decided setting the ship alight wasn't something he wanted to try, even with two Water Spinners on board, so he refrained from making any fires – although I was of the opinion that he had already mastered his Fire Magic to an extent, rather like Anise with his Earth Magic.

It was the morning of our third day at sea. While neither Rian, nor I, had had overly restful nights, our dreams had been nothing like what we'd endured in the past. A little unsettling, maybe, but not full-on nightmares, and when we woke, unnerved by their clarity, we had been there to soothe and lull one another back to sleep. Time was a great healer.

While watching the others out on the deck, I couldn't help but mull over the red shadow that still haunted the back of my mind – and, indeed, sometimes my dreams. Every time I thought of it, my heart started racing. My hands turned cold. I had to take deep breaths to calm myself – this was one prophecy that couldn't come true. But how to stop it when all the others had come to pass?

'What's the matter with you? You're very quiet,' Rian said, sitting beside me on a packing crate.

'Nothing,' I said.

'Yes, there is, I can tell, remember?' he said, taking hold of my hand.

'Just wondering about how we're going to catch Juniper and stop her destroying the Vortex – and start it going properly again, of course.'

He nodded, buying my story. 'It's playing on my mind, too. Especially the fact that you're going to have to control all our Magic at once. I really don't want you doing that. I'm concerned you might burn up.'

'I don't have much of a choice, though, do I?'

'I know. But I don't have to like it.' He sucked a breath in through his teeth.

'I managed to survive the Cursed Weapons,' I said, glancing at the purple sword and shield standing to attention beside me. 'I broke the Curse, with your help, and I can do this.' *I hope.* 'As long as you're with me, I'll be fine,' I said, squeezing his hand.

'I will be,' he said. 'There's nowhere else I'm going to be, and anyway, you can't do it without me.'

'Exactly.'

A shout went up from the Crow's Nest high above us. 'Doldrums ahead!'

I glanced at Rian. 'Now we see how well Mal and Sage have been doing.'

CHAPTER FOURTEEN

The Great Doldrums lived up to their name. The wind dropped without warning. The water calmed. The sea became like a millpond, silent and still, no waves, not a breath of air anywhere as the sun reflected on the glass-like surface that mirrored the azure sky.

'You ready?' Mal asked, looking at Sage.

Sage nodded. 'We'll start together, then you rest for a bit.'

'Let's do it.'

The two young men looked up at the slack white sails and concentration suddenly filled their faces. For a moment I thought their eyes were going to pop out on stalks, then the sails filled with a blast of air, and the ship picked up speed as we continued to head south-east.

Anise smiled. 'It's working. It's actually working.'

'Did you doubt it?' Tarragon asked. 'I didn't.'

Rian gave him a long look.

Anise screwed his nose up on one side. 'Not as such…'

Willow grinned. 'We'll be through the doldrums in no time. I'll be pleased when we get back to land again.'

'It'll still take us until sometime tomorrow, even if they can keep this up,' Rian said.

'Let's hope they can. Otherwise I'll need more of Anise's sea sickness remedy.'

'I thought you'd been doing very well, Willow,' Anise said. 'You haven't been asking for as much as on previous trips.'

'Bobbins. I still need your tea from time to time to keep it under control.'

'Even so, you're improving.'

'Perhaps you're finding your sea legs after all,' I said.

She flashed me a smile. 'Maybe I am.'

Sage and Mal took it in turns, two hours on, two hours off, as they continued to send us across the doldrums at a great rate of knots. By evening, Captain Pol reckoned we were a good third of the way across.

Mal sat near the bow, taking a rest. He glanced at me as I leant on the rail.

'You're still worrying, aren't you?' he asked.

Sometimes I wished he didn't know me so well. He could have a nasty habit of getting to the truth with the precision of a surgeon cutting through to the bone, something he'd always been able to do, but then, he was my brother and he knew me inside out. Only Rian came close. Very close.

'Maybe,' I said, looking out over the golden water as the sun set.

'Worrying isn't going to help. You know when it'll happen – in the cave – so deal with it then. Don't spend all this time fretting beforehand, you'll just wear yourself out.'

'Spoken like a true pragmatist.'

'You think it helps to worry?'

I turned towards him. 'No. But my mind won't leave it alone, especially because it's Rian's life at stake. I can't seem to shake it off, put it to one side for long before it slams back into the forefront of my mind.'

Mal nodded, glancing over my shoulder.

'I keep going through what I need to do, how I have to save him, not let this happen,' I said, sighing. 'I can't let him die. I *won't* let him die. Especially if I can do something about it.'

'By the Stars, Ama, you can't control everything.'

'I can try, though.'

Mal shook his head. 'Any one little thing could change, go right or wrong. You can't be in charge of it all. I think you should tell him. Especially as it's worrying you so much.'

'But how? How do I tell him what I've dreamt? That what I saw is slowly killing me inside because it was watching him die?'

'What's this?'

Rian's voice sounded right behind me, making me gasp. Had Mal seen him? By the look in his eyes, he had. He'd dumped me right in it. On purpose. I loved my brother, but right now he was a bastard. I twisted around.

'N—nothing,' I said. 'Just talking.'

Rian looked at Mal.

Mal let out a long breath. 'You two need to talk,' he said, getting up. He took my hand. 'It's for the best, Ama. Really.'

I glared at him as he walked off towards the cabin, past Sage who sat concentrating on the sails, Anise beside him.

Rian stood next to me and leant on the rail. 'Well?'

I couldn't do this. I didn't know where to start.

He put his hands on my waist. I looked into his amber eyes, eyes that seemed to already know the truth.

'I...' Where to begin?

'I heard most of what you were saying,' he said. 'Your dream – you saw me die. Why, by the Herbs, didn't you say so?'

'B—because I didn't know how to.' Tears suddenly came. A sob burst from my throat. He held on to me as I tried to control my emotions. If I couldn't even do that, how could I hope to control anything else?

'Come with me,' he said, leading me to our cabin. He sat beside me on the bed. 'Now, tell me. I thought you said there wasn't anything else to your dreams.'

'That was before.'

'Before what?'

'I had another dream, when Topaz stabbed me.'

'Which was?' He had his arm around my shoulders, pulling me close.

'There was this red shadow, with a blade, a knife.'

'You told me about that.'

'Yes, but this time it... it stabbed you. I couldn't stop it. I was frozen to the spot and all I could do was watch.'

'It was a dream – you'd just been stabbed yourself,' he murmured, kissing my head.

I pulled back. 'But everything else has come true. Even the pain in my stomach turned out to be Topaz stabbing me. I couldn't stop that, either. How am I going to stop this?' The tears came again. 'I can't lose you. Not again.'

He sighed, and when he spoke his voice was like silk. 'If it's what's meant to happen...'

'No! I won't accept that. Our lives aren't pre-destined in some way by my stupid dreams.'

'But your dreams are damn accurate.'

'Not this one,' I said, gritting my teeth. 'Maybe when we get to the cave you should stay outside. If you're not in the cave it can't happen.'

'You're going to need me in there for this to work.'

'I won't risk your life!'

'You're risking yours by trying to control all our powers and restart the Vortex. Even Zabell said it was dangerous.'

'I know, but that's different—'

'No, it's not.' He gently brushed the tears from my face. 'We're doing this for the Six Lands, for all its people.'

'Then maybe the people can go to hell. You're the most important thing to me.'

He raised an eyebrow. 'I know, but you want to save the people, too, don't you?'

'Not at the expense of your life. No!'

'Samphire Amethyst,' he said, looking deep into my eyes. 'You know in your heart what the right thing to do is.' He placed his warm hand gently over my heart.

I bowed my head in resignation. 'Of course I do, I just don't want to do it if the cost is your life. I know what we have to do. Save the Six Lands. Save the people. I do know that, but I'll stop if I need to, to protect you. I vowed to be your shield.'

Rian smiled. 'And I've sworn to protect you, too. We'll try and do both, but if we can't, we'll know that what we've done is for something far greater than the two of us.'

'That'll be cold comfort,' I muttered, looking away.

'But the right thing to do,' he said, turning me back to him and holding my face in his hands. 'And you know that, deep down.'

My shoulders sagged. He may have been right, but I didn't have to like it.

'We'll do what we have to,' he continued. 'But now I know to beware of death in that cave, I'll be even more alert. We'll tell all the others, too. Then that way I have the best possible chance of staying alive.'

I nodded slowly. 'I love you too much to lose you. Again.'

'I know. Same here. But we'll do what we must for our people.' He gazed into my soul. 'And for now we grab hold of every minute we have together, just in case.' He started by kissing my neck, sending hot, comforting sparks through my body.

We didn't leave our cabin until morning.

I stepped out into the bright sunlight. Frowned. The wind generated by Mal fluttered the sails high above. A lone seagull cried forlornly overhead. But something else made the hairs on the back of my neck stand to attention. Far off, but unnerving. A noise, strange and unfathomable. A deep rumbling.

'Hell's teeth, what is that?' I shuddered.

'What's what?' Willow asked, stepping out onto the deck beside me.

'By the Stars, can't you hear it?'

She frowned, concentrating hard. 'Oh.'

'We don't know what it is,' Onyx said, coming over. 'It's been there a few minutes now, in the distance, but it's getting closer.'

'Does your aunt have any ideas?' Willow asked.

'One, but she won't say what – and neither will Holm.'

'That's even more worrying,' I murmured, gazing out over the flat sea. I turned and looked up. No one was in the Crow's Nest. 'I'm going up to take a look,' I said, moving over to the rigging that would take me up high above the ship.

'Up there?' Willow winced. 'What if you fall?'

'I won't fall. Everything is quite calm.'

Onyx sniffed. 'I'm not sure you should go alone,' he said, a doubtful look on his face.

'Want to come?'

'Not really.'

'Then I'll go alone.' I started climbing up the rigging, taking it steadily, one step at a time. I hadn't gone far when I glanced down. *Idiot.* For a moment everything swam in front of my eyes. *Don't look down.* I closed my eyes and took a deep breath.

'You all right, Ama?' Onyx called.

'Fine,' I said between gritted teeth. How did sailors manage to climb the rigging in stormy seas? The ship glided smoothly across the water, no rolling or lurching, and it still made me feel a little sick, but I'd started and couldn't back down now – not with Onyx watching. I'd never hear the end of it. I opened my eyes and carried on climbing upwards, my sweaty hands gripping the dry, coarse rope.

'What's she doing?' Holm asked from far below.

'We wondered what that noise was, and there's no one in the Crow's Nest keeping lookout, so Ama went up to take a look,' Onyx said.

Holm swore.

I continued upwards, eventually arriving at the little wooden Crow's Nest and climbed in. I held onto the side, the wood smoothed by wind and rain, and gazed out over the blue sea. The sun reflected off it, casting little diamonds across the surface. I looked to both sides and behind us. Nothing – just flat water stretching out to the horizon. I looked ahead.

Swallowed.

The whole way across the horizon, water churned, white crests flying skyward in an angry display. But why? I squinted, trying to get a better look. I shielded my eyes from the sun with my hand.

The sea directly ahead moved in a great spiral, the water running faster and faster towards an invisible centre like a great wheel. But it was more than one wheel. Many huge spirals lay ahead of us the whole way across the sea, stretching from horizon to horizon in a great line. There didn't appear to be any way around them, only through. Between. But where one ended, the next began. The great rumbling increased, a throaty roar thundering ahead of us, warning of our doom.

I shook my head. How would we ever get through them?

A grunt came from the rigging below. Holm joined me in the Crow's Nest and looked out. He swore and looked below to where Captain Pol now stood, along with Onyx, Willow and Rian.

'Maelstroms!' he yelled down to the deck.

CHAPTER FIFTEEN

'What are maelstroms?' I asked, mesmerised by the churning water ahead.

'Massive whirlpools,' Holm said, his face pale. 'We come across the odd one, but nothing like this. It's probably all part of the Crystal Vortex decaying. There's no way around them,' he said, looking to the horizon.

'Then what do we do?'

'You need to get to Chroma?'

I nodded.

'Then we may have to run the gauntlet,' he said, climbing out of the Crow's Nest and heading down to the deck.

I glanced back to where the great waves circled and spiralled down towards the ocean floor. I shuddered, then followed him carefully down the rigging, keen not to fall.

'How many?' Captain Pol asked as Holm jumped down onto the deck.

'No idea,' Holm said. 'They're stretched in a line right across our path from horizon to horizon.'

'Is there room between them?'

'Maybe – just enough. But we'll have to have a good wind behind us to force us through or we'll get caught in the current.'

Rian helped me onto the deck as I stepped off the rigging. He gave me a fairly long *What do you think you were doing up there?* look.

I smiled and shrugged. 'I didn't go far.'

He shook his head and clasped my hand. Tightly.

The deep rumbling became a screech that grew louder, setting my teeth on edge.

'Right, I'll get in the Crow's Nest, give you directions. You get the men to adjust the rigging so we have the best chance of getting through, then get to the wheel,' Pol said to Holm. 'We may need last minute adjustments to our course. We need both our Air Spinners – and Water Spinners, too.'

'What can we do?' Onyx asked.

'Try and calm the water around us as much as possible for an easier passage between the maelstroms.'

'Will that work?'

'We can only try, lad,' Pol said, heading for the rigging and the Crow's Nest.

'I'll get Tarragon,' Willow said.

Onyx nodded. 'I'll get Mal.' The two disappeared below.

I looked at Rian.

'Not much we can do,' he said, looking out over the water.

'By the Stars, I don't like feeling helpless,' I said.

He raised an eyebrow. 'I've noticed that.'

I winced. Our conversation yesterday still made me anxious. On the one hand, I wished Mal hadn't set me up, that my dream was still a secret – but on the other, I was glad Rian knew, could be careful. And now that the others knew, too, hopefully between us we'd be able to thwart the prophecy.

We went to the bow, watching the seas ahead as they went from a mirror glass finish to rampant waves, in places almost thirty feet high. We'd definitely need our Water Spinners to calm those, if they could. How we were ever going to get through the maelstroms, I didn't know.

Tarragon and Willow joined us.

'I don't want to be in another shipwreck,' Sage said, walking over and standing at the bow, just to our left, still concentrating on filling the sails.

'Neither do I,' Anise said, looking out at the ever-growing waves.

I grabbed at the rail as we hit a large one, the ship lurching to the right, salt water spraying over us.

Rian grabbed me as I slipped. 'This is going to get nasty,' he said, letting go of me.

The water grew angrier, foaming white streaks beginning to appear around us as we cut through the raging water.

'What should I do?' Mal asked, moving over to join us.

'Keep the wind in the sails,' Sage said. 'We'll try and force our way through as quickly as we can.'

Mal nodded and stood at the bow to the right.

'Onyx, let's try and calm the water ahead and to our sides,' Tarragon said. 'You take the right, I'll take the left.'

Onyx nodded going over to stand on the same side as Mal, who was holding onto the rail, concentrating on the water. The foaming water began to calm a little, but despite Tarragon and Onyx's best efforts, they were up against the raw power of Mother Nature. It was an uneven battle as sweat ran down their faces. They valiantly did what they could to ease our passage, but they'd never be able to calm the maelstroms themselves.

The whirlpools loomed up ahead now as Mal and Sage forced us on. The water spun on both sides of us, ever faster, moving towards the centres of the whirlpools, then dipping down towards the ocean floor. How far down the centres went I couldn't see from where I stood on the deck.

'Starboard!' Pol yelled down to Holm who now stood at the ship's wheel. He spun the wheel, making a correction to our course.

'This isn't enough,' Sage said through gritted teeth, his earring jingling. 'We need more.'

I glanced at Onyx and Tarragon. Onyx had one hand over his Rose Quartz Ring, Tarragon a hand over the Rose Quartz in his black leather Wristband – they were both using their Artefacts to increase their powers. What we needed was an Air Artefact to help Sage and Mal, but we had none.

The ship lurched to one side as the ocean tugged at us.

I collided with Rian and we landed on the deck as a wave broke over the side of the ship. Almost everyone had fallen or lost balance. The sudden movement had caused the Spinners to momentarily lose their focus. They scrambled back to their feet.

'Bugger,' Tarragon muttered.

Rian pulled me up, staring over the rail. 'Damn.'

I turned in the direction he was looking.

We were caught.

The left hand maelstrom had us in its grasp. The ship started to circle the huge, gaping maw. I clung to Rian. Were we lost? He looked at me, fear in his eyes – from his inability to swim, or just the dire situation, I wasn't sure. Then he shook his head. It was because he knew, as well as I did, that we'd never break free of this now.

Sage and Mal grasped the ship's rail, trying to break us free of the whirlpool as the current took us around. The sails strained; the ship creaked. Tarragon and Onyx tried to steady the water around us, calm it enough to allow us to escape.

But it still wasn't enough, even with the Water Spinners' Artefacts.

The screeching whirlpool refused to let us go, intent on pulling us to its centre and taking us down into the depths forever. It wrenched us around again, a spinning top in some child's game.

'I love you,' Rian said in my ear.

'What?' I tore my eyes from the raging water and glanced at him.

'This is it. I want you to know I love you, and you'll be the last thing I think of.'

I swallowed. Clenched my fists. 'No. This isn't it,' I said. There was still something to try. Something I'd never done before. It gave me a wisp of hope, but I had to time it at exactly the right moment.

'What do you mean?' He held me up as another wave crashed into the side of the ship, making us all stagger sideways, spraying us with water.

'We need more!' Mal yelled at Sage. 'When we get around the other side, give it everything you've got. We have to break free, and this time around will be our only chance. Tarragon, Onyx – just concentrate on the water ahead of us, smooth our path out.'

My brother was right. This would be our last and only chance to escape the furiously spiralling water – after this, we'd be too far in to ever break free.

We reached the far side of the great spinning wheel. I glanced into it. I still couldn't see the bottom, but I could see it reached down a very long way – into hell itself, maybe.

'Now!' Mal yelled.

The four Spinners focussed on their jobs. The water in front of us calmed, and a path out of the churning water gradually appeared. The sails billowed with air, wind moving us towards freedom. The ship strained. Timbers protested as it was pulled in different directions at the same time.

'No!' Sage cried.

We'd gained momentum in the right direction, but were now about to be pulled around once more.

That couldn't happen. It would mean our deaths.

'I love you, Rian,' I said.

He looked at me, frowned. 'What are you do—' His eyes widened.

I stepped forwards.

Placed my glowing hands on Mal and Sage.

Help them.

My hands glowed white on their shoulders, the white spreading up my arms, across their backs.

'Be careful, Phire,' Rian said from behind me, his voice taut.

But I couldn't. If I was, we'd all die. All be sucked into the depths of the ocean and drown.

Take what you need.

'Blast it, Ama, what are you doing?' Mal asked, his voice strained as he glanced furtively in my direction.

'Helping,' I said. I'd give them all the energy they needed. All I had, if necessary. Give everything, to cut us free of the water's death spiral. 'Tarragon, Onyx!' I shouted at them.

They both glanced back at me, at each other, then placed their hands on my shoulders. Their hands, too, started to glow white.

I felt the raw power inside me, eager to get out. It sped from me, nourishing the other Spinners, giving them the extra power, the Magic, they needed to work.

The ship began to move faster, the sails taut in the wind, the wooden timbers creaking under the pressure. The rigging groaned, strained to its limits. The ship cried in pain as we pushed it beyond its normal constraints.

I gritted my teeth as I felt myself beginning to drain. My Quintessence continued to power us through the sea. The water around us calmed to a mirror as Tarragon and Onyx began to get the upper hand on the current.

Mal's knuckles turned white as he held onto the rail. Sweat ran down Sage's face. The sound of the water roared in my ears. The waves crashed over the side of the rail and across the deck. A great, shuddering vibration ripped through the ship. The timbers shrieked in protest and we broke free.

We kept hold of each other as the sails billowed in the Air Magic and the ship slid across the sea flattened by the Water Magic. *The Spirit of the Seas* slowly pulled away from the maelstroms that would pull us back and into their depths if we rested for one single moment. Perspiration covered my brow, my back. It was like running across Iolite from north to south. My heart thudded uncomfortably in my chest. My head ached. My arm muscles, tense from holding onto Mal and Sage, burnt. Even my shoulders hurt where Tarragon and Onyx held onto me. I forced air into my lungs as we moved away from the thrashing water.

'It's all right, we're free,' Pol shouted from above.

'Hear that? You can stop now,' Anise said, running over towards us.

'Phire, stop,' Rian said urgently.

Tarragon and Onyx released their grips on me, both slumping to the deck. Willow ran over to Tarragon who gave her a wan little smile. I let go of Mal and Sage, who both crumpled against the rail. Anise stepped over to them, checking they were all right.

A great surge of exhaustion swept through me. I'd given almost everything to help get us through. Maybe too much.

No. I *knew* I'd given too much.

I staggered. My legs gave way. Rian made a grab for me as I collapsed, catching me before I hit the deck.

'Phire?' He held me in his arms.

I couldn't speak – I was too busy gasping for air. My pulse thundered in my ears. Everything hurt. I started to shake. I looked up into his worried eyes.

Everything went dark.

CHAPTER SIXTEEN

I opened my eyes. I found myself lying in our bed, Rian next to me. The only light in our dim cabin came from a single candle flickering in a holder on the wall, casting soft light over the Cursed Weapons across the room. It must have been night. I turned over, my muscles protesting, and groaned. Rian's arms were wrapped around me, his body next to mine, soothing me.

'You all right?' he asked.

'Yes,' I replied, my voice a little croaky.

He sighed. 'You did too much.'

'I had to, or we'd all have drowned. You'd have drowned.'

He stroked my hair. 'You did too much,' he repeated, kissing my head.

'Thank you for catching me.'

'It's my job. I'm your husband.'

I smiled at him. 'I love you.'

'I love you, too.'

'How are the others?' I asked.

'They're all resting,' he said. 'We decided that once we were free of the maelstroms and a good distance away we'd stop, let Mal and Sage rest properly – and Tarragon and Onyx, too, for that matter. They're all really tired. Not as much as you, though. We'll start off again in the morning.'

I nodded. 'Good idea.'

'You want something to eat?'

'Not really, I just want to sleep.'

'All right then. I'll stay with you.'

'You can go and eat if you want to,' I said. 'I'll be fine here.'

He shook his head. 'Not only am I not leaving you, but I'd rather be here with you anyway.'

I shuffled a little closer to him, resting my head on his chest so I could hear his steady heartbeat and revel in his sandalwood scent. With his arms around me, I fell asleep in seconds.

Everything ached.

My head. My arms. My shoulders. My whole body.

Every movement caused pain, and through it all, I had no energy. Nothing. I could barely move out of bed, even with Rian's help,

"

though I insisted on getting out on deck. I needed the cool breeze on my face, the fresh salty air that somehow rejuvenated me. We sat on the deck, Rian's arm draped around me, and watched the sailors at work.

We were almost out of The Great Doldrums. Sage and Mal weren't having to do too much now to keep us heading south-east. They both looked quite grey and shared the load as the sails fluttered high above, sitting up near the ship's wheel. Tarragon and Onyx looked exhausted, too, their faces etched with their exertions as they lay on the deck, Willow sitting beside them. We made a sorry group as Anise went around with a tincture.

'Here, take this,' he said, handing me a small golden glass vial. 'It's the same as the one I gave you back in the palace dungeons.'

'That worked really well,' I said, taking it from him and swallowing it down in one gulp. The taste of rosemary, fresh mint and summer hit my tongue. Once again, the tincture immediately warmed me inside, sending a surge of energy through my muscles, my blood, my whole body. I felt more alert and quite refreshed. 'Thank you,' I said, passing the vial back.

'Hopefully it'll last long enough for you to feel better naturally.' He grinned. 'Especially if you rest this time rather than rescue princes from execution.' He wandered back towards Sage.

'How do you feel?' Rian asked.

'As strong as an Iolitian Ox,' I said.

Rian raised an eyebrow.

'Well, almost,' I conceded. I still had a lingering weariness in my bones, but nothing like it had been before.

'You all went down like flies,' Rian said, looking at the others. 'Everyone was lying on the deck, panting, although you were the only one to pass out. And I'm not surprised, after what you did.'

'I didn't have much choice.'

'Maybe not. You certainly saved us,' he said, pulling me to him. 'Again.'

I laughed. 'You've done your bit too,' I said, thinking of the fire in Fennel Town and the Dryad Forest – not to mention the whole Hematite and Sunstone incident.

He smiled. 'I have my moments.'

I sat leaning against him, thanking the Stars I'd met him, that I'd fallen in love with him – that he'd fallen in love with me.

'What had you heard about me? Before we met?' I asked.

'What?'

'When we met you said you'd heard of me – *what* had you heard?'

'Oh.' He rubbed the back of his neck. 'Well, I'd heard that the Master and Mistress of Iolite had a strikingly beautiful daughter with vibrant, deep amethyst eyes you could drown in, and hair the colour of flames.'

I elbowed him gently. 'Rubbish.'

'It's all true. Really, that's what I'd been told.'

'Who by?'

'Tarragon.'

'Tarragon?'

'He'd spent time in Iolite, if you remember. He must have heard about you, maybe even seen you.'

'He's never said he'd seen me before we met in that village.'

Rian shrugged. 'He'd definitely heard of you.'

'I'd seen him before, though.'

'In Iolite?'

'No, in Viridi on the day I... you know.' I still found talking about his sister's death difficult, even if he hadn't liked her much. 'I saw him on my way to the palace. Had to dodge out of his way.'

'So, what had you heard about me?' Rian asked, a quizzical look in his eyes. 'Or hadn't you?'

'Yes, I knew about you. I'd heard that there were two princes of Aerba, one extremely handsome, and one proud and opinionated.'

'And which was I?'

'Which do you think? The handsome one of course. But the description I was given didn't live up to reality. You're far more good looking in real life than Lord Flint said.'

He smiled a smug little smile. 'That's nice to know.'

'I'd heard Chervil was mean spirited, and so was Angelica.'

Rian's eyes were far away, back in the past, just for a fleeting moment. 'They were very alike, my brother and sister. I was the odd one out. We never got on, but thanks to Tarragon, and then Sage when I was a bit older, I still felt as if I had siblings. A proper family.'

'You and Tarragon have always been very close?'

He nodded. 'Always. Shared everything with each other.'

'So I heard,' I said, grinning.

'What?'

'Willow said you and Tarragon shared everything, even notes on sexual conquests.'

'Tarragon was the one doing the sharing. I had nothing to tell.'

'Willow said that, too.'

Rian's face turned pink. 'She knows I'd never... *you know...* before you?'

I nodded.

He sighed. 'I'm going to have to have words with Tarragon. He really doesn't need to tell Willow everything.'

'You tell me everything.'

'That's different. You're my wife,' he said, kissing my head.

'Would you have preferred a reputation like Sorrel, for being with lots of girls?' I asked.

'No! But everyone knowing my personal business, especially when the others had done it and I hadn't, well, it's embarrassing to know they all knew I was inexperienced.'

'Even though you were following the Blood Rules?'

'Yes, even though I was the only one following the Blood Rules.'

'Look, Willow isn't *everyone* – she didn't say Tarragon had told anyone but her, and I'm glad you were inexperienced, as you put it, because it makes what we have even more special because we've learnt together. Still are,' I said, casting him a little mischievous smile.

He grinned at me. 'You think so?'

'I know so,' I said, kissing his lips emphatically.

'That's all right, then,' he said, pulling me into a hug.

'Put her down,' Willow said, coming over to us and sitting beside me.

'How's Tarragon?' I asked.

'Exhausted. Although Anise's tincture seems to be helping. Using his Magic took a lot out of him.'

I nodded.

'The whole situation took a lot out of everyone, whether or not they were using Magic,' Rian said.

Willow rubbed her eyebrow. 'So do you think Juniper made it through the doldrums? And the maelstroms? Or is she languishing at the bottom of the ocean somewhere?' she asked.

'I, for one, pray the bitch is on the sea bed,' Onyx said with feeling as he joined us.

'You hope,' Mal said from where he sat concentrating on the sails.

Had he been listening to Rian and me? Blood rushed to my face and I avoided my big brother's eyes.

'It took us two Water Spinners, two Air Spinners and a Quintessence Spinner to get through that lot – you think she has that number of Elemental Angle Spinners with her?' Onyx asked with a sniff.

'I wouldn't put anything past our dear stepmother,' Mal said.

I sighed. Mal was right. She was probably still ahead of us somewhere. As much as two days ahead. We might have made up a little ground on her, but not enough to beat her to Chroma.

The Spirit of the Seas continued to cut through the calm water as the day wore on.

Sunlight caught the diamonds on Rian's ring that adorned my hand. I admired the fiery little rainbows shimmering inside the tiny stones. My mind wandered back to Ostianzis and the dream I'd had in his cabin before I'd come around properly from my trip down the river.

'Is your ring an Artefact?' I asked, gazing at it.

Rian turned towards me and looked at the ring. 'Not that I know of, why?' he asked, forehead furrowing.

'Something I dreamt when I was with Ostianzis, but I don't think it was a prophetic dream, otherwise I'd have mentioned it earlier.' I watched the mesmerising rainbows. 'I suppose the only way to find out is to try it.'

Wind suddenly flapped in the sails.

'We're clear of the doldrums,' Captain Pol announced.

Mal and Sage's shoulders slumped, relieved their work was finally done.

'Go below and get some rest, boys,' Holm said. 'You've earned it.'

They nodded and went below with Anise and Onyx.

Rian and I borrowed the map Zabell had given Captain Pol. We laid it on the deck and studied it. We had two more days at sea, then we'd reach the straits that would take us up to a large lake and Azure City, where we hoped to get new supplies. After that, we'd continue along the straits to Second Water and across it to Middle Isle and the town of Ecru. Once there, we'd have to travel by land to Teal and find a boat to take us across to the Central Isle and the Chromian capital of Magenta.

'It'll take us two and a half days to reach Azure,' I said, running my finger over the creases in the map.

'Then another two to Ecru,' Rian said, chewing his lip. 'Over land – a day with horses, maybe two without, to Teal – and two days across First Water to Magenta. Then we have to find the Fire Opal and get to the Cave of Crystals.'

My shoulders slumped. 'Maybe another ten days.'

'*Only* ten days,' Rian said, looking at me. 'After everything we've been through to get the Fire Opal, it won't be long now.'

He was right, of course. We'd been at this for several months, another few days wouldn't matter.

'You think it'll really be there?' I asked, giving voice to the whispers of doubt I could see in his eyes.

He shrugged. 'We'll have to pray to the Herbs it is.'

'And the Stars,' I murmured.

He nodded. 'We'll find out soon enough.'

CHAPTER SEVENTEEN

The Straits of Azure were narrow and calm. And busy. Merchant vessels sailed in and out to other parts of Chroma and distant islands. Chroma may have been hidden from the Five Lands, but there were other peoples that obviously still knew of their existence and traded with them. Towering grey cliffs rose to either side of us like great walls, seabirds nesting in their craggy sides, swooping into the water, fishing for their young that peered out at us from their twiggy, mossy homes. Their cries echoed around the cliffs as we made our way through.

When we eventually broke free of the straits, Azure City finally appeared in the distance, resting on the side of a huge U-shaped lake. It sat like a jade stone in the sun, its pale green stone walls and buildings surrounding a tall central building with spires that grazed the clouds. Beige-tiled roofs topped the homes and businesses, stretching into the distance. Great harbour walls of deep green granite protected the docks like arms, stretching out into the lake, curving towards one another to form a small entrance to the harbour itself. One wall jutted somewhat further into the lake, providing shelter for the ships entering and leaving the city. The harbour teemed with ships and sailors as they worked to load and unload their cargo.

'Not what I was expecting,' Pol said, coming to stand next to me at the bow where I was watching with Rian. 'More people know about Chroma than we've been led to believe.'

Rian nodded. 'Looks that way.'

'We'll resupply the ship and continue on,' she said as *The Spirit of the Seas* slid gracefully past the outer harbour wall, through the entrance channel and into an empty berth.

No sooner had the ship been secured dockside than an Official wearing a deep red uniform came running up to us. He was a short man with an oval face, deep umber skin, curly dark hair and the brightest of blue eyes. As I scanned the docks I could see his features were typical of Chromians.

'Papers,' he yelled.

'What papers?' Pol asked, striding down the gangplank.

'You need papers to trade here.'

'We aren't trading, we're just passing through and taking on supplies.'

'You still need papers.'

'And how do we get them?'

He narrowed his eyes. 'Up in the city, at the central government building, the one with the spires. You can get them there.'

Pol sighed. 'Very well.'

'Send someone – you can restock your ship while you're waiting.'

Pol nodded as he moved off.

I glanced at Rian. He nodded.

'We'll go,' I said. 'You deal with the restocking.'

'That would be best,' Pol said. 'If you're sure?'

'I'll go with them,' Onyx said, coming up behind us. 'Mal's resting – he's still tired from all his Magic Spinning.'

'Then be careful and don't be long,' Pol said. 'We'll get underway as soon as you're back.'

'See you soon,' Onyx said, leading the way up into the city.

'Do you know where you're going?' I asked suspiciously.

He shook his head. 'No. But this is the main street and the government building looks to be at the centre of the city, so if we keep going this way we shouldn't go far wrong.'

I couldn't disagree with his logic.

'Just stay alert,' Rian said. 'We don't know if Juniper or one of the Coterie are about. If we get separated, we meet back at the ship.'

Onyx nodded.

Rian slipped his hand into mine as we walked along the street, past market stalls, leaving the smell of dead fish and salt behind and replacing it with the smell of spices I couldn't name. In addition to the umber-skinned Chromians, there were other people here of lighter skin colours. A few looked almost Aerban.

'Where have all these people come from?' I murmured, glancing around.

'Ithia? Axandor? Calperion? Nyssia? I'm not sure Chroma has been as lost as we thought,' Rian said, watching the people passing us in their multi-coloured, jewel-hued clothes.

'Not this side of The Great Doldrums, anyway,' Onyx said. 'Do they have the Blood Decree here? Because I can't tell if there are different Blood Classes.'

'I don't know,' I said. 'Maybe they ditched the Decree.'

'Wouldn't mind doing that myself,' Rian muttered, his eyes clouding.

I glanced at him. 'One day.'

'Doubt it – but we can dream.'

We walked on, suddenly assaulted by the smell of rose, lavender and orange. I glanced at the shop we were passing. The large sign outside said "Perfumery". Thank the Stars Sage wasn't with us, or we'd never get him out of there.

I glanced ahead. A black metal railing with large wrought iron gates encompassed the government building. I squinted up at the spires towering above me. The height of them had my head spinning. We moved into the building, following other foreigners, and, having asked for assistance, were directed to a desk at the right end of the building.

A sharp sensation in my toe made me pause.

'I've got a stone in my boot,' I said. 'You two join the queue, I'll catch you up.'

Rian frowned at me. 'But—'

'I won't be a minute.'

He gave me a disapproving look and followed after Onyx. A staircase rose up from the hallway and I sat on the steps, removing my boot. As I tipped it up a small, sharp stone fell onto the grey carpeted floor. I started to put my boot back on.

'Is that them?'

A voice to my left had me shrinking into the shadows at the side of the stairs.

'The one with the maroony hair and the dark-haired boy next to him,' came a second voice.

I peered around the end of the staircase. There stood two men beside the wall, watching Rian and Onyx. One had a bald head, the other short black hair. They were both Chromian, though, and their eyes never left the two young men.

'What does she want us to do with them?' Short Hair asked.

'Stop them from leaving,' Bald Head said. 'Preferably permanently.'

'Scuttle their ship?'

'Either that or detain them in the prison.'

'On what charges?'

'Does it matter? The Mistress has paid us good money.'

I shivered. The Mistress? Of Iolite? I had to get to Rian and Onyx, and we had to get out of Azure City now.

'We'll let them finish here – don't want to cause a scene. We'll get them on the way back to the docks. On the main street.'

The two men took one last look at Rian and Onyx as they approached the red-coated Official sitting at the desk in front of them, and left the hall. I waited for Rian and Onyx to finish, then took them to one side.

'We have a big problem,' I said in hushed tones, quickly explaining what I'd overheard.

Onyx sniffed. 'Then the bitch has been through here,' he said, his eyes narrowing.

'We need to get back to the ship and out into the lake as fast as possible.'

'We'll split up,' Rian said, chewing his lip. 'Onyx, you head out to the left and back to the docks; we'll go to the right and meet you there, avoid the main street completely. Whoever arrives first, get Pol to set sail immediately.'

Onyx nodded. 'I'll see you back there.' He glanced at us. 'Be careful, both of you.'

Rian nodded. 'You, too.' He placed his hand on Onyx's shoulder. The two had come a long way since they'd first met, and it filled me with pride. 'Let's go.'

We let Onyx leave first before heading out the gates and into the noisy crowd beyond. We walked to the right, away from the main street and into a side street that ran parallel. Hurrying along, I checked around me for danger – but any one of the people we passed could've been paid off by Juniper. We moved quickly, doing our best not to attract attention. We'd both pulled our hoods up, keeping our heads low as we hurried along. No one paid us much attention as we moved towards the docks.

I glanced behind.

Was that Short Hair keeping to the side of the street, following us?

'This way,' I said to Rian, heading into a street on our right, away from the docks.

'What is it?' he asked, his voice taut.

'I think we're being followed,' I said, looking back again. We were. Short Hair was definitely following us, hand on his sword hilt. 'I think it's time to run.'

We turned left into an alley, making a break for the harbour.

My breaths tore at my throat as we ran, my heart pounding in my chest. I turned back. Short Hair was matching our pace. *Hell's teeth.* How would we get back to the ship and get underway without him right with us? Stop and fight? We couldn't delay, we had to keep going.

Rian grabbed my hand, pulling me into another alley. He yanked me into an alcove. As Short Hair turned the corner, Rian stuck his foot out. Short Hair yelled and hit the ground. Before he'd had a chance to get up, Rian hit him on the back of his neck with his sword hilt.

'Come on,' Rian said, returning his sword to its sheath and taking my hand. He led me back the way we'd come. We stopped.

Standing in the side street were four Chromians, all wielding swords. They looked at us and smiled. One stepped forward.

'We need to ask you some questions,' he said. 'You're to come to the Town Guard's Office with us.'

'Why?' Rian asked. 'We're just passing through.'

'Our orders are to detain you. If necessary we will use these,' the guard said, waving his sword.

I glanced at Rian. He nodded.

'Then you'll have to use them,' I said as Rian and I both drew our swords in one swift motion. Rian went for the man closest to us as I lunged at the other one in the middle.

The second guard parried my blow. But then, he was meant to. I let him come at me, allowing his momentum to do the work, sidestepping him as he plunged past me. I drove Deorwine's hilt into the side of his head.

Rian already had his first opponent on the ground, and had started engaging the next. The fourth guard raised his sword, aiming at Rian's back. I grabbed Glædwine and blocked his blow before Rian was even aware it was coming. I struck back at the guard, ducking as he swiped at me, falling to one knee and slamming Deorwine's hilt into one of his knees – I really didn't want to kill him, even to stop him. He fell to the ground, screaming in pain. That would do.

A shadow fell over me.

I twisted around, still on one knee, unbalancing myself. I reached my sword-hand to the ground to steady myself, only to find Short Hair standing over me. Rian hadn't hit him hard enough. The Chromian's sword fell towards me. I attempted to raise Glædwine.

Short Hair's sword glanced off my shield, biting into the dust beside me. I lunged towards him, ramming my body into his, knocking him over. As I rolled to my feet, a crunching sound made me hesitate. Short Hair lay still, blood oozing from a wound at the side of his head where he'd hit the wall.

'He's definitely out now,' Rian said, glancing at the unconscious man as he sheathed his swords. At his feet lay the other guard, blood soaking into the dirt. He held his hand out to me. I sheathed Deorwine, returned Glædwine to my back, and let him pull me up.

He flashed me his lopsided smile. 'I know what you just did for me.'

I smiled back at him. 'Just helping out.'

'Come on. We'd better get a move on before someone comes asking questions – or one of them wakes up,' he said, looking at the bodies littering the ground around us.

Holding hands, we ran on, twisting and turning through alleys, finally making it out onto the main street. We dodged and weaved our way through the crowd, their shouts and haggling at the various market stalls filling the air. As we reached the harbour, we both skidded to a halt.

'Hell's teeth,' I gasped. Between us and the ship stood a group of twenty soldiers, and at their front, Bald Head. I strained to see the ship. Onyx was already there. Pol was shouting orders, readying to cast off, even as another group of soldiers headed towards *The Spirit of the Seas*.

'Suggestions?' Rian asked, short of breath.

I quickly scanned the docks, trying to take in everything, trying to formulate a plan.

'This way,' I said, leading him towards the right of the harbour and the longer of the two harbour walls. I paused as we came out of the buildings' shadows and into the sunlight that streamed over the water, casting white diamonds across it. I pulled Deorwine free, took hold of its hilt and top of the blade, and twisted the Cursed Weapon, catching the light.

'What are you doing?' Rian asked.

'Signalling to them – they need to leave immediately.' I continued to send a flashing beam of sunlight towards the ship.

Holm pointed at us. Onyx ran up to the ship's wheel. I waved at him, pointing to the end of the harbour wall. He nodded and ran towards Pol. She started issuing instructions, and the gangplank retracted, the mooring lines released, and the ship began to move towards the main channel of the harbour, out of reach of the soldiers. But we weren't. Bald Head gesticulated and a group of men headed in our direction.

'What about us?' Rian asked, looking around anxiously as I sheathed Deorwine.

'We'll never get on board with all those soldiers in the way,' I said. 'We'll have to jump for it.'

'Jump?' His eyes widened. 'You said jump?'

'Yes, I did,' I said, pulling him along behind me as we started down the long wall of the harbour.

'You have remembered I can't swim, haven't you?' he asked breathlessly.

'I'm not likely to forget it.'

As we ran along the granite wall I glanced back into the harbour. *The Spirit* was slowly making its way to the entrance and freedom, but behind her two smaller, faster vessels were already following in her wake, grappling hooks and ropes being readied in order to board her.

'Can you do anything?' I asked, pointing at the chasing ships.

We paused.

Rian's eyebrows knitted together as he concentrated. A spark appeared in his hand, turning into a ball of raging flame. He hurled it at the ship closest to *The Spirit*.

CHAPTER EIGHTEEN

Rian's fireball hit the sails, turning them instantly into flaming sheets that dripped fire onto the deck, setting light to anything flammable. There were panicked shouts from the ship, sailors diving overboard as the fire took hold. The ship altered course abruptly, and the ship behind it helplessly rammed its hull.

Rian grabbed my hand and pulled me along. We sprinted towards the end of the wall, soldiers not far behind us now. *The Spirit* had passed the harbour entrance and now shadowed the long harbour wall we ran along.

'Keep going,' Rian gasped.

Bangs and cracks echoed around the harbour as the chasing ships collided, crashing into each other and wedging themselves in the gap between the two harbour walls, forming a flaming wall of orange and red.

'I'm not getting wet,' Rian said emphatically as the end of the wall loomed ahead of us.

'I really do need to teach you to swim,' I said.

The distance between the harbour wall and the slowly moving *Spirit* had to be twenty feet at least, even if the deck was lower than the wall. I may have miscalculated. Badly.

But maybe there was something else. Quintessence? Could it help?

I held his hand firmly in mine. 'When we get to the end, jump for all you're worth,' I yelled at him.

'I knew you were going to say that,' he said, a resigned note to his voice.

Help us!

We sprinted for the end of the harbour wall, my lungs bursting, my muscles aching. My hands glowed white. We jumped. Wind rushed through our hair. We flew across the impossibly wide gap towards the ship, landing hard on the deck, rolling, and coming to a juddering halt, the two ships aflame behind us in the entrance channel.

I groaned. Everything hurt as I came to rest. The glow faded.

Rian scrambled over to me. 'Are you all right?'

'Whacked my knee. You?' I asked, wincing as it throbbed.

'Sore elbow, that's all,' he said. 'Thank you.' He leant and kissed me. 'I think your Quintessence just saved us.'

The others dashed over.

'Are you all right?'

'That was amazing!'

'How did you do that?'

'Was that Quintessence?'

They pulled us to our feet, although I'd been quite happy where I was, lying on the deck with Rian. The moment I put weight on my leg my knee screamed at me. I gasped, my knee buckling under me.

Mal grabbed hold of me. 'Let's get you below deck,' he said, picking me up.

'Put me down, I can walk,' I objected, trying to free myself from his grasp.

'No, you can't,' Rian said.

'Blast it, Ama. Just let me carry you,' my brother said, staring into my eyes. Sometimes it was best not to argue with Malachite of Iolite.

'Fine. You can take me.'

He carried me into the cabin, Rian following, nursing his elbow – or he probably would've insisted on carrying me himself. It was nice that they wanted to be protective of me, but I was quite capable and they both knew it – they just liked to take advantage when I was slightly incapacitated to make a point, even if I could fend for myself.

Anise quickly retrieved his Herb Chest and, with tongue out, retrieved some salve for Rian and I to use on our bruised limbs.

'What happened?' Onyx asked.

We quickly updated them on our trip back down to the docks.

'We realised something was going on when a company of soldiers appeared on the docks,' Tarragon said.

'I managed to get onto the docks just before they arrived,' Onyx said.

'You were lucky,' Rian said, rubbing the salve into his elbow.

'You think you can heal yourself and Rian?' Mal asked suddenly, looking at me.

'What?'

'Well, you helped heal Rian when he was poisoned, by all accounts.'

'Well...'

'Give it a try.'

I frowned. 'Come here,' I said to Rian.

'What are you going to do?' he asked.

'Make it up as I go along.'

I placed my hand gently on his damaged elbow and shut my eyes.

Concentrated. Opened one and squinted at his bruise.

'Whatever you were trying, it didn't work,' Rian said.

I sighed. Turned to my own knee and concentrated harder. Nothing.

'Perhaps Quintessence only heals Magical wounds,' Tarragon said, rubbing his chin.

'What do you mean?' Willow asked, coughing.

'Well, Topaz's attack wasn't Magical in any way, was it?'

'Just brutal,' Rian muttered, glancing at me.

'And Zabell seemed to indicate Quintessence wasn't involved in healing that wound.'

'So it really was all me?' Anise asked, frowning.

'You were holding your Artefact,' Tarragon said. 'And I could've sworn I saw a green flash like the others.'

'I think it was just Anise's Magic that time,' Sage said. 'He's becoming more used to it, and his herbs, when enchanted, obviously have a powerful healing effect.'

'Very powerful,' I said, knowing only a small scar remained the next day after my stabbing.

'So you're sure you didn't use your Quintessence on yourself?' Mal asked, looking at me.

'I don't think I was in a fit state to be using anything.'

'There was definitely a white flash when I recovered from my poisoning,' Rian said. 'So Quintessence can heal – Zabell said that.'

'Yes, but I think the berries you ate weren't just laced with poison, Rian, but Earth Magic, too,' Anise said. 'I'm sure of it – that's why the poison moved so quickly.'

'And that's why I was able to do something, because it was a Magic-induced illness?' I asked.

'Makes sense,' Mal said.

Anise nodded.

Rian chewed his lip. 'So, Quintessence can either boost another Spinner's power—'

'Like through the maelstroms,' Onyx said.

'Or counteract another Spinner's power.'

'The berries,' Tarragon said, nodding slowly.

'But I almost died in the fire in the Dryad Forest,' I said, frowning.

'That wasn't Magic,' Rian said. 'It may have been started by Magic, but the fire itself was real, ordinary fire, not something you could do anything about.'

'I suppose.'

'In which case, no amount of Quintessence will do anything to your bruises,' Sage said. 'But Anise's Magic-enhanced salve should heal you quicker.'

'But there wasn't a flash as I was preparing it,' Anise said.

Sage shrugged. 'Perhaps it depends how much effort you're putting in and if you're using the Artefact or not.'

'Maybe.'

Rian nodded. 'We used the Amethyst Talisman when I had the poisoning – there was a flash then.'

'And when the Curse was broken,' Willow said.

'Both curses,' I said.

Mal glanced at me. 'I thought I was enchanted.'

'Cursed, enchanted, it's all the same.'

Anise had a broad grin on his face. 'I didn't see a flash, but I was holding my Amulet when I made up the salve. You should heal quite quickly, then.'

'Let's hope so,' Rian said, ''cause this damn well hurts.'

We sailed away from Azure City and across the great Azure Lake as the sun set, shards of pink and gold glittering on the water's surface. I sat in the cabin while the others chatted, thinking about what they'd said about my Quintessence, about it boosting and counteracting Magic. But it also had an energy of its own, according to what I'd learnt. How else could Rian and I have jumped across the gap at the docks today? There was still so much to learn, and I wished my Father's book was in a better condition to give me answers, but I'd read everything I could in it now. I regretted not reading it more fully when I'd had the chance, but back then, not all of it seemed relevant – not by a long way. He'd always had an interest in Magic – had he known about his children being Spinners? Did Mother know her heritage? I sighed. All questions I'd never have answers to.

One thing I did know was Juniper was ahead of us, just as Topaz had said, and she was doing her best to stop us from catching up with her. She couldn't be allowed to destroy the Crystal Vortex. With no one able to stand up to her and Chervil, they'd sweep the Lands and have everyone under their control in weeks, if not sooner. And who knew what havoc the Vortex's final destruction would have on the Elements? The dryads feared what was to come, and so did those that knew about the power of the Vortex. It would be chaos and destruction, and Juniper would step in as a benevolent Mistress to help clear it up, Chervil at her side, no one aware of the fact they'd instigated it all, or what their real intentions were, until it was too late.

The red shadow loomed in my mind. It was always there, at the edges. Threatening to overwhelm me. I was glad Rian knew, but that didn't mean it wouldn't happen. That he wouldn't die in front of me. A chill wind, like the first snowstorm of winter, swirled inside me. I couldn't be without him now, live without him, now. I understood how he'd felt when he thought he'd lost me.

My evening meal rose in my throat.

'Time for bed,' Rian said, getting up and offering me his hand.

I took it and smiled at him, rising and limping back to our cabin. My knee was already improving, but I still favoured it as the odd twinge would catch me out from time to time. We entered the small room and Rian closed the door behind us, then pulled his shirt off. I removed my tunic and glanced at his arm. It looked red, but not angry anymore.

'How's the elbow?' I asked.

'Much better.'

'Good.' I moved over to him, gently rested my hands on his arms and kissed his chest. 'I love you.'

He looked at me, grinning, his eyes alight. 'What's brought this on?'

I shrugged. 'Nothing. Just grateful for having you. Making the most of you.'

His eyes narrowed. 'I know exactly what you've been doing this evening, why you've been so quiet. You've been dwelling on things and you need to stop. Nothing is going to happen to me. Everyone knows what you dreamt now. Between us we'll stop it from happening.'

I prayed that was true.

He took hold of my hands and rested them on his warm, bare chest. I could feel the strong, steady beat of his heart under my fingertips. He leant towards me, his soft lips brushing mine, his heart rate increasing.

'Time to get to sleep, wife, and stop worrying,' he said. 'We've had a busy day.'

I nodded. He let go of me and we climbed into bed. I quickly cupped his face in my hands and brought him to me, kissing him. We lay in bed, arms around each other, drifting off to sleep as the ship gently rocked.

'We're well into the next set of straits,' Tarragon said, coming into the main cabin.

The mid-morning sun shone on the water as we glided across the surface. I was pretty sure Mal and Sage were on deck moving us along a little more quickly. Rian hadn't let me out of his sight this morning, and I wasn't inclined to leave him, either.

'They're wider than the last lot, so they're easier to navigate, or so Captain Pol says,' Tarragon added.

Rian nodded. 'When will we be through?'

'She thinks by late evening or the early hours.'

'Good.'

Tarragon sank onto a chair. 'You really think we can do this?'

Rian glanced at him. 'You think we can't?'

'I think it's not going to be as straightforward as we might all like.'

'Nothing ever is,' I murmured.

'That's true enough,' he said, grinning at me.

'You're having second thoughts?' Rian asked.

'Not at all, I just think we need to make sure we're all prepared for whatever lies ahead, that we all know what we're doing.'

'I'm not sure we do,' I said. 'I mean, how are we actually supposed to practise starting the Vortex up properly again?'

'You're supposed to bind our power together, once Willow's Released the Fire Opal. Send it into the Vortex.'

'And how exactly does that work?'

Tarragon shrugged.

'We'll work it out,' Rian said.

'Maybe it'll turn out to be an instinctive thing and we'll all know what to do when it happens,' Tarragon said.

'You hope,' I said. 'Because at the moment I haven't got a clue what I'm supposed to do. Binding everyone's power together, using it to restart the Vortex, is all very well, but I don't know how to do any of that.'

Rian rubbed his neck. 'When we get on dry land, we'll give it a go, see what happens.'

I swallowed. 'We could destroy half of Chroma.'

'Even more reason to practise.'

Tarragon scratched his chin. 'That's a good idea, actually. Then we'll have a better idea of what we're all doing.'

The whole suggestion filled me with aching dread. What if I got it wrong? What if I killed someone?

'We'll start slowly,' Rian said, looking into my eyes as if he knew my exact thoughts.

'Is mind reading part of Fire Spinning?' I asked suspiciously.

He laughed. 'Not that I know of – it's probably more because I know you, wife. We've been together long enough now for me to know what you're thinking – feeling, even.'

I wasn't sure if that was reassuring or not.

Tarragon buffed his fingernails on his tunic. 'It's the same with me and Willow. I know what she's going to say half the time before she even says it. She's like that with me, too – I don't even have to tell her what I'm thinking, I just look at her and she knows.'

'I can imagine,' I said, giving him a wink.

Tarragon turned a strawberry colour and got up. 'I think I need some air,' he said, and he left the cabin.

I smirked as he went.

'You're a bad woman, Samphire,' Rian said disapprovingly, although he was smiling, too.

'He needs to be teased from time to time. It does him good,' I said.

'You're not wrong.'

I sighed. 'And neither are you. We need to practise before we get to the Cave, it's just I don't want to kill anyone and totally ruin our chances of doing this.'

Rian frowned. 'You think someone will die doing this?'

'It's not exactly tried and tested, is it? Who knows what might happen?'

'Zabell did say it would be dangerous – particularly for you.'

'I'm not worried about me.'

'No, you're worried about everyone else, as usual.'

'It's in my nature.'

'I've noticed – and it's one of the things I love about you.'

CHAPTER NINETEEN

Rian's suggestion of trying out our powers before getting to the Cave made perfect sense. We all agreed that once we reached the Middle Isle, and were well away from any people, we'd give it a go. We sailed on through the straits and the next day swept out into Second Water.

'We'll reach Ecru tomorrow,' Captain Pol said as I joined her at the wheel. 'But I'm wondering if it might be prudent to stay out of the harbour, take you to land in the pinnace.' She pointed to the ship's boat – a small rowing boat that lay further down on the deck.

'I was wondering that, too,' Holm said. 'Might be safest all round.'

Rian, standing beside me, nodded. 'We can take supplies with us and walk to Teal, find a boat to take us across from there.'

'We'll wait for you out here in Second Water – you can signal us when you're ready to come back,' Pol said.

'Sounds good,' I said.

We sailed on through the night, until we were north of Ecru, where Pol dropped anchor. We said our farewells, and Holm and three of the sailors rowed us ashore.

Watching them row back to *The Spirit* made me shiver. This was all becoming very real. We just had to hope the Fire Opal really was in Magenta, or everything would be lost.

We pulled our packs onto our shoulders as the men climbed back onto the ship.

Rian took my hand. He really didn't want me wandering off now we were back on land, which made me smile and set off a warm cascade inside me. We made our way northeast towards Teal, hoping to soon come across the main road. The land here appeared dry as old bones, the plants scrubby and short. A few trees and stubby bushes, brown grass, and dust littered the gently rolling landscape. This had once been a lush land, but drought had turned it into a shrivelled husk of its former self.

'How long will it take to walk to Teal?' Sage asked.

'Why?' Tarragon asked.

'Because I'm getting a blister already,' his cousin replied sourly.

'Tomorrow, if we keep good time,' Rian said.

'Let's hope we can find a boat easily to get us across to Magenta,' Willow said.

'I never thought I'd hear you say you wanted to get aboard a ship.' Tarragon laughed.

Willow shrugged. 'I want to get this over with.'

'Me, too,' Onyx muttered.

I wasn't the only one who was nervous about what lay ahead. I glanced at Rian. He smiled at me and squeezed my hand reassuringly, but deep in his eyes his own anxieties shifted. I squeezed his hand back.

'Together,' I whispered in his ear.

'Together,' he murmured back.

'So we need to get to the Emperor?' Anise asked.

'Hopefully he'll know where the Fire Opal is,' Rian said.

'Maybe he has it,' Mal said.

'You think he might?' Onyx asked.

Mal shrugged. 'It's possible.'

'He's certainly the place to start,' Rian said.

A short distance ahead lay a wide river. Despite its width, it was shallow – probably from the drought. Rian wouldn't have to worry about swimming. We walked across the parched ground and made our way to the water's edge. The clear water rushed across the rocky riverbed, but from looking at the banks it was obvious the water level here was far lower than it should've been. We started to cross, splashing through the water which wasn't much more than ankle deep, kept at bay by our leather boots.

The ground trembled.

The water around us shifted and swirled.

'W—what's happening?' Willow asked, looking around nervously, eyes wide as the sound of continuous distant thunder surged across the countryside.

'I don't—' Tarragon began, twisting to look upstream. His eyes widened in alarm. 'Oh, bugger.'

I turned to where he was looking. Around a bend in the river, a huge wall of water rushed towards us, frothing and churning. Willow gasped.

'Move!' Rian yelled, pulling me towards the far bank.

'We don't have time!' Sage yelled as he followed us, splashing through the water.

'Onyx! Help me,' Tarragon said, planting himself firmly in the centre of the river.

Onyx ran over to Tarragon. 'What do we do?'

'Part it – send half one side of us, half the other.'

'I'll take the left.'

Tarragon nodded. 'Stay in the centre and get behind us,' he said to us.

Rian and I moved behind him, Anise, Sage, Willow and Mal joining us. This wouldn't be a matter of whether they had the strength to do this, but whether it was actually possible.

'I hope this works,' Sage muttered, his earring catching the light.

'Don't we all,' Mal replied, watching the approaching water with trepidation. 'If it doesn't, it'll take us back out to sea.'

'I've been swept down one river. I don't want to be swept down another,' I said, bracing myself.

'If you are, this time we'll go together,' Rian said, wrapping his arms tightly around me and pulling me close. I buried my head in his chest as the wall of water approached.

'Ready?' Tarragon stood, one arm raised, the other over his Wristband.

'Ready,' Onyx said, taking up a similar position, hand covering his ring.

The wave hit.

I shut my eyes, clinging on to Rian for all I was worth, waiting for the wall to crash into me. He bowed his head, resting it against mine as we braced for the inevitable.

Spray surrounded us. Thunder engulfed us. Onyx let out a groan of effort. I half-opened an eye. The wall of water had split around us, forming two smaller waves which sprayed us with cold mist as they rushed past. The foaming river settled and calmed.

I felt Rian take a shuddering breath, then he relaxed and looked around.

Tarragon wiped sweat from his face as Onyx stood beside him, shaking, looking at the receding water. Mal stepped over to his boyfriend and slipped an arm around his shoulders as Willow took Tarragon's hand.

'That was close,' Tarragon said, kissing the back of Willow's hand. She looked at him, her eyes full of love and admiration.

The glint of sunlight on metal made me look up. In the distance stood a black-haired figure, the sun illuminating his scarred face – a result of falling into the poisoned Viridi moat. His brown horse waited a short distance behind him.

I sucked in a breath. 'Sorrel.'

'What? Where?' Sage looked around, then tensed as he locked eyes with his brother.

I felt Rian's muscles go taut as he saw his cousin.

Sorrel sneered at us, his piercing green eyes hard as granite, his scruffy clothes straining against his muscular build as he limped over to his horse, mounted, and rode off, leaving a cloud of dust behind him.

'Bastard,' Sage said, his fists clenched at his side. 'I confess there was always a little bit of me that hoped he'd made it out of the moat at Viridi City, that he'd survived somehow – but after Flos, and particularly now, I wish he hadn't.'

'So he's a Spinner, too,' Anise said, screwing his nose up. 'A Water Spinner.'

'Looks that way,' Rian said, finally releasing me. 'We'd better keep going. They know we're here, so we need to keep moving and out of their sight where possible.'

'They're probably watching us from a distance,' I said, scanning the horizon. 'We may only be able to lose them once it's dark.'

Rian looked up at the sun. 'We've got a few hours yet,' he said. 'Let's keep going.' He grasped my hand and we waded through the river and up the bank on the far side.

The further we walked the worse the unbalancing of nature became, probably because we were getting closer to the Crystal Vortex. A feeling of gloom pervaded the very air we breathed, but still some hardy plants and animals survived amongst the arid hills. A deep sense of unrest fell on me and I was glad of Rian's warm hand as a coldness clutched at my heart. All the Lands would succumb to this if Juniper and Chervil succeeded in their scheme.

'We can't let them win,' Rian said as we walked along a little way behind the others. 'We'll have to do whatever it takes to stop them and stabilise the Vortex.'

He was only echoing my own thoughts.

'I know,' I said softly. 'And we will.'

He glanced at me. 'But we'll do it together. We'll watch each other's backs.'

'Of course.'

Rian looked ahead. 'You know Beryl might die, don't you?' he said quietly.

I nodded. 'Chervil, too.'

Rian sighed. 'He won't stop of his own accord – we'll have to stop him. I'll have to stop him.'

I looked at him. '*We'll* stop him,' I said. 'We'll stop Beryl – and the rest – together, all of us. None of us will be able to do this alone.'

'I'd rather we didn't have to kill them, though.'

'Me, too,' I said. The chill drove itself further into me. 'I don't want to kill anyone. I still don't know if I can.'

Rian squeezed my hand. 'Let's hope you don't have to find out.'

'Who's that?' Willow asked from up ahead, shading her eyes.

'Where?' Tarragon asked.

'On the ridge.'

I looked at where she was gazing as we caught up with the others. A young man stood on the ridge top some distance away, holding the reins of a bay horse that grazed on some of the few green blades of grass on the isle, swishing its tail. That wasn't Sorrel. Who was it?

He changed his stance. A chill ran down my back and I gasped. Mal made a choking noise beside me.

'The bitch brought him with her?' Onyx asked.

'If she's a Spinner, he's probably a Spinner, too,' I said, my voice resigned.

'Who is it?' Sage asked, squinting.

'Elm,' Rian said, his muscles tensing at the sight of my stepbrother. 'Juniper's son.'

'But what's he doing?' Willow asked.

Elm crouched down, one golden hand on the other, resting them on the soil, still holding his horse's reins. The smallest of green flashes lit the air around his fingers. The ground began to tremble.

'Hell's teeth,' I said, struggling to remain upright. 'Now what?'

'Earth Magic,' Anise breathed as his mouth gaped open.

From out of the ground started to rise great brown thorny trunks, covered in what could only be described as daggers from their size and sharpness. Elm glanced up, his scar pale in the sunlight, his yellow eyes shining with triumph. The thorns started breaking through the earth in front and on either side of Elm, kicking up dust, until they covered the land from horizon to horizon, forming a deep, impenetrable wall of blades covering Middle Isle from one Water to the other.

The trembling stopped. The dust settled. I stared up at the top of the thorn wall, mouth open. The thorns reached fifty feet into the air, their jagged edges clawing for the sky. There was no getting around it, over it, or under it.

'So what do we do?' Sage asked, looking sourly at the barrier between us and Teal.

'Look on the bright side,' Mal said with a little grin. 'Juniper sees us as such a threat that she's now throwing things at us to stop us from getting to the Vortex.'

'That's a good thing?' I asked him, giving him a long look.

He shrugged, then smiled wickedly. 'She's scared of us, and if she's scared, she might just make a mistake.'

CHAPTER TWENTY

'Mal has a point,' Rian said, staring at the thorn wall.

'Let's see if we can cut our way through,' I said. I wasn't going to be beaten, and especially not by someone as annoying as Elm.

We walked across the dusty yellow grass and up towards the top of the ridge. The thorn wall loomed over us as we approached. Stems the size of tree trunks made up the bulk of the wall, with branches as thick as a man's arm and thorns so sharp you could cut your thoughts on them. No sword would be able to cut through these, but I wasn't out of ideas yet. I pulled Deorwine free of its scabbard.

'You think that'll work?' Tarragon asked, glancing at the crystal sword.

'Only one way to find out,' I said, slicing down with it. It bounced off the thorns like they were diamond. 'What?'

'They're Magic, Phire,' Anise said, studying the wall.

'So's Deorwine.' I aimed at a branch in the thorns and slammed the crystal sword into the joint. Again, it glanced off. 'Maybe he used an Artefact.'

Mal made a strangled sound. 'He always had that jade ring on his index finger, remember, Ama?'

Onyx's eyes narrowed. 'An Artefact, like my Ring?' he asked, holding his hand out to look at the Rose Quartz ring on his finger.

'Hell's teeth, it must be,' I said, shaking my head. Maybe Rian's ring was an Artefact after all?

'I suppose we had to expect them to have Artefacts, too,' Rian said with a sigh.

I turned to Anise. 'Can you do anything?'

'I don't know,' Anise said. He reached out and gently touched part of a trunk. He cried out, stepping back and nursing his hand as if he'd just been burnt by the flames in a furnace.

Willow gasped as Sage grabbed his boyfriend's hand. Blood oozed from great sores on his fingers. Onyx grabbed a kerchief from his pack and pressed it to Anise's bleeding wounds.

'What the hell?' I looked at the wall.

'Blast. Earth Magic with a kick,' Mal muttered as Onyx and Sage fussed around Anise.

'Definitely an Artefact,' Rian said, wincing at Anise's hand.

I chewed a nail, not happy with how everything was taking shape.

'You know, Elm was covering one hand with the other when he conjured these thorns, and I'm pretty sure there was a little green flash – did anyone else see it?' Mal asked.

I nodded, although at the time I'd thought my imagination had decided to run riot.

'Artefact or not, we aren't getting through that,' Onyx said. 'Maybe we can go around.'

'That'll mean trying to find someone to take us across Second Water, and the men on the dockside in Azure City said there were only boats on the inside of Middle Isle, at Teal, when I asked them about it,' Tarragon said, scratching his chin.

Rian rubbed the back of his neck. 'Maybe I could do something,' he said, reaching a hand out.

I grabbed his arm, pulling him back. 'Don't touch it.'

'I wasn't going to – it's all right.' He gave me a wink.

I frowned, but let go of him and he stepped forward again, hand stretched out but not touching the thorn wall. His eyes narrowed as he concentrated. Flames erupted from his fingers, licking at the dead wood of the thorns. The fire began to take hold, starting to creep up the trunks, along the branches – then began to fade.

Rian shook his head. 'Damn, I thought I had it.'

'Do it again,' I said. 'But don't start a wildfire. Everything's so dry.'

'I won't.' He looked at me, an eyebrow raised. 'Don't use your Quintessence to control it – we may need it later, the way things are going.'

'I won't – but you can use the Amethyst Talisman.'

He smiled and fished the Talisman out of his tunic. Holding it in one hand, he reached out again, sending flames into the wall. This time the intensity of the fire was even greater, burning hotter than before. In seconds the orange-red flames had taken hold, but Rian didn't stop. He closed his eyes. The flames continued to burst from his hand as they started to devour the thorn wall. Instead of a wall of thorns it became a wall of fire as Rian's Magic took hold. We all moved back, apart from Rian, the heat becoming too much for us as the inferno raged across Middle Isle.

Onyx grinned. 'Bet Elm didn't see that coming.'

He didn't know we had a Fire Artefact – he would never have thought we'd get through this, and neither would Juniper. The flames continued to lick at the thorns until they slowly turned to ash, and the whole wall imploded in a smoking, charred heap.

Rian dropped to his knees, sweat running down his face. I crouched beside him.

'You all right?' I asked, passing him my waterskin.

He nodded and took a sip of water. 'A little tired, that's all. I'll be fine. Just give me a minute to get my breath back.'

'I'll go look ahead,' Mal said.

'I'm coming with you,' Onyx said.

The two young men picked their way through the ash pile and over to the other side of the ridge.

'That was impressive, y'know,' Tarragon said as I helped Rian to his feet.

Rian grinned. 'Thanks.'

'Is Anise all right, though?' Willow asked Sage.

Sage nodded. 'I think so.'

'Can we get you something from your Herb Chest?' I asked, kneeling beside Anise as he nursed his hand.

'I'm not sure I've got anything for something like this,' Anise said. 'I mean, it's a kind of Magical wound. Only Magic will heal it, won't it?'

'But what sort of Magic?' Sage asked. 'Earth?'

'I don't know.'

'Let me see,' I said as Sage gently removed the kerchief.

I rested Anise's hand in mine – his fingers looked angry, raw and blistered, and they were still bleeding.

So sore. They need to heal.

I hadn't meant it to happen, but a white glow appeared at my fingertips, quickly covering Anise's hand. In seconds it was gone, and all that remained of Anise's injury were pinkish marks. He looked at me, eyes wide.

'Thank you, Phire,' he said.

I let go of him, slightly shaken. I hadn't meant to do that. I was using my power without realising it. I needed to be more careful, more focused – even if it had been the outcome I'd wanted.

Rian pulled me up, a questioning look in his eyes.

I looked back at him, surprised and confused all at once. 'I didn't actually mean to do it. Not like that, anyway. But as Anise said, it was a Magical wound – it needed Magic to heal it.'

'You need to be careful,' he said. 'You might use your power up by accident.'

'I know,' I murmured, stifling a yawn. 'But it needed to be done.'

'I don't disagree. Just be careful.'

We followed after Mal and Onyx, reaching the far side of the ridge. I looked out across Middle Isle. Teal was still out of sight. It had to be a good day's walk still. Maybe we'd underestimated the distance, or our speed without horses. There wasn't a lot of cover ahead. About an hour away stood a wood of dying trees. To our right, well in the distance, lay Second Water twinkling in the late afternoon sun. I chewed on a curl, thinking.

'Stop that,' Mal said, pulling the hair from my mouth.

'She's still doing it,' Onyx said with a sigh, 'the chewing thing. Rian and I have both tried to stop her.'

'What makes you think the two of you can stop her when I've been trying since the day she was born?'

'She's always done it?' Rian asked, glancing at Mal.

'Always.'

'I am here, you know,' I said, irritated. 'I was just thinking. How about we head for the woods? We could rest until it's dark, start a fire, so anyone watching will think we're there, and head out towards Second Water under the cover of darkness. We could follow the coast and hopefully avoid any further attempts by our marvellous stepmother to stop us.'

Mal looked at Rian. 'Maybe we should encourage the chewing – that's not a bad idea.'

I sighed.

'What?' Mal asked innocently.

'It's the way you make it sound like it's the first good idea I've ever had in my life,' I said.

'I thought you were going to complain about me mentioning your chewing.' Mal grinned.

'It's a good thing I love you, Brother.'

'And I love you too, Little Sister,' he said, giving me a squeeze.

'Get off,' I said, backing into Rian, who grabbed me before I could step on his toes.

'Let's do it,' Rian said, leading the way and pulling me along with him.

'Are you ever going to let go of my hand?'

'I've been giving that some thought,' he said as we walked along.

'And?'

'No. Never. I shouldn't have let go of you before, so I'm making up for it now.'

'This may get awkward.'

'Why?'

'There are certain things that require privacy.'

Rian smirked. 'All right. I'll let go of you on those occasions, then, but I'll stay close – will that do?'

'Not too close.'

'Fine.'

We made our way to the woods, setting up a little camp on the far side, but not too far into the trees so that a fire could be seen at night. I collected firewood with Rian, we built a little campfire, and he set light to the wood. The others had also collected some wood, ready for nightfall. We ate a brief meal from our packs and rested against the trees, awaiting the darkness.

I sat with Rian, lying in his arms against an old oak tree. I still felt cold from nerves, but his warm body helped to quell the sensation. Despite the fact I wanted to sleep, I couldn't. My nerves were too raw from everything that had happened, not that that stopped Sage, Anise, Tarragon and Onyx from nodding off. Willow dozed from time to time, but Mal, Rian and I remained wide awake.

'She'll keep trying things,' Mal murmured so as not to wake the others. 'She'll do everything she can to stop us from getting to Magenta.'

'I know,' I said softly. 'That's why we have to outwit her.'

'Let's hope it works,' Rian said. 'I don't really want to have to fight for every step of the way.'

'Not my first choice, either,' Mal said, screwing his nose up. He threw another branch on the fire, sending a few sparks up into the dusky air. 'But I guess we'll do what we have to.'

'You've damn well got that right. By the Herbs, we can't stop now, we've come too far.'

'And if Chervil's with her?' I asked anxiously.

'I'll deal with him,' Rian said, resting his chin on my shoulder. 'You don't need to worry about him.'

'But I do. What do you intend to do with him?'

Rian shrugged. 'He can't stay King. It wouldn't be right. He's betrayed Aerba, its people – he can't remain in power.'

'That means you, then,' Tarragon said, opening an eye.

Rian grunted.

'You're next in line to the throne,' Tarragon continued.

'I've been written out, remember?'

'Then it's Bergamot.'

Sage sat up. 'If Father's crowned King of Aerba and Sorrel is Crown Prince, I'll lead the rebellion myself.'

Tarragon let out an amused snort. 'I volunteer as your deputy.'

'You want to be King?' I smirked at Sage.

His eyes narrowed. 'If it fell to me, I'd abdicate in favour of Rian.'

'Thanks,' Rian said drily. 'It's really an honour I'd like to forgo. It's not something I've ever sought. I don't want to be King of Aerba.'

'You may not have a choice,' Tarragon said, giving Rian a long look. 'You'll have to take it on – it would be your duty.'

Rian shook his head. 'Look, this is all just talk at the moment. We're a long way from that.'

'You hope,' I murmured.

'You wouldn't be alone, y'know,' Tarragon said.

Sage nodded. 'Tarragon's right, Rian, you'd have all of us to back you up.'

Rian's eyes glistened in the light of the fire. 'Thank you,' he said, his voice cracking with emotion. 'You don't know how much it means to me to hear you say that.'

'We'd all help you out,' I said, squeezing his hand.

'Probably,' Tarragon said, then turned and grinned at his cousin.

Rian shook his head and rolled his eyes to the velvet night sky.

I glanced upwards. Little white lights hung in the darkness, peering out from behind the passing clouds. No moon graced us tonight – that should help with moving unseen.

'Shall we go?' I asked.

'Let's just make the fire up a bit more so it keeps going for a while,' Rian said.

We woke the others, built the fire up and collected our packs. Moving quietly to the eastern side of the trees, we headed out across the dark, open countryside.

CHAPTER TWENTY-ONE

Waves rushed up the beach, almost to the base of the cliff we were hugging as we walked. We'd managed to reach the coast while it was still dark, and now, down by the cliffs, we couldn't be seen from inland. The smell of seaweed hung in the air, salt lingering on my tongue.

'The tide better not come up any more or we'll be swimming,' Sage said, screwing his nose up.

'First Water is a lake. There's no tide, not like the sea,' Anise said.

'Oh. Good.'

We walked along, our feet sinking into the soft, golden sand, leaving boot marks behind us.

'If they do find us, they'll be able to track us easily,' I said, gritting my teeth.

'Can't be helped,' Mal said. 'At least we're not out in the open now.'

'I suppose.'

Rian still had hold of my hand and I'd given up trying to reassure him I wasn't going anywhere, so I decided to just enjoy it instead. Seagulls squawked as they swooped over the cliffs and out to sea in search of fish. The waves ran up the beach, hissing as they failed to reach us and drag us back into their midst. The grey sky above us gave the water a menacing feel, and despite the lack of sun, the air was warm and humid. I'd removed my tunic a while ago, but my shirt still clung to me.

Late morning, we stopped for food and a short rest. I yawned. My body craved a nap. Getting no sleep was taking its toll, and after eating, I nodded off, my head resting on Rian's shoulder, his head on mine. A couple of hours later, we all roused ourselves and packed our things away.

'Would now be a good time to try our powers?' Tarragon asked, looking up and down the beach. 'There's no one here, and we're hidden from the land.'

Rian rubbed the back of his neck and nodded. 'All right. Let's try it.'

'So, how is this supposed to work?' Mal asked.

'You channel your powers to me and I'm supposed to control and focus them,' I said, my stomach flipping at the thought.

'You're sure you want to try this?' Rian asked. 'Without something to focus our powers into?'

'Ostianzis didn't seem to think it mattered whether you focussed your powers on me or the Opal, and I'd rather know what I'm doing now than leave it until we're doing it in a panic.'

He nodded. 'All right, then – you stand over there and we'll take it in turns to try and channel our Magic to you.'

I stood a good ten feet away from the others and they lined up next to each other.

'I'll stay back here with Willow,' Onyx said. 'You won't need me.'

'Or me,' Sage said.

I nodded, taking a deep breath, not really sure what I was going to do. I hoped it would come to me naturally.

'I'll go first,' Rian said. 'If everything's working all right, Tarragon can go next, then Anise and then Mal.'

Everyone nodded, exchanging nervous looks.

'Ready?' Rian asked me.

'Ready,' I said, swallowing.

He took a deep breath and stretched his hands out in front of him, one on top of the other, and closed his eyes. A red glow appeared at his fingertips, slowly covering his hands. I wasn't really sure what to do, so I held my hands out as if I were about to catch a ball. I hoped it would be that easy. Rian opened his eyes and a bolt of red energy shot from his hands to mine, and kept coming.

Control it.

I gasped as I took hold of his Fire Magic. It swirled around my hands. I could feel its heat – not painful, just hot – as it filled me, spiralling inside me as I took it in. He looked at me and I nodded.

'Tarragon,' Rian said, his voice tight as he concentrated.

'Here goes,' Tarragon said, taking up a similar posture to Rian. He closed his eyes. Blue light gradually lit his hands, spreading down his fingers, before hurtling towards me.

Control.

I tried not to gasp as the Water Magic joined the Fire Magic. It was a curious sensation as the cold of the water and the heat of the fire moved within me, the blue and red light swirling around my hands and fingers like snakes.

'Anise,' Rian said, sweat beading on his brow.

Hold it.

In seconds, a green bolt of energy joined the red and the blue. The Earth Magic swelled within me, nourishing and rich, joining the others in a strange, mesmerising dance, a dance I was beginning to find it hard to control.

'Mal,' Rian said.

My brother took a deep breath and closed his eyes. Yellow energy started to fill his hands. It gradually covered them up to his wrists and he released it towards me.

I—I can't—

'No!' I yelled.

The additional power surged into me. I fought for control. I tried to tame the Air Magic, hold it within me, but all four together had combined into a wild creature, wild and feral. I gasped. My heart raced. My breathing became ragged. I couldn't do this. The hairs on the back of my neck rose with the energy twisting and writhing within me.

'Everyone, stop!' Rian yelled.

I turned towards the sea, my hands out. A cry escaped my lips and a white beam of light shot across the waves with a crack like thunder in its wake. I dropped to my hands and knees, chest heaving.

The Spinners had all stopped, out of breath, Anise and Tarragon sinking to the ground. Mal staggered as Onyx grabbed him, keeping him upright.

'I'm sorry,' Mal said, breathing heavily.

Rian scrambled over to me, his eyes wild.

'Are you all right?' he panted, slipping his arm around my shoulders. 'It was taking you over.'

'I—I think so,' I managed to get out between ragged breaths. I felt full of power and yet drained. That wasn't how I'd been expecting it to go. I'd hoped to be in control of the Magic, but it had been in total control of me. 'I can't do it. I can't control it.'

'Don't worry,' Rian said, moving the hair from my sweaty face. 'It was a good first attempt.'

'But I couldn't contain it – when Mal sent me his, it was too much,' I said, my voice quavering.

The black spectre of fear shifted inside me. This was beyond what I could handle. I could never hope to contain all their Magic at once. I stood no chance of restarting the Crystal Vortex if I couldn't harness their power without losing control. How could I ever focus it enough to send it through the Fire Opal and target the Vortex? We were beaten before we started.

I shook my head. 'By the Stars, I can't do it. I'm not strong enough.' I forced myself to my feet, my body shaking from the exertion, and stumbled off ahead of the others, leaving Rian kneeling on the sand.

'Ama! Stop! It'll be all right!' Mal called after me, but I kept going.

I'm going to fail them. Rian, my friends, and the Six Lands.

Boots running through the sand crunched behind me. Rian grasped my hand, forcing me to stop, and he turned me towards him, holding my upper arms. He gazed at me, his amber eyes full of concern. 'You can do this. If anyone can, it's you, Phire. I have faith in you. You and your inner strength. You've shown it time and time again. You can do it here with this, too. I know you can.'

Tears sprang to my eyes. 'I can't.' My bottom lip quivered and the tears started streaming down my face. 'I'm going to fail you all.'

He pulled me to him and wrapped his arms around me. My head rested against the crook of his neck as I sobbed. He ran one hand over my head, the other holding me firmly as he whispered in my ear, whispered words of comfort, whispered words of love.

'Don't give up,' he murmured. 'We've come so far. We can face this together, like everything else.'

I pulled back. 'But what if I can't?'

He gave me his best lopsided smile. 'You'll find the strength you need when you need it. Like you did in the dungeon, at the scaffold, when facing Mal. I know you can do this. I know *you*,' he said, leaning towards me, one hand now caressing the side of my face as he brought his mouth to mine and kissed me. The kiss was salty and wet, one full of love and solace. He leant his forehead on mine. 'You all right?'

'Yes, as long as I've got you,' I said. His warm hand still rested on my cheek.

Mal cleared his throat. I looked over towards him. The others had come to join us and for a moment embarrassment filled me as I felt blood rush to my face.

My brother covered his eyes in an exaggerated fashion. 'You two are awful,' he said, peering over his hand, a flicker of a smile on his face. 'Shall we carry on?'

Rian looked at me, totally unabashed, not even a tiny hint of embarrassment in his amber eyes. I nodded and he took my hand, leading me on up the beach in the afternoon sun.

It took me a while for my heart rate to go back to normal. Every step was now a monumental effort. Trying to control the Magic had exhausted me. I only really wanted to sleep, not spend the rest of the day walking. I couldn't help but drag my feet slightly as we walked through the sand. My pack and the Cursed Weapons seemed heavier on my back now, and my shoulders sagged under their weight, my muscles beginning to ache. No one spoke as we walked, and other than the sound of the waves, silence surrounded us for a good while.

A strong gust of wind ripped along the beach, whipping my hair into my eyes and scattering sharp pebbles and sand.

'What the hell was that?' I turned around, but we were alone on the beach.

Rian's hand tensed in mine. 'Not sure,' he said, scanning the shoreline. 'Let's keep going.'

Another gust made me look to the sky. Was a storm coming towards us that we couldn't see – from the land side? The wind continued to rise, but it appeared it was a land breeze now, rushing from the cliff tops out to sea, but the way it began to intensify sent a chill down my spine.

'It's not natural,' Mal said suddenly.

'What?' Tarragon asked.

'This wind. It's not natural.'

'Air Magic?' Anise asked.

Sage frowned. 'It must be. Should we do something about it?' he asked, looking at Mal.

'Not sure there's much point,' Mal said, shaking his head. 'It's not stopping us from moving.'

'Then what do we do?' Willow asked.

'Nothing, just keep going,' Rian said, increasing his speed.

'They're looking for us,' I said.

He nodded. 'They've realised we're not out in the open countryside anymore and their Air Spinner is trying to flush us out.'

'I wonder who their Air Spinner is,' Mal said, scratching his head.

'Not Sorrel or Elm,' Onyx said. 'Or Juniper.'

'Rather narrows it down to Beryl or Chervil, then,' I said.

'You think they're the other two?' Mal asked.

'Process of elimination, really.'

We hurried along, the wind continuing for some time before finally abating.

'Whoever their Air Spinner is, I'll wager they'll be rather tired by now.' Sage grinned.

They weren't the only ones.

'Let's hope so,' Tarragon said.

As we walked on, the cliffs slowly receded until sand dunes and a rough, grassy bank shielded us from the land. The parched, spiky vegetation rippled in the sea breeze. The afternoon wore on, but there was still no sign of Teal, and my legs began to turn to lead weights as I walked. I wasn't sure how much further I'd be able to go before I collapsed.

'I'd hoped we were going to get to the city by tonight,' Onyx said.

'Not sure we will now,' Rian said, squinting at the coastline ahead.

My heart sank. I glanced out to sea. There were a couple of little fishing boats bobbing up and down in the water. We were getting closer, but not close enough to see the city yet.

'Do we keep going or camp for the night?' I asked, hoping he'd say camp.

Rian rubbed the back of his neck. 'I'm not sure. I mean, we really want to be in and out of Teal as quickly as possible so Juniper and her cronies don't spot us.'

'Then we go in at night, make our way to the docks and try to find passage at first light?'

Rian glanced at me and nodded. 'Might be best. We'll find somewhere to camp for a while up ahead at dusk.'

We walked on until Teal City finally appeared ahead of us. It sat on the edge of First Water, its buildings in the same pale green stone as Azure, with the same beige roof tiles. It, too, had towering spires that scraped at the sky. Dusk was rapidly approaching, as were more cliffs – with a path that led up to the top.

I looked at the beach ahead. 'Let's stop at the base of the cliff, past the path. We'll be well out of sight, and we can light a fire and rest until the early hours. After that, we can make for the town.'

Rian nodded.

'Good idea,' Mal said, and he started to collect driftwood as we walked along.

By the time we stopped, we had a good pile, and we set it up ready to light as the sun vanished. I let Deorwine and Glædwine fall to the ground with my pack and rolled my aching shoulders. I sank slowly to my knees, relieved to finally have a chance to rest a while. Everything ached, including my head. I wasn't sure I'd have the energy to eat before I slept, though my rumbling stomach said otherwise.

I glanced at Rian's ring, the last pink rays of sunlight casting their light into the diamonds and changing their colour. Was this ring an Artefact? I stared at it, concentrating.

Are you?

Nothing.

Maybe I was wrong and it wasn't – or maybe its power just needed to be woken. Perhaps a Waker had never Released its Quintessence, and its power still remained sealed within, waiting to be brought to life.

A red-orange glow flickered on the cliffs beside me, catching my attention. I glanced at the wood, then at Rian. That was odd. There were no flames there yet, and the sun had gone. Where was it coming from? I turned.

A column of spinning flame sped towards us along the beach.

'Hell's teeth, what's that?'

CHAPTER TWENTY-TWO

Willow gasped, her eyes widening in the light of the red flames as I struggled to my feet, heart skipping.

'Fire tornado?' Sage asked, stepping back, his face strained.

'Magic,' Anise said, sucking in a breath.

'We need to get off the beach,' Rian said, urgency in his voice as he grabbed my arm.

'We can't,' Tarragon said. 'We're too far from the cliff path. We'll never make it before the flames get to us.'

The sound of angry wind mixed with flames reached us as the fire tornado's roar echoed around the cliffs.

'So what do we do?' Onyx asked.

'Water,' Mal said, grinning. 'Use your Magic to put it out.'

Tarragon grinned back. 'Excellent idea – Onyx, let's use the sea. We won't have to conjure anything up, then.'

Onyx nodded, and they both stretched their arms towards the water. Two columns rose from the sea, swiftly moving towards the fire tornado. They twisted around the flames, but the moment they tried to extinguish the flames the wind pushed the water away, flinging it across the beach. I turned away as the water hurtled towards us, wetting our hair and clothes.

'Bugger,' Tarragon swore.

'Sage, maybe we can stop it,' Mal said, his eyes brightened by the light.

'I'll help,' Rian said. 'See if I can put the flames out at the same time.'

The three Spinners stepped forward, raising their hands. Wind started to swirl in the opposite direction to the tornado that was now level with the path. Sweat broke out on Rian's forehead as he tried to quell the fire. I watched in horror as the tornado continued inexorably towards us.

'They're using Artefacts,' I murmured.

'What?' Anise asked from beside me.

'They're using Artefacts – how else could it be so strong?'

'Maybe Juniper is using Quintessence.'

'Then perhaps I should, too.'

Rian stepped back, dropping his hand. 'You can't, you still haven't recovered from this afternoon. Don't think I haven't noticed the way you've been traipsing along, and how your shoulders have been sagging. You've been dragging your feet for

ages. You can't help this time. If you do, you could kill yourself –
and I'm not having that.'

I wanted to protest, but everything he'd said was true.

'Then we'll use ours,' Anise said, a steely look in his eyes. He
took hold of his Amulet, raised his hand, concentrated.

Rian nodded and took hold of the Amethyst Talisman.

Mal and Sage stood back as the Fire Spinner and the Earth
Spinner stepped forwards, their muscles tense, both holding their
Artefacts. They closed their eyes, raised their hands and focused.

I glanced at Mal. He stepped towards me and slipped his hand
into mine. If this didn't work we'd all be burnt to death – unless I
did try to use my Quintessence. My free hand balled into a fist. If I
had to, I would. I'd give my life to save the others, if that's what
was needed.

The roaring, rapidly advancing column of fire suddenly began to
shiver. The swirling flames stuttered and slowed. The roar faltered.

Rian's body shook with the effort.

Anise suddenly dropped to his knees.

'Are you all right?' Willow asked anxiously.

'Fine,' he said, placing one hand on the beach, the other still
firmly clasped around his Amulet.

What was he up to?

The sand began to shift. Tremble and shake. Mal held on to me
tighter, just to keep us both upright. Then a huge wall of sand rose
up in front of us as the spiralling flames approached. The wall built
and built, then collapsed on top of the fire tornado, smothering the
flames.

A shriek of pain and frustration rent the night.

Beryl.

I looked at Mal.

'Blast.' He blinked then stared back at me, his eyes wide.

Silence filled the air, broken by the lapping of waves and the
panting of Rian and Anise.

'You did it,' Sage said, grabbing his boyfriend into a hug.

Anise nodded, his face red and sweaty.

Rian staggered as he lowered his arm, his broad shoulders sagging
from the effort. I rushed over to him, ducked under an arm and
helped him to stay upright. His body trembled from the effort of
trying to control the flames. He gazed at me, a lopsided smile
appearing.

'Juniper won't win,' he murmured.

I frowned. He looked more exhausted than me now.

'No, she won't,' I said.

'We need to move,' Mal said. 'They know we're here. Let's get to Teal. Maybe we can hide there, lie low somewhere.'

Rian nodded. 'Let's go.'

'You need to rest,' I said.

'I can rest later.'

'But—'

'Mal's right. We have to go.'

I screwed my face up, but helped Rian collect his pack, then pulled the Cursed Weapons and my own pack on. We walked back to the cliff path, Sage helping Anise, Mal helping me with Rian.

Thankfully, we were only a half hour from Teal, or we'd have been carrying Rian. It was fully dark as we entered the city through a side gate. A friendly, although surprised, guard at the gate directed us to a couple of inns.

'I'd love to stay at an inn, but maybe we should stay somewhere else,' Tarragon said, scratching his chin.

'There must be some warehouses near the docks,' Onyx said.

'Exactly what I was thinking.' Tarragon grinned.

We had enough food with us to make it unnecessary to stop somewhere to eat, so we made our way towards the harbour. Down near the water we found an old warehouse full of wool and textiles. A musty, sweet smell filled the building's cool air, reminding me of sheep. We made ourselves comfortable at the back of the building behind large piles of material on some wool packs.

Rian sank on top of two packs and was asleep the moment he hit the soft wool.

'That was Beryl, wasn't it?' I said quietly to Mal. 'I didn't imagine it?'

He nodded. 'I thought so, too. Anise and Rian stopped her in her tracks. I wonder if she's a Fire or Air Spinner.'

'I don't know, but she's dangerous, whichever she is.'

My brother nodded, then grinned. 'So are we.'

I smirked at him. 'Let's hope so.'

We ate a small, cold meal and I snuggled up next to Rian, my bones weary from the day's trials.

'I'll go out and see what I can find out about passage to Magenta,' Onyx said. 'Back soon.'

'I'll come with you,' Mal said. Onyx nodded and the two slipped out of the warehouse.

I wanted to stay awake, hear what they'd found out, but sleep claimed me.

'Ama, wake up.' Mal nudged me awake. 'We've got a ship. They're sailing on the next tide. We thought we'd go on board while it's still dark.'

I nodded and yawned. Rian lay with his arm around me – whether he'd woken or done it in his sleep, I didn't know, but it made me smile. I sat up, my stiff, tired muscles protesting. I'd had several hours' sleep, but my bones still ached.

'Wake up, sleepy head,' I said, kissing him.

A little smile spread across his face. 'You should do that every morning.'

'I'll remember that.'

He opened his eyes. 'What time is it?'

'Just before dawn. Mal and Onyx have found us a ship and we're getting on board while it's dark. Fewer eyes about.'

He sat up and yawned. 'I feel as if I've been hit by a wagon.'

'Join the club,' I said, pulling him up.

We all collected our things and followed Mal and Onyx out the warehouse and across the docks towards a small ship where sailors busily readied their cargo.

'The captain says he can take us to Magenta,' Onyx said. 'And the price is reasonable.'

Rian nodded. 'How long will the voyage take?'

'We'll arrive the morning of the day after tomorrow.'

'Plenty of time to rest,' I said to Rian.

'I'm fine now,' he said, but his slower-than-usual movements said otherwise – rather like my own.

We boarded the ship, and the First Mate showed us to the cabins below. They were small and airless, but considering the trip would be reasonably short, and I intended to sleep as much as possible, they were adequate. We had a small breakfast as the sun rose, and Rian and I climbed into our narrow bed. He immediately had his arms around me, pulling me close. The ship glided out of Teal harbour as we fell asleep.

Late afternoon, Rian went out to join the others on deck. I slipped into the main cabin in search of a drink to find Willow sitting there alone, an unused bucket near her.

'Have you seen Anise?' I asked, nodding at her bucket.

'Yes. And I took one of his teas a little while ago. I'm already beginning to feel a little better.'

'Good.' I smiled, absently turning Rian's ring around my finger. I paused, looking at it and the little diamonds that ran around it, sparkling in the light. 'Willow, would you try something for me?'

She frowned. 'What?'

'I think Rian's ring might possibly be an Artefact. Can you try and Release it?'

'Wake its power? I can try, but I don't know how, and I don't even know if I'm really a Waker at all.'

'Then now might be a good time to find out, and a great opportunity to practise – when we get to the Fire Opal, you're going to need to know what to do.'

She nodded. 'I'll try. You're sure it's an Artefact?' she asked as I pulled the ring off and passed it to her.

'No, it's more of a feeling, really.'

She held it in the palm of her right hand. 'What do you think I should do?'

I shrugged.

She stared at it.

Nothing.

Her brow furrowed as she concentrated. Perspiration beaded on her face, but nothing happened. She let out a long breath.

'I can't do it,' she said. 'Maybe I'm not a Waker, in which case we're in a lot of trouble.'

I chewed a nail. She was right. If she wasn't a Waker after all, we were in deep…

'Ask it to wake up,' I said.

'Ask it?' she giggled. 'Bobbins. Are you serious?'

'It doesn't hurt to be polite. Just try asking it rather than forcing it. Maybe that will work.'

'You're serious?'

I nodded. 'Just try it. At worst, nothing will happen.'

'All right, let's see then.' She stared hard at Rian's ring. 'Please wake up,' she said, concentrating on the ring. 'Release your Magic Angle.'

CHAPTER TWENTY-THREE

A little splutter of light, like a hiccup, flared from the ring. A bright flash. The diamonds around the ring suddenly burst into light before dying down again, back to their normal sparkling selves.

Willow gasped. 'By the Herbs. Did I do it?'

I took the Ring from her palm. It felt different now. Like the Weapons on my back, that spark of power inside them, almost as if they were alive… and in some ways they were.

'I think you did it,' I said, my voice quiet and in awe as I slipped the ring back onto my finger. I could sense the power in the Ring rivalled the Cursed Weapons – maybe even exceeded them. Was that possible? I studied the little diamonds. Peered at the vines of Thyme.

Thyme.

I swallowed. Not the Time Ring, but the *Thyme* Ring. Was this the powerful Artefact Ostianzis had mentioned? It had to be. But if it was, why hadn't he said something? *Of course.* I'd been wearing those fingerless gloves Onyx disapproved of – the Senex wouldn't have seen me wearing it. So, it had been brought back to Aerba from Calperion.

Willow's eyes were wide as she beamed at me. 'I have powers, too.'

'Yes, you do – and possibly the most important ones of all of us, because without you Releasing the Fire Opal when the time comes, we'll be sunk.'

'Maybe.'

'There's no *maybe.* If we can't use it, we can't restart the Vortex.'

Tears suddenly glistened in her eyes as the light sienna skin around them crinkled. 'You know, I've never been needed for something before. Not properly. And certainly not like this.'

'But at the palace—'

'Doing what I did was just a job. I tried to work hard at it so I could be a King's Warrior–Attendant. Show I was worth something. But I was never special.'

I took hold of her hands. 'You are special. For just being you. Let's face it, no one can pick locks the way you do, for a start,' I said, smiling. 'Or keep Tarragon in check.'

She shook her head. 'Bobbins. I don't have any value, not like a High Blood or a Spinner.'

'I think Tarragon would have something to say about that,' I said, looking deep into her brown eyes. 'It doesn't matter what Blood you are – Onyx is a Low Blood, but do you think any less of him?'

She shook her head. 'But he's a Spinner, so he's really a High Blood like you. You're not Middle like you thought.'

'But you have High Blood, too – you're related to Onyx, you share a bloodline.'

She frowned. 'I'd forgotten that.'

'But Blood Classes are a load of twaddle. It's you as a person that matters, not the blood flowing through your veins that makes you who you are. So you don't have Magic? So what? You can do something none of the rest of us can do – you can Release Artefacts. You're a Waker. None of us have that power, even put together. And even if you couldn't do that, before we even knew it was a possibility, you were a good friend to me, an important friend to all of us, and to no one more so than Tarragon who loves you to distraction, whether or not you're a Waker.'

She looked at me through her long eyelashes, her face flushing. 'He does, doesn't he?'

'He'd do anything for you.'

She sniffed and wiped away her tears. 'I'm sorry. I guess I've always felt a bit of a hanger-on, deep down. That I was tolerated at the palace, nothing more. But you're right. The others are my friends, true friends. And now you, your brother and Onyx are, too. Things have been very overwhelming recently.'

'Since I came on the scene.' I grinned.

She smiled. 'You've definitely caused some excitement.'

'That wasn't all me,' I said, ruefully. 'But if I hadn't been sent to kill Angelica, none of this would have happened.'

'And you'd never have met Rian.'

I nodded.

'I told you once he'd never had any interest in girls or romance,' Willow said. 'I think deep down he was waiting for the right girl. For you.'

My face grew warm. 'You think so?'

She nodded. 'He almost seemed to be waiting for some*thing*. For some*one*. It was you, and none of us knew. Not you. Not even him.'

'Are you talking about destiny?'

'Kind of,' she said. 'I think the two of you were destined to be together. That's why you came to Aerba. You were fated to meet. To fall in love. To change the world.'

I choked. 'Change the world? What, the whole of Elvedon? I'm not sure about that.'

'But if we do restart the Vortex, you will change the world. You will keep Elvedon safe.'

'With all of you, too – Rian and I can't do this alone. This is going to take all of us.'

'And after that?'

I frowned. 'What do you mean?'

She looked at me, a strange flicker in her eyes. 'He'll be King of Aerba.'

I shook my head. 'As Rian says, Chervil's written him out of the line of succession.'

'You think that'll make any difference to the people? There'll be riots in the Viridi streets if Rian is passed over. The people love him. They always have. Of all of King Finule's children, he's the one who has a special place in the people's hearts. Didn't you notice how they reacted at the scaffold when Chervil was going to execute him? If we hadn't done something, I don't believe for one moment the people would've let Rian's execution go ahead. And certainly not unpunished. Chervil would've had a revolution on his hands.'

'You know the Aerban people better than me – they really love him that much?'

She nodded. 'He's always been kind, fair and popular with them, unlike his siblings and father. I think that has irked Chervil over the years more than anything. Although that's his own fault. Chervil wanted to force the people to love him, but that's not how it works. You can't do that. You can't make someone love you at knifepoint. They love Rian for who he is. For his actions. And by the same token, Chervil has just alienated them with his brutality and excesses.'

I chewed on a fingernail. 'But Rian doesn't want to be King of Aerba.'

'He may not want it, but it's his duty. Maybe even his destiny. And if I know anything about him, he's always taken duty very seriously. He'll step up and do it even if he hates the idea. Even if he's terrified of the responsibility. Even if it's the last thing he wants. But he will do it. For the people. For Aerba. And you'll have to do it with him, because without you at his side, I don't think he'd cope now.'

'You'd be surprised by what he can cope with.' The Mandragora Berries and their side-effects gnawed at me.

She raised an eyebrow.

'You know about that, too?' I asked, slightly aghast.

'Tarragon talks.'

Good old Tarragon. They must all know.

'And from what Tarragon says, Rian has only coped with it because of you. Because of your love and understanding,' she continued. 'No other woman alive could have helped him like you have. You're his one true love.'

Tarragon definitely talked too much, but was what she said true? Rian was stronger than he'd ever been, but I had a sneaking suspicion she was right. We were stronger together. Apart? Not so much, as had been proven not so long ago. Together we could take on the world.

'But you're right, Phire. If he can cope with that, he can cope with being King. But he'll need your support, and love, to do it. You two need each other. You're like two parts of a puzzle. You just fit. Lock into place and become one. Solid. Rather like me and Tarragon. I think it's Rian's destiny to be King, and yours to be his Queen.'

Queen of Aerba.

The whole idea sent shivers through me. Maybe it wasn't so much whether Rian could do it as it was if *I* could. I sighed.

'We're a long way from that happening,' I said.

'Not that far. And if it does, the two of you really could change the world. You could revoke the Blood Decree, make things fairer for everyone. Stop this stupid situation with Flos. Heal the Five Lands.'

'That's some task,' I said, chewing another nail.

'One you'd do together.'

'Don't think the rest of you would get away without helping,' I said.

Willow's eyes widened. 'You'd really want us, too?'

'I'd definitely need *you.*'

'Then I'd be there.'

'I think we all come as a team now, a family, don't we?'

She smiled. 'Yes, I think we do.'

I stepped forwards and gave her a hug, her frizzy hair tickling my face. The door to the cabin opened, and Tarragon walked in. He raised an eyebrow.

'Is there something the two of you want to tell me and Rian?' he asked, grinning mischievously.

'Bobbins,' Willow said, letting go of me. 'Phire and I were having a little girly chat.'

I headed for the door. 'It's all really about destiny, Tarragon, and yours is waiting for a hug,' I said, nodding towards Willow. 'Probably wouldn't mind a kiss, too, while you're at it.'

'You think so?' he asked, gazing towards Willow, a besotted look in his eyes.

'I know so.'

I closed the door behind me and paused for a moment. There was the low murmuring of voices. A giggle. A soft moan followed by a low groan. I left them to it.

Magenta City loomed up out of First Water, it's pale green stone like that of the other cities, but here there were more spires, more towers, more of everything on a grander scale than we'd seen before. Something from a book of fables. This island also looked even more desolate than the rest of Chroma. Dead trees rose out of the dry land like crooked fingers, and dead grass waved in the breeze along the dusty brown shoreline. The heat here was greater, too, and I wiped the perspiration from my brow as the ship slowly slid into Magenta harbour.

'We go straight to the Emperor?' Tarragon asked, scratching his head.

Rian nodded. 'I think that's where we should start.'

I glanced down at the docks where we were about to berth. A large number of men in black uniforms were running towards our ship. Soldiers. Their deep umber skin glistened in the sunlight, and their oval faces were framed by dark curly hair. Bright blue eyes watched our every move as the ship came to a juddering halt.

'Rian.'

He glanced at me, then at where I was looking.

'I think we're expected,' I said, my hand instinctively reaching for Deorwine's reassuring hilt.

'Looks that way, doesn't it,' he replied, his voice tight.

'The bitch got here first,' Onyx said.

'The question is, what lies has she been pouring out?' Mal asked, coming to stand between me and Onyx.

'I don't think we'll have to wait long to find out,' I said as the gangplank was lowered and a group of the men, swords drawn, boarded the ship, the rest remaining on the quayside, longbows trained on us.

'You are under arrest by order of Emperor Xanthos,' a man in a highly embroidered uniform said, coming towards us.

Rian stepped forward. 'I am Prince Valerian of Aerba, and I have business with the Emperor,' he said, standing tall and noble.

The soldier chuckled. 'Indeed you do, Your Highness. We're to take you to see him immediately. Now, hand over your weapons, and don't try anything clever, any of you, or at least one of you will die,' he said, glancing towards Willow.

Tarragon took a protective step towards her.

I winced. Handing over my weapons would be easier said than done.

Rian glanced at me. I shrugged. We didn't have much choice, really.

'Very well.' Rian nodded and unsheathed his swords and knife. The others followed his lead, and I reluctantly did the same. Even though he was complying, a vein in Rian's neck fluttered. He clenched his fists. He was angry. So was I. This wasn't how we wanted to see the Emperor – as prisoners – but now wasn't the time to fight, either. We had to pick our battles, and this wasn't one of them. We needed information, and that currently outweighed our capitulation.

As I handed over the Cursed Weapons, I looked at the man taking them. 'They're bound to me—'

'We know,' he said curtly.

He did? Was this because they knew what they were, or because of Juniper? I didn't know. Topaz's knife rubbed my leg inside my boot. No need to mention that to them.

We were marched off the ship, our packs carried by other soldiers – I caught Anise looking anxiously at his Herb Chest – through the docks and up into the city. Our escort was rather extreme – maybe sixty men, all told. They obviously weren't taking any chances with us.

Sweat gathered on my brow at the heat in the city centre, my heart pounding from a combination of exertion and anxiety. City folk cleared a path for us, their blue eyes curious, their jewel-coloured clothes fluttering in the breeze. I couldn't tell from their outfits if there were Blood Classes here or not. If there were, their distinguishing features weren't as overt as the Five Lands.

The palace rose ahead of us, its highest towers painted gold and silver, the great windows, some of stained glass murals and patterns, reflecting the sun. I glanced at Mal. His face was taut, jaw set, as we walked along. He was thinking the same thing I was thinking.

Where was the bitch?

CHAPTER TWENTY-FOUR

We walked through great golden gates and into a large paved square, the slabs of polished white marble reflecting the bright light, making it hard to look at. The palace's round towers climbed skyward, the green stone in stark contrast to the azure sky. We moved up a set of steps into the main building. I was immediately grateful for the coolness that greeted me inside its walls. I looked at Rian who walked beside me. For once he wasn't holding my hand. His fists were still clenched as he contained his anger at our arrest.

They escorted us along a wide corridor with ornate candelabra and gold-framed mirrors, silver leaf in the ceiling cornices. I'd never seen such opulence anywhere. In front of us, two huge, white-painted doors, both elaborately carved with swirls and spirals, opened.

The Throne Room.

I swallowed, wiping my sweaty palms on my tunic as they ushered us in. At the far end, on a large raised dais, sat a throne of gold. Perched on it was a slight man, his deep umber skin in contrast to the white robes he wore, his piercing blue eyes immediately alighting on us. His face became tense, his eyes narrowed, his skin taut over his knuckles as he grasped the arms of his throne.

We were brought to a halt in front of the throne, Rian on one side of me, Mal on the other. Emperor Xanthos sat and looked at us. The guards around us held swords, and it seemed prudent to speak only once the Emperor had spoken first. A flash of light took my attention for a moment.

I stifled a gasp.

On a table at the side of the room sat the Aerban Fire Opal.

It was the first time I'd seen it up close. The only other time I'd had a glimpse of the Opal was from a distance in the Aerban Throne Room, a long time ago when I'd first arrived in Aerba. I'd thought the stone to be faceted, cut by master jewellers, but it was nothing of the sort. It was simply the way the light caught the uncut, glittering gemstone that made it appear that way. A bright, yellow-red glow emanated from it, flashes of purple and green twisting inside it.

The Opal sat watching, a living thing with fire burning at its heart. It appeared to be observing the proceedings, as one question filled my mind.

Had it been Released?

It didn't look any different to the last time I'd seen it. So maybe it hadn't, but I couldn't be sure.

'So, you are the ones who have come to destroy the Crystal Vortex,' the Emperor said, his deep voice resonating around the chamber.

Rian frowned. 'No, your Imperial Majesty, we're here t—'

'Silence!' a guard behind us snapped.

'It wasn't a question, Prince Valerian,' Emperor Xanthos said. 'I already know why you're here and who your companions are.' He looked at me, then glanced towards the Cursed Weapons that a soldier not far from me was holding.

Rian shifted his feet, his whole body tense.

'Who told you?' I asked, standing defiantly.

Emperor Xanthos turned his gaze back to me, then looked towards a side room. 'King Chervil of Aerba, and your stepmother, Lady Merciless.'

I swallowed.

Chervil and Juniper strode out of the side room, hand in hand, Juniper in her usual yellow gown that fell back at her wrist to expose her Quintessence Spinner birthmark. Elm, Beryl and Sorrel followed in their wake. Sauntering behind them came Carnelian, his right eye twitching, and Topaz, flicking her brown hair over her shoulder.

Juniper caught me in her gaze, her yellow serpent eyes dead and calculating as usual, and around her neck, catching the light, hung her diamond and agate necklace. Holding her hand, Chervil looked even shorter than normal next to Juniper's tall, willowy frame, his brown eyes narrowing as he looked at his younger brother, his long black hair, in its Aerban ponytail, swishing as he walked. He still had his goatee, which did nothing to alleviate his shifty appearance, despite his regal-looking burgundy and gold Aerban High Blood coat.

Beryl glowered at me, her hazel eyes boring into me as she twirled a curl around a finger. She held firmly onto Elm's arm, and was surrounded by a puffy blue gown – was this the image I'd seen in my dream? Elm looked lustfully at my sister before turning towards me. The scar on the golden skin of his cheek caught the light as he leered at me, his yellow eyes glinting as his free hand fiddled with the hilt of his sword.

Now I was the one clenching my fists.

'Then you've been lied to,' I said, unable to contain the venom in my voice.

Emperor Xanthos raised an eyebrow. 'Don't be ridiculous, Lady Merciless. The King of Aerba and Mistress of Iolite are here to heal the Vortex, restart it for the good of all six Lands.'

'They've lied to you,' Rian said, glaring at Chervil. 'They're here to destroy it and take control in the chaos that follows.'

Chervil just smiled at Rian and adjusted the sleeve of his coat.

'Strange, that's what they said you'd say,' Xanthos said, tapping a finger on his throne. 'However, I think the word of the King of Aerba and Mistress of Iolite has more weight than that of a prince who has committed regicide, and an assassin guilty of murdering a Crown Princess, don't you?'

Hell's teeth.

'We didn't do either of those things,' I said, my jaw set.

'I'm afraid your reputation precedes you, Lady Merciless.'

Carnelian grinned. I really wanted to wipe that smile off his face.

I locked eyes with Beryl. Her head was tilted to one side as she looked up at me, her white-blonde curls swinging gently as her hazel eyes hardened. To think we'd once been the greatest of friends and confidantes – or at least that's what I'd thought. Her betrayal still tore at my heart.

Mal moved a fraction beside me, but I flung my arm out in front of him before he could do anything. Beryl smiled back at us, a vicious, nasty smile that, rather than chill my bones, made my blood boil.

'That's not my name,' I said. 'My name is Samphire.'

Xanthos waved his hand dismissively. 'I don't care what you want to call yourself. What I *do* care about is the safety of my land. The Crystal Vortex needs to be restarted. As enemies of Chroma you will be cast into the dungeon until the Vortex has been healed. Then I will decide what to do with you all. I know of your Elemental Angle Spinning abilities and I wouldn't want any of you to get ideas about escaping, so we will take this one as insurance against you trying anything *unwise.*' He signalled to the palace guards, and one of them took hold of Willow and pulled her across towards Juniper, holding a knife at her throat. She started coughing.

'No!' Tarragon lunged after her before stopping abruptly, a sword at his chest.

'If you try anything, she will die,' Xanthos said.

'We need a Waker to save the Vortex, and she will be it,' Juniper said, her yellow eyes sparkling in the light.

Did this mean Carnelian and Topaz weren't Wakers? Or did she just want a spare in case something went wrong?

Willow took a deep breath in an attempt to control her coughing, probably brought on by the tense situation.

'I can't do anything,' Willow said, shaking her head. 'Not all Middle Bloods are Wakers. I've already tried.'

Tarragon half raised an eyebrow in surprise.

'It's true,' I said. 'I was with her when she tried. Nothing happened.'

'Looks like it's down to you after all, Carnelian,' Juniper said. 'But the Emperor will keep the girl as hostage to make sure the rest of you don't try to escape and interfere.'

Tarragon's face was puce red, a vein throbbing in his neck. His body was actually shaking, and for a moment I thought he might explode, or at the very least flood the place.

'Bobbins. I'll be fine, Tarragon,' Willow said, staring into his eyes, stifling a cough.

'You better be,' he said. I'd never seen Tarragon like this before – so fired up. His love for Willow was as strong as Rian's for me.

'It's all right,' Willow said, shaking her head at Tarragon.

'No, it's not,' Tarragon said. He looked over at the Emperor. 'If you harm her…'

'You'll what? You're in no position to make threats, young man,' Xanthos said.

Tarragon glanced back to Willow. The distress in his eyes would've melted the hardest heart.

'Now, the rest of you will go to the dungeon until I am ready to decide your fates,' Xanthos said, gesturing to his men.

'You're making a big mistake,' Rian said.

'Shut up, Valerian,' Chervil snapped, taking a step forward.

Xanthos raised his hand.

Chervil hesitated as the Emperor narrowed his eyes.

'I think you're the one who has made the mistake, Prince Valerian,' Xanthos said.

I glared at Juniper as soldiers led us towards the door. She smiled her serpent's smile, her yellow eyes drilling into me. Her hand went subconsciously to her necklace, which she absently toyed with, as her long, blonde hair cascaded over the golden skin of her shoulder.

Sage glanced back at the side table. His earring jingled. He spoke in a low voice. 'Did you see—'

'I saw it,' Rian murmured as we reached the doors, his jaw set.

'If Your Imperial Majesty will allow, I'd like to escort them down, just to make sure they cause no trouble,' Chervil said from behind us.

'Of course,' Xanthos said.

Chervil and Carnelian followed the soldiers as they marched us out of the Throne Room and away to the far side of the palace, down two sets of stairs and into the dim passageways of the palace dungeon.

'I was surprised to hear you were still alive, Lady Merciless,' Chervil said, smoothing his short goatee.

'Revenge is a powerful motivator,' I said, glowering at him.

'Still in love with her, Little Brother?'

Rian didn't answer, just looked straight ahead as we walked.

Chervil chuckled, swishing his black hair in its high Aerban ponytail. He was three years older than Rian but never acted it. 'I'll take that as a *yes*. I thought you might have tired of her by now.'

Rian still didn't reply.

'Maybe it is love, after all, and not an enchantment,' Chervil continued.

'And what do you know of love?' Rian asked, contempt thick in his voice.

'I know what love is.'

'You know what power is, what control is, but not love.'

Chervil snorted. 'Shut up, Valerian. You don't know what you're talking about. Love, power, control, it's all the same.'

Rian shook his head. 'No, it's not. It's not even close.'

Chervil laughed. 'You really are beguiled, aren't you?'

'No, I'm not.'

We entered a corridor with cells on one side, their bars fronting the passageway. Sunlight shone down into the cells from grated windows that lined the top of the outside wall, providing a view out to the palace stable yard.

Tarragon was forced into the first cell and a soldier locked the door. The key grated in the rusty mechanism, making me wince. Anise and Sage were pushed into the second, and Mal and Onyx in the fourth at the end. We were to be put into the third.

Carnelian opened the metal door. It creaked, setting my teeth on edge as we stopped.

'You know, you've been a thorn in my side since you set foot in Aerba, Lady Merciless,' Chervil said, fidgeting with his cuff.

I turned.

'You've destroyed my family, set my little brother against me and angered the people with your devious, underhanded tricks.'

'And I thought you were the one being devious – setting Aerba against Flos for no reason other than your own desire to rule,' I said.

Chervil shook his head. 'All lies—'

'I overheard Sorrel and Monkshood – it's not a lie.'

The King of Aerba tensed, his brown eyes narrowing. He slowly pulled out a small push dagger from his robes. Little red spinel stones covered the hilt, catching the light even down here.

'Pretty, isn't it?' Chervil said, inspecting it. 'You recognise it, of course, Valerian?'

Rian stiffened.

'It's actually an Artefact,' Chervil continued. 'One for Fire Spinners, like me.'

'You're a Fire Spinner?' Rian asked.

Chervil smiled. 'Quite a good one, actually. I tried it on a town back in Aerba once. They blamed it on a lightning storm, but it wasn't. I was practising.'

An Aerban town? A lightning storm? No.

'Fennel,' Rian hissed. 'You set light to Fennel?'

Chervil raised an eyebrow. 'You know about the fire there?'

'We arrived after you'd started it.'

'I was quite impressed with myself. I'd had no idea I might be able to do something as magnificent as that. Until Juniper told me, that is.'

A bitter chill slammed into my chest. How long had this web of lies and deceit been going on? Well before any of us had known anything about it.

'You murdered innocent people,' Rian said. '*Our* people.'

'All for a good cause.' He looked up at me as he drew himself to his full height, trying to make himself look taller.

'You bastard,' I said, shaking my head in disbelief.

'Then you came along and almost spoiled everything, Lady Merciless. Well, no more.'

The blade flashed in the dim light.

'No!' Rian stepped in front of me.

The small Spinel Dagger slid into his chest.

Rian cried out.

I screamed, catching him from behind as he staggered backwards into the open cell. I fell backwards under his weight, breaking his fall.

I couldn't breathe – was this what I'd dreamt? Nothing to do with the Cave of Crystals at all? A red spinel dagger? An Artefact? It couldn't be, could it?

I'd failed Rian.

Completely.

Chervil snarled, his blade dripping scarlet in the light. 'That wasn't meant for you, Brother. But I suppose it will have to do.' He turned on his heel and left with the guards.

Carnelian chuckled, slamming the door shut. The key shrieked in the lock, the sound echoing shrilly inside my head.

CHAPTER TWENTY-FIVE

'You're a bastard, Chervil!' I shouted after him, holding onto Rian who writhed in pain, clutching at his chest wound. 'I've got you, my love,' I whispered to him.

I pulled Rian up to lean against me, and I wrapped my arms around him, straining to get a good look at his wound over his shoulder.

'Phire? What happened?' Tarragon called.

I swallowed, looking at the blood seeping out between Rian's fingers where he clutched at his wound. I pressed my hand over his. He gasped.

No.

This wasn't right.

My dream had been nothing like this.

'Chervil stabbed Rian,' I said.

'Is he all right?' Anise asked from the next cell.

I didn't know.

The light in the cell was dim, but enough came in at the grate near the ceiling to tell me that no, Rian was not all right. He lay in my arms, groaning in pain as his life blood left his body.

Not like this. I couldn't lose him like this.

'Stay with me, Rian,' I said, struggling to keep my voice steady as I pressed on his hands, on the wound, trying to stem the blood flow.

'If—if this is it, I… I… y—you need to know how much I love you,' he said, his voice halting, breaking. 'Y—you changed my life, m—made me whole. I love you with all my heart and I wouldn't change a thing, even this.'

'Shh, save your strength,' I murmured, pressing down onto the wound in a futile attempt to stop the bleeding. My skin quickly became sticky and warm with blood. My husband's blood. His tense body shook with the pain, his rapid heartbeat thudding, stuttering through his chest and into my body.

'Phire?' Anise's voice drifted into the cell.

'It's bad,' I replied. I didn't know what else to say, other than *Rian's lying in my arms, dying, and there's not a cat in hell's chance of me doing anything about it.*

'Try and stop the blood. That's all you can do,' Mal said from next door, his voice tense.

I needed Anise. I needed his Earth Magic, but he was in the next cell and might as well have been back in Aerba.

I needed him – or did I?

This was a wound caused by a Magical Artefact. Quintessence couldn't heal regular injuries – that was the domain of Earth Magic – but could it heal this Magical wound?

It was supposed to be the purest of all Magic. The strongest.

I had to try.

'Just lay still,' I said to my groaning husband.

'W—what?' Rian's voice was thin with pain. His eyelids flickered. Closed. Each breath he took was like a gust of wind going through a copse of trees as his body shuddered. He flinched as a wave of pain rolled through him. To me, this was worse than the poison had been. He gasped, his breaths coming quicker. I could feel his heartbeat – fast, erratic. He was slipping from me. If I was going to do something, I had to act now.

'Stay with me, Rian. Just hold on a few seconds more,' I said, wrapping both my arms under his, moving his hands and resting mine over his gaping, bloody wound.

He came to for a moment. 'You can do this,' he whispered in a raspy voice. 'I know you ca… I lov…'

He went limp. Heartbeat faltering. Breathing shallow – *was* he even still breathing?

I swallowed. 'I love you, husband.'

Heal. Please heal.

I concentrated on the thought, willing Rian's wound to stop its profuse bleeding. His body to knit back together.

Heal.

A white glow began at my fingertips. It spread until both my hands were glowing.

The light moved from my hands to Rian's chest until his torso was covered in white light. I focused on his wound, concentrated on it healing, on him getting better, being healthier than ever.

He tensed.

Groaned.

He gasped in a shuddering lungful of air. Started to take deep breaths. His eyes snapped open. His heartbeat steadied and his body relaxed.

I released my concentration.

'Th—thank you,' he murmured as he watched the glow subside. After a few moments he sat up, looking at his healed chest.

My shoulders sagged. Using the Quintessence had drained me. My muscles ached, my energy sapped. That had taken more from me than I'd expected – or had I just given more because it was Rian?

'That's amazing. I feel amazing.' He turned and looked at me, wiping his bloodied hands on his clothes.

'It was a Magical wound – if it hadn't been...' I couldn't finish my sentence. I swallowed, wiping my hands on my britches. 'Why did you do that?' I asked, tears in my eyes. 'You almost died.'

'I vowed to protect you,' he said sheepishly, kneeling on the floor in front of me. 'I stand by that vow. And there was also the fact that the dagger was an Artefact. Magical. I couldn't have healed you, but there was a chance you could heal me.'

My eyes widened. 'You stepped in the way on a *hunch*?'

He shrugged. 'For you, I always will, no matter the cost.'

I sniffed. 'That cost was very nearly too high.'

'I had to do it. Because I love you,' he said, reaching out and cupping my face in his hands.

'I almost lost you,' I said softly. 'I truly understand now. How you felt when I fell off that cliff. Between this and your poisoning, I at least have an idea of what you went through on Trew.'

'And on the archipelago,' he murmured. His shoulders slumped. 'I'm sorry.'

'D—do you think we love each other too much?' I asked, fearing the answer.

He looked up, smiling, shaking his head. 'No, wife, I don't. It's just when you love someone as much, as strongly, as we love each other, the risk is that much greater.'

I nodded. 'But it's so worth it,' I said, pulling him to me. Our kiss was salty and wet, but also warm. He gently ran his fingers through my hair as I clung onto him. 'I... I don't want you dying for me.'

'I wouldn't want to live without you. I've learnt that much.'

'And I wouldn't want to live without you, either – don't you see that? I couldn't bear it.'

'I'll try and make sure we get stabbed together next time, then,' he said, grinning, breaking the intensity of the moment.

I sighed. 'That's not quite what I—'

'Phire! What's happening?' Sage shouted impatiently.

'Everything's fine,' Rian said loudly, looking into my eyes. 'I'm all right.'

A sigh of relief sounded from further down the passageway.

Rian smiled at me. 'We're fine,' he said, his lips skimming mine, then kissing me again. 'Aren't we?'

I nodded, wiping a stray tear from my eye.

He frowned at me. 'You look tired.'

'Using the Magic has worn me out,' I said.

'You probably used more than you needed. I don't think I'll need to sleep for a week, from the way I feel.'

I gave him a wan little smile. 'I'd use all my Magic to save you.'

'I know,' he said. 'Just don't let that be your undoing. Now, come here,' he said, sitting against the wall and pulling me to him. I leant against him, glad of his Fire Magic to soothe my aching body.

Only then did I notice my sword and shield resting against the wall opposite our cell. That explained why they hadn't come to me. Topaz's knife was still in my boot, but that would be of no use at the moment. We sat in silence, listening to far-off sounds of doors banging, water dripping and the odd yell. I shivered.

'What do you think's going to happen to us?' I asked.

He shrugged. 'I don't know. But whatever it is, it'll be in Juniper's best interests, not ours.'

I snuggled against him, hoping I'd be able to regain some strength before Xanthos decided what to do with us.

'Will I have a scar?' Rian asked suddenly.

'I don't know,' I said. 'You're alive. That's what matters.'

His lips brushed my ear. 'I thought you might be able to kiss it better if I did, like I did yours.'

I rolled my eyes to the ceiling. 'You almost died, we're imprisoned, running out of time to save the Vortex and that's what you're thinking about?'

He curled one side of his lips up into a little mischievous smile. 'Can't help it. It's something you do to me.'

I shook my head, suppressing a smile. 'Hmm, you do it to me, too.'

We sat on the cold stone floor in each other's arms, Rian keeping me warm, as the day wore on. The light faded and night filled the dungeon. Pitch torches were lit in the corridor and a meagre meal of dried bread and hard cheese delivered to our cells, along with mugs of water.

'You think it's safe?' Onyx said from the cell beside us.

'If they wanted to kill us they'd have done it already,' Mal replied.

Onyx grunted.

'He's right,' Tarragon said. 'But it doesn't taste good.'

The evening wore on.

'We need Willow to get us out with her lock picks,' Sage said.

'They were the first thing they took from her,' Tarragon rumbled. 'She won't be coming to get us.'

I glanced at Rian. Their forced separation must have been driving Willow and Tarragon mad. Rian's eyes glimmered with the same thoughts.

'I wonder what they're doing to her,' Tarragon said.

'They won't hurt her, they need her for leverage,' Mal said.

'Mal's right,' I said. 'The moment they do anything to hurt her they know we'll come at them, and they won't dare do that.'

Onyx sniffed. 'Not until they've destroyed the Vortex, at any rate. Ow! What was that for?'

'Don't say that to him,' Mal hissed.

'Sorry,' Onyx said.

But he was right.

'Then we have to get out as soon as they leave,' I said. 'Then we go after them.'

'But how long will that be?' Tarragon asked, his voice strained. 'I can't bear to be away from her like this.'

I glanced at Rian. We both knew Tarragon's pain.

'She's strong, Tarragon, she'll be all right,' Rian said.

A sigh came from down the corridor. 'I seem to remember saying something similar to you a few weeks ago,' Tarragon said.

Rian gazed into my eyes. 'And you were right,' he said, burying his face in the crook of my neck, planting a little kiss there. He lifted his head. 'She'll be all right. We'll free her, don't worry.'

Footsteps echoed down the passageway. *Now what?*

Rian didn't move and I stayed in his arms, waiting to see who it was. The golden flicker of torchlight illuminated the corridor outside our cells. The footsteps came closer.

'The two of you have more lives than a cat,' Carnelian said, stepping into the light outside our cell, holding a torch.

'What do you want?' I asked, glaring at him.

'Oh, don't be like that, Amethyst–sweetie.'

'Then let us out.'

'You know I can't do that.'

'Then go away.'

'But we've so much to talk about.'

'Like what?' Mal asked.

'I'm sorry about what happened to you, Malachite,' Carnelian said, turning his attention to the next cell. 'I did try to stop Juniper from fiddling with your mind with that diamond necklace of hers, but she wouldn't listen.'

'What?' I sat bolt upright.

'I don't remember that,' Mal said.

'By the Stars, I'll kill her,' Onyx said.

'I told her she'd regret doing it, but she refused to listen and almost killed herself using her Artefact,' Carnelian said, shaking his head. 'Turns out, doing that to someone's mind takes a lot of energy.'

'I wish she had died,' Mal muttered.

'Still, look on the bright side, everything's fine now.'

'We're in a dungeon, Carnelian. It's hardly fine.'

Carnelian shrugged and turned to Rian. 'Sorry about your sister and father. Orders – you know how it is.'

Rian tensed slightly. 'No, I don't.'

'I know Lord Wintergreen arranged the commissions, and we were happy to take his money, but someone had actually already got there first,' Carnelian said, a glint in his eye.

'Really? Someone had already arranged Angelica and the King's deaths?' Sage asked, surprise in his voice.

'Angelica's, Finule's, and yours, too, Valerian, to be done over a period of time.'

I swallowed.

'Who?' Rian demanded, sitting up.

'I don't want to spoil things for you,' Carnelian smiled.

Rian got to his feet and went over to the bars of our cell, grasping hold of them. 'Who?'

CHAPTER TWENTY-SIX

'Oh, all right, you've twisted my arm.' Carnelian grinned. 'Chervil.'

Rian's body trembled at the news, but whether from shock or anger, I wasn't sure.

I got to my feet and stood beside Rian, resting an arm on his back. 'Chervil arranged it all?'

'He arranged things first, then Wintergreen's commission came in to kill Angelica, Finule and Chervil. It was all rather laughable, actually.'

'I thought Beryl wanted Rian dead,' Onyx said.

'She did,' Carnelian said. 'So did Juniper. They wanted Rian and Amethyst dead.'

'Is there anyone they didn't want to kill?' I asked sullenly.

'Not really. Still, going to Aerba to kill Angelica gave me the opportunity to steal the Fire Opal.'

'That was you, too?' I asked. 'Why did you do it?'

'I was asked to.'

'Who wanted it?' Rian asked, his voice grim. 'By the Herbs, who wanted it?'

'The Emperor of Chroma. He asked me to steal it – the money was good, and I was going to Viridi to kill Angelica anyway, so it seemed quite a good deal. Amethyst couldn't be trusted to kill anyone, and Juniper had already imprisoned Malachite. I was the obvious choice for the mission, and the Fire Opal was just a bonus.'

Rian looked as though he wanted to break down the bars and strangle Carnelian, but I didn't think even his Magic could do that.

'You evil bastard,' Sage said, the sound of rattling bars echoing down the corridor.

'The Fire Opal is Aerba's,' Rian said, teeth gritted.

'You really care so much about a rock?' Carnelian asked.

'It's part of our heritage. Our history.' Rian shook with anger. I knew how much the Fire Opal meant to him, how much Aerba and its people meant to him. '*My* history,' he said through gritted teeth.

I glared at Carnelian. 'When did you become a common thief?'

Carnelian laughed. 'I like to freelance from time to time – I'm actually quite a good thief, if I say so myself. And the extra money's handy – Topaz has expensive tastes. Still, killing Angelica and stealing the Fire Opal in one night just before you arrived at the Viridi Palace was quite a challenge,' he said. 'And a joy. And so was setting up the trail for Valerian to follow.'

'You've told them enough, Carnelian.'

A voice I recognised only too well rang out along the passageway. Footsteps sounded before Beryl appeared in the flickering light.

'Brother, Sister,' she said, inclining her head towards Mal then me. 'I heard you were dead, Amethyst.'

'I heard you were a bitch,' Onyx muttered.

'Rumours can be exaggerated,' I said, my hand instinctively going to my stomach.

'Go away, traitor,' Mal said.

She pouted. 'That's no way to speak to your little sister.'

'He's right, though,' I said. 'Just leave, Beryl.'

'But this is supposed to be a happy family reunion.'

'By the Stars, the only blood family I have now is Samphire,' Mal said.

I started. That was the first time he'd ever called me that.

Beryl raised an eyebrow. 'You're calling her that, too? Do you want a new name as well, Brother? An Aerban one, perhaps? What about Mugwort?'

'Shut it, Beryl,' Onyx spat.

'Leave him alone,' I said as Rian let go of the bars and took a step back, his hands in fists, muscles strained.

Beryl tilted her head. 'You still with her, Prince Valerian?'

'As you can see,' Rian said, his jaw set.

'She's never been much to look at, with that shock of red hair and hideous coloured eyes.' Beryl smiled sweetly at me.

'She's beautiful,' Rian said, slipping his arm around my shoulders, 'and kind, which is more than I can say for you, on either count.'

Beryl's smile slipped from her face. 'I'll pretend I didn't hear that.'

'It's true, though, she's always been kinder than you,' Mal said.

She turned sharply towards him. 'You taking sides, Brother? You always did like her more than me.'

'That's not true. I treated you both the same.'

'No, I always knew you loved *her* more than me.'

'That's ridiculous – although it's true now.'

Beryl glared at him. 'You were all the same, preferring Amethyst to me – that's why I asked to join the Coterie.'

'You asked?' Mal's voice was full of disbelief.

'It was the only way to get what I wanted.'

'And what was that, exactly?'

'Iolite – and revenge.'

I laughed scornfully. 'And how would you get Iolite?'

'Join Juniper, kill Father, get rid of you and Malachite.'

'You're delusional.'

'I think it's all worked out quite well. Mother will now leave everything to me, and my husband, Elm, in due course. We'll rule the Six Lands together – well, I'll rule and he'll do as I say.'

Carnelian chuckled.

I almost choked as she once again referred to Juniper as "Mother". Mal made a strangled sound from the next cell. He hadn't heard her refer to our step-mother like this before.

'You really think Elm will do as you say?' I asked.

'I know he will. After all, Mother did.'

'What do you mean?' I asked.

'She agreed that killing Father was a good idea.'

I grabbed the bars, swearing at my sister in disbelief.

'It was *your* idea to kill Father?' Mal asked, his voice scarily quiet with anger.

Beryl grinned, twirling her hair around her finger. 'Yes.'

I clenched my teeth. 'I thought Juniper killed him because she wanted control of Iolite, and so she could keep the Coterie going after Father found out and told her to stop.'

'Well,' Beryl said, 'Mother was happy to go along with my idea for those reasons, yes.'

'So you got her to kill Father?'

Beryl frowned. 'No. Of course not. I did it.'

For a moment complete silence enveloped us like cotton wool.

Mal swore.

Onyx choked.

My heart stuttered. '*You* did it?' My knuckles went white as I held the bars, and Rian slipped his arms around my waist. 'You cold-hearted bitch.'

Beryl smiled again. 'Mother provided the poison, but I administered it. She really is quite wonderful.'

'She's not our mother!' I hissed at her.

'Blast it! She's nothing like Mother,' Mal said. I could just see his hand gripping the bars like mine. 'Nothing like her at all.'

Beryl shrugged. 'Our mother was weak. Juniper is strong.'

I shook my head. 'You have absolutely no idea what you're talking about.'

'Mother was far stronger than Juniper,' Mal said.

'Whatever, I don't really care,' Beryl said, going back to twirling her hair. 'Our mother's dead. Juniper is alive. Those are the facts.'

'Well, good luck to you and your new husband,' Onyx said. 'He's going to need it.'

'What's that supposed to mean?'

'One day he might wake up and realise what he's married.'

'Unlikely. He loves me.'

'Loves you?' Mal laughed. 'You're just using each other to get what you want, strengthen your claims to Iolite.'

'Iolite belongs to Mal, not you, Beryl,' I said. 'He should be Master now.'

I felt Rian's grip on me tighten. He knew it was true. Mal should be Master of Iolite.

'But he's not, is he?' Beryl purred. 'And one day I'll be Mistress.'

'And one day Elm will get bored of you, once he's Master, and he'll throw you out of Iolite,' I said. 'Even he has his limits.'

Beryl's face rapidly turned red. 'Quiet, Amethyst. Anyway, it doesn't matter, he's mine.'

'But for how long?' I asked.

'Don't listen to them,' Carnelian said, obviously amused by the whole thing. 'They're trying to wind you up.'

From the look on Beryl's face, Mal and I had succeeded.

'Come on, let's go,' Beryl said, flicking her hair. 'We've got an early start tomorrow, and we haven't eaten yet.' She turned back to us. 'This is all your fault, both of you. If you'd treated me properly I never would have felt the need to kill Father and take your place, Mal.'

'Treated you properly?' I gasped.

'Yes. Put me first. I was the youngest.'

'By mere minutes.'

Beryl ignored me. 'It was only right, but you didn't – none of you did, and now you're all paying for your misdemeanours. Enjoy your time here, both of you.' She stormed off down the corridor with Carnelian in tow.

'Hope you choke on your meal!' Onyx called after them.

I let go of the bars, suddenly overcome with shivering. The revelations were on the verge of overwhelming me. I looked at Rian. His eyes were full of horror. His brother had arranged to have him murdered even before I'd arrived in Viridi City. Beryl and Juniper wanted him dead. My own sister had asked to join the Coterie and had murdered my Father.

'Don't take any notice of her. None of this is your fault, Mal, or yours, Ama,' Onyx said. 'She made her own decisions, not you two, and not your father.'

'He's right, Phire, this wasn't us,' Mal said. 'It was all Beryl. I just wish we'd seen it sooner.'

Breathing was suddenly difficult, and I started gasping for air. I couldn't get it into my lungs quickly enough. The walls of the cell started closing in on me. Nausea gripped me, and my pulse thundered like an Iolitian folk drum in my ears.

'Hey, I've got you,' Rian said, grabbing me before I could fall. 'Deep breaths. Take slow, deep breaths. In through your nose, out through your mouth.'

'I—I can't,' I said, shaking as the panic gripped me.

'Yes, you can. Come on. Slowly in through your nose, and slowly out through your mouth. In through your nose, out through your mouth.' He held me in his arms, holding me to him as I tried to follow his instructions.

'Is she all right, Rian?' Mal asked.

'She will be,' Rian said. 'It's all been a bit much.'

'You can say that again,' Sage said.

'Keep going,' Rian said, urging me to continue as the overwhelming sensations began to very slowly ease.

'How could she do that? Kill your own father?' Onyx asked.

My breathing faltered at his words.

'I don't know,' Mal said, his voice broken.

'Concentrate,' Rian said, holding my face in his hands. 'Look at me – don't listen to them, just to me. Breathe in, breathe out. In… out…'

I gradually took control of my breathing again. The walls returned to their proper places and the nausea receded, but the shaking continued.

'I'm sorry,' I whispered as we sat down.

'Don't be,' he murmured back. 'It's all been a shock for all of us.'

Silent tears began to run unchecked down my cheeks. Rian tenderly brushed them away, but there were too many, and I buried my face in his chest, sobbing quietly.

'What can I do?' he asked, his voice breaking.

'Just hold me,' I said.

He held me closer, his warmth nourishing me, sandalwood slowly calming my soul.

'I will kill her before this is over,' Mal was saying.

'Who? Juniper or Beryl?' Onyx asked.

'Both of them.'

'If there's a queue, can I join?'

'I don't think there'll be a need for a queue. I intend to finish those two myself,' Mal said grimly. 'But you can stay in the queue for Carnelian.'

'I really think you should reconsider and let me help – why should you have all the fun?' Onyx moaned.

'If you insist.'

'I do.'

'I can't believe Chervil was trying to have Rian killed,' Sage said.

'I can,' Anise said.

'But the King and Crown Princess, too?' Sage asked.

'He's always craved power, y'know that,' Tarragon said.

'Yes, but to commission the Coterie to kill three members of your own family… Really?'

'It's Chervil all over,' Tarragon said.

Silence fell for a moment.

'Are you two all right in there?' Anise asked.

I looked up into Rian's face. His expression was one of anger and sadness, his eyes glistening with unshed tears. His brother had wanted to have him assassinated. A few hours ago, Chervil had almost killed him – admittedly by accident as he'd tried to kill me. This had become even more personal for Rian. He looked at me, took my hand and kissed it.

'We're all right,' Rian said. 'Aren't we?'

I nodded. 'As long as we're together we can take on the whole world of Elvedon.'

CHAPTER TWENTY-SEVEN

I rubbed an itch on my forehead. 'At least Beryl let slip one useful piece of information,' I said.

'What was that?' Rian asked.

'They're leaving early tomorrow morning. Once they've left we can make our move and rescue Willow.'

'Unless they decide to take her with them,' Tarragon said mournfully.

'Let's hope they don't,' Sage said.

'Why would they?' Anise asked. 'She's of no use to them, they've got Carnelian.'

It was a long night, and I barely slept. Rian nodded off a couple of times, but I don't think any of us rested particularly well. Shortly after dawn, a commotion out in the stable yard made me stir.

'What's going on?' Tarragon asked anxiously. 'I can't see.'

'Climb on,' Rian said, getting to his feet then crouching down.

'What?' I looked at him.

'Get on my shoulders – you'll be high enough to see out the grating.'

'I'm too heavy for you.'

'Are you saying I'm not strong enough?'

'No, but—'

'Get on.'

I scrambled up, climbing onto his broad shoulders. He stood up, lifting me with ease. Maybe I wasn't as heavy as I thought – or he was just very strong. I gently held on to the top of his head to keep my balance and looked out the grating. I could see horses' legs, people's legs – stable boys? Further away, a group of people were approaching, dressed in fine clothes. Juniper and Chervil. Beryl and Elm were with them, Carnelian and Topaz walking behind. They were talking, but they were too far away for me to hear what they said. I relayed the information to the others.

'Anyone else?' Tarragon asked, voice tense. 'Is Willow there with them?'

'No, she's not… Wait,' I squinted, trying to see as a small group of soldiers came out escorting someone. Yes, she was there, and she didn't look happy. Her hands were bound in front of her and she had a dark scowl on her face. She was hoisted up onto a horse and Carnelian got up behind her. 'Yes, she's with them.'

'Bugger.'

'Damn, is she all right?' Rian asked.

'She doesn't look particularly happy about things, but she doesn't look harmed in any way,' I said.

Tarragon let out a long sigh.

Emperor Xanthos appeared in the yard. From his clothes, he wasn't going anywhere – was he really trusting them to restart the Vortex without him there? Then a rumbling filled the air and a carriage appeared. Maybe he was going after all. He climbed in, and with half a dozen soldiers surrounding him, they set off.

Rian ducked down and I climbed off, reporting the details.

'Let's go,' Tarragon said.

'No, we have to wait until they're far enough ahead,' Rian said. 'If not, it'll put her in danger.'

'More danger, you mean,' Sage said sourly.

'Give it half an hour and we'll make our move,' I said.

'What are you planning?' Mal asked.

'We'll get out and follow them to the Crystal Cave.'

'You know where it is?'

'We can track them. We have one of the best trackers alive with us.'

Rian looked at me. 'Who?'

'Me,' Onyx said in a smug voice.

'It pains me to say so, but it's true,' Mal said. 'He once tracked a dog all the way across Iolite.'

'Why?' Anise asked.

'It stole my dinner,' Onyx said. 'They've got a carriage with them. This will be easy in comparison.'

'Let's hope so,' Tarragon said.

That half hour was the longest of my life. Patience wasn't my thing. Although being an assassin had meant learning to wait, I'd always found it incredibly hard. I liked to get on with things.

'You ready?' Rian asked eventually.

I nodded. 'How are we going to get out? We don't want to set fire to everything.'

'I've an idea about that, Phire,' Anise said.

'You do?' Sage asked. 'You haven't said anything.'

'That's because I wasn't sure, but I am now.'

'And?'

'I'm going to do this.'

'Just don't be too enthusiastic – anyone – we won't be able to rest once we get out,' Rian said, a warning note in his voice.

'This doesn't take much effort,' Anise said.

'What doesn't?' Sage asked. 'Oh. That's impressive, Anise.'

'I thought so.'

'I knew I loved you, but didn't realise quite how much.'

Anise and Sage appeared outside our cell.

Rian raised an eyebrow. 'How did you…?'

'Like this,' Anise said. He took hold of the barred door and closed his eyes. Suddenly the metal bars disintegrated into dust.

'Hell's teeth,' I said, awed.

Anise shrugged and grinned. 'Earth Magic. I just reduced it to its smaller parts.'

Rian looked at me wide-eyed as Anise moved on to Mal and Onyx, before releasing Tarragon. Sage glanced at us, shrugged, and grinned proudly.

I looked over towards the crystal weapons. Might as well let them attach themselves. We quietly headed for the end of the passageway and peered out into the next corridor. It was empty.

'Let's go,' Rian said.

'Which way? We don't want to end up in the Throne Room again,' Tarragon said.

'We'll find someone and ask,' Onyx said.

'We'll what?' Sage asked, eyes wide.

'You heard.'

'Make sure you ask nicely,' I said. 'The screams will echo down here.'

'Yes, Ama.' Onyx grinned at me, then led the way down the passage. As we hurried along, Deorwine and Glædwine joined me.

Mal swore. 'I'm never going to get used to that,' he murmured.

'You will,' Rian said.

We carried on along the passageway, ducking into a side room as two guards patrolled. I glanced at the wall: a small bunch of keys rested on a hook. They might be useful. We waited until the guards had gone by. Just as we were about to step out, another guard appeared out of a side passage.

'I think that's your man,' I whispered in Onyx's ear, my heart beating rapidly as we watched the guard move towards us.

He nodded.

As the guard got level with us, Onyx stepped out and grabbed him, pulling him into the side room, his hand firmly over the man's mouth to stop him from calling for help. He grabbed a knife from the guard's belt and held it at his throat. The man looked at Onyx, wide-eyed.

'I'll slit your throat unless you answer my questions, understand?' Onyx said menacingly.

The man nodded mutely.

'How do we get out?' Onyx asked.

The man pointed towards the way we'd come.

'There must be another way,' Onyx pressed. 'A back entrance, secret tunnel.'

The man swallowed. Nodded. Then pointed the other way.

'There's a small passageway,' he rasped. 'Takes you out beyond the city to the forest above the main road.'

'Does this road lead to the Crystal Cave?' I asked.

The man looked horrified. 'I can't tell you that.'

'But you will,' Onyx said, tightening his grip on the guard's knife and holding it firmly against his throat. 'Does it?'

The man swallowed as best he could. 'Yes, but you need to take the first track north after you've followed the road through the forest for a while. If you leave the trees behind, you've gone too far.'

Onyx nodded. 'If I find you've lied, I'll come back and kill you.' He hit the man on the head with the hilt of the knife.

Mal caught the unconscious guard, and he and Onyx lowered him gently to the ground as Rian relieved him of his sword and another knife, passing it to Tarragon.

'You get worse with age,' Mal said, looking proudly at Onyx.

Onyx grinned. 'That's why you love me.'

Mal nodded, grabbed Onyx's tunic and pulled him towards him, kissing him soundly on the lips.

I rolled my eyes, looking at the ceiling. 'There's no time for that.'

Mal beamed at me. 'There's always time for *that*.'

'See what I've had to put up with all these years?' I said to Rian, giving him a long-suffering look.

He grinned back at me. 'And now you've got me.'

I frowned. 'Not sure that's entirely an improvement.'

He glanced at Mal, then followed his lead, kissing me on the lips, lingering to make his point.

'Surely *that's* an improvement,' Rian said.

Blood rushed to my face. 'Maybe,' I murmured.

'There really isn't time for any of this dithering,' Sage said, peering out into the passageway. 'Come on, the way's clear.'

We left the unconscious guard, closed the door behind us, and moved on, heading into the side passageway the guard had spoken of. Unlit torches lined the dark and narrow corridor, and Rian quickly lit two of them to illuminate our path. The passage took us down a short set of steps and on for some distance.

A bell rang far off, back in the dungeons.

'They know,' Mal said.

We increased our speed. By the Stars, I hoped the guard was right about this.

Finally, having passed a number of side passageways and store rooms, we reached the end of the long tunnel. A large door blocked our way. Halfway up the door a small peephole let in a shaft of light. I peered through it.

'We're out of the palace and the city,' I said. 'It looks like open countryside, a forest like the guard said.'

Tarragon took hold of the handle and turned it. It screeched, making my hair stand on end.

'Locked,' he said.

'Anise?' Rian said. 'Can you do something about this?'

'If we disintegrate the door they'll know we've gone this way,' Onyx said.

'Then let's see if one of these work,' I said, producing the bunch of keys and starting to work my way through them.

'Where did you get those from?' Mal asked.

'That side room we hid in.'

'Always keep your valuables hidden when my sister is about.'

'I've never stolen anything in my life.'

'What do you call this?'

'Borrowing.'

One of the keys turned. I grinned at my brother. He shook his head, and gave me a disapproving look.

The door creaked open – obviously seldom used. It took a moment for our eyes to adjust to the bright light, but once they did, I took in a forest of mostly dead trees that extended before us.

As we stepped out, I glanced at Rian. Only now did I realise the full extent of his blood loss from the day before. Black, dried blood covered the front of his tunic. If I'd known at the time how much he'd lost I might not have been able to do what I did. Thank the Stars I hadn't realised. I looked at my hands. They weren't much better, and neither were Rian's, despite the fact we'd both tried to clean them. He saw where I was looking.

'We'll find a stream,' he said, his face going slightly pale as he also realised the significance of what he was seeing. So did the others.

'I didn't realise it was that bad,' Tarragon said quietly. 'I thought it was just a little flesh wound.'

'It wasn't,' I said, trying to push the awful memories aside.

Rian shrugged. 'I'm fine now.'

'You were lucky you were with a Quintessence Spinner and Chervil's knife was an Artefact,' Tarragon said.

'I'm very lucky,' Rian said, gazing at me.

I smiled back, but a little shiver swept down my spine.

'Let's get this door locked and move on,' Rian said, nodding to Mal who started into the trees with Onyx, Sage and Anise.

Rian started to push the door to, then hesitated.

'Damn, there's no lock on the outside,' he said.

The sound of distant footsteps echoed in the corridor behind us. I looked at Rian. We had to do something or they'd catch up with us in no time.

Tarragon snatched the key from my hand.

'I'll lock it, then get rid of the keys,' he said, stepping back into the passage. 'Then I'll hide.'

'You can't do that,' I protested.

'It'll give you all a chance to get away,' Tarragon said, scratching his chin. 'But you must promise me you'll save Willow.'

'No, I'll stay,' Rian said, moving towards the door. 'This is my responsibility.'

'You can't,' Tarragon said, holding his hands out to stop Rian. 'Not that I'd let you even if it was. You're needed to start the Vortex.'

'We need you, too,' I said.

'But you don't. You've got a Water Spinner, you've got Onyx. Let me do this, Rian. Please. By the Herbs, just save my Willowherb. Please.'

Rian nodded mutely and grabbed Tarragon in a hug. 'Thank you, cousin,' he whispered. 'Try and get to safety.'

Tarragon nodded. 'I will. Give this to one of the others,' he said, handing me the guard's knife Rian had given him. 'And tell Willow I love her with all my heart.'

'We will,' I said, giving him a quick peck on the cheek. 'Be careful.'

'I'm always careful,' he said with a grin, waving me away.

'No, you're not,' Rian said, the footsteps getting closer.

'Campfire,' I said, reminding Tarragon of our first fight together.

He smiled. 'I know, no heroics,' he said, and he shut the door. The key turned in the lock and his footsteps moved away.

I turned to Rian. I wasn't sure whose eyes were more glassy.

'I'll tell Willow,' he said, taking my hand and squeezing it.

'No, I'll do it,' I said as we turned and raced into the trees after the others.

CHAPTER TWENTY-EIGHT

'Where's Tarragon?' Sage asked, looking behind us as we caught up with the others.

'He stayed to lock the door,' Rian said. 'There was no lock on the outside.'

Sage's face blanched. 'But why?'

'To give us time,' I said, handing Mal the spare knife. 'So we'd better use it.' I held on firmly to Rian's hand and we sped through the dead trees, kicking up dust as we went. We hurried between the lifeless trunks, up a small incline, and there, below us, was the main road, just as the guard had said. We moved cautiously down to it – but it lay empty in both directions.

'Now we see if what that guard said was accurate,' Sage said.

We followed the road, keeping a good pace, well aware Juniper and Chervil had a good head start on us. We reached the fork in the road the guard had spoken of; it continued through the dead trees towards the centre of the island.

Onyx crouched down and ran his fingers along a shallow groove in the road. 'A carriage and horses have been this way recently,' he said. 'We're going the right way.'

'But how long will it take to get to the Cave?' Sage asked. 'We have no provisions, nothing to drink, no blankets if we have to camp.'

'We'll worry about that when it happens,' Rian said.

'But we're only going to fall further behind.'

'Then we need to find some horses,' I said, plodding on through the trees. 'Maybe we'll find a farm where we can borrow some.'

Mal raised an eyebrow. 'Borrow?'

'Yes, borrow – I'm not Onyx.'

'By the Stars, I am here, you know,' Onyx said, scowling at me.

I grinned back.

A short while later we paused at a stream. Rian and I washed our hands and cleaned his tunic as best we could, then we carried on along the road.

'We'll never catch them up at this rate,' Sage muttered, a sour note to his voice.

'Interesting. Look, over there.' Anise pointed. 'Looks like a homestead of some sort.'

We'd reached a break in the trees and a large open plain stretched out before us, a small farmstead on one side, the forest crowding in again in the distance.

'Let's stop there, see if they can help us,' Rian said.

'We don't have any money,' Anise pointed out.

'I've my ring,' Mal said, fingering his malachite ring. 'If you don't mind, Phire.'

I swallowed. The thought of Mal giving it up tore my heart, but I knew he was right.

I nodded. 'I'll get you another one, one day.'

He smiled. 'Sounds good.'

Rian looked at me, then Mal. 'Are you sure?'

'We don't have much choice. Onyx's Ring is an Artefact, so's your Talisman and Anise's Amulet. We can't give them up, and there's no way I'd keep my ring and let you two give up your wedding ring.'

Bearing in mind it was an Artefact, too, I was grateful to my brother for offering up his ring. *I should really mention that to Rian.*

We walked up to the homestead. A man was tending some half-starved animals in the back fields, although they were more dry, dusty fields than lush green grass. He turned towards us and tensed.

'Put your hair up,' Rian said.

'What?' Sage asked, raising an eyebrow.

'We can say we're with King Chervil,' Rian said, almost choking on his brother's title. We quickly did as he said so we were all the same.

'I'll go and speak to him,' Mal said, brushing his hair over his shoulder.

'I'll come with you, Mal,' Anise said, and the two went over to talk with the man.

'He's got some horses there,' Onyx said, trying to look disinterested.

'Let's hope he'll part with them willingly,' Sage said.

He did more than that. He gladly took Mal's ring in payment for three horses, food, waterskins and three blankets. As we rode away, we now stood a much better chance of catching up with Willow and the others. As usual, I rode with Rian; he insisted on me sitting in front of him again. Mal rode with Onyx, and Anise and Sage shared the other horse. We cantered along, kicking up dust behind us.

'Juniper came through here a couple of hours ago,' Mal reported.

'They aren't going at much of a speed, according to the farmer,' Anise said.

'Probably think they've got us trussed up sufficiently and don't need to hurry too much,' Onyx said.

'That carriage of the Emperor's won't go that quickly on a road like this,' Mal said. 'There are too many ruts. If it was a paved road they'd be a long way ahead of us.'

'Did the farmer say how far the Cave was?'

'He didn't really want to say anything about it until we said we were with Chervil and on urgent business for the Emperor,' Anise said. 'Seems it's about another day's travel. If we keep going, rest tonight, we'll reach it tomorrow morning.'

'Can we afford to rest, though?' Sage asked.

'We can't arrive exhausted or we'll never be able to fight or restart the Vortex,' I said.

'We haven't even all got weapons,' Onyx said, shaking his head.

'Funny you should say that, Onyx,' Anise said. 'I was able to procure a couple of short swords and a knife, so we've all got weapons now.'

'Procure?'

'Steal.'

Sage sat up a little straighter. 'That evens the odds a little, then.'

'We'll rest early evening, continue again after midnight so we get there early tomorrow,' Rian said. 'We'll need to give the horses a break anyway.'

We rode on until the early evening when the final rays of the golden sun were breaking through the dead branches of the trees. Rian lit a small fire in a dip not far from the road, and we ate from the farmer's provisions. We also took advantage of a little stream running through there to stock up on water.

Mal sat next to me, gazing into the fire.

'Don't dwell on what Beryl said. None of this was our fault,' he said. 'We never treated her any different to you.'

'I know that,' I said, throwing a twig on the fire. I sighed. 'I used to tell her everything. That was a mistake.'

'She made her own decisions in all of this – she chose to join the Coterie, to kill Father, to marry Elm. I can't believe she's constructed this story to excuse her behaviour and blame it on us.'

'By the Stars, I can,' Onyx said, coming and sitting beside Mal. 'She always had a mean streak.'

'You think so?' I asked.

He nodded and sniffed. 'When she was small she used to torment me when she could, got me into trouble for things she'd done and, being the son of kitchen staff, I couldn't argue back.'

'Why didn't you say?' Mal asked, resting his hand on Onyx's knee.

'You think your father would have believed me over his daughter?'

'Probably not.'

'So I never said, just did my best to avoid her.'

'I'm sorry.'

'Doesn't matter now. I survived, and now I've got you.'

I grinned at them. 'I am pleased for you both, you know.'

Mal grinned back. 'We know.'

A short while later we settled down to rest. The warm night meant we didn't really need blankets, so Rian and I lay on top of ours and looked up at the stars peeping out through the branches. My mind was full of tomorrow's challenges.

I swallowed. I couldn't lose Rian in that cave. I'd find a way to stop it. I had to. The others may be looking out for him, but I was the one who'd lose everything if he died. If my dreams came true. I couldn't let it happen. My palms turned cold and sweaty, the muscles in my neck and shoulders tight and achy. I couldn't relax, let alone sleep.

Rian glanced at me, a wisp of a frown clouding his face in the flickering firelight. 'You remember the pool in Flos, where we first... you know,' he whispered to me.

I knew at once he was trying to distract me from my ruminations. Sometimes, I thought there were occasions that he knew I needed him before even I did, and I loved him for it.

'That's not something I'm ever likely to forget,' I murmured.

'I deliberately came to find you,' he said, taking hold of my hand. 'I knew what you were doing.'

I turned towards him. 'You mean you knew I'd be naked?'

'I was hoping.' He grinned mischievously.

I gave him a long look. 'It could have happened any night, you know, seeing each other like that.'

'But it hadn't, for one reason or another, and I'd waited long enough to see you – all of you.'

I raised an eyebrow. It'd been a calculated move on his part? 'You could've said something, I wouldn't have minded. I was looking forward to seeing all of you, too,' I said, my heart skipping a beat.

'I know. Skinny dipping with you seemed the perfect opportunity, though.'

'Even if you can't swim?'

'Goes to show how much I love you,' he said with a grin, lying on his side and pulling himself up onto one shoulder. 'What did you think?'

'That it was a little sneaky.'

'No, not about what I *did*. I mean, about *me*.'

I turned towards him. 'What did I think of you? What, in all your glory?' I asked, trying to stifle a giggle.

He nodded, still grinning at me.

I sighed. 'You're trying to take my mind off things, aren't you?'

'Would I do that?' he asked, feigning shock.

'Yes, because you're wonderful.'

'And is it working?'

'Not really.'

'Then I need to try harder,' he said, leaning towards me and kissing me gently on the lips. 'So… What did you think of me in "all my glory", as you so eloquently put it?'

I could see I wasn't going to get away with it, and maybe he was right, trying to divert my attention – especially with something as heart-warming as this.

'I thought you were quite exquisite,' I said, seriously.

'And I thought you were the most beautiful thing I'd ever seen,' he said, leaning towards me and kissing me again, lingering as he rested his hand on my cheek.

'You did, did you?'

'I knew you'd be gorgeous, but I wasn't prepared for quite *how* gorgeous. You were – *are* – even more beautiful than I'd expected.'

'Because you've had a lot of experience in that area, haven't you?' I teased.

He rubbed the back of his neck. 'You know I had none, but Tarragon talks, and when he starts describing things sometimes, you really don't need to see it for yourself to know what to expect – but you were so much more than anything he'd described, and over the years he's described quite a bit.'

'I can imagine.'

'And had you? Imagined?'

'If you're asking if I'd imagined you without anything on, then, maybe… a little,' I said, glad he couldn't see my red cheeks in the dim light.

'And?' he asked, gazing into my eyes.

'And what?'

'Did I meet expectations?'

'Are we really having this conversation?' I shook my head in disbelief. 'You surpassed all expectations quite emphatically.'

He grinned smugly.

'Have I ever told you that sometimes you can be impossible?' I asked, smiling.

He shrugged, a little playful frown on his face as he shook his head. 'Not that I can remember,' he said, grinning again as he leant in to give me yet another kiss. He drew back and lay down, staring up at the sky and the twinkling stars above us. 'Do you know their names?' he asked, keeping his voice low so as not to disturb the others.

'I know some of the constellations, but not all,' I said, gazing skyward.

'Show me some.'

I looked at the sky and pointed to a little group of stars. 'That's The Cat, with those two big bright stars as the eyes, and its tail going west. Those seven stars right above us are The Brothers, and over there, the two clusters are The Lovers. It's said they were two people who lived in the mountains of Iolite and fell in love, but their families disapproved so they ran away together to sea, but were lost in a storm at night. The Stars themselves were so moved by their great love for each other that they set them in the sky with them so they were never alone, always together and always remembered.'

Rian took my hand, looking at the pinpricks of light above us. 'You think the Stars would do that for us? So our love will last an eternity?'

I turned towards him. 'It's just a story.'

He smiled. 'I know, but it's quite romantic. And I think our love is strong enough to last forever, don't you?'

'Longer.'

We set off again in the early hours, continuing along the roadway. Rian's attempts at calming me had worked to an extent, and I'd managed to sleep a little in his arms, but my dreams were full of red shadows and I woke stiff and achy. A couple of hours after dawn we broke free of the forest, and a short distance further on spotted the remains of a camp at the side of the road. The fires were still smouldering, and the evidence of a number of people lay scattered over a small area.

'We aren't far behind,' Onyx said, gazing into the distance. The road ahead crossed a plain before reaching a brown, hilly region.

I took a deep breath. We'd soon find out if our powers were a match for Juniper and the others, and whether we'd be able to restart the Crystal Vortex, or if, instead, Juniper and Chervil would succeed in destroying it. I shivered involuntarily. Rian increased his grip on me.

'You all right?' he asked, leaning forward and whispering in my ear.

'I will be when this is all over,' I said quietly.

'I know what you mean. It'll be all right, though. We're together.'

The thought of the red shadow loomed large in my mind.

'I don't suppose you'd consider staying outside the cave when we get there, after all?' I asked.

'You know I can't.'

'I don't want to lose you.'

'You won't – the others all know what to look out for, and so do I.'

Sandalwood swept around me.

'I hope so,' I murmured.

The road wound into the hills, hardly more than a sparse track now. The wheel marks from the carriage were deep and easily seen, and Onyx didn't need to track them at all. As we rounded a small hill, voices drifted towards us. We all stopped and dismounted.

'I'll take a look,' Onyx said, heading for the hill and keeping low.

We tethered the horses and waited for him to return. Rian, Mal and Sage all had swords, Anise and Onyx knives. The Cursed Weapons sat ready on my back. I wiped my sweaty palms on my leggings. Mal glanced at me.

'We'll keep an eye on him, don't worry,' my brother said, looking towards where Rian was talking to Sage and Anise.

'Thank you,' I said. 'I'm so worried something will happen.'

Mal slid his arm around my shoulders. 'We've got his back. It'll be fine.'

I nodded, still not convinced.

'The bitch has just gone in the Cave with them. They've left six soldiers outside,' Onyx reported.

Hell's teeth.

Sage sighed. 'So we've got to get past them first?'

'We might be able to slip in around the back of them – they don't seem to be doing much in the way of guarding. They're more interested in gambling amongst themselves and playing dice, from what I could see.'

Rian nodded. 'Let's go, then. I'd rather not fight unless I have to.'

We followed Onyx around the base of the hill, keeping to the shadows, rocky outcrops and scrubby dead bushes. The cave mouth sat at the base of a small cliff, its yawning entrance a black hole into hell. The soldiers were totally engrossed in their dice game, wagering money and arguing with each other as the dice were tossed. Using rocks as cover, we slipped behind them and into the cave.

A tunnel led into the side of the cliff, water dripping down the walls and a musty odour filling the cool air. I unsheathed Deorwine as the others drew their weapons, and cautiously moved along one side of the wall opposite Rian, the others following. The tunnel curved. A flickering light glowed up ahead – blues, purples, greens and reds, all punctuated by a stuttering bright golden light, and the intermittent sound of what could have been breaking glass.

We pressed up against the damp walls, peering into the cave. Great crystal stalagmites and stalactites, bigger than a man, filled the huge space, all glowing softly in every single colour you could imagine. At the far end of the cavern the stuttering golden glow continued. The Crystal Vortex. A spinning column of golden light that stopped and started, flickered, died and started again. The sound I'd heard came from the Vortex each time it faltered: it had a shrill, high-pitched note when spinning well, but as it stumbled the sound of glass breaking into a million pieces filled the cavern. The column was unbalanced, failing, and we needed to restart it, but for that we needed the Fire Opal.

Voices came from ahead of us.

'You can't do this! You said you were going to restart it, not destroy it!' Emperor Xanthos' voice was filled with anger and dismay.

I crept along the tunnel a little further and peered out. Carnelian had a rope in his hands and was busy tying the Emperor of Chroma up like a chicken while Topaz held a knife to his neck.

'We lied,' Juniper said from her position in front of the failing Vortex. 'We've come to destroy it.'

'But why?' The Emperor strained against his bonds.

'For so many reasons,' Juniper said. 'But mainly for personal revenge and the satisfaction of taking over rule of all Six Lands.'

'But if you destroy the Vortex the Lands will fall further into chaos. There will be great floods, storms, droughts. The people will be decimated.'

'And they will need guidance and a firm hand to bring them back together,' Chervil said, coming to stand beside Juniper and taking her hand.

Out of the corner of my eye, I caught Rian shuddering as he quietly moved to stand next to me.

'And who better to restore order than Elemental Magic Spinners?' Juniper asked. 'The people will love us for saving them.'

'But you're the ones endangering them in the first place!' The Emperor tried to pull away from Topaz, but the knife in her hand nicked his throat and he stopped moving.

I heard Sorrel's amused laugh before I saw him. He stood holding the Fire Opal. Rian tensed as he saw his cousin and his heritage. The Fire Opal glowed with its usual yellow-red light, purple and green twisting gently inside.

'The people are already endangered because of the failing Vortex.' Beryl's voice came from my left side, from behind a stalagmite. She stepped out with Elm. 'We will save them.'

Elm nodded. 'And the people will be eternally grateful.' He played with the hilt of his sword. 'And those that are not will be dealt with by the Coterie.'

Rian tapped my shoulder and pointed to the right. I turned to see Willow tied to a glowing red stalagmite.

My heart skipped a beat. Icy hands clutched at my heart. Red. I looked around wildly for a red shadow, my hand on Deorwine's hilt – nothing.

At least, there wasn't a red shadow yet.

CHAPTER TWENTY-NINE

'Mal and I will get Willow,' I whispered to Rian. 'I don't want you anywhere near that red stalagmite.'

Rian gave me a long look. 'All right, but, by the Herbs, be careful.'

'Of course. The rest of you, look after him,' I said, nodding towards my husband.

Rian grabbed my hand. 'Stop worrying.'

'It's my job. I love you.' I kissed him quickly on the lips and slipped out the tunnel with Mal right behind me. We crept along the side of the cavern, keeping to the shadows where possible, moving from huge crystal to huge crystal.

I glanced back. Rian and the others were moving along the far wall. What were they doing? They were supposed to be staying where they were. Mal looked at me and shrugged. I turned back towards the red stalagmite and moved silently on.

The Emperor struggled, but he was now firmly tied to a blue crystal. 'You don't know what you're doing,' he said, fighting unsuccessfully against the ropes. 'You'll kill us all.'

'I don't think so,' Juniper said, staring into the stuttering Vortex, her diamond and agate necklace glittering in the golden light. 'Bring me the Fire Opal.'

Sorrel limped over to her carrying the large gemstone. At five inches across, the Fire Opal rested in the palm of his hands with a kind of reverence. Perhaps Sorrel felt the history of the Aerban Artefact, too. He held it out and Chervil took it from him.

'Carnelian,' Juniper said.

The assassin stepped forward.

'See what you can do,' Juniper said, staring at the Fire Opal.

Carnelian reached out and touched the Fire Opal. He closed his eyes. Nothing happened. Not even a hiccup.

Mal and I edged closer to Willow.

'Useless after all,' Elm said, shaking his head. 'Aren't all Middle Bloods Wakers?'

'Apparently not,' Beryl said, looking at Carnelian with disdain.

'We always knew there may be setbacks,' Juniper said. 'That's why we've got her – bring her here.'

Mal grabbed me and pulled me down behind a purple crystal as Topaz walked over to Willow, cutting her bonds. I glanced across at Rian. His forehead furrowed in frustration.

'Let go of me,' Willow said, coughing, pulling against Topaz's grip as the assassin dragged her over towards Juniper. 'Why don't you get her to try?'

'I already have, and I couldn't do it, either,' Topaz said, positioning Willow in front of Chervil.

'Come now, Willow, you're doing this for the good of Aerba,' Chervil said, smiling his best smile at her.

'Liar,' Willow spat. 'You're no king. Rian is worth a hundred of you.'

Chervil's face changed to thunder. 'He is worth nothing, do you hear me, nothing! He's weak and gullible. Look how he fell for Lady Merciless. He's a fool, and when we get back to Magenta I intend to make sure he dies – and her, too, for that matter.'

'You're a bastard, Chervil. I won't help you.'

'Oh, I think you will,' he said.

Topaz rested her knife at Willow's throat. 'Unless you'd prefer to die, of course.'

'If you don't, I'll make sure Tarragon is tortured for a nice long time before I kill him,' Chervil said, his voice menacing and determined. 'I believe Juniper has just the person for the job, a man named Serpentine.'

Hell's teeth. I very nearly choked.

'You wouldn't dare,' Willow gasped.

'Yes, I would. I am King of Aerba and I will do whatever I want. Now, awaken the Fire Opal – Release its power, now!'

Mal and I moved a little closer. Maybe Rian and the others were right to have moved up on the other side. We were going to have to take them all on now.

Willow's face contorted with indecision, and she coughed again.

'Do it,' Juniper ordered.

Willow reached out her trembling hand and touched the Fire Opal. With tears falling down her cheeks, she closed her eyes. 'Wake up,' she murmured.

The Fire Opal's internal flames suddenly flared. A flash of purple and green momentarily filled the cavern, making us duck for cover in case they saw us in the bright light. The flare died down and the Fire Opal sat in Chervil's hands, its inner flames far more vibrant than ever before, just as Ostianzis had said, dancing furiously to some internal heartbeat.

Sorrel looked at it, his eyes wide. 'I think it's worked.'

Chervil grinned, his eyes lighting up in the glow from the Fire Opal. 'Magnificent,' he said, studying the gemstone as Topaz dragged Willow out of the way.

'Let's get to work,' Juniper said. 'The Crystal Vortex must be destroyed utterly so no one can ever bring it back. Give me the Fire Opal.'

'No!' Rian stepped out from behind a large green stalagmite, Anise, Sage and Onyx right behind him.

What was he doing?

'How the devil did you get here?' Chervil snarled, still holding the Fire Opal.

'That doesn't matter,' Rian said, brandishing his sword. 'Put the Fire Opal down, Brother.'

Chervil sneered at him. 'Why would I do anything you say? It's you who need to put your weapons down or we kill her,' he said, indicating Willow.

Topaz had her knife at Willow's throat.

I glanced at Mal. He shrugged, then stepped forward, sword in hand, and tapped Topaz on the shoulder. She started to twist around towards him.

'Hello, Topaz, did you miss me?' he asked, and hit her on the head with the hilt of his sword. Mal always was fairly direct with things. Topaz collapsed to the ground. Willow jumped back to stand with Mal, grabbing Topaz's fallen knife as she went.

I stepped out to join them. Sorrel glanced at me, looking me up and down lasciviously. There was a bit of me that wished I'd finished him off in the Viridi Palace dungeon. Mal tensed beside me and Rian bristled, both noticing Sorrel's look.

Juniper glared at me. 'Hello, Daughter.'

'Stepmother,' I said. 'Time to surrender.'

Juniper laughed. 'Never.' She looked hard at me. 'You were never supposed to find out about your Magic. That's why I inducted you into the Coterie, to cover up that mark of yours so not you or anyone else would ever know. The moment I saw you I knew what you were capable of, but I also knew you'd never follow my path, unlike Beryl. Your father was a means to an end, my way of getting revenge on Trew and the Blood Decree.'

Chervil raised an eyebrow as he turned to her. 'What?' he asked, his wedding band glinting in the golden light of the Vortex.

'As soon as I have control over the Lands, the Blood Rules will be torn up.'

'You mean *we* have control – and we'll need to talk about this. The Blood Rules control the people and we need to maintain control.'

Juniper glared at him. 'They're oppressive and they will be revoked.'

Chervil's jaw set. 'We'll talk about this *later*,' he growled.

I glanced at Rian. Trouble was brewing between the two of them.

'Whatever happens, you won't stop us from destroying the Vortex, Daughter,' Juniper said, taking the Fire Opal from Chervil.

'Watch me,' I said, lunging towards her with Deorwine. Elm stepped between us, deflecting my blow.

'I don't think so, Sister,' he said, his lip curling.

'Get out of my way.'

He grinned and slashed at me. I parried his blow as Rian ran forwards to meet a challenge from Chervil. Mal and Onyx were suddenly locked in a deadly battle with Carnelian as Sorrel lunged towards Sage and Anise. Over to one side, Willow moved to free the Emperor from his bonds. Juniper and Beryl looked around wildly as their plan collapsed around them.

I parried Elm's blows. I stepped back, letting the momentum of his next strike move him past me as I twisted out of the way. He let out a howl of frustration as he slammed into a stalagmite.

'Bitch,' he yelled at me. 'I'm going to kill you!'

I didn't grace his words with a reply. Instead, I swung Deorwine at him. He blocked the blow awkwardly, staggering back against the crystal. He roared and moved forwards again, his sword aiming for my head. I ducked. Swung Deorwine across his body as I spun past him. Elm sucked in a breath, bending over, his free hand going to his stomach. He moved his hand away, his fingers covered in blood. He looked at it as if he couldn't believe what he was seeing, holding his hand up in the light. He turned to me, his eyes like granite pebbles, dark and hard.

'You'll die for that, Sister,' he snarled.

'You're not my brother,' I snapped at him.

'No. If I had been, you'd have toed the line years ago, but Malachite's soft, let you get away with things. Well, not anymore.' He grasped his sword in both hands and swung it violently towards me, a brutality to his movements I'd never seen before, even from him.

I parried his blow, but barely. He'd used such force that he knocked me backwards, and although I stayed upright, Deorwine jarred from my hands. I found myself within ten feet of the Vortex that continued to spiral and stutter behind me. I glanced to my right where Rian fought in some macabre dance with Chervil. Carnelian and Mal were to his left, still slugging it out, but Sage now had the upper hand on Sorrel. Rian glanced at me for a split second, but Chervil immediately commanded his attention again.

Elm sneered at me. Lunged. His sword glinted in the light of the cavern. I grabbed Glædwine from my back and prepared myself for his great blow. His sword skittered off the crystal shield as I twisted to one side.

'Bitch!' he screamed.

He tripped. Staggered.

He disappeared into the Crystal Vortex.

A great golden flash, followed by a loud bang, rang out around the cavern.

'Elm!' Juniper screamed. 'My son!'

'No,' Beryl yelled, horror written across her face.

Suddenly Juniper started concentrating on the Fire Opal, muttering to herself, her spare hand going to her necklace.

I froze.

She was going to use the Artefact against us. An Artefact with the power of the Fire Opal, combined with Quintessence, would obliterate us all.

'To me,' Juniper shouted, and Chervil, Sorrel and Carnelian backed away towards her side of the cave.

Mal looked around, confusion filling his face.

'What…' Rian began.

'Behind me,' I said, running towards them. 'Get behind me!'

Thankfully none of them hesitated and all ran to me just as Juniper unleashed her pent-up Quintessence.

I raised Glædwine. The shield was a Diamond Artefact. A Quintessence Artefact. I prayed to the Stars it would be enough.

Juniper's Magic hit Glædwine. I stood firm, holding the shield steady, channelling my own Quintessence into the diamond. The shield's influence extended beyond the crystal to protect us all, but my power wasn't enough to hold both her and the Fire Opal back.

Hell's teeth. I wasn't strong enough. I was losing.

A flare of red Magic surged around me. Suddenly Fire Magic mingled with my own, pushing back against Juniper's onslaught. The Amethyst Talisman glowed purple as Rian held it. He slipped a hand around my waist and the power increased again.

Juniper screamed as her power began to consume her. She was using too much. The brilliance of her diamond necklace faded to nothing.

'Stop, Mother, stop,' Beryl pleaded.

But Juniper had no intention of stopping. She continued to vent her Magic at us.

'Stop!' Beryl yelled, grabbing Juniper's shoulder.

A roar reverberated around the cavern, echoing in every corner of the stone space. I flinched as a huge white flash filled the cave.

Juniper screamed.

Beryl shrieked.

Glædwine disintegrated into sand.

The light faded and the Magic stopped abruptly.

Juniper lay on the cavern floor, a smouldering corpse, the Fire Opal rolling from her grasp. The smell of burning flesh almost made me vomit. Beryl lay beside our stepmother, convulsing.

'H—help me!' Beryl screamed.

'Damn,' Rian murmured, his hand still around my waist.

Neither Mal nor I moved.

I looked down at my hands in disbelief. The Cursed Shield had shattered into infinitely small pieces. I looked at Rian. He frowned, shook his head, a bewildered look in his eyes. My Amethyst Talisman winked at me from Rian's hand.

'Thank you,' I murmured.

Rian gave me a wan little smile and moved forward to inspect the remains of the Cursed Shield, kicking the shattered pieces with the toe of his boot.

Mal lunged at Carnelian. Sorrel took one look at the smoking remains of Juniper and bolted. Beryl continued to convulse for a couple of moments longer, then stopped. I shuddered. Was she dead? She had to be.

To my side, Chervil swore. 'What have you done, Lady Merciless? What have you done?' He shot towards me, sword raised in his smooth, unblemished hands that spoke of a life of luxury – something my husband hadn't enjoyed.

I had no shield, no sword, and Topaz's knife would never block his oncoming blow. I recoiled as his sword swept towards me.

A ring of steel cut through the air. A flash of flame. I looked up. *I'll love you and protect you until my last breath.* Rian had sprung forward and blocked his brother's blow, meeting his strike with his fiery sword. Chervil initially looked shocked at the sight of the flaming blade, then glowered at his younger brother.

'I should have expected as much from you, I suppose,' Chervil said, jaw set, face taking on a demonic look in the flames and shadows cast by Rian's blade. 'I still don't understand what you see in that disgusting assassin.'

'And, thankfully, you never will,' Rian said.

Chervil swiped at Rian, who parried before delivering his own devastating blow. The brothers continued their titanic battle as I scrambled out of their way.

Mal spun around behind Carnelian and smashed his hilt into his head, just as he had with Topaz. Carnelian fell to the ground, poleaxed.

Rian slashed at Chervil, changed direction, brought his sword down hard on his brother's, jarring it from his hand. He now had Chervil against the cavern wall, his sword pointed at his elder brother's chest.

'You're going back to Aerba to answer for your crimes against the people of Aerba and the Six Lands,' Rian said, his voice unwavering as the flames faded.

'Shut up, Valerian, you can't tell me what to do. I'm the King,' Chervil spat.

'Exactly. And responsible for our land. And by the Herbs, you've damn well done all you can to bring war and destruction to it and our people. You'll be charged with treason.'

Chervil glanced down at the dull blade, its point resting on his chest, then looked Rian in the eye. 'No, I won't,' he said.

I guessed what Chervil was about to do a split second before he did it. 'No—'

Chervil grabbed Rian's hands and plunged the sword into his own chest.

Rian let go of it in horror, stepping back as his brother slid slowly to the cold stone floor, gurgling horribly. Chervil smiled at him, then lay still, a trickle of blood running from the corner of his mouth as it had Angelica's, his face fixed in a hideous grin.

I swallowed.

Sage swore.

Anise and Onyx looked as though their eyes were going to pop out of their heads. Mal glanced across at us, disbelief in his eyes.

Rian shook his head. 'I didn't want him to die, despite everything, I didn't want this.'

I stepped forwards, slipped my hand into his. 'I know.'

He turned and looked at me, his eyes glassy. He'd just lost the last member of his immediate family. My heart tore for him. I glanced over at Beryl's prone body. I only had Mal now. I wasn't entirely sorry, but at the same time she was still my sister – probably rather what Rian was thinking about Chervil.

My gaze moved to the flaming Fire Opal that had come to rest on the ground near Juniper's smoking body.

The Crystal Vortex suddenly flickered, shrieked.

'It's going to collapse,' the Emperor yelled. I'd almost forgotten about him. He stood beside Willow, who had cut him free from the ropes. 'If you're going to save it, you have to do it now!'

CHAPTER THIRTY

Rian ran forward and grabbed the Fire Opal, doing his best to avoid looking at either Juniper or Beryl as he picked the Artefact up.

'We know what to do,' Rian said, coming back to us. He glanced at me.

I stared at the faltering golden Vortex, doubt creeping in. I couldn't control the Magic last time; why would I be able to now? But there was no one else who could do it. I had to. I had no choice. I had to do this for Iolite, for Aerba, for the Six Lands, for the people – for Rian.

'Mal and I have already talked about this and he's going to be the Air Spinner,' Sage said.

Anise looked at him. 'Are you sure, Sage?'

Sage nodded, reached out and squeezed Anise's hand. 'Really. I know you'll be okay – I'll be over here,' he said, moving over to join Emperor Xanthos and Willow.

The others all lined up behind me.

'Here,' Rian said, carefully passing me the Fire Opal. 'You know what to do, and you *can* do it.'

My heart thudded uncomfortably in my chest.

'I hope so,' I murmured, taking hold of the Fire Opal. The gemstone didn't have anywhere near the weight I'd expected. The stone was warm, the flames inside spiralling and dancing. I could feel the power in it, the raw energy – the life. Like the Amethyst Talisman and the Malachite Dagger, it lived, but its power was on a far larger scale than either of them. On a magnitude even greater than the Cursed Weapons and Rian's Thyme Ring, and they were some of the most powerful Artefacts that had ever been in existence.

I gazed into my husband's eyes.

He smiled at me. 'I love you, remember that,' he said, kissing my forehead before joining the others.

'Focus your powers directly into the Fire Opal,' I said. I hoped that way I might be able to contain them better.

'Mal, you go first this time, I'll go last, just in case,' Rian said.

'In case?' Onyx asked.

'I'll gauge how Phire's doing, increase the Magic if she can take it.' Onyx nodded.

'Let's go, then,' Mal said, looking at me. 'Ready, Phire?'

'Are you actually going to stop calling her Ama now then?' Onyx asked, turning to his boyfriend.

Mal shrugged. 'Everyone else calls her Phire now.'

'I don't.'

'I've noticed.'

'Now really isn't the time for a discussion about my name, boys,' I said, the anxiety welling in me making me irritable. 'You can decide what to call me later. For now we need to concentrate.'

Anise grinned and nodded.

Onyx and Mal exchanged a smile and faced me.

Rian nodded at Mal.

'Get ready,' Mal said, closing his eyes. He stretched his hands out in front of him. Focused. His hands started to glow yellow. A great beam of yellow energy surged from his hands towards me and the Fire Opal. The Magic slammed into the Fire Opal, making me take a step back to brace myself.

I took a deep breath.

One.

I looked at Onyx and nodded.

He closed his eyes, and a blue light filled his hands. Then a bright blue bolt of Water Magic joined the Air Magic in the Fire Opal. The colours in the Fire Opal swirled brighter than ever as it soaked up the raw power.

Two.

Anise's green Earth Magic was the next to join the power swelling in the Fire Opal. The three colours swirled within the blazing stone, periodically escaping and wrapping around my arms like snakes. I gripped the Fire Opal tightly, acutely aware of the great power building within.

Three.

I was beginning to struggle. How could I contain Rian's Fire Magic, too?

I had to do what I could.

'Go on,' I said to Rian, perspiration building on my brow, my heart racing.

He nodded. Fire Magic immediately swirled at his fingertips. A red pulse of energy surged into the Fire Opal. I staggered backwards.

'Phire?' Rian's voice was tight.

'It's all right, keep going,' I said, gritting my teeth.

Four.

The raw power of four Magic Spinners filled me with awe, and not just a little fear. I took a shuddering breath and turned towards the Crystal Vortex, the energy from the four Spinners still cascading into the Artefact.

The Vortex faltered. Shrieked. Flickered as if someone were trying to put out a fire that refused to die. Then began to fade away.

'Now! Do it now,' the Emperor shouted.

I reached out my hand, holding the Fire Opal in the other, still receiving the Magic from the Spinners who now strained to continue, sweat beading on their brows, their faces strained, muscles taut.

From the hand cradling the Fire Opal, I released my Quintessence into it. Raw power surged through me, and a burst of silver white light broke from my outstretched hand, inundating the stuttering Vortex with Elemental Magic.

Hold it. Hold it.

My muscles tightened. My body began to shake from the effort. I couldn't hold, couldn't contain, this amount of power for long. As I directed it into the Crystal Vortex I feared burning up, just like Juniper. But I had to hold it for as long as I could, until the Vortex was balanced once more. It was my destiny. Like being with Rian was my destiny.

I can do this.

I *had* to do this.

The Vortex started to stabilise.

Spluttered. Wobbled.

This wasn't enough. Even if it burnt me up to restart the Vortex, we needed more Magic.

'Use your Artefacts!' I ordered.

Rian frowned, sweat beading on his forehead. 'You won't be able to take that power, too.'

'I have to. We won't restart the Vortex without it.'

He muttered something I didn't hear. 'Do as she says,' he said, taking hold of the Amethyst Talisman.

Mal turned to Rian then looked at me, forehead furrowed, then nodded at Onyx. Onyx placed his hand over his ring as Anise took hold of his Amulet, his tongue slipping out his mouth as he concentrated.

I gasped as their additional power hit me, making me stagger with the force of it. I wouldn't be able to take this, or control it, for long. I focused on the Vortex, sending everything I had into it.

Suddenly, the Vortex became brighter. Began to steady again. Its stuttering became less pronounced as it spun, beginning to regain its proper rhythm. We were almost there.

'I can't!' Anise said, and he fell to his knees, severing his Magic link with the Fire Opal. Sage ran over to him as he knelt on the ground, shaking violently.

Onyx was next to drop. As his power broke its link with the Fire Opal, I began to suffer. I couldn't continue to channel as much power from the Fire Opal.

Mal cried out and fell.

I glanced towards him. He lay on the floor, his chest heaving as he took in great gasps of air, his hair plastered to his head by sweat.

Suddenly Sage was standing in my brother's place, focusing his own Air Magic into the Opal. He gave me a little nod as a new burst of power rushed through me and into the Vortex.

My eyes flicked to Rian. He was only just holding on. I turned back to the Vortex. We were so close. The spiralling column of golden light was almost in balance again.

But not quite.

Rian dropped to his hands and knees, shaking. 'Damn. I'm sorry.'

Sage continued until he, too, was exhausted and on the ground.

I turned fully towards the Crystal Vortex, my outstretched arm aching, trembling. I released everything I had left into the spinning golden light.

The flames inside the Fire Opal died.

I collapsed to my knees, utterly spent.

I took deep breaths, my whole body shuddering as I tried to control my breathing and my heart rate. After a few moments I looked up. The Vortex was spinning, and rather than screeching it sounded more as if a thousand people were tapping on glass all together. But it still wobbled slightly on its axis and the smell of burning filled the air.

'It needs something else, it needs more power,' Rian shouted over the tapping from somewhere behind me, his voice tired and strained.

'But we don't have anything else,' Onyx yelled back.

I had nothing more to give. The Fire Opal was dead. There was nothing else. I let go of the Fire Opal.

A flash of light caught my attention.

Over near the Vortex lay Deorwine, winking in the golden light.

Dear Friend.

Would it work? I had to try.

I half-crawled, half-scrambled over to the Cursed Sword. I grasped its familiar hilt.

Thank you – for everything.

I hurled Deorwine like a spear into the brilliant column of light.

A bright golden light swept from the Vortex, making me shield my eyes as an explosion rocked the cavern, bringing pieces of crystal flying down at us from the ceiling. I curled into a ball as shards of rock rained around me. The whole cave shook with the energy now swirling inside the Crystal Vortex. I covered my head, wishing I was next to Rian. I tried to get up, tried to get over to him, but the shaking ground and the falling debris made it suicidal. I could just make him out about twenty feet away, curled up like me, hands over his head.

Gradually the shaking and the bright light receded. The noise stopped.

I turned towards the Crystal Vortex.

It spun silently. Stabilised. Balanced once more.

I took a long breath and looked back at the others.

Willow was some distance away with the Emperor, his expression somewhere between fear and awe. Mal and Onyx lay on the ground together, holding hands, breathing deeply. Anise held Sage in his arms, heads together.

Rian had propped himself up against a stalagmite. He looked over at me and smiled a wan but happy little smile. His eyes had a dazed look about them.

I sighed with relief. I wanted to go over to him. Hold him. But I had no energy left. Nothing. It was all I could do to sit up and smile at him.

Mal sat up and swore. 'Ama,' he shouted. 'Carnelian!'

I twisted around.

Carnelian unleashed a feral snarl and moved out from behind a crystal and towards Rian, sword raised over his head.

Hell's teeth.

Everything suddenly seemed to slow.

Was Carnelian the red shadow I'd seen in my dream? Had the answer been there in his name all along? The shadow had been the same deep red as the assassin's namesake, and he carried a blade in his hand – only it wasn't a knife, as I'd assumed, but a sword.

I finally understood my dream.

Things sped up.

I gasped. I had one chance.

Help me!

Rian's Ring glowed white on my finger, the tiny little diamonds responding to my Quintessence, giving me the burst of energy I needed. With all my concentration on the Fire Opal before, and saving the Vortex, I'd forgotten all about it. Now it flared into life.

Mal's warning propelled me to my feet and across the cavern floor towards Rian as he shook his head, trying to clear it. My only weapon was Topaz's knife, and I didn't dare throw it from this angle in case I missed. Rian looked up towards Carnelian, eyes blurry, blinking, trying to clear his vision. A look of horror dawned on his face as he realised the danger he was in, and his inability to do anything about it. Carnelian started to bring the sword down, right into Rian's unprotected body. Rian threw up a hand in a futile gesture of defence as the sword plunged towards his chest.

'No!' I yelled, barrelling into Carnelian, knocking him away from Rian. We both hit the rocky cave floor, hard. I scrambled back to my feet as he got up. The assassin's sword lay on the ground.

I'd outwitted the prophecy. Or had I?

Carnelian unsheathed his knife, snarling like a rabid dog as his right eye twitched. I pulled Topaz's blade from my boot.

'Let's finish this, shall we, Amethyst-sweetie?' Carnelian asked.

He lunged at me. I sidestepped. He swiped his knife at me again, and I dodged out of the way, passing behind him, catching his arm with my knife.

'Bitch,' he hissed as blood seeped into his clothing.

'Too slow,' I said, goading him. Maybe he'd make a mistake. He swiped at me again and I jumped backwards.

Rian was slowly pulling himself to his feet, still suffering the after effects of using his Magic. I stood between him and Carnelian, and I was going to stay there. I would be Rian's protector as he was mine. My vow to him – *I'll care for you, defend you and be your shield* – was as true now as it had been when I'd made it months ago.

Once more, Carnelian came at me. I blocked his arm with my own, pulling him around, away from Rian, but he suddenly lunged in Rian's direction, knife raised, the blade catching the golden light from the Vortex and the multiple colours of crystals that glowed around us.

No. I wouldn't let the prophecy win this time. What's more, I now knew what was most important to me.

And what I would do to keep it.

I did the only thing I could.

I ducked under the assassin's raised arm. I'd expected Carnelian to twist away as I moved. But he didn't. He was too focused on Rian, too intent on killing him.

Topaz's knife – my knife – slid into Carnelian's chest.

CHAPTER THIRTY-ONE

It was all so easy.

Far easier than I'd expected.

The look of total surprise on Carnelian's face was mirrored in my own. I let go of the buried knife. Stepped back. Swallowed.

'I never thought you had it in you,' Carnelian said, his voice gravelly. 'Never thought you'd do it.'

'To save Rian I'd walk into hell,' I said quietly as Carnelian dropped his knife harmlessly on the cave floor, staggering slightly.

'I'm proud of you, Amethyst-sweetie.'

I shivered, nausea welling in my throat.

Carnelian looked at the hilt sticking out of his chest, thrumming to the faltering beat of his heart. 'Topaz,' he murmured, looking at the stone-encrusted hilt, and collapsed.

What had I done?

I'd stepped over that invisible line I always swore I wouldn't. But I'd done it for Rian. To thwart the prophecy. To save his life. I stared speechless at Carnelian's dead body lying in a pool of ever increasing blood. Warm arms had me in their grasp.

'Damn, you did it – thank you,' Rian said, his breath tickling my neck.

I continued to shiver, despite his warmth. Thank the Stars and the Herbs he was safe.

He frowned as he turned me to look at him. 'You're shaking – it's fine, you're all right. I'm all right. The prophecy's broken.'

'I—I...' This wasn't how I thought it might be. Great regret. Remorse. Guilt. I'd wondered if I might feel all those things if I ever killed, and yet I didn't really feel anything.

'Shh,' he said, stroking my hair. 'You'll be all right.'

Would I ever be all right, though? I'd killed someone, even if that someone was Carnelian.

Rian took my hand and pulled me into an embrace. I buried my head in his shoulder, shaking, glad he had hold of me because my knees were threatening to buckle from shock and exhaustion. The horrors of the last hour cascaded through my mind like water slipping through my fingers. I could just barely grasp that the Crystal Vortex had been saved, that Rian was alive – and I had killed.

The cave shook again as the Vortex settled into its new rhythm. More rocks, loosened by the first tremors, fell around us in a shower of dust and grit. I ducked and dropped to the ground. Rian did the same, covering my body with his, shielding me from the worst of it. The shuddering stopped.

He raised himself off me a little. 'Are you all right?' he asked, moving dusty hair from my face.

I nodded. 'Thanks to you.'

He smiled. With the cave stable again, we gingerly stood up, clinging to each other.

'Thank you, thank you,' Emperor Xanthos said, rushing around to each of us in turn to shake our hands gleefully. 'It will settle now – you needn't worry about further tremors. I will never be able to repay you all for what you've done – and neither will the Six Lands.' He paused as he got to Rian. 'I'm so sorry, Prince Valerian. You told me I was making a mistake. I didn't realise how big a mistake it was. I and Chroma are forever in your debt,' he said, and bowed.

There were so many things in Rian's eyes, but he just nodded.

'My men will clear up here – will you want any of the bodies transported back to Iolite or Aerba?' Xanthos asked.

Mal looked at me and Rian. 'No. Bury them here.'

Rian nodded. 'I think it's best.'

I scanned the cave for Beryl's body. She lay crumpled on the stone floor. I wanted to feel something, wanted to grieve my twin sister, but her betrayal ran so very deep I couldn't. I wasn't angry with her anymore, just disappointed. And annoyed with myself for not seeing it sooner.

Xanthos frowned, then nodded. 'Come with me, come – we'll go back to Magenta immediately.'

Rian slipped his arm around my waist as if he realised I was having trouble standing and guided me from the Cave of Crystals. My legs were like lead. I wanted to sleep for a week. I glanced at my wedding Ring. It was as dead as the Fire Opal, which Anise had collected before helping Sage to his feet.

'You better take care of this,' Anise said, passing the Fire Opal to Rian. 'Aerba still needs it.'

Rian nodded and took hold of it in his spare hand. The vibrancy, the heartbeat, was gone, the colours inside now back to the flickers from before. When I'd first seen it in the Aerban Throne Room, I'd thought it alive. I now knew that was just torchlight playing on it. Its true essence had only been awoken when Willow touched it. That was when it had truly come alive. Now it was just a simple fire opal.

I glanced at Mal on our way out into the tunnel. He stood holding Onyx, and looked over at me.

'Thank you,' I mouthed. Mal nodded, throwing me a little grin and a *told you so* look.

I'd never hear the end of this now – how Mal had been right and my dream could be beaten. I didn't care, I was just relieved Rian was alive.

I glanced back one last time at Carnelian's broken body, and entered the tunnel just as Topaz came around. She took one look at Carnelian and screamed. I kept walking, looking straight ahead as bile rose in my throat.

Outside, the Emperor's soldiers were running about, preparing for our departure. To one side I noticed a bound figure, hands and feet tied. Sorrel.

'We caught him trying to steal one of the horses, Your Majesty,' one of the soldiers said. 'What would you like us to do with him?'

Xanthos glanced at Rian. Sage looked over towards his brother and scowled.

'What do you normally do with horse thieves?' Rian asked.

'Hanging, or life in prison,' Xanthos said. 'We take horse theft very seriously here.'

Rian glanced at Sage. He looked back at Rian and shrugged.

'Life imprisonment then, if that's your law,' Rian said.

'A wise choice, Your Highness,' Xanthos said.

Sorrel's face blanched. 'What? For stealing a *horse*? That's ridiculous!'

'Really? You'd prefer death, Brother?' Sage asked.

Sorrel's eyebrows lowered and he glowered back at his brother as his feet were unbound and he was attached to a rope behind one of the soldier's horses. Sorrel was going to have a long walk back.

Willow came out of the cave with Anise. He draped his arm protectively around her as she walked along, her face ashen. She attempted to stifle little coughs as she went, her eyes searching all the faces for one in particular.

'Where is he?' she asked, her voice trembling as she looked around desperately. 'Where is he?' She coughed again.

'He stayed behind to let us escape,' I said, taking her hand. 'Don't worry.'

'Of course I worry. Bobbins. You know what he's like. He's being heroic again.'

'He told us to tell you he loved you, with all his heart.'

She promptly burst into tears between coughs.

I winced.

'See? He's being heroic,' she sobbed as Anise took her into a hug.

'I'm so sorry I can't make you anything for your cough, Willow,' Anise said. 'My Herb Chest is back at the Palace.'

'That's all right,' Willow said. 'It's not too bad, really.'

'It'll improve once you've had a chance to calm down and rest,' Anise said.

I stepped back and looked at Rian. He had a worried look on his face. I hoped his cousin was all right, and had either escaped or been thrown into a cell rather than anything else, and I could tell Rian was thinking the same.

'Rian,' Onyx said, coming over to us with Mal. 'I wasn't sure if you'd want this or not... I found it lying on the ground next to your brother.'

In Onyx's out-stretched hand lay the Spinel Push Dagger that had so nearly ended Rian's life. I swallowed and glanced at Rian. His face paled as he looked at it.

'It is an Artefact – it probably shouldn't be left lying around,' Mal said.

Rian sighed and took it from Onyx. 'Thank you, Onyx.'

Onyx nodded. 'I wonder where it came from, originally?'

'It belonged to my mother,' Rian said.

I looked sharply at him. 'What?'

'Mother kept it in a drawer in her bedchamber – a family heirloom of her mother's, from what I remember her saying.'

'Then it's rightfully yours,' Onyx said. 'Even if it did nearly kill you.'

'That was Chervil, not the Dagger,' I said, keen to differentiate between the act and the object for Rian's sake.

He looked at me. His eyes were full of all sorts of emotions, too many to sort through. He nodded.

'You're right. I'll look after it from now on,' he said, slipping it into his boot.

The Emperor offered us his carriage, but Rian preferred to ride, and although there were now enough horses, we rode together. We were back in the forest by twilight and camped early in a little clearing. Topaz and Sorrel were tied up on one side of the camp, guarded by six soldiers; the Emperor wasn't taking any chances.

We were all weary after our exertions, but also relieved that everything had turned out well – more or less. After a hot meal I sat looking into the campfire. I wasn't numb, exactly, but I didn't really feel much of anything. Carnelian's death filled my mind.

'I didn't know what to do the first time after I killed someone, either,' Sage said, sitting beside me, the scent of violets and lemons swirling around us.

'I'm sorry?' My brain was finding it hard to function.

'I didn't know how to deal with it. You know, killing. Although, I think it depends on *why* you killed. That has a lot to do with processing the emotions. Whether you've trained to do it or not, whether you're prepared.'

'I was trained for it, all right,' I said bitterly. 'That's all Juniper had me do the last few years.' I turned and looked at him, his earring glistening in the firelight. 'Onyx said sometimes it can be like a millstone around your neck.'

'Really?' Sage nodded slowly, staring into the fire as he thought. He looked at me. 'But I think in the end, though, it's about understanding what you're prepared to do – to win, to live, to protect someone. If you find yourself in a fight, you need to be ready to do anything, absolutely anything at all, or you – or someone you care about – might die. That doesn't mean you should instigate the fight, but what we did today was to save the Vortex, save the Six Lands. It had to be done. And we had to win, and in the end, you had to save Rian. Thwart your prophetic dream. You had no choice. If you hadn't acted in the way you did, an evil assassin would've lived and the rightful, good King of Aerba would be dead – how would you have handled that?'

I glanced over at Rian. He sat talking to Anise and Xanthos, deep in conversation about something or other.

'Very badly,' I said.

'Exactly. What you did – it was the lesser of two evils.' Sage tugged at his earring. 'You know, the first time I killed, I did it to save Anise.'

'You did?' I asked, glancing at him.

'We were attacked by thieves outside of Tansy Town – the King had sent us to escort some Merean diplomats from Tansy to Viridi. Anyway, just outside the town we were attacked. One of the thieves came at Anise from behind. He had no idea the bastard was even there. I killed him with my sword, ran him through.'

Sage paused, looking over towards Anise.

'It was Anise or the thief, and I far rathered it was the thief. And I'm glad I did it.' He turned towards me. 'Saving someone is the same as self-defence, really. You didn't go out looking to kill Carnelian – he came to you looking for trouble. Sometimes you have to give them some back.'

'You're saying I did the right thing and I'll get over it?' I asked, glancing away from Sage and towards Rian, then back to Sage.

Sage smiled at me. 'That's exactly what I'm saying. It does get easier after the first one – not that I'm suggesting you'll have to kill again, but as long as you don't start it, you're purely defending yourself or someone else, then you have no choice. It's not your fault. Sometimes it can even help to view your attacker as not human, as a creature, like a powler or a mynogre. You wouldn't hesitate with one of them, would you?'

'No,' I said, shaking my head. He was quite right. 'I'm not really sure Carnelian was human, the way he carried on.'

'There you go, then. Just be kind to yourself. You saved your husband's life. That's the most important thing, isn't it?'

I let out a long breath as I looked back at Rian. 'Most definitely.'

Sage gave me a quick hug – not his normal style at all – and got up, starting to move away.

'Sage?' I grabbed his hand.

He turned back. 'Yes?'

'Thank you.'

He smiled as I let go, nodded, and walked over to Anise as Rian came to join me.

'You all right?' he asked.

I nodded. 'I will be, at any rate.'

Rian looked over at Sage. 'He doesn't usually hand out hugs.'

'He was handing out a bit of advice, too. Rather good advice, as it happens.'

Rian glanced at me. 'The first time he killed, saving Anise's life?'

I nodded.

'Hmm. I was there when it happened. He did the right thing. Just as you did.'

'But I always hoped never to kill,' I said, bowing my head.

'You did it to save me.'

'I know, but – do you think any less of me? For killing Carnelian?'

Rian slipped his arm around my shoulders and pulled me into a hug, my face resting in the warm, comforting crook of his neck. 'No, I think more of you, because when you had to act, you did. You didn't hesitate. You saved my life and I'll always be grateful for that and cherish you even more because you went against your principles for me.' He rested his head on my forehead. 'You could've let me die.'

'Never. That's one thing I could never do.'

'And so whatever the personal cost was going to be to you, you put it to one side to save me. And I love you even more for it. If that's possible,' he said, kissing my forehead.

My brow creased. 'I thought you might—'

He reached out and lifted my chin. 'Do you think less of me for the times I've killed to save your life?'

'Of course not. Why would I?'

'Well then, that answers your question. I love you more than ever. It wasn't your fault – Carnelian made the decision to attack me, not you. You just defended me – you were my shield, as you said you would be. Now, stop thinking and kiss me,' he said, leaning towards me.

I could never say no to him now, and our lips met, his hot tongue exploring as he gently kissed me, making me tingle all over at his touch. I kissed him back, just as deeply as he kissed me. He held me close, running his hand over my hair.

'What I want to know is how you found that final burst of energy,' he said. 'I had nothing left. When Carnelian came at me I truly thought that was it.'

'It was your Ring,' I said, holding up my wedding Ring. 'It's an Artefact – or at least it was. The Thyme Ring, Ostianzis called it, although I didn't realise that's what it was at the time. One of the most powerful Artefacts. It gave me the strength to save you when I had nothing left, no energy.'

Rian took my hand and looked at the Ring, frowning. 'How did you find out that this was the Thyme Ring?'

'I just had a feeling about it, that it was special, and when we found out about Willow being a Waker, we decided to get her to practise on it. That's when I realised what it was – the Thyme Ring.'

'We?'

'Me and Willow. It was the first time she'd woken anything. I thought it would give her a little practice before the Fire Opal, if I was right – and I was. I just hadn't realised it was *the* Ring until I saw the diamonds glowing in amongst the engraved Thyme. I never found the time to tell you.'

'And you used its energy to save me?'

I nodded. 'It gave me the strength I needed, when I needed it, to save you.'

'I'm even more glad I gave it to you now,' he said, smiling. 'Mother would have been pleased. I don't know how old the Ring is, but it's from far back on her mother's side of the family.'

'Your mother was Aerban, though?'

'Yes, and no. She was born in Aerba, and her father was an Aerban High Blood, but her mother came from the Azurene Isles, out in the Southern Ocean, or so I understand. She was their equivalent of a High Blood. But other than that, I don't know. We've never had much to do with the Azurene Isles.' Rian bowed his head. 'Father forbade anyone speak about the Isles after Mother passed.'

I frowned. 'Ostianzis said the Thyme Ring was once owned by the Aerban Royal Family but during the Great Pestilence the Queen, Cicely, gave it to the then Queen of Calperion for safekeeping. Calperion is way out east, so I wonder how it ended up in the Azurene Isles and in the hands of your mother's family?'

Rian frowned, then shrugged. 'Who knows? But it obviously did, or Ostianzis was wrong about what happened to it in the first place. I believe the Azurene Isles did trade with the Far Eastern Lands at one time, so they knew about Calperion. It's amazing to think the Ring has come full circle and been returned to the Royal Family without us even realising.'

'I doubt Ostianzis was wrong in what he said. Had you heard of the Thyme Ring being in your family?'

'No, not that I recall. It was probably assumed lost, and forgotten about.'

'What do you know about the Azurene Isles? Are they a large land?'

'I think they're a series of sizeable islands, overall about the size of Aerba, but cold and snowy.'

'Snow? I've only ever seen that on mountains. They have that at low level, too?'

He nodded. 'Apparently so.'

'But you've never been?'

'No one in the family has ever been, as far as I know. I asked once...'

'But your father forbade it?'

'Not so much *forbade* as refused to even talk about it.'

'Oh.'

'Nothing I could do.'

'Perhaps we could go one day.'

A little smile played on his lips. 'Maybe we could. Although it's quite a long sea journey – two to three months each way – so I don't think Willow and Tarragon would come. Not willingly, anyway.'

I smirked at his words, gazing at the Ring again. The dream hallucination I'd had of the woman and Rian's Ring nudged into my mind.

'Your mother, what did she look like?' I asked quietly.

Rian smiled, a lingering sadness in his eyes. 'Rather like me.'

'Maroon hair, but wavy, and amber eyes?'

He frowned. 'Yes, how did you know?'

'I think I saw her, in a hallucination, after I'd fallen off the cliff. She had your Ring, but gave it to me.'

Rian chewed his lip. 'Did she look happy?'

'She smiled as she gave it to me.'

A little grin spread across his face. 'I'll take that to mean she approves.'

'I hope she would've, if she'd got to know me.'

'Was there anything else?'

'I thought she was beckoning to me for a moment, but then this circle of coloured lights appeared and she vanished.'

He shrugged. 'Not all your hallucinations have been prophetic – and this one certainly can't be. Maybe it was just your injuries, and perhaps Tarragon, or one of the others, had described her to you.'

'Maybe. How did she die?'

His forehead furrowed, eyes clouding. 'She was on her way to Saffron, on the east coast, for a Royal Visit. The weather suddenly turned and… She was caught in…' His voice almost cracked as he spoke. He took a deep breath. 'She was caught in a flash flood. Swept out to sea. We never found her body.'

I gasped. 'That's why you were so cut up about me, wasn't it? Because I'd been swept away, too?'

He looked out into the trees and nodded.

'Oh, Rian, I'm so sorry.' I slipped my arms around him, holding him tightly.

'Hardly your fault,' he said, kissing my cheek. 'But yes, your loss hit harder because of Mother.' His eyes had a haunted look about them.

'I'm sorry – I shouldn't have asked…'

He shook his head. 'It's fine. I should've told you long ago.'

I paused. 'I never told you what happened to my mother.'

'That's true. What did happen?'

'She drowned, too, in a storm. She was on her way to Flos when it happened.'

Rian pulled me closer. 'Never found her?'

'No.'

He sighed. 'That's one thing I'd rather we didn't have in common.'

'Me, too,' I said, a twinge of sadness sitting in my gut. I took a breath. 'Well, at least your mother's Ring saved you.'

'You did that,' he said, tilting his head slightly and kissing me again. I relaxed into his arms, into the kiss, giving myself over to it, and him, and the comfort it gave us both. His warm mouth and gentle tongue made me melt inside as I kissed him back. We lingered for a while.

'Are you all right?' I asked.

'Couple of bruises, but I'm fine,' he said.

'No, I meant about your brother.'

'Oh,' he said, and sighed. 'I suppose it was inevitable, really. Looking back, we were never both going to make it out of that cave alive, but I didn't expect him to do what he did. I'd hoped to take him home to Aerba to stand trial. Maybe this way it's better.'

'You'll miss him?'

'Will you miss Beryl?'

For a split second my eyes teared up, but the tears quickly vanished. 'There would have been a time when I would have said yes, very much, but I didn't know then what I know now. I suppose I might a bit, sometimes, but rather miss what we had as children, what we could've had now.'

'Mal said something similar to me earlier while they were preparing the meal.'

I nodded. He'd said that to me while we ate – but I think for him, too, her betrayal ran too deep to forget. Forgive? He thought maybe one day, but it would take him a while. And me, too. Maybe then the two of us would be able to grieve.

'I'm sorry she's dead. I didn't want that, but we'd never have been friends again, let alone sisters,' I said.

'Chervil and I were never really brothers – not like you are with Mal,' Rian said, raking his fingers through his ponytail. 'Until you and Mal, the only examples I had, other than my family, were Sage and Sorrel. Not good touchstones. Now I see how it can be. I never had that with Chervil or Angelica. Tarragon, Sage and Anise have always been my brothers, even though they're not all blood.' He paused, looking into the firelight, the dancing flames reflected in his amber eyes. 'No, I don't think I'll mourn Chervil particularly. He always made my life a damn misery. What about Juniper and Elm?'

'If Chervil made your life a misery then Juniper and Elm made mine and Mal's nothing short of pure hell,' I said. 'There was never any love there, on either side. Juniper wanted to use us. Elm, I think he just enjoyed antagonising us. Mal gave him that scar during a fight Elm started. Mal finished it.'

'I can believe that,' Rian said, chuckling quietly.

A sudden thought struck me, something we'd talked about before, something Sage had said earlier but hadn't fully registered at the time. I sat up straight.

'What is it?' Rian frowned.

'Are you the King now, then?' I asked.

'I…' His forehead furrowed, his face blanching. 'I don't know. I mean, I don't think so. We know Chervil removed me from the line of succession.'

'So Sage's father is King of Aerba?'

CHAPTER THIRTY-TWO

'I heard that,' Sage said from where he now sat near the fire with Anise, a sick look on his face. 'As I've said before, I believe for everyone's sake it would be better if Father wasn't King.'

'No, Rian, you're the rightful King now,' Anise said, a firmness to his buttery voice. 'Surely, Chervil's heinous decrees won't stand?'

'They shouldn't,' Sage said.

'But we're not the ones making the decisions, though, are we? And I'm not sure I'm good enough to be King – not really. Not worthy.' Rian rubbed his head.

'Not worthy?' I asked. 'Utter rot. You've saved the Six Lands from chaos, from your brother's evil schemes, and wrested them from Juniper's clutches. You're more than worthy.'

'Then so are you,' he said, glancing at me. 'And what's more, you saved the King's life.'

'Oh.' Queen Samphire. I swallowed. Maybe there'd be no cottage in the hills for us after all, no crystal-clear pool, no "just the two of us", but a whole palace full.

'Phire's right, though,' Sage said. 'It should be you. You'd make things right with the Blood Decree, Flos, Iolite – all of it.'

Rian winced. 'Like I say, it's out of my hands.'

'W—will you still want me if you're King of Aerba?' I asked quietly.

He turned to look at me. 'By the Herbs, what do you mean?'

'If you're the King, you should have a Royal wife, shouldn't you? One of Royal Blood.'

'I have a Royal wife already, and I don't want anyone else.'

'But I'm not legally Royal, or your wife.'

'I don't care. We stick together – that's what we promised each other, isn't it?'

I nodded, relieved. 'As long as you want me, I'm yours,' I said. 'And I'll always want you – prince, king or pauper.'

He grinned. 'Together.'

'Together,' I said, smiling, and I kissed his nose, wondering how I'd ever get used to the idea of being a queen – if it happened.

We arrived back at Magenta late the following morning, having called in to see the farmer and retrieve Mal's ring. I wasn't sure how much the Emperor paid for it, but it was a lot more than we'd sold it for.

As we rode into the palace courtyard, Onyx dismounted and came over to help me down from our horse. Rian raised an eyebrow, but let it pass.

'You all right, Ama?' Onyx asked. His dark eyes were troubled, and I knew why. 'I've not had a chance to speak to you.'

I nodded. 'I will be. I don't think it will be one of those millstones you spoke about – at least, not for long.'

Onyx shook his head. 'No, Carnelian's not one of the millstones. Just as long as you're okay?' He glanced at Rian, who slipped his hand into mine.

'I'm sure.' I nodded.

Rian gave me his lopsided smile. *Absolutely sure.*

The first thing the Emperor did when we got back into the palace was to send Topaz and Sorrel to the dungeons. I wasn't sorry to see either of them go. Sorrel cast me a last angry glance, but Topaz, still grieving Carnelian, just shuffled away without protest. For a moment my heart skipped a beat, but Rian, who'd seen where I'd been looking, took my hand into his.

'Not your fault,' he murmured in my ear.

'I know,' I replied.

The Emperor immediately had the recaptured Tarragon released. As soon as he was brought into the Throne Room he ran towards Willow and she flew into his arms.

'Thank the Herbs,' Tarragon said, his voice cracking with emotion. 'I thought I'd never see you again.'

I'd never seen two people so happy to see each other. They embraced, he spun her around and then they kissed – I wondered if they might pass out from lack of air the way they carried on. Their reunion was almost surpassed by Anise's with his Herb Chest, but not quite.

Our weapons were returned to us – at least, the others had theirs returned to them. Not having my War Fan or the Cursed Weapons felt incredibly odd, and I was given a sword to wear at my waist, courtesy of a grateful Xanthos.

The Emperor wanted us to stay a while, but Rian was keen to get back to Aerba. Mal wanted to return to Iolite and take up his position as Master as soon as possible. I also thought my brother wanted to put Flint and Serpentine in the Crimson Castle dungeons as soon as he could before they got wind of what had happened in Chroma and escaped. And then there was the dismantling of the Coterie and the Iolitian Blood Rules. Mal and Rian had a number of conversations about the Blood Rule Decrees as we sailed back home with Captain Pol.

We agreed with Xanthos to keep in close contact from now on, and the balancing of the Vortex made that easier – the Great Doldrums were no more and the maelstroms gone.

'It's interesting, I can really feel nature rebalancing now,' Anise said one afternoon as we sailed across calm water. 'Everything feels more settled. I think the dryads will be pleased.'

'Let's hope it stays that way,' Tarragon said, glancing across at Willow, who for once stood happily at the ship's rail, staring out across the glistening waves. 'You know, Nacea will have been most put out to miss all this excitement.'

'Excitement?' Rian raised an eyebrow. 'There are many words I could use to describe the last few months, and excitement wouldn't be one of them.'

'Who's Nacea?' I asked, frowning. 'I don't remember him. And I've never heard of a herb called "Nacea".'

'It's short for Echinacea,' Rian said.

'He's really nice,' Tarragon said. 'Between Rian and me in age, and very handsome, too. The girls all love him.' Rian gave him a long look. 'What? They do. And you can't be worried about your wife straying?'

Rian huffed. 'I'm not,' he said, wrapping an arm around me. 'I trust my wife implicitly. Next to you, Anise, and Sage, he's pretty much the only King's Warrior I'd trust with my life – and my wife.'

'Well then,' Tarragon said, buffing his fingernails on his tunic. 'Lord Lemongrass' nephew, Bay, will probably be a little upset as well. He's a good lad, too.'

Rian nodded. 'He is.'

'So why haven't I met them?' I asked.

'Father decided a permanent detachment of the King's Warriors was needed at Tulsi. He liked to visit there quite regularly – he enjoyed the climate.'

'Bit warm for me,' Tarragon muttered.

'Me, too,' Rian said with a nod. 'Anyway, Nacea and Bay have been stationed there for the last nine months or so.'

'Who knows where they are now.'

'We'll find them when we get back – I'm going to need them.'

We stopped in Spindle to update the Royal Family and make arrangements for Captain Hyssop to meet us at Sycamore in southern Trew to sail us back to Aerba – Pol was going to take Mal and Onyx back to Iolite. Princess Hazel was thrilled to see Anise. She was looking well and insisted on joining us for meals.

'I can never thank you enough for what you did for me,' Hazel said.

'You've recovered well, Your Highness?' Anise asked.

'Yes. I still get rather tired, but I'm so much better.'

'You will always have our deepest gratitude,' Queen Photinia said. 'You will come back with Sage and visit often, won't you?'

'Of course, we'd love to,' Anise said.

'I'd like you to have this, in recognition of your great service to my family,' King Ash said, passing Anise a small book.

Anise took it in his hands, gently turning it over. His eyes widened and his hands started trembling.

'But this is your book about the Chamber of Earth and the herbs inside, Your Majesty,' Anise said. 'I can't accept this.'

Ash held his hands up. 'It's a copy I had made of mine while you were away. I think it will be of great use to an Earth Magic Spinner and Master of Herbs such as yourself.'

'Thank you.' Anise grinned, his eyes glistening.

'Now we'll have to go to the Chamber of Earth,' Onyx said, digging Sage playfully in the ribs.

'No,' Sage said.

'It wasn't that bad, was it?'

'You have no idea.'

'Perhaps we could get Rian to clear the forest of the mynogres first?' Onyx suggested brightly.

'And just who would he find stupid enough to volunteer to do that?' Sage asked, frowning.

Mal flicked his hair over his shoulder. 'I could lend him the Coterie, or whatever I decide to call them now,' he said, his face absolutely straight. 'Give them something to do now they're not going to be killing innocent people for a living.'

'You're not Master of Iolite yet,' I pointed out.

Mal shrugged. 'Details.'

Onyx grinned. 'I think that's an excellent suggestion.'

Sage groaned.

I glanced at Rian, who looked towards the ceiling in disbelief as Anise grinned broadly at the prospect of returning to the Chamber.

I had a tearful farewell with Mal and Onyx when we arrived at Sycamore. They promised to visit Aerba just as soon as things were settled in Iolite and Mal was ensconced as the new Master. Not long after they sailed, Captain Hyssop's ship, *The Sea Urchin*, arrived at the quayside.

'Your Majesty,' Hyssop said with a grin, bowing, as we alighted on deck, his deep green eyes sparkling like the sea. Hyssop was in his mid-thirties, a dependable Aerban man, with skin weathered by his time at sea.

'Not yet,' Rian said, shaking the captain's hand. 'It's not a foregone conclusion – Chervil changed the succession. At the moment, the Kingdom of Aerba passes to Lord Bergamot.'

'Then you haven't heard?' Hyssop asked, glancing from Rian to me and back again. 'Lord Wintergreen has arranged for the Royal Council to repeal all laws passed by Chervil.'

'He what?' Rian asked, wide-eyed.

'Chervil has been branded a traitor to Aerba and his reign stricken from the records.'

'By the Stars, that was quick,' I said.

'I don't believe they wanted to be associated with him at all once news reached Aerba of Chervil's betrayal and treacherous deeds, and your victory and your restartin' the Crystal Vortex,' Hyssop said. 'I've already noticed that the Elements are more balanced, particularly at sea, but even the droughts have stopped and the unseasonable onshore storms have receded. They're callin' your brother Chervil the Unjust.'

'Hell's teeth,' I said.

Tarragon came running up the gangplank. 'Have you heard? The people are calling you "King Valerian the Great",' he said to his cousin. 'And when they're not doing that, you're "The Opal King" because you're bringing the Fire Opal home.'

'Damn, they're what?' Rian asked, turning pink.

'I was gettin' to that,' Hyssop said. 'And Samphire's "The Merciful" or "The Benevolent", dependin' on who you ask.'

'Why?' I asked, startled.

'Because after your treatment at Finule and Chervil's hands, they all feared you'd go back to Aerba and level it with your Quintessence, particularly after King Finule tried to kill you with the Cursed Weapons. They're countin' their good graces that you didn't immediately head in their direction to take revenge.'

'People know about my Quintessence?'

Hyssop grinned wide and bright as the sky. It was a look full of hope and of awe. 'Everyone knows.'

The voyage back to Aerba was uneventful. Hyssop insisted that Rian and I have his cabin on the journey for some privacy. Rian protested, saying we were quite happy in the main crew's cabin like before, but Hyssop was having none of it. He said it wasn't appropriate for the new King of Aerba and his Queen to sleep in hammocks in the crews' quarters, and to be fair, he was probably right, not that I minded. Rian eventually gave in, which pleased Hyssop no end. After all, he could now say the King and Queen had used his cabin. Bragging rights amongst the other ships' captains, I supposed.

Anise made Willow her seasickness remedy. I spent time on deck looking out over the calm water as Sage helped to move things along with his Air Magic. My hand went absently to my shoulder, but rather than the familiar hilt it grasped air. I sighed. I hadn't realised how much I'd miss the Cursed Weapons. I was so used to them on my back that I felt naked without them. I'd got quite attached to them.

'You still pining after your weapons?' Rian asked, wandering over to me, a serious look on his face.

I nodded. 'I guess I'd got used to them.'

'They had almost become a part of you.'

'Like you, then,' I said, wriggling my arm into his. He didn't resist, but didn't exactly make it easy. 'What's the matter?'

'I don't want to be King of Aerba.'

I rested my head on his tense shoulder. 'I know,' I said quietly. 'You could abdicate, but I know how much you love the people – *your* people – and your land. You can do this.'

'Only with you by my side – if I don't have you, I can't,' he said, now wrapping his arms around my shoulders.

'Good thing I'm here then.'

'You'll really be my Queen?' he asked, anxiety resting behind his eyes.

'I don't want to be a queen any more than you want to be a king. In truth, I'd rather have that cottage of yours up in the hills next to the crystal-clear pool, where we can be alone together, rather than the luxuries of Viridi Palace, but...' I took a long breath. 'That's only ever going to be a dream, now, isn't it? I want to be wherever you are, and if that means I have to be your Queen to do it, then I will. So, yes, I'll be your Queen.'

He took hold of my hand and kissed it. 'Maybe I can arrange a cottage in the foothills of the mountains near Nettle, one that has a pool. It's quite beautiful there and the weather's always good. After all, we will need to get away from Viridi from time to time, or we'll go mad.'

I smiled at him. 'Hmm, that sounds delightful.'

His leather wrist strap that had covered my Coterie tattoo for so long slipped and exposed the symbol. I glanced at it and hurriedly covered it up again. Rian looked at me, a troubled expression in his eyes.

'Maybe it's time to get rid of that,' he said quietly.

'How? There's no easy way of removing a tattoo without leaving a nasty scar,' I said, although getting rid of it was my dearest wish.

He frowned a moment. 'Do you trust me?'

'Implicitly.'

'Then let me try.'

'I don't see how you can do anything.'

He smiled at me. 'Just let me try.' He took my arm and removed the wrist strap, handing it to me. He glanced at me. 'I'm hoping this won't hurt too much.'

'What are...' My eyes widened as he balanced my upturned wrist in one hand and placed the other a hair's breadth from the tattoo, closing his eyes. A sensation of warmth spread across my wrist. His hand glowed a comforting red as the heat increased. My skin felt as if it was beginning to burn, but I stayed still. I trusted him. After a few more moments he moved his hand and opened his eyes, inspecting his handiwork.

The skin on my wrist glowed pink from the heat, but the tattoo was gone, revealing the birthmark underneath that marked me out as a Quintessence Angle Spinner. My eyes were wide as I stared at the mark that had been hidden for so long. Rian could really control his powers well now.

I looked up at him. 'Thank you,' I said, my voice crackling with emotion as tears welled in my eyes. 'I never thought I'd be rid of it.'

He smiled at me, his eyes alight. 'I always wanted to free you from it, and today I have. I didn't hurt you?'

I shook my head, leant towards him, and kissed him.

'No, just a little warmth,' I said, hugging him. 'It means the world to me to be free of it.'

'Glad I could help.'

'You know, Mal and Onyx might appreciate theirs being removed, too.'

Rian coughed. 'Well, actually…'

I narrowed my eyes as I looked at him. 'You practised on them first, didn't you?'

'I might have done,' he said, rubbing the back of his neck.

'And it worked?'

He nodded. 'Onyx complained that I'd burnt him, but it really wasn't that bad – it healed really quickly once Anise gave him some salve. When I did Mal's, it was the same as yours, just a little pink.'

I shook my head. 'I didn't even know.'

'We wanted to keep it as a surprise for you.'

I smiled. 'Well, you did that.' I looked at the wrist strap I still held in my hand. 'You want this back?'

'No,' he said, shaking his head. 'It's yours now.'

I smiled and he helped me put it on, but this time we placed it on my other wrist.

Despite our talk, the closer we got to Aerba the more distracted and distant Rian became. The day we were due to arrive in Tansy, we all dressed in our Aerban clothes, hair up in high ponytails. Rian stood at the bow of the ship, an agitated look in his eyes as the coastline appeared on the horizon.

'Tell me what it is?' I asked.

He turned to me, took my hands and looked deep into my eyes. 'I need to ask you something. Will you marry me?'

'I thought I already had – sort of.'

Rian shook his head. 'That won't be good enough for the Royal Council. It needs to be completely one hundred percent legal for them to acknowledge you as Queen. They'll say whatever we pledged to each other doesn't count and they'll start trying to forge an alliance with a princess of Flos or Mere or any of the other lands, and that's not happening,' he said, a steely determination in his voice. 'I'm married to you.'

'Surely, if you're the King you're in charge,' I said.

'You'd think so, but my experience is that that isn't always the case – so will you? Will you be my Queen Samphire Amethyst – properly? I'd be so honoured if you would, and quite frankly I need you. You already know I can't take on being King without you to help me. It's going to be a huge job and, honestly, it frightens me, but with you by my side as my wife, my proper wife, I think I can face it, be a good king. So what do you think? Will you? Please?

You can think about it for a while if you want.' He looked over my shoulder at the Aerban coast appearing in the distance. 'You've probably got an hour to decide.'

I gave him a long look. His eyes were full of fear, hope, love and so many other emotions that I couldn't help but lean forward and kiss him gently on the lips.

'A whole hour? I don't even need a whole second. Of course I'll marry you – again.'

He grinned a relieved sort of grin. 'As soon as we arrive in Tansy we'll find a priest, although I'm not sure if there's a priest in Aerba who'd marry us. I don't know what to do. Damn. I should've thought of this ages ago,' he said, rubbing the back of his neck with one hand. 'I'm a damn idiot. But I'll walk away from the throne rather than lose you.'

I looked at him, wide-eyed. I knew how much Aerba meant to him – the land, the people. Even if he'd never liked the idea of being King, it had fallen to him. It was his duty now, even if he'd never have chosen it for himself, and Rian being Rian, he would never shirk that responsibility, even if it weighed heavily on him. The fact that he was even contemplating giving that up for me if they wouldn't let us be together made my heart swell with love.

'It won't come to that,' I said, squeezing his hand.

'We do need to get married properly,' he said. 'We haven't even... *you know*... so I want to make sure there are no arguments once we're back in Viridi.'

'We've all but,' I said.

He grinned impishly at me.

'Anyway, they hardly need to know if we've...' I waved my hands.

'They have their spies,' he said sullenly.

'In the Royal Bedchamber?' I asked, aghast.

'I'm dismantling the Nightshade the moment I get back to Viridi, and having all the passages in the palace sealed – permanently – as soon as possible.'

'Then we'd better do something about getting married, and quick – just in case.'

Hyssop walked up to the bow. 'We'll reach Tansy within the hour,' he said.

I chewed my lip for a moment. 'Hyssop – will you marry us?' I asked.

Rian's eyes widened. 'Of course, how daft of me.'

Hyssop looked from Rian to me and back again. 'I am able to do such a thin' – but wouldn't you rather it was in Viridi City with all the pomp and circumstance?'

'No,' we said together, looked at each other and grinned.

'I'm not sure the Royal Council will be in favour,' Rian said. 'The new King of Aerba marrying an ex-assassin Middle Blood from the family of a Demoted Aerban High Blood – they won't be keen, but I don't care about any of that. Samphire is of Royal Blood – a little diluted, perhaps, but nevertheless worthy. Will you do it for us?'

Hyssop grinned. 'It would be my pleasure, Your Majesty,' he said, giving a little bow.

Standing on the deck of a ship, wearing Aerban clothes, surrounded by a few friends and sailors, wasn't how I'd ever thought I'd be officially married, but in all honesty, it was more wonderful, more intimate than I could ever have imagined. Rian and I repeated the vows we'd said in the dungeons so long ago, at last able to pledge ourselves to each other formally and in front of witnesses.

After the ceremony, and "The Kiss", we collected our things from the cabins while Hyssop quickly drew up the formal document and we all signed it, proving our marriage. He gave it to Rian. I glanced at it and smiled. Hyssop had dated it the day we left Aerba months ago, the day the Curse had been lifted.

Rian looked at it, then at me. 'Appropriate – the day we were both freed.'

I nodded. 'Thank you, Hyssop. For everything.'

'It's been my pleasure – Your Majesty,' he said, grinning.

I swallowed.

Rian took my hand and gave it a squeeze. 'You're going to have to get used to that now, my Queen,' he said, kissing my cheek.

I took a deep breath. 'I'm not sure that's something I'll ever get used to.'

'Not sure I'll get used to this "Majesty" business, either, but we don't have much of a choice, do we?' he whispered in my ear. 'Just as long as we're together.'

'True.'

Rian turned to Tarragon. 'Cousin, I want you to look after the Marriage Document. And when we get back, I want you to be my new Chamberlain.'

Tarragon blinked. 'Bugger me. You do?'

Rian nodded, and Tarragon took hold of the Marriage Document, his hands trembling slightly. I smiled. In truth there was no one I'd trust more with it - Tarragon had become like a brother to me, as he was to Rian, and I couldn't be more pleased with Rian's first proper appointment.

'If you're sure, I'd be pleased to serve the new King of Aerba as Chamberlain,' he said. I'd never seen Tarragon look quite so emotional, other than when he emerged from the Magenta dungeons and greeted Willow.

'Don't lose that.' I nodded at the piece of parchment in his shaking hands. 'Or it's the dungeons for you,' I teased.

Tarragon looked at me and grinned. 'Don't worry, Queen Phire, I won't lose it.'

'Sage, will you command the Army?' Rian asked.

Sage looked a little wide-eyed at the prospect. 'Really? It would be my honour.'

'And Anise, can you organise the Royal Household, be its Head?'

Anise grinned. 'As long as I can be the Royal Herbalist, too, Rian.'

'Is there such a position?' I asked.

'There is now,' Rian said, smiling. 'Willow, my Queen is going to need a Lady-in-waiting, one married to Royal Blood who will run her affairs – do you know of anyone suitable?'

Willow's eyes darted between Rian and Tarragon. 'I…'

'And just to let you know, the first thing I'm doing is tearing up the Aerban Blood Rule Decree,' Rian added.

Tarragon scratched his chin thoughtfully. 'Willowherb of Viridi, will you do me the great honour of becoming my wife?'

'Are we doing this *now*?' Willow asked, wide-eyed, although she looked as though she was about to melt as he used her full name.

'Yes, right now,' Tarragon said, suddenly crashing down to one knee. 'Will you make me the happiest man alive, my love?' he asked, offering his hands out to her.

Willow blushed, looked at him through her long eyelashes and nodded. 'Yes, Lord Tarragon, of course I will,' she said, taking hold of his hands. He stood up and kissed her.

At last.

Willow turned back to Rian, still holding on to Tarragon. 'Your Majesty, I wonder if I might apply for the position as Queen's Lady-in-waiting myself?'

'I'd rather hoped you might,' Rian said, squeezing my hand. 'As long as my good wife is happy with the arrangement?'

'Yes, I couldn't be happier, but that title's all wrong,' I said. 'Lady-in waiting sounds like a glorified maid, and Willow can't be my servant like that – how about Queen's Companion?'

Rian grinned. 'Perfect. So, Willow, you'll be the Queen's Companion?'

'Bobbins. You're really sure?' Willow asked, her eyes bright.

'Yes.'

Willow nodded.

I beamed at her. 'Excellent.'

'You'll all obviously be on my Royal Council – you, too, Willow,' Rian said.

Willow gasped. 'I'd be honoured.'

A knock sounded at the cabin door and a sailor peered in the room. 'Captain, we've just docked – and, Your Majesty, Lord Wintergreen is on the quayside waiting with an escort,' the sailor said.

'Thank you,' Hyssop said with a nod. 'Looks like news of your arrival has spread already and your country is awaitin' you, Your Majesty.'

'Right, then,' Rian said, straightening his coat and taking a deep breath. 'Let's go and meet Lord Wintergreen.'

'You did all this to stop him from arranging things himself, didn't you,' I whispered in Rian's ear.

'How well you know me, wife,' he murmured back. 'I'm not sure I can let him continue in his position after what he's done, even if it was for me. I'll have to come up with something else for him.'

'Retire him. He deserves it. Then make him a Royal Adviser – he'll still be involved but not *too* involved, and you won't be seen as totally condoning his actions.'

'I think you should be a Royal Adviser, not him.'

'I already am. I'm your Premier Royal Adviser – but then, I'm your wife.'

'I'm coming to realise that quite quickly,' he said, smiling. 'Now, take my hand. I'm going to make it quite clear where we stand from the outset. I'm not having any arguments about you.'

'Rian, you'd better take this,' Tarragon said, coming over and handing him the Fire Opal.

'Thanks,' Rian said. He looked at the dead stone. It still caught the light, but not like it had when Willow had Released it.

We followed Hyssop and walked out on deck. Rian took my hand, interlacing his fingers with mine as if to stop me from running off. But the time for running off was well past; we'd both passed the point of no return and were now committed to our new roles. Maybe we hadn't sought them, didn't even really want them, but we'd been called and we would meet our destiny together, do our best to rule Aerba and look after its people.

We moved down the gangplank, hand-in-hand, Rian holding the Fire Opal in his other hand.

The Royal Escort stood to attention as Lord Wintergreen bowed. Finule's old Chamberlain adjusted his burgundy and black coat as he stood upright again, ready to greet his new King.

'Your Majesty,' he said, his eyebrow rising as he noted our joined hands. 'How relieved we are to have you back home in Aerba, King Valerian. And the Fire Opal,' he said, acknowledging the Artefact.

'It's good to be back, Lord Wintergreen,' Rian said, then turned to me. 'You know my wife, Queen Samphire.'

I smiled sweetly at the Chamberlain. He swallowed, his face draining of all colour, his grey eyes aghast.

'W—wife?' Wintergreen stammered. 'But, I'd heard it wasn't official, Your Majesty, and surely a wife of Royal Blood and a delicate disposition would be far more suitab—'

'It's a little late now,' Rian said firmly. 'Everything is legal.'

I took a little step forward so only he and Rian could hear. 'You wouldn't want your new King of Aerba, Valerian the Great, tangled in a web of intrigue with a Royal bastard on his hands before he's even been in power for a year, would you?'

'Royal ba…' Wintergreen looked wide-eyed at Rian, then back at me. 'You're pregnant already?' His voice went up an octave.

'One can never be entirely sure of these things at the beginning,' I said quietly. 'But it is very possible. After all, we have been—' I coughed delicately— 'doing what's required to make it happen, *very* frequently.'

The Chamberlain swallowed again and scratched his nose. I'd hit a nerve. This was the last thing he wanted. A scandal. Obviously he wanted this transition to be smooth, not complicated by divorce or annulled marriages and babies before he'd had the chance to marry Rian off to someone he considered more suitable – assuming this phantom fragile princess of his even existed.

Wintergreen's shoulders sagged in defeat and he bowed, his long salt-and-pepper hair shifting in his high ponytail as he moved. 'Your Majesty,' he said to me. 'I am sure you will be a great asset not only to the King, but to Aerba as well.' He sighed.

'A Quintessence Magic Spinner would have to be of High, if not Royal, Blood, wouldn't they?' Rian asked, attempting to smooth things over. 'Or she wouldn't have that power?'

Wintergreen frowned. 'Now you come to mention it, Your Majesty, you are quite correct. Queen Samphire is obviously an extremely suitable match.'

'She'll also help relations with Flos, having Flosian ancestry as well as Aerban, not to mention her connections with the new Master of Iolite and his partner, a relation to the Queen of Mere.'

Wintergreen nodded slowly as he mulled over the information. 'Of course, that paints everything in an entirely different light. Welcome, Queen Samphire.' He looked at Rian. 'There will of course have to be a formal Coronation Ceremony.'

'Of course.' Rian nodded as I groaned inwardly. 'I would like you to involve Lord Tarragon in the arrangements.'

Wintergreen frowned. '*Lord* Tarragon?'

'There are going to be some changes at Court. I feel that you have worked so hard for the Royal Family over the years that it's high time you were rewarded.'

'Rewarded, Your Majesty?'

'You have earnt your retirement, Lord Wintergreen, and your son will take your place as Chamberlain – with initial guidance from you, of course,' Rian said, smiling.

A vein popped out on Wintergreen's neck. 'Your Majesty, if only you knew what I'd done to get you on the thr—'

'I do know, Lord Wintergreen,' Rian said, locking his eyes with Wintergreen's – the older man shrank backwards slightly. 'All done with the best intentions, but for Aerba to move on from my father and Chervil, we need a new Royal Council, although I would be pleased if you would become a Royal Adviser and still remain close to Court.'

The vein in Wintergreen's neck faded back down. 'As Your Majesty desires. It would be my honour to serve you as such, Your Majesty. I'm sure my son will make a worthy replacement,' he said with a little bow. He looked up as Tarragon walked down the gangplank arm-in-arm with Willow. The vein popped out again.

'I also intend to revoke the Blood Rule Decree,' Rian said, glancing at Tarragon and Willow. 'I think it would be to everyone's advantage,' he finished as Sage and Anise joined us, hand-in-hand.

Wintergreen almost choked as his face blanched. 'Are you sure, Your Majesty? I mean—'

'Positive,' Rian said in a voice brooking no argument. 'It is my decision and my right. As is the choice of Royal Council. Where is Lord Bergamot?'

'I regret to tell Your Majesty that King Chervil sent him to the dungeons for refusing to lead the army against Flos. He was tortured on the King's orders b—by Sorrel.' He glanced up at Sage. 'He's alive, but not the man he was. He wouldn't be able to lead your army now.'

Sage's face tightened. He had no real love for his father, I knew that, but even so it was disturbing to hear Sorrel had been complicit in such heinous crimes.

'Sorrel is in prison in Chroma for crimes against the Emperor, the same crimes that saw the death of Chervil as they attempted to destroy the Crystal Vortex,' I said. 'He won't trouble Aerba again.'

Wintergreen nodded, a look of relief on his face.

'Lord Sage will take his place,' Rian said quietly. 'Lord Bergamot will be cared for.'

'Thank you,' Sage murmured from behind us.

Rian nodded. 'Lord Anise will take over the Royal Household, working with the new Lady Willowherb, who will be in charge of the Queen's affairs.'

For a moment Wintergreen looked as if he was going to protest, then thought better of it and scratched his nose. 'As Your Majesty desires.' Wintergreen bowed.

'Now, let's get back to Viridi City with all haste,' Rian said. 'There is much to do.'

Wintergreen led the way to where horses waited for us. Rian helped me into my saddle.

'You're quite seductive when you're so formal,' I said quietly.

Rian raised an eyebrow. 'I'll have to remember that.'

CHAPTER THIRTY-THREE

Upon our return to Viridi City, Rian quickly set about dismantling the Nightshade and the Blood Rule Decree. Blood Classes were banned and the people free to wear what they wanted, in the colour they wanted – although many started wearing purple, the colour of my coat. The Flosian Ambassador was called to the palace almost immediately and relations with Flos smoothed over, especially once Rian pointed out my Flosian ancestry.

Priest Cardamon was released from the prison, given a Royal Pardon and new rooms in a wing of the palace. He blessed our marriage at a private service in the Temple, just so there were no future arguments.

Rian quickly found Echinacea and Bay and had them return to the palace. Nacea was made Head of the King's Warriors – as Tarragon had said, he was a handsome young man with long black hair, a muscular build, and a friendly personality. Bay was made his deputy – he was smaller, wily looking, and a couple of years younger than Nacea, with light brown hair and a big grin. I immediately liked them both.

A small, informal ceremony was held to return the Fire Opal to the Cedarwood Throne. The Aerban treasure, fabled for its luck, abundance and protection against danger, once again sat in pride of place.

Rian also banned Saliivia.

The Aerban people immediately took their new King Valerian to their hearts, just as Willow had said. They cheered whenever they saw him in the City. There would be shouts of "The Opal King! Long live King Valerian the Great!". Initially, Rian just looked embarrassed, but as time went on he took it with good humour, and smiled and waved back. Willow had been right – the people loved him. And much to my amazement, they also took me to their hearts, too. It was a slightly slower process, but they began to wave when they saw me; initially it was a little subdued, but very quickly they began to smile and cheer for me as well. I found it hard to come to terms with at the start, and a little disconcerting.

'I can see why they love you – you're their prince – but not me,' I said to Rian one evening. 'An ex-assassin from Iolite.'

He smiled back. 'They know they've got a lot to be grateful to you for. They know about your Magic, your relationship with Mal, and the fact that you saved them from war with Flos. And you saved their world.'

'I didn't do it alone.'

He shrugged. 'They also know about your Aerban ancestry, so I think they see you as Aerban rather than Iolitian. And they know you didn't kill my sister. But I think, most of all, they can see that you make their King very happy, so they're obviously going to fall in love with you, too.' He beamed at me.

'Hmm.'

But it did appear that he was right.

After a few weeks we received word from Iolite that Mal had been installed as the new Master with little protest, and he had confined Serpentine to the dungeons on a permanent basis. Unfortunately, Lord Flint had somehow escaped and was nowhere to be found.

Mal had also disbanded the Coterie, as he said he would. In fact, he was considering setting up a new Fellowship, giving the ex-assassins new jobs as special protection details for the Royal Families of the Six Lands and the Crystal Vortex. There was no mention of clearing out the mynogres from Cilantro Forest, though, much to Anise's dismay.

The calming of the Elements continued, and reports of fair weather came in from across the Six Lands.

Priest Cardamon agreed to preside over the Coronation Ceremony in the Temple, which took place three months after we returned to Aerba. The arrangements went on and on, almost driving me insane, the only good point being that Mal and Onyx, the other Royal Families, my relations from Flos, and Onyx's grandfather, were all going to be in attendance.

'So, remind me why do we have to go through this again?' I said one afternoon after another round of discussion.

'Formality and tradition,' Tarragon said, buffing his fingernails on his new coat.

Rian grunted.

I'd hoped we might be able to escape the whole Coronation thing, but apparently not.

The ceremony itself was abbreviated, at Rian's insistence, but still went on for three long hours. By the time we left the Temple of Herbs, I was ready to scream and Rian looked bored to tears.

The banquet and ball afterwards went on for several more hours, but at least the whole event had given me a chance to apologise to Erica for the dress I'd borrowed from her in Flos and ultimately ruined – and to give her a new one. My cousin brought news about Prince Monkshood. After his treachery had been made known, King

Narcissus of Flos had had him arrested, along with his associates – it turned out he hadn't been working alone. They were all executed a few days later. I shuddered when she told me. Rian wouldn't have done something like that, but then, Flos wasn't Aerba, and there, treason came with the death penalty rather than life imprisonment.

We settled into our new roles, hesitantly at first, but soon found a kind of rhythm to them. A lot of our duties revolved around meetings and diplomacy, although that was more Rian than me, which I was initially rather put out about, but took with good grace. After all, he was the King and it was his country, so maybe I didn't have the right to get involved like I might want to. What I was included in was all the formal dinners and balls. Some of it I enjoyed. Some of it I tolerated. So did Rian. On the very odd occasion we were able to escape the palace for a ride or a picnic, we often went with Tarragon, Willow, Sage and Anise, but those times were few and far between. I really enjoyed our outings together. We reminisced about our travels and adventures, and spent time enjoying each other's company.

It had been two months since the Coronation, and the morning held Rian's first formal Audience with his Court, exactly as Aerban tradition dictated after the crowning of a new king. And, of course, the new Queen of Aerba was to be in attendance, too.

I woke early, my stomach doing somersaults. Rian lay beside me, still fast asleep, so I left him alone in our rooms, slipped on a tunic and a pair of leggings – Willow would have gone spare if she knew – and ventured into the empty Throne Room. I looked at my throne. A new one had been commissioned for me from the Master Carpenters of Trew so I could sit beside the Cedarwood Throne. Mine was of sandalwood – I'd insisted, much to Rian's amusement. It was hand carved with beautifully ornate flowers of Valerian and Samphire, which was Rian's suggestion. I was yet to sit in it, so I climbed the dais steps and sat down. It wasn't too uncomfortable – as long as I didn't have to sit here for too long at any one time I'd be all right. Maybe I could suggest cushions for both of us if Audiences proved to be protracted.

I twisted around and looked at Rian's newly painted throne. My gold and diamond Ring caught the early morning light streaming through the large windows that faced the gardens where flowers bloomed and fountains laughed.

'We've been through quite a lot together, us three, haven't we?' I said, looking at the Ring and the Fire Opal. 'I'm sorry the two of you aren't like you were.'

My memories of the feelings I'd had from the Ring and the Fire Opal when they were Artefacts of Elemental power filled me for a moment. I missed how I'd felt when they were *living*, when they'd had their power inside, before we'd used it in our hour of need.

I touched the Ring with my other hand.

If only.

A warm sensation grew in my chest, my hands. My fingertips glowed white, then a spark jumped from them to the Ring. I sat up straight, surprised. The diamonds in the Ring flickered then sparkled brightly before returning to how they'd looked before I'd used all their power up in the Cave of Crystals, when I'd been desperate to save Rian.

'What the…?' I touched the ring again. The sensation of a living thing once more resided in Rian's Ring. Could I have revived it somehow? Could Quintessence Spinners not just use Artefacts, but recharge them, too?

I looked up at the Fire Opal, nestled in its home at the top of the King's Throne. 'What about you? Will it work for you?' I got up and knelt on Rian's throne, reaching up to touch the dead opal with both hands. 'Are you still there, too, old friend?' I asked, closing my eyes as a warmth built in my chest and hands.

Come home.

The warmth swept from my fingers. I gasped. It felt as if something had tugged inside me, and I opened my eyes, breathless and tired.

The Fire Opal winked back at me, its centre once again swirling with a vivid green and purple flame heartbeat – if anything, brighter than when Willow had Released it. I looked behind me – the room stood empty. This was going to be hard to explain, especially as I wasn't sure quite what had happened or how I'd done it. Father's book had probably had a whole chapter on it. If only I'd read it when I'd had the chance.

Maybe I needed to write my own book.

I stood back up, pleased to see the Fire Opal in all its magnificence once more. Although, quite how this would go down, I didn't know. I suddenly felt like a small child who'd done something terribly wrong and now hoped no one was going to notice – but there wasn't a chance they weren't going to notice *this*. It wasn't some vague change like the diamonds in my Ring. This was blatantly obvious. Maybe I could plead ignorance if I left now? I slipped out the side entrance.

Knowing I should tell Rian what had happened before we had

our Audience, I headed back towards our rooms, taking the slightly longer route via the corridor with the views over the gardens that shimmered in the early morning sunlight. I glanced out at the flowers and shrubs. A short distance away, at the far side of the gardens in an area I hadn't visited when I'd first been here, sat the Lapis Tower. It was the palace library, stuffed full of all sorts of Aerban histories and documents. I'd only been in there a couple of times, but I was pretty sure I could lose myself in amongst those books for days on end, given half a chance. I just never seemed to get the opportunity. The sun glistened on the Lapis Lazuli that coated the tower, hence its name, making the deep blue of the stone more vibrant than ever.

A heavily-built figure stepped out in front of me.

'So, I finally get you alone, Your *Majesty*,' said a deep, grating voice.

I gasped as my blood froze. *Hell's teeth*. Lord Flint stood in front of me, knife raised, his beady brown eyes hard. His black hair hung into his eyes and he flicked it away.

It suddenly dawned on me that we'd come full circle, only this time it was a knife, not an oar.

'What do you want?' I asked, trying to sound like a queen as my pulse thudded in my ears, racing along at an uncomfortable speed.

He laughed. 'I'm going to kill you, Lady Merciless.'

I tried not to flinch, and held my ground. 'You wouldn't dare, not here in the palace.'

'It wouldn't be the first assassination within these walls.' He smiled, lip curling unpleasantly. 'I should have made sure I killed you the first time. If I had, none of this would have happened. That was a mistake on my part and one I intend to rectify now.'

'You told me Mal was dead that day – was that another mistake?'

He shrugged. 'I captured him in Flos. He didn't even realise what was happening, but then, he always was too trusting. After that, it was easy. I sent him to the Malign Prison with Feldspar and Topaz. I'd drugged him by then and he was no trouble. Then I came for you.'

'Bastard.'

He grinned. 'That's not very queenly.'

'It wasn't meant to be.'

'This is one of Serpentine's knives,' he continued conversationally. 'It's laced with poison. One nick, and you'll die slowly and in agony.'

I didn't doubt it. Flint and Serpentine had always been good friends. I thought about all the innocents they'd killed over the years, some in quite excruciating ways, and shuddered. I refused to be another.

He looked down the corridor. 'Well, as much as I enjoy standing around chatting…'

Unfortunately, this was a quieter route back from the Throne Room – the servants would be out in force on the other side of the building, but here, I was alone. And unarmed. I'd stopped carrying my weapons with me around the palace, and now regretted that decision. I still had something I could use, but it was a sledgehammer to crack a proverbial nut, but that couldn't be helped. I'd apologise to Rian later for the mess.

I concentrated on my newly-Revived ring. My hands started to glow white. The Quintessence swirled around my fingertips. I'd have to try and contain it so it didn't bring down half the palace.

Flint raised an eyebrow. 'I don't think so.' He raised his foot, preparing to lunge forward, a vicious, gleeful grin on his face. 'Your time is up, Amethyst.'

'No, it's not.'

A blade slipped out from between Flint's ribs. His face took on a surprised expression as blood seeped from the wound in his chest. The blade withdrew. Flint choked, blood speckling his lips as he dropped his knife, staggered forward, then fell to the carpeted floor. He looked up at his assailant.

'You,' he rasped.

'Me.'

I looked in shock at Malachite, who stood over Flint with a grim expression, his sword red with blood.

'You really thought I was going to let you get away?' Mal asked. 'After what you did to me? What you did to Amethyst? And to so many others?'

'I… I…' Flint gurgled, and lay still.

I took a deep breath, the Quintessence that had been swirling at my fingertips dissipating.

Mal turned and grinned at me. 'Good morning, Little Sister.'

I ran forward and flung my arms around his neck and hugged him. 'Thank you. But what are you doing here? And at this hour?' I asked, my heart still racing.

'Catching up with some unfinished Iolitian business,' he said, glancing back at Flint. 'I am the Master now, after all. Although I'm going to have to apologise to Rian for the bloodstain on his carpet.'

I stepped away and looked at Flint's body. Blood was soaking into the luxuriously deep-piled carpet. At least the palace building had remained intact, though.

'I think he'll forgive you, seeing as you saved his wife's life,' I said, suppressing a shudder.

Mal glanced at my hands. 'That's not to say you couldn't have dealt with things, but this was my responsibility – and pleasure.'

'I didn't realise it was Flint who captured you in Flos?'

'I only remembered myself a couple of weeks ago,' he said, wiping his sword on Flint's body and sheathing it. 'Not to mention how he was the one that forced that drug on me.'

I looked into my brother's eyes. In many ways he was still recovering, but maybe this would give him some closure.

'Are you here alone?' I asked.

He shook his head. 'Onyx is here, too – we came to… deal with him, amongst other things.' An anxious wisp slid across his face, making me frown. He quickly recovered and poked his foot into Flint's body, just to make sure he was dead. 'He won't give anyone any more trouble.'

A servant appeared at the end of the corridor. He saw us and gave me a little bow. I recognised him – one of the new servants.

'Could you have this dealt with please, Coriander?' I winced as I gestured at Flint's body. 'And please take special care of the knife when disposing of it – it's poisoned.'

Coriander's face blanched. He nodded mutely and hurried away.

'I'd better tell Rian what's happened,' I said. 'You coming?'

Mal shook his head. 'No, I'd better find Onyx. He'll wonder where I disappeared to, but when I caught sight of Flint I had to come after him.'

I nodded. 'And I'm glad you did. I'll see you later?'

'Of course.' Mal grinned and walked off down the corridor.

I took a last look at Flint's prone body and headed back to our rooms. Unfortunately, Rian had already left by the time I returned. I yawned. Doing whatever it was I'd done to the Artefacts, as well as my close encounter with Flint, had worn me out. I decided to take a quick nap – I could speak to Rian later – so I took advantage of the small amount of time I had and curled up on the bed.

About an hour and a half later, Willow arrived with a maid to get me ready.

'Why are you so tired?' she asked as I tried to look lively.

'Didn't sleep well,' I replied, the maid tugging a comb through my hair.

'Rian said you were up before him.'

'I couldn't sleep so I went for a walk, had a little adventure, then took a nap. Is he coming back before the Audience?' I asked, keen to speak to him about the Fire Opal and Flint.

Willow shook her head. 'No. He's been in some meeting with the Trewan Ambassador all morning. He said he'd meet you in the anteroom to the Throne Room in half an hour.'

Hell's teeth. I really wanted to speak to him first in private. I hoped I'd still get the chance. The encounter with Flint had rather shaken me, though I was doing my best to carry on as normal.

When I arrived there a short time later, Rian was already in the anteroom with Tarragon, a guard standing by the Throne Room door. They both looked quite relaxed. They couldn't have heard about Flint yet.

'You look lovely,' Rian said, admiring the purple dress with gold embroidery that Willow and the maid had encased me in.

'I better, because this thing is extremely uncomfortable,' I muttered. 'I think I may have to start a new trend in queen's clothing that doesn't involve dresses for formal occasions, and just traditional Aerban coats.'

'You're beautiful, whatever you wear.' He kissed my hand, which I suddenly realised was trembling slightly. A little frown flickered across Rian's face.

Tarragon grinned. 'Save it for later, you two.'

The guard at the door raised an eyebrow.

'Is he allowed to talk to his King and Queen like that?' I asked, still desperate to speak to Rian alone. Tarragon being there was one thing, but I couldn't say anything with the guard there, especially about the Fire Opal. I'd also prefer to be the one to tell my husband about Flint, and preferably alone, because I knew how he'd react and I didn't want Tarragon in trouble about palace security. Flint was a professional. Nothing Tarragon could've put in place would've been able to guarantee Flint's capture before he got to me. It would've been nigh on impossible to stop the master assassin getting in and finding me.

Rian shrugged. 'He's always talked to me like that, don't think he's about to change now.' He looked at me, his forehead furrowing. 'Are you all right? You seem a little "off".'

'I need to tell you something,' I said. 'A couple of somethings, actually. But in private,' I continued, flicking my eyes surreptitiously towards the guard.

'Oh?' Rian asked. He turned to the main door as a Palace Guard came in and whispered something in Tarragon's ear.

'Do you know why?' Tarragon asked.

The guard shook his head.

'Seems Mal wants to see you,' Tarragon said as the guard left.

'Mal's here?' Rian asked, looking towards the door. 'He's only just left after the Coronation, or at least it feels like it.'

'He's been gone over six weeks now, but he wasn't due to visit again yet.'

'Show him in,' Rian said.

'Er, it appears he wants to have a proper Audience with you,' Tarragon said.

'Why?' I narrowed my eyes. Mal hadn't said anything about an Audience earlier. This had the smell of something very odd, and it put me on edge. My brother didn't typically do things like this. What was he up to?

Tarragon shrugged. 'The guard didn't know.'

Rian sighed. 'Better go and see what he wants, then.'

I'd missed my chance to say anything to Rian.

He held his hand out to me and led me into the noisy Throne Room, where the waiting nobles and Courtiers were assembled. I walked as regally as I could in the hellishly long dress Willow had insisted I wear. The awful bodice that laced up the front constricted my chest making it harder to move, not something I was at all used to. We turned towards the dais and for a split second I felt Rian tense, hesitate, then continue. To anyone else nothing had happened, but I'd sensed it. Was it the Fire Opal? Had he seen it? He couldn't really have missed it. We stepped up onto the dais where our thrones were positioned.

We sat and faced the Court, now totally silent. Rian nodded to Tarragon.

'Your Majesties, Lord Malachite, Master of Iolite, and Lord Onyx wish to speak with you,' Tarragon said loudly.

Despite my worries, I had to suppress a smile. I wasn't sure how good I was going to be at Audiences, especially when Mal and Onyx were introduced like that.

The two young men appeared from between the Courtiers wearing formal Iolitian attire, and stepped forward in front of the thrones. Mal looked less than comfortable, and nervously flicked his hair back over his shoulder. He glanced at me, then looked at Rian. Onyx appeared more poised, serious-faced, but perfectly relaxed.

'Your Majesties,' Mal bowed. 'We are here at the behest of the other Five Lands.'

"Behest"? Where had he learnt that word? I struggled even more to keep my face straight.

'Indeed,' Rian said. 'Go on, Lord Malachite.'

'We would have you grant us a boon,' Mal said, his face strained, his body tense. In fact, he looked rather like a rabbit who's just realised it's about to become someone's supper. Onyx continued to look relaxed.

What was going on? What was he doing, and was this why he was *really* here? Had Flint been a bonus?

'A boon?' Rian asked, his eyes narrowing.

'Your Majesty, the Empire of Chroma, the Queendom of Mere, the Kingdoms of Flos and Trew, and the Island of Iolite all join together in asking you if you will take the title of "King of All".'

Now Rian looked like someone's supper. Where the hell had this come from? Rian wasn't keen on being King in the first place, but knew it was his duty – but to be King of All? He sat, not moving or speaking. The whole Court stood in silence – after the initial gasp that had reverberated around the room had died down, that is.

I stood up. 'I believe my husband, the King, may need time to consider your request, seeing as it is one of such great—'

Rian reached out and took my hand. I looked at him and sat down.

'It's all right,' he whispered to me, then raised his voice. 'Tell me, Lord Malachite, is this title to be used as it was in ancient times? King of the Hexad – all Six Lands? As the ruler of All? Or do you mean it in some other form? A figure-head, perhaps?'

Mal hesitated, and glanced at Onyx. 'Um, I—I...' He was struggling. He liked formal things even less than Rian. I was surprised that the other Lands had been able to convince him to come here and formally make the request in the first place.

Onyx sniffed and stepped forward. 'Your Majesty.' He bowed – he'd definitely been practising. I suppressed a smirk. 'What my esteemed Consort wishes to say is that the title would be more in the form of a figure-head to enable you to guide the Six Lands, to intercede in any disagreements and other such issues. The Rulers wish to acknowledge your service to the Hexad – both you and Queen Samphire. They would continue to self-govern, but with the knowledge that your advice and direction would be there if needed.'

I narrowed my eyes. Consort? Had I missed the wedding invitation? Or had they been speaking to Moonstone and Agate, having lessons in etiquette? After all, who else could have coached them? I glanced at Rian.

'Spoken most eloquently, Lord Onyx.' Rian nodded. His eyes clouded in thought for a moment. 'Very well, Lord Malachite, you may advise the other Lands that I am touched by their proposition and humbly accept their offer. From now on I will be King of All, and Samphire, Queen of All.'

We would? Did I get a say in this? I looked at Rian. *Obviously not.* I smiled in a queenly way and made a mental note to speak to Rian, Mal and Onyx about this later. At length.

After the Audience, Rian was immediately called away to see the Merean Ambassador, and Mal and Onyx had a meeting with the Flosian Ambassador, so I had no chance to speak to any of them. I received a message in the early afternoon to say that Rian had called a meeting of the Royal Council, as well as Mal and Onyx, at four o'clock.

I went to Rian's private study a little ahead of time, hoping to catch him alone. Mal and Onyx were already there, but no Rian.

'You weren't here for Flint at all, were you,' I chided as I gave my brother and Onyx a hug, noting an unfamiliar bag on Rian's desk.

Mal flinched. 'Not exactly. Coming across him was serendipitous, though.'

I squinted at him. 'You've been spending too much time in the library with Moonstone and Agate.'

He laughed. 'Maybe I have.'

'So why didn't you tell us you were coming?'

'We wanted our visit and request for an Audience to be a surprise. In fact, we were under orders from the other countries not to let you know ahead of time, and to only reveal our request in a formal setting. They wanted it to be official when we asked. As far as Flint was concerned, I just happened to notice him heading into the servants' entrance when we arrived, so I followed him. I guessed what he was up to, and I knew I had to stop him. Anyway, he was a traitor to Iolite and needed to face justice.'

'So, you were really here for the Audience, then, not to tell me you've got married and forgotten to invite me to the ceremony?' I asked, raising an eyebrow suspiciously.

Mal blanched. 'We're not—'

'I think she means because I called you Consort,' Onyx said, placing a hand on Mal's shoulder. 'I meant as in *companion*, not husband.'

'Oh, sorry,' I said. 'Well, that's all right, then. Otherwise, I'd have been most upset with you both.'

Mal rubbed his chin. 'It's not a bad idea, though. What do you think, Onyx?' He looked at his partner, obviously quite serious, not to mention besotted.

Onyx swallowed. 'Do you mean that?' he asked, his eyes wide. 'You're actually proposing to me?'

'We both know we're serious about each other – but if you don't want to—'

'I didn't say that,' Onyx said quickly. 'I don't know what to say, actually, other than, yes.'

Mal grinned and pulled Onyx into a hug and kissed him.

'You want me to leave?' I asked, grinning.

My brother stepped back. 'No, but I would like you to put a note in your diary for next spring to visit Iolite.'

'Next spring?' Onyx frowned.

'Don't you fancy a spring wedding?'

Onyx beamed from ear to ear. 'Sounds wonderful.'

'Consider it inked in my diary,' I said.

'The others, too,' Mal said.

'Hold on – we want to send out formal invitations, don't we? Otherwise it won't feel official. After all, you are the Master of Iolite,' Onyx said.

'That's true, you know,' I said to Mal. 'You'll have to do it properly and invite all the Royal Families, not to mention our Flosian relatives and Onyx's Merean ones.'

Mal screwed his face up. 'Blast it. But you had a nice quiet, intimate wedding aboard ship – and I'd just like to add I didn't get an invite.'

'It was all rather last minute. Rian didn't want any arguments when we got back here – but we were already married, at least as far as we were concerned, and the first wedding was even quieter.'

'The first?'

'I told you about that – in the palace dungeons, Rian and I pledged ourselves to each other. We were the only ones there, so you didn't really miss out.'

'I was otherwise detained at the time,' Mal said ruefully.

Onyx sniffed.

My heart twisted in my chest. 'I'm still sorry we didn't get to you sooner,' I said.

'You came as quick as you could,' Mal said with a smile. 'I'm just glad I didn't kill you.'

'You gave it a good go,' Onyx said.

Mal winced.

'Thankfully, not quite good enough, though,' I said. 'Although, that had more to do with my Quintessence than anything.'

'I'm still sorry, Phire,' Mal said.

'Don't be daft, you weren't in any fit state to know what you were doing,' I said, stepping forward and giving him a hug.

'True.' He nodded as he let me go.

'We may have had a quiet wedding, but you didn't have to endure the three hour Coronation Ceremony that we did,' I said sourly.

'I seem to recall almost every excruciating minute of it.'

'You were just a guest, Malachite. Rian and I were on parade, and those Coronation Crowns weigh a ton – I was practising with it for weeks beforehand to make sure it didn't fall off or break my neck.'

'That's true, I suppose. When we got back to Iolite, Onyx and I just marched straight into the Crimson Castle with Pol, Holm and her men, and took it.' Mal grinned. 'And that was that. No Coronation. No formal ceremony. Nothing.'

'Serpentine wasn't happy about it,' Onyx smirked.

'That's because your aunt took him by the scruff of the neck, locked him in the deepest dungeon she could find, and then threw the key away. Do you know what she did with it?'

Onyx shrugged. 'Don't know, don't care.' He sniffed again.

'So, how's your new Fellowship going?' I asked. 'Did you decide to set it up in the end?'

Mal nodded. 'Arrangements are well underway, and I have to say, the bulk of the Coterie were very happy to change profession. Those that weren't were dealt with.'

'Dealt with?'

'Pol found cells next to Serpentine's and threw those keys away, too.' Onyx chuckled. 'Feldspar was the first volunteer.'

'Are you feeding them at all?' I asked, raising an eyebrow.

Onyx glanced sideways at Mal. 'When we remember.'

Mal frowned at his partner. 'Of course we are, we're not barbarians.'

Onyx rolled his eyes to the ceiling. 'Although they all deserve to starve after what they've done.'

'Maybe, but we're not Juniper.'

'No,' Onyx said, clenching a fist for a second. 'We're not.'

'I meant to ask you, what did you and Xanthos decide to do with Topaz?' I asked.

'We decided it was best all-around if she stayed and kept Sorrel company,' Mal said. 'She may not have stolen a horse, but she did try to deceive the Emperor and kidnap him, not to mention attempt to murder you.'

'She definitely deserved some sort of punishment.' Onyx nodded.

Mal reached into the bag that lay on Rian's desk. 'I did have another reason for wanting to come and see you, as well as to pass on the request from the Six Lands – I wanted to give you this.' Mal handed me something wrapped in a deep malachite-green silk cloth.

'What is it?' I asked, taking it from him.

'Open it and see.'

I narrowed my eyes as I looked at him, wondering what, by the Stars, it was. I placed it on Rian's desk and unwrapped it. I gasped. In front of me lay a fan. Its gold outer cover shone in the light, highlighting embossed flowers of Samphire and Valerian that were punctuated with inlaid vibrant purple amethysts, deep green malachite, and creamy-beige onyx.

I looked at Mal. 'It's beautiful,' I said, my voice quivering.

'Open it up, Ama, open it up,' Onyx said, barely containing his excitement.

I picked up the fan. Just like my old Fan, it had an amethyst stone at the base. I gently opened out the leaves and couldn't help but gasp again. Rather than Iolitian Malachite leaves, this fan had deep purple amethyst leaves – but with the same design of cut-out stars as my old Fan. I pressed the amethyst button at the bottom and, sure enough, with an audible click, thirteen knife points emerged from the top of each of the spokes, and one each from the two covers.

'The amethyst leaves make it stronger than your last one,' Mal said. 'There's also a special fastening for your belt, so hopefully you won't lose it if you fall into any more rivers.'

'Thank you so much,' I said, closing the War Fan and flinging my arms around my brother, kissing his cheek for good measure.

'My pleasure.' Mal grinned at me.

'I helped,' Onyx muttered.

'I'm sure you did,' I said, giving him a hug, too. He grinned, satisfied.

Willow, Sage and Anise arrived, with Tarragon bringing up the rear. No sooner had they closed the door than Rian burst in, the Fire Opal in his hands.

'Why didn't you tell me?' he demanded as he looked at me.

'What's this?' Tarragon asked, glancing between Rian and me.

I squinted at the Fire Opal. 'Well—'

'Lord Flint got into the palace this morning and tried to kill Phire. Didn't you know?' Rian thundered. 'You're my Chamberlain! You should know these things!'

Oh, that. Not the Fire Opal, then.

'What? I haven't heard anything about that,' Tarragon said, looking aghast. His face drained of all colour as he glanced at me in shock. 'That piece of information seems to have slipped people's minds.'

'How did it even happen? Do we actually have any security here?' Rian took a breath, trying to calm himself. Only once had I seen him so annoyed with Tarragon, and that was after Prince Monkshood almost got the better of us back in Flos.

There was a knock at the door. A guard stepped in and handed a piece of parchment to Tarragon, leaving quickly and shutting the door. Tarragon opened the note and groaned.

'Now they tell me,' he said. 'I'm sorry, Rian. I'm still having trouble with certain lines of communication and people who still prefer to report to my father rather than report to me.'

'Maybe I can help with that,' Anise said. 'As Head of the Royal Household I can make things quite unpleasant for people if they don't toe the line.'

Sage raised an eyebrow. 'You're becoming quite devious in your new position.'

Anise grinned. 'I am, aren't I?'

'Thanks, Anise, I'll take you up on that offer,' Tarragon said with a nod, then turned back to Rian. 'Don't worry, heads will roll over this, I can assure you, and Anise and I will make sure nothing like it ever happens again.'

'Good,' Rian said, shoulders relaxing slightly.

'Look, I'm fine,' I said. 'Mal appeared and dealt with Flint, not that I couldn't have done it myself. And I did try to tell you earlier, but I didn't get the opportunity – and I don't want Tarragon getting in trouble for any of it. Flint would have managed to get in however many guards we had patrolling to keep him out.'

Tarragon shot me a little smile.

'She's right,' Mal said, nodding. 'Flint would've got in somehow.'

'He was one of the Coterie's best, particularly when it came to stealth,' Onyx said in agreement. 'You wouldn't have kept him away, Rian. At least this way he's been dealt with.'

'Maybe,' Rian said begrudgingly. 'Sorry, Tarragon, it's just where Phire's safety is concerned—'

'You're madly overprotective, I know,' Tarragon said with a smile. 'Just like I am with Willow.'

Willow blushed and grinned at him.

'Look, I'll make sure the Queen, and you for that matter, are properly protected in future, and I'll start by increasing the guard,' Tarragon said. 'Maybe we need an actual Queen's Bodyguard. After all, the King's Warriors are supposed to protect you. It's only fair that Phire has her own men.'

'I'm fine,' I said.

'No, you're not,' Rian said. 'And today proves it. Tarragon, we'll speak to Nacea about it.'

Tarragon nodded as I groaned inwardly, but could see this was one argument I was not going to win with Rian. Or Tarragon, for that matter.

Mal scratched his head as he thought. 'You know this sounds like the perfect opportunity for the Fellowship to get involved, provide some training for your guards. What do you think?'

'Rian?' Tarragon glanced at his cousin.

Rian nodded. 'I think it sounds an excellent idea.'

'I'll arrange it as soon as we get back to Iolite,' Mal said, grinning at Onyx.

'Are you sure that "Fellowship" is the right name for the Coterie now?' Sage asked. 'It sounds a little too cosy to me.'

'Fellowship is fine,' Mal said firmly.

Onyx wiggled his nose. 'What about the "Iolite Society of Ex-assassins", then?'

'No.'

'Surely the "Iolite Mob" would be more appropriate,' Sage said sourly.

Mal gave him a long look. 'No. I've already decided – the Coterie is now the Iolite Fellowship. And it's meant to be less threatening. That's the whole idea,' he said, staring down Sage and Onyx.

I laughed. 'I think it's a very good choice.'

Onyx narrowed his eyes. 'You know, I think I know just the assas... *Fellowship* members to entrust with this training.'

I raised an eyebrow, wondering who he was thinking of.

'Let me know and I'll make arrangements with Nacea.' Rian gave him a nod, then looked at me. 'You need to tell me these things when they happen.'

'You weren't around to tell,' I said. 'You have so many meetings these days, and most of them without me.'

He winced. 'I've been thinking maybe I need to do something about that, make sure you're included in them all, too.'

'Really?' I asked, my eyes widening. This was something I really wanted to get involved with. 'That would be wonderful.'

He nodded and smiled.

'It might raise a few eyebrows,' Tarragon said. 'But you two really need to put a stamp on your new reign, and that's probably one way to do it. Up until now the Queen of Aerba has been very much in the background. It would be good to change that.'

'You'll be happy to attend these things with me?' Rian asked. 'I warn you, though, some of them almost have me in tears because they're so boring.'

'I don't mind, really,' I said with a smile.

'Good.'

'I'll make the arrangements, then.' Tarragon nodded.

'You never know, my sister might just liven things up,' Mal said, grinning.

'I'm not sure how to take that,' I said, frowning.

'Neither am I,' Rian said. 'But you're sure you're all right, though? After your encounter with Flint?'

I nodded. 'I won't say it didn't shake me a little at the time, but I'm fine now.'

Rian glanced at Mal. 'I owe you a debt of gratitude.'

Mal shook his head. 'No, you don't. I should have caught Flint when I first got back to Iolite. Finding him was my responsibility as Master of Iolite, no one else's. But it's done now. I'm just sorry about your carpet.'

'Forget that, I'm just relieved you saved my wife's life.'

'Nonsense. Phire's my sister. And besides, I owed him for what he did to me and Phire, so there's no debt between us.'

Rian didn't look convinced, but let it go.

'Are you still lugging that thing about with you?' Onyx asked with a grin as he watched Rian place the Fire Opal carefully at the centre of his desk.

'Not as a matter of course, no,' Rian replied, slipping an arm around my waist and pulling me protectively towards him. 'But I wanted you all to take a good look at it.'

'Looks fine to me,' Tarragon said, gazing at the swirling green and purple fire blazing within the crystal like a strong heartbeat.

'That's rather the point.'

Willow gasped. 'It's like it's woken up again.'

'Anything to do with you?' Rian asked, raising an eyebrow.

She shook her head. 'I can only Release Artefacts. Not bring them back to life once their power's been used. Bobbins. I don't have that kind of power.'

I could see Rian wasn't going to let this rest. Owning up would be the only way.

'Are the Nightshade all gone now?' I asked, looking towards the walls.

Sage nodded. 'They've been gone since before the Coronation, and the passages all blocked. I've checked them myself.'

'I was with him, Phire,' Anise said. 'No one can listen to us in here.'

'Why?' Rian asked, narrowing his eyes as he looked at me.

'Well, it's about the Fire Opal,' I said, squirming slightly.

'Yes?' he said, his full attention on me.

'It seems that once an Artefact is dead it can be – well, Revived.'

'Interesting,' Anise said, peering at the gemstone, tongue out as he inspected it.

'Revived? Why didn't you tell me?' Rian asked, eyes wide.

'Because I only found out myself this morning, just before I ran into Flint, and as I've already pointed out, I haven't been able to talk to you in private yet,' I said. 'I didn't want to say anything in front of unwanted ears, like the Palace Guard.'

He flinched. 'Sorry about that – so *you* did this? You revived the Fire Opal?'

I nodded. 'It was an accident, really. I was talking to it early this morning and—'

'By the Stars, you were talking to it?' Mal asked, his eyes widening.

'Don't look at me like that. You don't understand.'

'My sister's finally lost it and is going mad.'

'After everything I've been through it wouldn't be a surprise.'

'No, Phire's right. I talk to the Artefacts when I Release them,' Willow said.

'You do?' Tarragon asked.

She nodded.

I looked back at Rian. 'Anyway, I was talking to it, and your Ring, this morning and it just kind of happened,' I said, shrugging.

'My Ring?' Rian asked, taking my hand and looking at my wedding Ring, the diamonds around it sparkling in the light coming in from the gardens. 'Damn, you've Revived that, too?'

'Yes.'

'Maybe it's best if we keep this to ourselves,' Tarragon said, rubbing his chin. 'We don't want everyone knowing Phire can bring Artefacts back to life, or who knows what sort of trouble that could cause.'

Rian nodded, looking into my eyes. 'You think you can do something about the Amethyst Talisman?'

I smiled at him. 'I can try,' I said as he pulled it from his shirt.

'It's time we rewrote the history of the Six Lands,' he said. 'Time we righted wrongs, made the world fairer for everyone and used our power to help those in need.'

Mal nodded. 'That's exactly why the other Lands want you as King of All.'

'I can't say that was something I wanted, or expected,' Rian said. 'You rather put me in a corner, seeing as you did it in public like that.'

'I'm sorry,' Mal said, fidgeting slightly, 'but the other kingdoms wanted me to do it publicly, to show we were serious, rather than in some quiet conversation over dinner.'

'You could've thought about it,' I said, looking at my husband. 'No one would have minded.'

Rian shook his head. 'No, it had to be done there and then. It had to be an immediate response or I'd have looked as if I was hesitating.'

'Now this really does give you the opportunity to do what you always wanted.'

He smiled. 'It does, doesn't it? Mal, I'm going to need your help as Master of Iolite.'

Mal grinned. 'Anything you need, Rian.'

'It might be a good idea if the new King and Queen of All tour the Lands before too long,' Onyx said with a sniff. I could see he was going to make an excellent diplomat.

'I'm just going to worry about ruling Aerba first,' Rian said. 'There's a lot to sort out here after Father and Chervil's reigns before Phire and I go off gallivanting around the Six Lands on some extended trip.'

'Perhaps we should send out an invitation to the other Lands for them to visit us, then,' I said, twisting Rian's Ring around my finger.

'That's an excellent idea, my Queen.'

'I thought so,' I said smugly.

'Do it Tarragon, send out invitations. We'll have a formal meeting of the Six Lands here in Aerba. It'll give me the opportunity to really sort everything out with them.'

I cleared my throat.

'And for my Queen to give her suggestions, too,' Rian said. 'Obviously, when I said "I" what I actually meant was "we". Slip of the tongue, wife. We're one these days, you and me,' he said, placing the Amethyst Talisman in my hand. 'At least, I think of the two of us as one.'

'Very smooth,' Tarragon said.

'It was, wasn't it?' Anise grinned.

Rian ignored them. 'But we'll start with this,' he said, looking at the Talisman. 'Can you Revive it?' His amber eyes were full of hope and love.

I looked at the dull purple crystal lying in my hand, its fire long since gone out. 'Maybe. If you can revive the Six Lands, I think I can probably do something about this.'

The King of Aerba smiled at me. 'I thought you might,' he said, leaning forward and kissing me. 'But then, Amethyst always has enhanced Fire Magic.'

'So I've heard,' I said, concentrating on the purple crystal. 'I believe they complement each other nicely.'

'Because they're together.'

EPILOGUE

Over a year had passed since we'd first left Aerba, and preparations were well underway for the first meeting of the New Hexad to be presided over by the King and Queen of All. Rian now made sure I was included in all his meetings – it raised a few eyebrows amongst the older members of the Court for a while, but they soon got used to me being there.

Both Rian and Tarragon commented on the fact the meetings now ran far more smoothly with me in attendance. Rian thought they were all on their best behaviour because the Queen of Aerba was there; Tarragon muttered something about how having an ex-assassin in their midst kept everyone affable and in order. Whichever it was, no one ever looked bored.

Having had the preliminary meeting with the Ambassadors six weeks after Mal and Onyx had had the Audience with us, we'd arranged to make it a biannual event to be held in different Lands, starting with Aerba, two months after the preliminaries. Those two months had flown by, and the first meeting would soon be upon us. The whole thing made me quite nervous.

Another thing Rian had done was make arrangements for us to have a place to retreat to, away from Viridi, where we could escape and relax every now and then. Somehow, he'd found a beautiful valley in the hills southeast of Nettle, with a small lake of crystal-clear water. He'd immediately set about having a cottage built for us. Admittedly it wouldn't be the permanent home he'd once dreamt of, but it would do; a place for the two of us to be alone and pretend, at least for a while every now and then, that we were just an ordinary couple.

It was also somewhere I could finally teach him to swim. The building work was almost complete, and soon we'd be able to go out and inspect it, something we were both incredibly excited about.

I looked out of the window, staring into the gardens as I thought about our upcoming trip. A maid was just drawing me a bath, under Willow's watchful eye. The mid-afternoon sun shone through the windows, making the rooms Rian and I shared warm and full of a mellow, golden light.

'Anything else, Phire?' Willow asked as the maid left the room, closing the door behind her.

'No, thank you,' I said. 'How are you and Tarragon getting on with married life?'

She beamed at me. 'Wonderfully. Do you know it's been two months now? I can't believe it.'

'He's still going around with a silly big grin on his face, have you noticed?'

'I have,' she said, nodding. 'Mind you, so have I.'

Rian opened the door to our sitting room and two servants came in carrying something large, covered with a black velvet cloth.

'Over there will be perfect,' Rian said, pointing to the sitting room wall next to our bedchamber door. The two servants carefully placed the large item against the wall, nodded to Rian, and left.

'I'll see you later, then,' Willow said, smiling at Rian as she followed after them and shut the door.

'You're back early,' I said. 'I was about to take a bath. And what's that?' I pointed to the velvet cloth.

He leant on the door and locked it. 'A present for you.'

I narrowed my eyes at him. 'What sort of present?' I glanced at it, trying to work out what it was. 'A painting?'

A little smile played at the corner of his lips. 'Maybe.' He walked over to it and took hold of a corner of the cloth. 'It's to go in our bedchamber on the wall opposite the foot of our bed. I had it commissioned especially for you, to commemorate this day.'

'Why today? Have I missed something important?'

'No, you haven't missed anything, and you'll find out what I'm talking about very soon. Now, do you want to see it?'

'Yes, show me what it is,' I said, intrigued and suddenly quite excited. Rian wasn't a great one for grand, romantic gestures, and this had taken me by surprise.

'Ready?'

I nodded, coming to stand in front of it.

He gently pulled the black velvet cloth off and came and stood beside me.

'What do you think?' he asked, a note of trepidation in his voice.

My breath caught in my throat and tears welled in my eyes. 'It's beautiful,' I said, looking at the portrait in front of me. The image showed Rian standing face to face with me, his hand resting on my cheek as we looked lovingly into each other's eyes. 'I'll cherish it, thank you.' I flung my arms around his neck, hugging him fiercely.

He slipped his hands around my waist, hugging me back. 'I thought you might like it. It's called "Forever Free".'

'Did the artist name it that?' I asked, pulling back slightly, wiping a happy tear from my eye.

'No, I did,' he said, his eyes glistening with delight at my reaction.

'It's very appropriate.'

'I'm so glad you like it.'

'I love it,' I said, giving him a quick kiss before letting go and stepping forward to have an even better look at the painting. Whoever they were, the artist had produced an exceptional likeness of us. The brush strokes were elegant and crisp. Rian was dressed in his burgundy coat and me in my purple. The artist had perfectly captured our eye colours, and the emotion resting there – our love.

He sighed. 'It's us. Together. Just as it should be,' he said, gazing at the painting. 'As it should've been from the start.' His forehead furrowed.

From the start? What did that mean? I raised an eyebrow. 'Something wrong?'

Rian turned to look at me, a strange expression on his face. 'No, I'm fine.'

'You know, you were rather distracted at this morning's Audience. Was it because of this or something else?' I asked. 'Are you sure you're all right?'

'I think I may be better than all right,' he said, a sparkle in his eye now.

'Oh?'

He held his hand out to me and I took hold of it. He trembled slightly as I touched him. What *was* wrong with him? He pulled me towards him, the scent of sandalwood swirling around us. He reached towards me and rested his hand on the side of my face, gazing into my eyes, into my very soul, just like the portrait.

'I wanted to give you the portrait on this day in particular. The day that we first...'

'First what?' I frowned, totally confused.

He hesitated a moment and took a deep breath.

'Will you do me the honour of kissing me, my Queen?' he asked.

'Are you changing the subject?' I asked, raising an eyebrow.

'No, actually, I'm not.'

'Then if King Valerian the Great is going to ask with such formality, I have no choice but to yield.'

'You did say you found it seductive when I was formal.'

'Hmm, I did, didn't I?' I grinned, then looked at him more closely. Something shifted deep in his eyes. A want. A hunger. Something I'd not seen there for so long because...

Did this mean...?

I started to tremble as he took me in his arms. I turned my head up towards his and he kissed me, almost hesitantly at first, before moving me so my back rested against the wall, carrying on kissing me as I wiggled my fingers into his hair. He leant against me, shaking slightly, his eyes closed and forehead furrowed as his tongue gently parted my lips. His warm mouth tasted sweet from pine tea, his Fire Spinner's tongue hot.

I traced a little path of kisses up his beautiful rose-beige neck to his ear and nibbled gently at it. His body quivered for a moment. He gasped, then gave a relieved, satisfied little moan. My eyes widened and I pulled back, looking into his amber eyes.

I gasped. 'Was that…?'

'Do it again,' he murmured, an urgency in his tone. A look of such joy and excitement lit his eyes that a little shiver ran down my spine as he pressed against me. I did as he asked, kissing his neck and ear. He groaned as he pulled me even closer. I felt his body respond to me as I kissed him, in a way it hadn't for so long. He went taut, his breathing changed, growing heavier, and then he gave a moan of such pleasure and relief that a little butterfly fluttered in my lower stomach. He tilted my head upwards and captured my mouth with his, kissing me urgently. We both succumbed to the intensity of the kiss and what this meant for us. He sighed happily as he pulled back and looked at me, his pupils dilating.

My breath caught. 'You meant the day we first made love, properly?'

He nodded and smiled. 'I think the last of the poison has finally burnt away,' he said, brushing my hair over my ear. We were both shaking a little as he rested his forehead against mine, his hand caressing the side of my face.

'Anise said it would eventually,' I said, smiling at him.

'Today is going to be our first time, and it's been so long coming I wanted to make sure we marked it properly.'

'With the painting?'

He nodded, smiling shyly. 'As long as you're ready?'

'I'm *so* ready.' My breath hitched again.

'So am I,' he said softly, gazing into my eyes. 'Finally, I can truly make you mine,' he said, looking into my very soul.

'I've always been yours,' I said.

'I know, but now I feel as if everything is finally falling into place after so long.'

I nodded. 'It is – and you'll be mine fully, too.'

He took a deep breath. 'You know, it's been exactly a year since…'

I shuddered at the memory of his poisoning and frowned. 'Is it really a year?'

'Exactly, give or take a day or two.'

'You've been keeping track?'

'That's not something I'm ever going to forget. That day changed our lives, but perhaps now we can get back to where we should be, so if you're not too busy right now, Queen Samphire, I believe we finally have the time and the bed to make it quite special,' he said, looking at me, his pupils dilating further as his eyes darkened. 'We have a whole year to make up for.'

My heart clamoured in my chest – just as well I had some of Anise's Silphion powder to hand in case this ever happened.

'We need to start making up for all the lost times we should have been sleeping together,' he continued, grinning.

My face burnt. 'Very well, King Valerian. As it happens, I'm not busy at all – other than my bath,' I said, looking through our bedchamber into the little room beyond where tendrils of steam escaped. 'Of course, we could both put it to good use first,' I said archly. 'A nice, long bath – you wanted it to be unhurried.'

'Does it have to be long?'

'What happened to unhurried? You can't wait after all, can you?'

He smiled. 'I still want to take my time, but I also think we've waited long enough, don't you? We'll take it slow – or as slow as I can manage…' He swallowed. 'The first time, anyway…'

'Oh…' My face reddened further. My heart lurched in my chest, pulse racing, butterfly fluttering. I frowned. 'The first time, you say?'

'We've got plenty of spare time, so I don't intend to stop at once.'

'Really?' My heart skipped a beat as I raised an eyebrow.

He rubbed the back of his neck. 'You know, suddenly I'm quite nervous about it all.'

I smiled at him. 'Don't be,' I said, kissing his nose. 'You never need to be nervous around me.'

A little lopsided smile returned to his velvet lips as he stroked the side of my face with his trembling hand. 'I know, it's only that – we've waited so long for this. I want it to be just right.'

'We're together. Whatever happens, it'll be just right,' I said, my lips brushing his as my hands slid under his shirt, then drifted down his body, caressing his warm skin. 'Maybe I should get my rose perfume out.' As my hands slipped lower, he gasped and went taut just like a harp string. Just like I'd hoped. 'Hmm,' I murmured, looking into his eyes as he let out a little groan of pleasure. 'Maybe I don't need to.'

'Hmm, indeed,' he said, his breath hitching, his eyes full of desire. He grabbed my hands. 'Not yet.'

I pouted at him. 'Killjoy.'

'You'll thank me for it later,' he said, grinning impishly at me. 'And we can get the perfume out in a while. I've been planning this for a very long time. We'll just need to put in as much practice as possible to perfect it – hence, more than once.'

I frowned. 'Have you been talking to Tarragon again? I told you not to listen to him,' I said, scowling for effect as an initially-suppressed grin spread across my face.

He beamed at me. 'He mentioned something a while ago.'

'Practice, you say?' I asked, raising an eyebrow. 'Then perhaps we'd better get started,' I said, grasping Rian's hand. I took a last glance at the portrait – he'd actually commissioned it to remember this day? My husband was a true romantic at heart. I'd make sure it was up on our bedchamber wall as soon as possible. I led him towards the bath, locking our bedchamber door behind us. 'I don't want Tarragon to disturb us.'

'Neither do I, especially not this time, but don't worry. I've just sent him on an errand that will take him a couple of days – and he'll be taking Willow, and her lock picks, with him.'

'Have you indeed?' I grinned mischievously. Then frowned. 'Have you known about this for a while?'

He rubbed the back of his neck again. 'Let's just say I knew something was changing, and once I'd spoken to Anise and I was certain, I decided to make sure Tarragon was out of the palace for a couple of days. I've put Anise in charge and he understands things completely. This whole wing is totally empty and he'll keep it that way for us.'

I smiled and nodded.

'So, you see, wife, we'll be completely alone for a while and we can finally make love, uninterrupted, and make as much noise as we like.'

I raised an eyebrow.

He smirked. 'I think you hold back.'

'Not this time, I won't.'

'And neither will I. I've got you all to myself.'

'No more aching?'

He shook his head. 'No more aching.'

'Well, then...' I started to undo the laces on the front of my dress, but he pulled me back towards him for a hug. I took the opportunity to pull his Aerban coat off. The Amethyst Talisman slipped free of his shirt, dangling on its chain and catching the afternoon light. At its centre a deep purple glow, soft, yet pronounced, once more showed the power resting in its depths. As Rian released me I looked into his eyes and cupped his face in my trembling hands.

'I'm yours for always and forever,' I murmured, repeating our vows from the dungeon so long ago.

He smiled, taking hold of my hands and kissing them. 'I'm forever yours, my Samphire Amethyst, and no one else's,' he said, repeating his own vows. He gazed at me, desire resting firmly in his eyes, and tilted his head, leaning towards me, kissing me, his lips as intoxicating as ever as I draped my arms around his neck, his hands firmly planted at my waist. I let out a soft little moan, which only seemed to encourage him, and his hands started to caress my back and shoulders. I tugged at the tie in his hair and it fell loose around his shoulders. He looked even more attractive like that.

'I'll always love and cherish you, wife.'

'And I'll always love and cherish you, husband,' I said. I narrowed my eyes as I looked at him. 'If things work out the way we hope, you do realise you won't be getting *any* sleep tonight?'

A lopsided grin appeared as he gazed adoringly at me, freeing my own unruly hair, running his fingers through it and making me shiver. 'Sounds good to me. I've rearranged everything so we've nothing planned until late the day after tomorrow, and who needs sleep when we've got this to attend to?' he asked, chewing his bottom lip thoughtfully as he pulled his shirt off. He started tugging on my bodice laces, working them free with a determined look in his eye.

'The day after tomorrow?' I asked, my eyes widening.

'It's all right, Anise will bring us food when we want it.'

'I wasn't worried.' I smiled. 'I love you, King Valerian.'

'I love you too, Queen Samphire,' he said as he finished undoing my laces. My dress fell to the floor. His gaze wandered over my body as he drank me in, then he took a deep breath, and when he spoke his voice had a husky quality to it, his face full of love. 'Now, about the next couple of days... you see, if you want to perfect something, you have to do the practice, which means putting the time in.'

'Hmm. Have I ever told you that you're impossible?' I asked, running my fingertips down his bare chest.

He trembled at my touch, sighing contentedly, and smiled, making me melt inside. 'I think you might have mentioned it once or twice,' he said, tenderly stroking my cheek. 'So I've been working hard at it, just for you. How am I doing?'

'Exceptionally well, but there's always room for improvement, so don't ever stop trying,' I said, taking his hand and kissing it.

'In that case…' He ran a finger gently over my lips, want filling his eyes. 'I'm going to spend the next couple of days showing you exactly how much I love you, wife, in a way I never have before,' he said, his voice soft like a summer breeze. 'I want you. I need you. I need you, *now.*'

My heart skipped a couple of beats, a silken thread beginning to knot in my stomach. 'And I need you, too, now, because I can't wait any longer for you – for *this*,' I said, my voice catching. I kissed his hand again. Hesitated. I looked into the amber-rimmed eyes of my husband, of the young man who was my best friend and soulmate. 'What will it be like?' I whispered, now inexplicably nervous, too.

He didn't answer immediately, but instead leant towards me again, his warm arms encircling me as his searing mouth claimed mine, his lips tender and velvety as our tongues explored and we held each other close – but the kiss changed, became feverish, deepening further as our deep love for each other took over. His kiss became ardent with a fiery urgency, a burning hunger flickering within it as our bodies touched, his hot skin pressed up against me. The kiss had the same intensity as the one we'd shared after his nightmare back in the Dentro Settlement. It took my breath away. *He* took my breath away with his passion and love as he held me close, our bodies pressed against each other. I could never ask or want for more than him, for more than *my* Rian. The silken thread tightened into a knot. He moaned into my mouth, and a wildfire swept through my veins. My love for him filled me to overflowing. His love for me, unyielding and strong, could never be questioned. He drew back, his pink lips a hair's breadth away from mine, smiling at me, his amber eyes glowing in the afternoon light as his trembling hands started to caress me.

'Let's find out, shall we?' he murmured in a husky voice, his breath hitching.

And we did.

Together.

DRAMATIS PERSONAE AND GLOSSARY OF TERMS

ELVEDON

The world where the events of our story take place.

LAND OF IOLITE

Agate – Librarian at the Iolite University.

Amethyst/Samphire (Phire) – Wife of Valerian. Ex-assassin. Daughter of the late Master of Iolite. Younger sister of Malachite and twin of Beryl. Legendary member of the Iolite Coterie of Assassins and known as Lady Merciless.

Beryl – Twin sister to Amethyst, and sister of Malachite.

Carnelian – A notorious assassin. Member of the Iolite Coterie of Assassins.

Citrine – Dead assassin. Sister to Carnelian. Member of the Iolite Coterie of Assassins.

Elm – Son of Juniper. Member of the Iolite Coterie of Assassins and involved in Coterie business.

Emerald – Dead Mistress of Iolite. First wife of Lord Peridot. Mother to Malachite, Amethyst and Beryl.

Feldspar – An assassin and member of the Iolite Coterie.

Flint – Chief Assassin of the Iolite Coterie of Assassins.

Juniper – Mistress of Iolite and Leader of the Iolite Coterie of Assassins. Mother of Elm. Widowed second wife of Lord Peridot and stepmother to Malachite, Amethyst and Beryl. Originally from the land of Trew.

Malachite (Mal) – An assassin. Older brother of Amethyst and Beryl. True Master of Iolite. Member of the Iolite Coterie of Assassins.

Moonstone – Librarian at the Iolite University.

Obsidian – An assassin and member of the Iolite Coterie.

Onyx – An assassin and member of the Iolite Coterie. Best friend to Amethyst and Malachite.

Peridot – Dead Master of Iolite. Father to Malachite, Amethyst and Beryl.

Topaz – An assassin. Carnelian's girlfriend and member of the Coterie.

Zircon – An assassin and member of the Iolite Coterie.

LAND OF AERBA

Angelica – Dead Crown Princess of Aerba. Eldest child of King Finule and Queen Myrtle. Older sister of Chervil and Valerian.

Anise – Herbalist and ex-King's Warrior.

Bergamot – King Finule's cousin and Chief of the Military. Father of Sage and Sorrel.

Chervil – King of the Land of Aerba. Second child of King Finule and Queen Myrtle. Younger brother to Crown Princess Angelica, older brother to Valerian.

Finule – Dead King of Aerba. Husband of Queen Myrtle. Father of Angelica, Chervil and Valerian.

Hyssop – Captain of the ship *The Sea Urchin*.

Myrtle – Dead Queen of Aerba. Wife of King Finule. Mother of Angelica, Chervil and Valerian.

Sage – Cousin to Valerian and ex-King's Warrior. Younger brother to Sorrel.

Sorrel – Older brother of Sage, cousin to Valerian and King's Warrior.

Tarragon – Cousin and best friend to Valerian. Ex-King's Warrior.

Valerian (Rian) – Husband of Amethyst/Phire. Exiled Prince of Aerba. Third and youngest child of King Finule and Queen Myrtle. Ex-Head of the King's Warriors.

Willowherb (Willow) – Ex-King's Warrior-Attendant.

Wintergreen – King Finule's cousin and Chamberlain. Father of Tarragon.

Wormwood – Head of the Nightshade.

LAND OF FLOS

Erica – Cousin of Amethyst/Phire and Malachite. Wife of Gladiolus.

Gladiolus – Husband of Erica.

Hyacinth – Husband of Jasmine.

Jasmine – Cousin of Amethyst/Phire and Malachite. Wife of Hyacinth.

Narcissus – King of Flos.

Monkshood – Prince of Flos.

LAND OF MERE

Calder – Flosian spy working with Erica.

Holm – First Mate on *The Spirit of the Seas*.

Lynn – Inn owner and friend of Onyx.

Onyx's Grandfather – member of extended Merean Royal Family.

Pol – Captain of the ship *The Spirit of the Seas*. Aunt to Onyx.

LAND OF TREW

Ash – King of Trew.

Birch – Prince of Trew.

Hazel – Princess of Trew.

Ostianzis – A Senex with long life and a feel for Elemental Magic.

Photinia – Queen of Trew.

PAX ARCHIPELAGO

Zabell – Friend of Pol and Holm.

LAND OF CHROMA

Xanthos – Emperor of Chroma.

CAPITAL CITIES

Adamas – Capital city of Iolite.

Magenta – Capital city of Chroma.

Muscari – Capital city of Flos.

Rill – Capital city of Mere.

Spindle – Capital city of Trew.

Viridi – Capital city of Aerba.

CREATURES

Dryads – Creatures from the forests of Flos.

Powlers – Lake dwelling creatures, now seldom seen in Aerba.

Merean Blue Death Worms – Great worms that live out in the deserts of Mere.

Morgens – Creatures of the sea and lakes that take their victims down into the depths and drown them. Their beautiful song is as enchanting as it is dangerous.

Mynogres – Legendary creatures that once roamed the forests of Aerba.

Senex – Long-lived individuals with a feel for Elemental Magic.

TERMS

Artefacts – Crystals that could enhance the power of an Elemental Magic Spinner.

Blood Class System – Hierarchical system you are born into. Your Blood Class cannot be changed. Each Blood Class has particular rules and a dress code they must adhere to.

Blood Rule Decree – Laws governing the Blood Classes, including rules on relationships and naming of children.

Crystal Vortex – The source of all the Artefacts, located in Chroma. It keeps the Elements and nature in balance.

Elemental Angle Spinners/Elemental Magic Spinners – Ancient High Bloods who could wield Elemental Magic.

High Bloods – The Royal Family and extended relations.

Iolite Coterie of Assassins – Order of Assassins led by Mistress Juniper and run from Iolite.

King's Warriors – King Finule's best Warriors.

Low Bloods – All citizens that do not fit into the High and Middle Blood Classes.

Magic Angle – The Element a Magic Spinner could wield: Air, Earth, Fire, Quintessence or Water.

Middle Bloods – Lesser nobles, high status citizens and priests.

The Nightshade – Aerba's spy network.

Thyme – Aerba's sacred herb.

ACKNOWLEDGEMENTS

Firstly, I want to thank Peter and Alison, aka Elsewhen Press, for rescuing Phire and Rian, and giving them a fantastic new home. You have my eternal gratitude, and I'm so glad you've loved their story as much as you have.

My biggest thanks go to my husband and daughter for their never-ending love, support, and supply of chocolate! To my sister who inspired me with the idea of Magic Angles and Spinning, I couldn't have done it without you.

To my original editor, Lauren Dooley, thank you for believing in me, Phire, and Rian – this amazing journey wouldn't have started without you. Editor Nicole Lindsay has travelled the entirety of the Six Lands with me, and my thanks go to you, too.

Two of my writer friends, Emma Bradley and Estelle Tudor, continue to offer great inspiration, and are amazing sounding boards when it comes to ideas and writing in general. Thank you both!

To everyone who has read and enjoyed Phire and Rian's story – THANK YOU! I hope you've had fun on their adventures, and with the various twists and turns along the way. If you want to know more about my writing and books, then please visit my website www.aerinapeltun.com and sign up to my newsletter!

Happy reading!

Aerin

Elsewhen Press

delivering outstanding new talents in speculative fiction

Visit the Elsewhen Press website at elsewhen.press for the latest information on all of our titles, authors and events; to read our blog; find out where to buy our books and ebooks; or to place an order.

Sign up for the Elsewhen Press InFlight Newsletter at elsewhen.press/newsletter

CURSED WEAPONS TRILOGY BY AERIN APELTUN

BOOK 1: THE AMETHYST TALISMAN

Within a world broken by an ancient civil war, skilled assassins will kill anyone for a price. Known as Lady Merciless, the greatest assassin in the Five Lands, Amethyst hides a terrible secret from the Coterie of Assassins that hold her in thrall - one that could mean her death.

When she is falsely implicated in the murder of Aerba's Crown Princess and the theft of their legendary Fire Opal, Amethyst is hunted down and captured by the princess' brother, Valerian. Things only get worse when his father makes her carry the Cursed Weapons of Aerba as a punishment.

Forced together, Amethyst and Valerian set out to find the Fire Opal and the assassin. But as they work towards their goals, their destinies now entwined, things spiral out of control as dark forces move against them. With the Curse hanging over Amethyst, and the Coterie after Valerian, both their lives, and their hearts, are in danger.

ISBN: 9781917507332 (epub, kindle) / 9781917507233 (304pp paperback)

BOOK 2: THE MALACHITE QUEST

Having escaped the land of Aerba, Samphire, Valerian, and their friends continue in their quest to find Samphire's brother, Malachite, and Aerba's legendary Fire Opal. But their travels are complicated by Aerba and Flos teetering on the edge of war.

Now knowing of the existence of Magic, and the Fire Opal's possible power, they continue on in the hope that they can recover the stolen Artefact, and Malachite – but hope is fading fast.

With a long journey ahead, and time against them, Samphire and Valerian find their love tested, and heartbreak before them. And when a friend from Samphire's past reappears and new tensions arise, can they not just overcome them, but also stay one step ahead of the assassins that dog their steps as they try to reach Malachite before they're out of time?

ISBN: 9781917507349 (epub, kindle) / 9781917507240 (288pp paperback)

BOOK 3: THE OPAL KING

With Malachite rescued, Samphire and Valerian's attention turns to the rapidly failing Crystal Vortex. With their friends at their side, they must forge on across treacherous seas and foreign lands in search of Valerian's stolen Fire Opal, even as they come to terms with their new Elemental Spinning powers.

Samphire fears that she may be confronted with her greatest nightmare, and it becomes apparent to Valerian that he may yet have to take on his biggest, and most unwanted, challenge. As they reach the end of their desperate quest, they must face their families and confront their fears.

Can they save the Crystal Vortex, and the Six Lands? Through their love for each other, can they both find the strength to accept their fates? And will the assassins sent to destroy them succeed, or can their love save them one last time?

ISBN: 9781917507356 (epub, kindle) / 9781917507257 (308pp paperback)

Visit bit.ly/TheCursedWeapons

AN ORCHID IN MY BELLY BUTTON

KATY WIMHURST

Offbeat short stories that explore our fragile world

These stories savour the surreal, flirt with magical realism, dabble with dystopia. A boy sees the ghosts of dead crabs. A girl with a fox tail is bullied. A disenchanted woman sprouts orchids from her belly button. Fashion models pursue the trend of having plants as hair. Electronic goods amassing all over London herald an apocalypse. Darkness and wonder, the strange and the ordinary, interweave to offer an environmental and social portrait of our times. Guaranteed to evoke a response, whether a giggle, a gasp, or a nervous gulp, these stories will stay with you, enriching your perception of the world.

Surreal, absurdist, magical realist; Katy Wimhurst writes speculative fiction that meditates on our reality. Although bleak themes are examined – dystopian futures, the climate crisis, bullying – a quirky imagination and wry humour lift the tales above the 'realm of grim'.

ISBN: 9781915304797 (epub, kindle) / 9781915304698 (160pp paperback)

Visit bit.ly/AnOrchidInMyBellyButton

Adventures of a Gnome by P.R. Ellis

1 – An Extraordinary Tale:

A Gnome's Odyssey

A gnome, a mouse and a skeleton meet on a train

The Fairy Queen's electrum, the most valuable material in the world, has been stolen. By chance Philbrach Hohenheim, a gnome, finds himself on the trail of the thief. A motley fellowship is formed between the gnome and other creatures. The pursuit crosses lands, times and realities until finally a major puzzle at the borders of the world is solved. On the way, Philbrach encounters giant pigeons, a sentient fungus, a seafaring merman, the Sun's chariot driver and other helps and hindrances.

ISBN: 9781915304353 (epub, kindle) / 97819153041254 (290pp paperback)
Visit bit.ly/AnExtraordinaryTale

2 – The Mage Returns

She's Back!

As Philobrach Hohemheim and his companions relax after their adventures recounted in *An Extraordinary Tale*, they receive an urgent message. The Sorceress Carmine, The Red Mage, has returned to their world. What mischief does she plan this time?

Soon, the Gnome, Bones the skeleton, Hugo the Ogre and a brave mouse called Mortimer, find themselves on a quest that takes them across both land and ocean, into the moon, and through it to another universe. They discover that their own world is in danger of fading away, unless they can find enough electrum to re-start magic!

ISBN: 9781915304957 (epub, kindle) / 97819153041858 (230pp paperback)
Visit bit.ly/TheMageReturns

3 – To the World's Edge

Coming soon

ABOUT AERIN APELTUN

Aerin Apeltun is an English writer based in the East of England. She started writing stories as a child, and has always loved reading about fantasy worlds. Aerin now loves to develop and write about her own worlds and mythologies.

Having been listed in a number of writing competitions, Aerin's Upper YA Romantasy, *Crystal Bloods,* was published by Elsewhen Press in February 2025, with a sequel to follow in 2026. Upper YA Fantasy Romance trilogy, *The Cursed Weapons*, out now, will be followed by a New Adult Historical Romantasy duology scheduled for 2026/7; she is always busy working on something!

A Second Class Archer, Aerin has had various careers in school/university administration and insurance, as well as a stint at the local library, but writing is her passion. She also loves to draw, and is a keen fantasy cartographer, designing maps for her worlds. Aerin enjoys travelling, taking inspiration from nature and landscapes for settings and characters in her books.

www.ingramcontent.com/pod-product-compliance
Lightning Source LLC
Chambersburg PA
CBHW030608170726
48283CB00002B/510